THE MONARCH OF DRAHN

S.T. WOODS

First edition 2024 – Published by Rindmark – http://www.rindmark.art

Cover design and artwork by Diz Williams Tattoo – http://www.dizwilliamstattoo.com

the praise

In recognition of my dearest wife.
She has my sincerest thanks and appreciation for her contribution to this story. Endless hilarious hours were shared creating this alien world and its people. As my soundboard from the beginning, she corralled many crazy ideas and filled even more plot holes.
But, I am mostly thankful for her enduring the untold hours of edits and rewrites alongside her tyro author husband.

the warning

The characters portrayed within are alien beings. They are a tripedal genderless people with an alternative perception of normalcy due to their physicality, environment and culture. The story contains imagery and concepts that are familiar yet exotic. At best, the attitudes and behaviours depicted are odd. At worst, the descriptions of sex, violence, and death are graphic.

This is high fantasy. Sometimes lurid entertainment is worth the risk of being affronted, and wickedly delighted at the same time. This is an adult's tale aimed at a mature minded audience. Enjoy.

PART ONE - ORIENNA

PART TWO - MEZZINA

PART THREE - OXXIA

PART FOUR - MUNIKA

PART ONE

ORIENNA

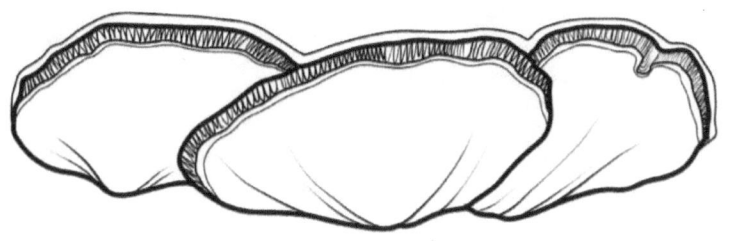

1.0 - THE BANISHED SUMMONS

A new day began as the shadow of the plaza sundial swept from the ninth hour to the first.

Erected as the foundation stone of the new capital, the gnomon was a tall triangular obelisk forged from black glass darker than the shadow it cast. Palama ran across the mosaic icons of the nine ancient heroes that decorated each hour. He passed the belfry under the spire and flinched when the smirking chronister struck the clock's chime. Its deafening knell rang in his ears long after the tubular bell fell silent.

This summons was a first, something had changed. The monarch had never allowed him in his presence since childhood. Sent away young, and raised by the League of Barren Uncles, he studied law. For the past decade he had contented himself with the anonymity of a lowly public arbiter settling minor legal disputes. He had always lived in virtual obscurity, forever shunned by the royal family.

Now and then he would perform some altruistic duties, but only when his parent insisted that it might count for something one day. *Was today the day?* he wondered. The President of the Consultorium publicly praised him for his renovations to the country lodge for lust-spawn waifs. Perhaps he was due for a promotion. He yearned to join the finance league or the legislative sector. Both were plush posts, well paid and respectable. Either would do. At last, he was to be rewarded. He had finally earned a place in the bureaucratic corps and he knew he was ready for it.

Beyond the malls, and by the palace gardens, lay the Monarch's Hall. It was a vast indoor stadium built generations ago by Xendaka the Monofier. Before then, the seat of power sat in the old capital of The

Kataraxs, the city behind the western waterfall. A seniarch straddled the plynth back then. A position vacated by death or retirement at the age of forty-five, which ever came first. Eventually, it was seldom the latter. After a dozen centuries, sybling rivalry devolved into incessant civil wars between the clandoms. Countless kin died in the endless conflicts so that one selfish doyen after the other could mount the lofty perch. Within a corrupted and exhausted kindom, an idealist rose to end the chaos. He subdued the clanlords by purge or reward until they all pledged their allegiance. Any future ambitions were thwarted by installing himself as monarch for life. A royal standing army was formed to ensure his descendants succeeded him, and thus maintained an unbroken royal line. It was all done for the sake of national stability. How selfless the royal family was.

The enormous dome loomed above Palama. Red stained funglstone curved in a seamless arc and met high above the city. The base was ringed with tall thin arched entries thrice his height. Each was flanked with sculptured columns and topped with an ornate vaulted lintel. Through the open doorways, the low sun shone through and lit the polished floor with long bright reaching fingers.

It was a grand space, a testament to the power and sovereignty of the pedigree nation. It was built of wood and stone and glass, for the body and mind and spirit. A place for the affairs of state, and to exhibit the power of the monarchy. Where law was dispensed and coronations performed. A place to gather the kin of the realm to feast and celebrate themselves. Most importantly, during seasonal aurora, it was the primary site for the national conjugation.

As Palama stood on a threshold, his elongated shadow stretched halfway to the centre where the plynth stood. The seat of power. The sovereign's throne. Sculpted from white-veined indigo marble, it resembled the stump of a felled tree. From the base of the wide trunk, gnarly roots crawled out across the floor. Monarch Soltoro, his cousin, sat upon it.

His heart jumped to his throat. Until now, Palama had not realised the magnitude of this meeting. He would soon be in the presence of the

4

three most powerful people in the whole kindom. The Monarch, the Chancellor and the President of the Consultorium all cast their gaze to his silhouette. He assumed they had suspended their conversation, but he could not tell. The hall was too vast and they were too far away. With an encouraging gulp, he straightened his back and strutted toward them.

Above him, the ceiling disappeared into its own shadow. The enormous dome was supported by massive petrified buttresses. They curved down like mighty ribs to rest between the tall, narrow archways around its base.

A wide stonewood veranda ringed the interior and stood above the doorways on glass columns as clear as water. Congested shelves held two thousand years of Drahn's legal history. Millions of paperbark scrolls sat sealed in clear glass tubes. Legislation, wills, property sales, criminal cases and other assorted histories all collected dust. They were only gaudy copies, displayed to show off the kindom's pride in their rule of law.

'Let no mob dictate, nor tyrant decree' was the legal maxim from millennia past branded onto the heart of every Drahni sybling. The precious originals were securely stored directly underground throughout the deep cavernous libraries. They were in the meticulous care of the city curators.

Palama joined his betters. He wore his legal suit, and he was glad of it. It befitted the occasion. His bright scarlet toga wrapped him like a thin blanket and reached the floor. A jet black feathered boa draped about his shoulders like a mantle.

His cousin out-dressed him, as expected. The monarch flicked a hem of his royal gown. Encrusted with smolderstone powder, the black velvet shimmered as the wrinkles smoothed themselves. The plush fur twinkled like the stars in the southern sky. Split at the waist and edged in pure white fur, the tails rippled about Soltoro like a shadowlit stream tumbling over rocks. But, the elders were not so fussed about dressing up. Both wore their drab duty clothes. Their brown robes hung off them like crumpled sheets draped over doors.

Palama curtsied and lifted his head face up. He stretched his neck high to display the extent of his esteem. Before he could verbally express any respectful greetings to them, the monarch grunted...

"Should I start again, or will he catch up?"

"I am late. I do apologise, thyre," said Palama. "The case I heard went over time. A fickle witness delayed the procee..."

"Good," said Soltoro. "Dispensing the monarch's rule is reason enough."

Palama flashed his uncle a daring glance. Quetono winked a goading grin.

"With all due respect thyre," said Palama, "the monarch's rule is your own to impose. My area is seniocratic law." Soltoro stared at him with a face that would melt stone. Despite the frightful glare, Palama continued. "While the monarchy controls the highest level of government, the seniocratic system is still embedded within everyday life. The syblings live under the old laws and customs. Xendaka was wise to leave the ancient statutes intact..."

"Palama. Now is not the time for a political lesson," hissed Vondaka.

"He sounds like a seniocrat," said Soltoro. "Is he always like this?"

"I would not know, I hardly see him. You have forbidden him from the palace all his life," scowled Vondaka.

"You never visit your own child?"

"I am your Chancellor, thyre. When do I have time to squander?"

"Well, you're squandering it now!" roared Soltoro. "Let us waste no more of it. Palama, you are aware of the Miokhi problem?"

"Thyre, as a simple magistrate, I am ignorant of current events. I judge by law, rather than by rumour."

"This is no idle gossip," snapped Soltoro. "Allow me to enlighten you... we are facing a national disaster."

"I think you exaggerate, thyre. The Mio..."

"Do not interrupt me Vondaka. I am sick of your interference. I know what you are doing," said Soltoro. Vondaka narrowed his eyes and shut his mouth. The monarch cleared his throat. Assured he had

6

silenced his insolent assistant, he continued. "Over the past four years they have stolen our Oxxian sand."

The precious dunes were a national resource of immense revenue. Far too valuable to allow it to be taken without recourse. The grains were blacker than the deepest pit and harder than the oldest rock. Once forged, the dark grains were cast into a vitreous stone. A weapons-grade glass that cannot shatter. Phasha, a wandering sandwright from the Vitron Shores beyond the eastern border, perfected the shardsmith's craft. He privately sought fame and riches in a foreign war. The wily outlander chose Xendaka. The new glass blade hacked through traditional funglstone bladestaffs like fruit. He embraced the new battle shard as the ultimate tool to hasten Monofication. Now, centuries later, Drahni royalty decided who bought their treasured black sands.

"We tried diplomacy. We even threatened them, but the Miokh Premier did nothing to stop his dredgers from crossing the border. His barges cruised up and down the coast stripping our black beaches."

"Remember Yontala? He chased them for three years," said Quetono.

"The disgraced commander?" asked Palama.

"He did put an end to the theft," said Vondaka.

"Yes, and the idiot drowned the Premier's only child while he was at it," said Soltoro.

"Bent on revenge, the foreigners intend to claim the beaches for themselves as compensation," added Quetono.

"When?" asked Palama.

"My sources tell me they intend to invade soon after Pannatalia," replied Vondaka.

"Did you want my legal advice, is that why I am here?" asked Palama.

The eruption of the raucous laughter startled him. Palama squeezed a faint smile as if he should join in the joke, but he did not get it. His face flushed hot. They all looked at him and paused for a moment, then burst into a second round of hilarity.

"No you fool," said Soltoro. "I have a much better use for you."

All Palama knew was seniocratic law. He could magistrate theft, fraud, assault and even murder, but he could not see himself of any use other than that. Maybe if he knew his cousin, he might be able to glean an inkling of this 'better use' he referred to. As it was, they were embarrassing him.

"Tell him quickly," said Quetono. "I have an expedition to prepare."

Soltoro grunted and stood up from his seat. It was a blatant attempt to delay the conversation. He fluffed up his green woolly cushion and plopped it back on top of the blue stump like a large patch of forest moss.

"Uncle. I have still not granted your resignation," said Soltoro.

"I was not aware it was offered to you," said Quetono.

"It wasn't. I queried the secretary, he blathered on about volunteer advisers, elders only, members' business."

"You already knew that. So why?"

"Because I would prefer it, that you hadn't," confessed Soltoro.

"You have left the Consultorium in the hands of that idiot Krantolo," said Vondaka.

"He was vice-president," said Quetono. "His promotion was automatic."

"He is far too ambitious. It's bound to end in disaster," said Vondaka.

"Why did you resign, uncle?" asked Palama.

"Yes, we would all like to know that," said Soltoro.

"I wish to accompany the north-eastern recruitment drive," said Quetono. "Other than that, my reasons are my own."

"Your own reasons. They lead you on a fool's errand," scoffed Vondaka.

Both the monarch and the chancellor stared at Quetono as if their silence might coax an explanation from him. It didn't.

"Palama," said Soltoro, returning his attention to the business at hand. "I have an errand for you. We prepare for war. The Royal Army needs many more recruits to bolster its forces, and the call to duty went practically unheeded. So, we shall enforce a voluntary enrollment.

I have already sent enlisters across three of the four provinces. After weighing our uncle's arguments, I have assigned you Commander of the Far- Eastern Rural Draft. A purely ceremonial position, you understand. You will travel across the more remote areas of Orienna and oversee the conscription of all eligible recruits. A hectary and a security team are assembled as your support. Quetono insists he guides you, so follow his advice. You must arrive at Churon's Pen within two hundred days. You leave at once."

In that instant, everything went dark. All sound disappeared like a sudden deep breath. Reality evaporated, and time stood still. Palama gawped like a dumbstruck statue at Soltoro. This was nothing like he expected. Had his ears betrayed him? Travel the eastern province, recruiting yokels? Please, no! His place was here. He was city, not rural. The monarch was getting him out of the palace, out of the city, out of the way. Again. His blood pumped like lava, and brutal images flooded his mind. He would return surrounded by his own army and usurp the regime. He would smash the royal torkh and mount the senioral plynth himself. They will all regret ever snubbing him. Soltoro shall watch all his monarchist toadies skydance around him before being hoisted up himself. Perhaps Palama might make himself the prophesied hero foretold in the Paladin's Bode. Cheerfully lost in the fog of this morbid fantasy, Palama frowned an evil sneer. After a moment he sighed a pleasant smile, and just as quick, the imaginary mists cleared. He blinked, and focused at the bewildered monarch glaring down at him.

"What is wrong with you?" roared Soltoro. "Do you understand?"

"Yes, cousin. I am merely overwhelmed at the honour."

Quetono pulled Palama's arm. "Come nephew, we go east."

I.I – THE AFFLUENT PAUPER

Every time Drolla left those filthy caves, he vowed he would never return. Yet the treasure within always ensured he would.

The Red Spore fungus is deliciously narcotic. The size of a hand, its broad flat blade of white flesh is lined with scarlet gills along one edge from base to tip. It only grows on the sodden rock within these dark stifling caverns. Considered by all as 'the lord of the wildfruits', it commanded a high price. The desire for its euphoric effects made it a relish for the wealthy and a luxury for anyone else. But only known to the harvestors, until it was dried it smelled like fresh vomit.

Dank, humid caves were the perfect habitat. Moth Bats had stolen every whiff of air and their guano carpeted every surface. The stench was impossible. Hot, stale air seared the throat and tore the lungs. It reached down the gullet to grab and twist your innards. The belly ached from constant dry retching. Even after a decade of harvesting, it still made him sick. His light dimmed. He clacked the geode against the cave wall, and the white smolderstone crystals glowed bright again.

"Pluck a few more," said Drolla. His whispered voice echoed off into the dark. He pretended that greed might sooth the nausea. This harvest was a good one, and might hopefully improve his parent's apathetic opinion of him. He knew it wouldn't. The thought of it made him ill. He balked. His mouth watered and he spat. Nope, there was nothing left to puke.

One last slab filled the basket, and he sheathed his little sickle. He hawked and spat more bile as he emerged from the gloom. The light stung his squinting eyes, but his wheezing lungs thanked him for the deep breath of fresh, forest air. Out of one nostril after the other he shot brown stringy snot. He smiled and watched the heavier globs of mucous tumbled end over end before they spattered across the rocks. Within a moment, corpseflies landed and squabbled over his nasal slime. This putrid drudgery was all he knew. He craved something else. Anything else.

The Mauve Forest surrounded Drolla's peaceful, little village. It was nestled amongst the fertile shade of the Perse Hills, hidden within the north-eastern region of Drahn. His clan had always owned this little cluster of fetid caves, drip fed from highland streams. After Monofication, the country opened up trade with foreigners, this expensive delicacy had lifted his clan up and out of subsistence farming. Nowadays, the lonely little clan turned to hoarding wealth, thanks to the roving traders.

The Tamzi Kith were foreigners, and the merchants of the world. Business was the tradition of their nation, from the mightiest company to the lowly salesman. They bought and sold anything everywhere. Sole traders visited often to buy up all the fungus they could. They would haggle, jostle and often scuffle, but they would always leave behind huge piles of cash. Before then, the unknown wealth was used to compost the village fruit gardens.

Behind Drolla, the cave's black mouth smirked. It knew he would be back, and always looked forward to torturing him in the heat of the airless dark. Beneath him, the green moss crushed underfoot like a soft downy rug. Before him, the sunlit path led down to the village at the foot of the forested hills. Through the gap between the treetops, the view stretched for weeks across the flaxen meadows of the Amber Valley all the way to the distant, hazy Blue Hills. He spent many lonely lunches wondering who lived among them, and often vowed to visit them and find out. Somehow. Someday.

"Unka Dwolla," called Sroddi.

The seven year old ran toward his naked uncle with reckless joy and dove into his arms. Drolla dropped the basket and scooped up his little nephew. Face to face, mutual adoration smiled back.

"You're wet!"

"It's sweat!"

"Eeeewww..." They threw their heads back and laughed at their own hilarity.

"As mad as the other," smiled Kwinno.

His pregnant sibling waddled out of the purple shade. Two years younger and their parent's favourite. He was everyone's favourite. He was pretty, pleasant and decent. He oozed charisma and charmed everybody. Already blessed with one child, he was about to present another, thus further securing his lineage. Once again proving his fertility and value to the clan. Unlike Drolla, who was deemed the family's dead-end. He assured himself that the animosity their parent showed him was his own childlessness. *What else could it be?* he often thought. Never forgiven for never breeding.

"We brought a picnic," said Sroddi. He unrolled a tanned pelt and spread it onto the cool mossy forest floor. He took his parent's hand and steadied him as he squatted on his haunches. Kwinno pinched the fluffy yellow wool between his grateful toes.

"It's way past mealtime, you must be famished," said Kwinno.

"I missed the bell," said Drolla.

The child began to empty his shoulder packs. With solemn formality, he unfolded a woven grasswood mat and laid it beside them. With practiced care, he placed a stack of bowls on the mat and handed out glass goblets. They were as clear as air and shaped like a tusk. From a tall carafe, he filled each with sparkling citrus water. He removed the lids of the bowls and passed eating prongs to his parent and his uncle. With his own, he pointed to each bowl.

"Pickled jelly mushrooms, fermented oily fish and fresh fruit salad in syrup." He stabbed a thin fillet and giggled as he wiggled it above his open mouth.

"You excel yourself, young thyre," said Drolla. "What a wonderful picnic." The little one smiled at the praise. "I was a good little servant like you once." He soured at the thought. "So good, I still am."

"You should have kids, uncle. Then they can serve you too," said Sroddi.

The innocent child embarrassed Kwinno. He winced a sympathetic smile at Drolla and gently hushed the little one.

A sudden sadness fell upon Drolla. His heart groaned and threatened to collapse under the weight of his bygone grief. A loss forever mourned. His child who never was. His one and only, born dead. Bretto was the name he never took, but the cairn above his grave did. Haunted memories returned. A lifeless face. His tiny grey body slumped on the birthing pillow. The gasps of horror from the natal aides, and the glare of disgusted disappointment from his parent for delivering him a dead grandchild. He was only fifteen, it was his first and no one cared to console him. Anguish sent him into the caves to find solace in his loneliness, but his sanctuary soon became his prison.

"Maybe next conjugation. I might fall then, and you might get a new cousin," said Drolla without a shred of hope. He spiked a chunk of fruit, and fed it to the kid to shut him up.

Drolla was ranked an adult. He bred, or tried to, but had never fallen again since. Every season he would travel to the capital to attend the annual mating orgy. He would fuck as many syblings as he could while the colours ran across the sky. For nine seasons he was barren. Perhaps that one miscarriage broke him forever. At twenty-four, he was nearly too old to breed and no one he knew took anyone who was childless seriously. If you were not a parent, you were still a child. A dead child did not count, and he was never allowed to forget it.

He shrugged off his sorrow and smiled at a frowning Sroddi. Kwinno looked on with kind understanding. Despite his own sorrow, the emptiness within Drolla never coaxed him to begrudge the good fortune of his darling younger sibling. He adored him. He was his only ally within their heartless clan.

"We expect Vrune any day now," said Kwinno. "Par' had the cousins packing the dried fungus earlier today."

"I bet they loved that. The mighty, village clanguards reduced to manual chores."

"Yes," he laughed. "They do think they are too good for it. They complained about it the whole time. They said this was your work."

"What? They could help pick the damn things. I am the only harvester here."

"Drolla, it is far too disgusting. No one will help."

"Well, I am sick of it. It's not right. It's servant's work. It's children's work."

The air split with a thwack, and a long dart quivered in the tree behind them. A peal of laughter burst from the purple shade. Kwinno let out a squeal of surprise while Sroddi crawled to him for a reassuring hug. Drolla leapt to his feet and the startled pair gawked at the feathered shaft.

"Drord's Guts. You kladgers nearly hit the doyen's heir," he roared.

Three young adults emerged from the foliage, and strode bold into the little clearing outside the cave. Their short tunics of brindled black and purple hugged their lean, damp bodies. All three sported a quiver of long arrows and a throwing stick. They were on patrol duty and were meant to be invisible and silent, unseen by villager and intruder alike. As usual, a chance to bully their favourite victim had forced them into the open. They all looked down at the picnic, blushed and curtsied at Kwinno.

"Apologies thyre, we meant no disrespect to you," said Zonna. He pointed his woomera at Drolla. "Merely jesting with the kid here."

"He's older than you's" squawked Sroddi.

"Is he?" smirked Zonna. "He's an overripe fruit that's yet to flower." He stepped closer to Drolla and stared him down face to face. "You're still serving like a child, while the rest of us grew up."

"Yeh, we do the adult's work around here," boasted Flutto.

"And when we're promoted to seniors and run things, where will you be?" asked Zonna.

"In the caves," said Tromma.

"And when we retire as elders, where will Drolla be?"

"In the caves," said Flutto and Tromma in tune. All three burst into another round of taunting laughter.

The veins in Drolla's head throbbed as the fury pumped through them. He hated his cousins and he hated this one the most. Zonna relished teasing Drolla about his impossible predicament. The core of the seniarchy was the progression of learning and responsibility. A 'child' from five years old was trained to serve. They learned the arts of obedience and the duty of servitude. Once they came of age at fifteen they were expected to breed. As an 'adult' until thirty, they worked. All means of production and protection was performed by adults. As a 'senior', they ruled and directed everyone under their own sphere of responsibility. As head of the family or the clan leader, his word was law. Retirement at forty-five allowed 'elders' to advise those who succeeded them. Most joined a consultorium. They considered their advice indispensable, despite it not being mandatory. Drolla still served like a child. He was a slave to his own parent who did not consider him an 'adult'. Thus, he was enthralled for as long as the doyen wished. He was trapped.

Drolla pulled the dart from the tree, it was as long as he was tall. The fletching whispered as he twirled the shaft, spinning it from one hand to another. Zonna jerked back as the tip stabbed at his face.

"The brave patroller flinches," scoffed Drolla.

He spat at the coward's feet and broke the shaft across his knee. As he threw it aside, Zonna lashed out. His fist landed squarely in Drolla's mouth. A bell rang, and for a moment a smolderstone flickered behind his eyelids. He shook off the dizziness and licked the blood from his split lip. Drolla pounced at his aggressor. He knocked him off his feet, and pinned him to the ground. As quick as lightning, his little sickle was out of his belt and the curved glass blade pushed across Zonna's throat. A thin trickle of white blood crept across his neck and disappeared as it dripped into the moss beneath them. The cousins pressed two arrow heads onto Drolla's ribs.

"Stand back, or you'll watch this coward die," yelled Drolla. They did not move. "Don't wriggle. One slip and you will drown on your own blood."

Zonna's eyes bulged as Drolla applied a little more pressure to the stinging cut.

"Do it!" Zonna hissed through gritted teeth. A murderous smirk crossed Drolla's mocking face. He adjusted his body weight to accept the challenge. "Not you," he bleated. "Them! Stand away!"

"You pests have interrupted my picnic long enough," said Kwinno. He waved his hand above the picnic bowls, pretending to shoo flies.

The comrades complied. They stepped back and nodded their deference to Kwinno. Zonna grabbed at his neck and covered his tiny wound. He checked his fingers for blood. Drolla sheathed his little sickle and slapped him hard across the face. Defeated, Zonna bounded to his feet and led his peers back into the forest, clutching again at his weeping throat.

"The doyen will hear of this," cried Zonna. "You cannot assault a clanguard."

"Go on, run back home," called Drolla. "Tell everyone you were bested by a child."

Sroddi's impish laughter chased after them.

"What an idiot," said Kwinno. "Fruits don't flower."

1.2 - THE FIRSTHAND HEARSAY

Sroddi was chuffed.

He was allowed to stay behind and help Drolla lay out the Red Spore slabs in the drying sheds. Kwinno often encouraged them to spend time with each other, to whose benefit was debatable. Drolla appreciated the gesture. He loved his nephew, but he was no substitute child.

"I wish I could help you all the time," said Sroddi. "Even in the caves." He floated in the pond-tub, arms splayed wide. Only his cheeky face bobbed above the water.

"No, you don't. You are destined for better things."

"I like the dark, and the stinky mud."

"You'll soon grow out of that. Besides, you are the grandheir of the doyen. He would never let you help me."

The child blinked in thought.

"Grandpar' Hlammi is very mean, isn't he Unka Dwolla? He's always angry at you, even when you're not there. He doesn't like you very much, does he?"

"Sometimes, parents can love you and be nasty to you at the same time."

"Well, that's just silly. He's never nasty to par'."

"No one is ever nasty to our darling Kwinno," said Drolla.

"Never mind Unka Dwolla, I love you."

"I love you more, little fella." Drolla cupped two hands and pushed them hard onto the water. A mighty splash erupted and rained down onto them both. Moments like these helped Drolla forget his misery.

A sweet fermented breeze blew uphill from the shade of the parley awning. The alcoholic waft of his favourite brew was unmistakable, saporous and pert. It seemed the Tamzi trader had arrived earlier than expected. If the booze was flowing, then the haggling was done.

"Brewberries," Drolla salivated. He deemed it the greatest invention in Meladonian history. From millennia past, the ancient hero Menex studied and collated all the established methods of agriculture, harvest and culinary techniques. Food was his passion, but his perfecting of the fermentation process earned him an eternal place as the second hour on Throthm's sundial. He also earned the eternal gratitude of the merry generations that followed.

A grey linen canopy covered the circular plaza in the village central. It gently flapped as freely as the breeze shifted. Striding down the ramped path through the forest, what seemed like mocking laughter from the awning met Drolla as he approached. At the bottom of the ramp, Sroddi saw his par' and ran ahead. The laughter stopped when every face turned toward Drolla. He sighed and ignored his suspicions, what difference would it make if he was worried or not? They will think what they like. He strode between the planter boxes that ringed the plaza, and took one step under the awning.

"At last, you decide to join us," said Hlammi. "You were expected to help load the Red Spore."

"I..."

"I do not care about your excuses. What I care about, is you performing your tasks as required. Furthermore, I do not appreciate my patrollers attacked and their equipment damaged."

Drolla's face flushed hot. The gloating smirk of the coward Zonna, the embarrassed stare of the trader Vrune, and the judgmental gazes of everyone else stabbed holes in him. The seniors and elders lounged about on the doyen's best cushions. Entitled, arrogant and careless, they sipped from clear glass bowls and dripped bright red brewberry syrup on the woolly, yellow rug. Hlammi, the clan doyen sat in the centre of the group. His audience sat in rings around him. From those he favoured near, their ranks radiated out, to some who were barely eligible. Hlammi was dressed in his finest silken toga, fading top down, from the darkest green to the lightest, it shimmered while he roused on Drolla.

"Fortunately, the noble Kwinno has vouched for you. Again. But I insist you avoid any further confrontations and stick to your chores."

"Par', I was protecting Kwinno. But, thank you for the public scolding."

"Yeh, do as you're told, child," said Zonna from across the plaza.

"I'll do you proper next time."

"Enough," the doyen spat. "Drolla, take the cash box and sit. Kwinno will count it later. Vrune has important news."

The little chest was heavy and clinked as he sat it on his lap. Drolla opened the lid and his eyes squinted shut at the dazzle of a hundred glass rods. Each one could feed you for a month, or last a week spent on a brewberry binge. The size of a finger and as clear as water, each rod was forged from the purest sands from the Vitron Shores. A core of smolderstone powder lit its precious spine from end to end. Mined from an extinct volcano encircled by Zharkhon Island, the powder shone more brighter and far longer than the broken crystal rocks ordinary folk struck to light their homes. Exported and minted by the merchants of the Tamzi Kith, they would trade no other currency. Thus, their glash became the monetary standard everywhere. A dozen decades have passed since the volcano erupted, and sank the island. The mine is gone. The precious value of these shiny glass rods was guaranteed. Every year, they could buy a little more. He snapped the lid shut and blinked at the wriggling purple shadows behind his eyelids.

Ten years ago, Hlammi gave sole purchase rights to his harvests of Red Spore to Vrune. Of all the Tamzi traders, he was the most reliable and consistent. He often praised us as his favourites. 'Purple trees. Best place Vrune visit,' he would often boast with a hand on his heart and a lump in his throat. Raised goblets engendered trust between the trader and the doyen. Despite being a foreigner, Vrune was always granted pride of place in Hlammi's presence. Everyone was wise to show him due respect.

Squatting beside Vrune, the winsome teen glowed. His scanty poncho hung lopsided off his rounded white shoulders. A green breast glinted under the tawny linen. Kwinno's blue breast flash was starting to show, but the chest of the heavily pregnant southerner was as bright as an emerald sun.

"Thyre, you like Krodanga?" asked Vrune. Drolla's fascination did not go unnoticed, his face warmed and he realised he was staring at the ripe young chest. "Rescue from Zintrix. Last year. Orphan begging plaza. Poor beautiful thing. Mine now. Safe now."

"Yes, how good of you. But, I am more curious about the flash," said Drolla.

"Oh? Krodanga green?" He frowned, as if amazed he had to explain. "Me Tamzi, yellow. You Drahni, blue."

"It's not the colour Vrune. He looks pregnant. Too pregnant. He won't last until Pannatalia."

Vrune laughed loud, and the village prudes whispered behind their palms.

"I no wait Conjugation. Me pleasure young beauty," said Vrune. The naughty smile fell from his face the moment Hlammi decided to be indignant.

"Well, I am shocked to hear this Vrune," said Hlammi. "Is this customary for the Tamzi, or just your own personal lechery?"

"We trade. Private life no matter," said Vrune.

"Conjugation is a sacred act of procreation. The mass orgies during the mating season are essential to ensure the anonymity of the seeding parent. A pedigree family line is born only through the birthing parent."

"Paf," said Vrune. "My people. Tamzi Kith breed seven islands. We no pureblood nation. We mesh all people. Not you. Drahn selfish blue racists."

"You are right Vrune. We do favour ourselves," said Drolla.

"Yes, Drahn pure nation. Tradition. All good. But not Fronst and filthy Zharkhon, they too pure. Only breed own family."

The Drahni audience groaned with collective disgust. Vrune laughed at his hosts' pretended snobbery. They loved his naughty stories from abroad. Yet he agreed, correctly so, that incest is dangerous. Intrabred rivalry had always collapsed clans from within. It was revolting.

"But, how could you mate outside conjugation?" asked Drolla. He already knew the answer, but sought to embarrass his elders. "The annual auroras start the mating season for everything. That's the only time normal passion rages."

Vrune winked at Drolla and mouthed hidden words from behind his palm, "Red Spore". He took a sip from an invisible cup.

"Desire come. Urge too strong. Must act." He erupted into laughter and slapped Drolla's shoulder.

"This has all been very enlightening Vrune," said Kwinno, "but, might we hear your news before I retire underground? I believe I am done here for the day, par'."

Hlammi bowed a nod.

Vrune cleared his throat and adjusted his cushion.

"Thyre. For sixty days. Travel ahead. Your army come. War come."

"War, coming here? Did you know about this par'?" asked Kwinno.

"No," said Hlammi. Concern furrowed deep across his brow.

"But surely as clan leader, and the monarch's doyen, you were told," said Drolla.

"There have been no couriers," said Hlammi. He flashed a vicious glare at Drolla. "Please continue Vrune."

"Miokhi raid Oxxia. Steal black sand."

"Why?" asked Drolla.

"Who cares why," roared Brokka. His interjection startled those paying attention.

"Grandpar', please," said Kwinno. "A war is heading our way."

"They are not bringing warriors here, Kwinno. They are recruiters, they come to take them away. They scour the provinces and round up as many as they can, then send them all off to war."

"What about the royal army?" asked Drolla.

"They are career soldiers," said Brokka. "They are no better than peace-keepers these days. This is an inter-national war, they will need thousands more fighters."

"Grandpar' true," said Vrune. "Huge mob come. Recruit hundreds."

"Press-gang, you mean. They're not raising a volunteer army." Brokka punched his palm and scowled.

"Surely they won't take us," said Zonna. He pointed to himself and his fellow patrollers. "We are essential to the safety of the village."

"You are exactly who they will take. Start packing kids. You'll not escape the royal draft," said Brokka.

Drolla smirked at Zonna. The coward and his cousins rose and left the gathering.

"Off you run, the forest won't hide you," laughed Drolla.

As for himself, his innards buzzed. This was wonderful news. It could be his escape. Finally, a chance came for him to get out of the caves, out of the village, and out of Hlammi's grip.

Vrune's squire approached and squatted next to his master. He softly spoke his message in the Tamzi tongue. Vrune nodded and shot his eyes at Hlammi.

"Fungus loaded. Caravan ready. We go." He slapped his knees and stood. He extended a hand to Hlammi. They grasped palms. Middle fingers lay up either wrist, both thumbs folded top and bottom over the back of the other's hand. Their grip squeezed mutual admiration.

"Thank you once again for an excellent visit," said Hlammi.

"Always pleasure. Always good trade. Me leave now. Scouts see army. Here tomorrow. Me not. Farewell."

The villagers watched the caravan of porters trundle their overloaded litters along the forest road.

Drolla's cheeks ached.

Hlammi scowled at him. "Wipe that stupid grin off your face."

I.3 - THE YOUTHFUL ELDER

Drolla squat outside his fungal lair. A laden basket nestled between two ankles.

Cave sweat oozed from every pore, and the cool forest air freshened his wheezing breath. Orange sunbeams streaked through gaps in the mauven woodlands. High on his hidden hill, the forest fell away with the sloping ridge. Across the top of the trees his lazy eyes scanned the yonder meadows. A lone churning white cloud dawdled up the valley toward the village. His realisation was far slower than its lazy approach. He slapped his forehead at the cloudless sky, shadows are not white. Vrune's tidings had arrived. The army was here. He shot to his feet. His pounding heart stretched his smile wider than his excited eyes. He scooped up his things and ran straight to the bath house.

In the deserted village plaza, Drolla waited for his visitors. He relaxed in the shifting shade of a jewelfruit tree. Not one day ago, his supposed betters sat here under the parley awning. Today he sat alone. Everyone else lazed below in their darkened chambers, drowsy after their daily meal. They were all completely unaware their uninvited guests had arrived.

A lone stooping elder shuffled toward the empty plaza. He stopped at the edge, spied Drolla and nodded him a friendly greeting. Not far away, a war horn sounded. Long and forlorn, it announced its impending woe. The elder made his way over to Drolla, his long brown toga rustled like dry leaves.

"Greetings young thyre. An unexpected welcome," he said.

"We knew you were coming," said Drolla.

"Yet, you wait alone."

"I am always alone."

"Are you?' The old fellow smiled. "Well, not for long I trust. Do you know the doyen of this clan?"

A second, closer pair of blasts from the army war horns sounded.

"Unfortunately, I do," said Drolla.

"Yes, same here." The elder grinned again. From underground, the curious, dozy villagers began to gather on the plaza. The growing crowd took his attention. "Oh, good. Time to begin. I shall see you later." He winked.

A tall guard stood at the far edge of the plaza. Ten more flanked him, five a side. They wore sheer, jade green tunics, split at the waist. Each tab hung between thick, protruding thighs. A belt of woven black leather tied the garment to their middle. Hanging from it was a sheathed war-glass shard, a warrior's long blade. With two arms folded in front, they presented an intimidating pose. Their arm behind held an upright battle lance. They formed a semi-circular guard of honour, and watched the clanfolk cluster behind their doyen.

The old official in the brown toga took centre stage. Bright eyes scanned the gathered villagers. With one hand, he leaned on a long staff. A twisted tree branch carved into a spiral spear-lizard. In the other hand, he held the royal baton. The short shaft of black Drahn glass was topped with a flying tri-winged bat carved from beige grasswood. A glint of sunlight rolled across its lacquered sheen. Drolla recognised the thing from his grandpar's stories. This was the national symbol of authority. It was once the seniarch's baton. Adopted by the monarchy, it exploited the tradition that everyone acknowledged and respected the power of those who bore it.

Sroddi tried to pull his hand from his parents' grip. He huffed at his own failure, and he pinched the back of Kwinno's hand. In his surprise, he let go and looked down to scold the brat. But Sroddi was gone. He bolted over to the old official and looked up in awe.

"What happened to that arm?" asked Sroddi, pointing at the stump. "You've only got two now."

"Grandchild," Hlammi hissed.

The elder raised a dismissive palm and crouched to speak with the child.

"It got chopped off a long time ago," he said.

"Did it hurt?"

"Yes. A lot. But I got better, see." He wobbled the scarred flap of skin dangling from the elbow stump. Sroddi grinned wide at the silly looking thing. "Now, be a good kid and go back and cheer up your grandpar'. He looks cranky." The elder stood, with his gaze fixed on the doyen, and called, "Dandaron."

The tallest of the guards unfolded his brawny arms and scooped up the child. He held him high and allowed the child to stand on his shoulders. Sroddi was delighted. Dandaron playfully passed him over to Kwinno's outstretched arms. The little rascal and the gentle giant swapped a friendly smile and they both retook their proper places.

The elder thrust the baton into the air. Silent attention was expected.

"Greetings, syblings of Drahn." His voice boomed. The seasoned orator immediately commanded the attention of the spectators. After a pause, he continued. "My name is Quetono. My enforcers and I are the regal representatives of our great kindom. We have been sent by our exalted monarch, Soltoro, to draft recruits into his royal army.

"The monarch's law mandates all adults from the ages of nineteen to twenty-nine are conscripted. Seniors may volunteer. Everyone else, including the pregnant are exempt." He paused to allow the inevitable chatter to erupt and suppressed a sliver of a grin. Before the muttering could get out of hand, he continued. "Failure to comply with this royal order is a capital offense."

This was far more than the villagers had expected. Vrune's news had spread throughout the clan, but the families decided it was merely travelers' gossip. Yesterday, they scoffed and belittled any effect it might have on them. They believed their village was far too remote for the monarchy to ever notice them. Today, this reality caused an uncomfortable ruckus. The little mob started to voice denials, many sobbed and the rest prattled among themselves. It was obvious that Quetono had seen these reactions before. He allowed them to carry on for a while and let it all sink in. His face flitted here and there, delighting in the variety of reactions. It almost appeared he enjoyed their anguish before he interrupted their distress one last time.

"When you settle yourselves, could all eligible adults please come forward. I would ask you all to fetch any not present. While you do, I shall see the doyen first under that marquee." He pointed behind the audience. To their surprise a domed tent five paces wide had been erected on the grass beyond the plaza. The people had all been so distracted by the upsetting news that no-one noticed the sappers' silent labour. When Quetono was satisfied everyone understood the situation, he called out. "Clan doyen. Now, if you please."

The audience parted as he and his guard boldly strode forward between them. As they strutted past, Drolla stared at the tallest of them. Dandaron flicked a curious eyebrow in return. Quetono dipped into the tent, flicked his skirt, and sat in the shade.

1.4 - THE VOLUNTEER CONSCRIPT

The entrance flap of the recruiter's tent was tied low.

Hlammi grunted with contempt. He was indignant at being forced to duck and curtsy his way inside. Drolla and Kwinno followed him into the shade, and a corner of Quetono's mouth pinched into a snide smile.

The old drafter sat on the central plynth. The small stool was curtained by a linen skirt painted white and grey and resembled a fluted column. He leaned toward them, hands on his knees, as smug as a strict parent. A nervous secretary stood aside. His white silken toga wrapped tight up his burly frame. Looped around his neck, a braided cord held a writing tray in place. With ink, paperbark scrolls and a stylus poised, he was ready to take the minutes. Drolla dipped to curtsy proper, but Hlammi lifted him with a palm under his armpit.

"You have already done that."

An awkward silence resounded within the marquee. Staring into each other, the doyen and the recruiter spoke with their eyes. Neither seemed to like what they saw. Quetono's smile disappeared and Hlammi's frown furrowed. The scribe's innocent scratchings stole their gaze.

"Hinkara, what are you writing?" asked Quetono.

"Describing the atmosphere, thyre."

"Just record the conversation." He rolled his eyes at the idiot and scanned the trio in front of him. "Hello, and welcome."

Hlammi nodded, short and sharp.

"Hello thyre," said Drolla and Kwinno together.

"Could you state your name and status?" asked Quetono.

"You know who I am," spat Hlammi.

"For the record, please." He smiled and nodded to the scribe.

"My name is Hlammi, senior and doyen of clan Tro. These are my offspring Drolla the eldest, and Kwinno the younger."

"Good, thank you." The old recruiter stared hard at Drolla. He tore his eyes away to glance at the scribe. "Did you get that?" The scribe blushed and nodded. Quetono addressed the doyen. "It is good to see you again."

"I cannot say the same," said Hlammi. "I would have preferred it if you had passed our district over all together."

"Ha. If only, eh? How long has it been, four years, five?"

"Six. At a doyen's summit."

"Ah yes, in the capital. Vondaka was there as well, remember? You made quite a name for yourself, didn't you?" said Quetono.

"I don't remember."

"Yes you do. You complained that you were over taxed. You argued that because you were only a tiny little clan hidden away up here in your purple hills, that your tax rate should be reduced to reflect that. You ignored the well-known fact that you generated five times more wealth than many other larger clans. You and your greedy mushrooms. I was glad to see the delegates voted to ensure you paid your fair share."

"I have always paid my tithe, and more," said Hlammi.

"Yes, and the treasury is eternally grateful. I am sure you are grateful too, for the exemptions it bought you."

Throughout this banter, Quetono's eyes had shifted to Kwinno. His iridescent blue flash started at the base of his neck and spread across the top of his chests. It proudly displayed Kwinno's prenatal condition. In the shaded marquee, it dazzled sapphire in the light of the scribe's smolderstone.

"You're pregnant," said Quetono.

"Yes, with my second. You met my other one earlier."

"Ah yes, sweet child. I hope I live long enough to recruit him too one day." His joke fell flat.

"You would take them all if you could," said Hlammi.

"Only if they're eligible," said Quetono. He winked at Drolla.

"Kwinno is here as living proof he is not eligible," said Hlammi.

"I can see that, but there was no need. I would have trusted your word. We give everyone the chance to be honest and obey the edict. I did mention it earlier that is a capital offense not to. Once all your eligible adults are enlisted, and before we depart, my guards will thoroughly search this village above and below."

"Trust my word," Hlammi scoffed.

"I said I would, not my enforcers. Any shirkers they find, will be gathered to face justice."

"What sort of justice?" asked Hlammi.

"Instant. For example, the last clanburg back. Tuskfoot was it not?" He paused to ponder. "Doesn't matter. The enlistment there was so meager, it raised our suspicions. It did not match our census records at all. I challenged the elders, but they were obstinate and refused to give up their quota. So we searched the place. We found so many cowards hiding that after we impaled them all, they encircled their entire city plaza. We nicknamed the town 'Sky Dance City'." Again, he laughed alone for a moment.

"We know those people," whimpered Kwinno.

"Knew," said Quetono. "Like you, they were warned. Yet they chose to defy their monarch."

Drolla wondered what harsh world this old fellow had lived in to be so glib about a massacre. It was obvious he had seen battles before. His missing arm must surely be a war wound. He understood people could be evil with one another. His parent often beat him when he was young and was cruel all the time. He had suffered bullying all his life and often wore bruises from fighting his cousins. In the heat of the moment he threatened to kill them, but he could never actually do it. Could he? Soon he might face that doubt.

"You will have our complete co-operation," said Hlammi.

"I expect no less." Quetono waved a palm. "Kwinno, you are excused. Return to your parlour."

Kwinno curtsied and stole a glance at Hlammi. He nodded his assent and watched his pregnant child waddle out of the tent. Quetono turned to address Drolla, but before he could continue Hlammi spoke.

"We need to talk. In private."

"In private?" Quetono flicked his eyebrows and smiled a cheeky grin.

"What I have to say is for your ears only."

"Out of the question for anyone else. But with you Hlammi, I am happy to indulge you. Dandaron, escort everyone out and tie down the flaps."

The giant gave the scribbling secretary a shove and motioned Drolla to the exit. Once outside, Drolla shrugged at the anxious glares of his waiting cousins. As he gave them no new information, they ignored him and resumed their whispering gossip. Dandaron ordered the enforcers to widen their perimeter around the tent. They herded the folk until he was sure they were out of earshot of the conversation within.

Drolla moved to stand in Dandaron's shadow. He was taller and broader by a head and shoulders. Standing at attention, he pretended to ignore Drolla but his roving eyes betrayed him.

"How tall are you?" asked Drolla, looking up.

"Why? How short are you?"

"Ha. You must get asked that a lot."

"Being stuck out here on the edge of nowhere, you probably don't."

"Sure don't. There is no one here worth talking to, and no one new."

"Well, you will be meeting a thousand new syblings soon enough."

"You think so? You're sure I will be going with you?"

"It is why we are here. Now be quiet, I am on duty."

The awkward silence seemed to last an age, but soon enough a shrill whistle chirruped from within the tent. Their private chat was over. The giant trotted to the entrance and tied up the flap. He called for the scribe and ordered the guards to regroup around the marquee.

"Drolla. Inside. Now." Hlammi was as severe as ever.

Both the elder and his parent watched him approach. One face beamed, the other was as stern as stone. The scribe tapped his inkwell.

"Drolla, are you pregnant?" asked Quetono.

"No."

"Silly question I know, but it must be asked. Any children?"

"One. Stillborn, years ago. I have never fallen since."

"I am sorry to hear that. The loss of a child is a terrible thing to bear." He lost his smile and paused a moment in reflective thought. "Well, as you are fit and of legal age, you will be joining the monarch's army today. Bring nothing, we provide everything. Go with this officer to swear in."

"That's it? I'm leaving with you? Now?" asked Drolla.

"The recruits will be given time for goodbyes. You will be expected to muster when the war horn calls again in a few hours."

"Thank you for this chance. I won't let you down," spluttered Drolla. His heart pounded, and excitement tingled through him. Quetono laughed.

"This is a compulsory draft, there is no nee..." he interrupted himself, "...no one yet has thanked me for dragging them off to war." He threw a glare of disbelief at Hlammi.

"I know, it's just..." Dandaron grabbed Drolla's arm so hard his skin bulged between his fingers. He winced and glared in disbelief at his strength. The giant pulled him to the scribe and motioned Drolla to stop talking.

"Just like that, you take him," said Hlammi, standing alone, glowing with fury.

"He seems rather keen to leave. Why would that be?" replied Quetono.

"How long will he be away?"

"Recruits are discharged when the warring is over. What they do after that is their own business."

"I expect regular bulletins on his well being."

"We go to war. Personal news sent home is not a concern for the army."

"I meant from you."

"Thank you Hlammi, I must move on. Could you please inform the rest of your clan that I am ready to receive the next in line?"

"You are as cold as stone," said Hlammi.

He peered over at his child with such a sad and longing look that it unsettled Drolla. He had never seen such anxiety before. After an awkward moment, the glum parent moved to exit the tent. Before he could go, Quetono had the last word.

"Hlammi, as a favour to me and a warning to the others, please tell those waiting outside all about Sky Dance City."

I.5 - THE WELCOME FAREWELL

After the village adults had pledged their lives to the monarch's baton, Quetono allowed the new recruits some time to farewell their loved ones.

They can wait, thought Drolla. His toes fondled the soft, cool moss. The cave behind him seemed dejected. An imagined mournful sigh rose from its darkest depths. The era of their mutual hatred was over. The stinking hole could find a new stooge. Someone else could sweat, and sneeze and spew.

He pitied whomever it might be. His shoulders slumped, who was he kidding, he envied who it might be. Despite everything, he would miss it. He enjoyed the solitude up here. He was used to it.

For years he meditated away the misery of his hopeless life. Here was one place he could be sure of privacy. It was his refuge, a place to avoid his annoying cousins and his oppressive parent. What a ridiculous cruel irony. Taunted for laziness, he would retreat to the caves and work alone, just to do the task he was chided for avoiding. Every day he had dreamed of escape and today, at last, he would. He was going to leave it all behind. It was almost surreal. His eyes daydreamed across the tops of the purple trees down to the umber meadow. The dirty white cloud loitered by the shaded, roadside knoll, and his gaze drifted into the horizon. Soon he might discover the secrets of those distant hazy Blue Hills.

An unexpected clatter came from the drying sheds. It was always deserted. This was his other domain, the stink of the drying fungus ensured no one else shared it. Drolla peered through the slats and a silhouette glided across the mist cloth. It cursed again after another clumsy crash. Drolla tore aside the entry fold. Garlands of fresh fungus swayed, festooned on strings like festive bunting. From between the gauze tables, Brokka peeked.

"Grandpar', are you alright?" asked Drolla.

"I tripped over these stupid poles." He stood, and bundled the sticks to his chest like a faggot.

"Let me stack them for you. What are you doing in here?"

"Where are the driest slabs?" He pulled one from the drying line and sniffed it. "Phwoah," he kecked.

"Not those. They're not cured yet."

"Then where?"

"In the barrels, under the tables. Why?"

Brokka squatted and waddled along the rows, his head bobbed at every step. He opened and sniffed one container after the other.

"This one. Throw me that pack. There, that one, hanging right next to you," said Brokka. His impatient finger stabbed through the air. A slinger's satchel made of orange suede leather hung by a grey braided fur cord. A small bone carved like a fang, linked through a grasswood woven ring, latched the flap shut. Brokka caught it and stuffed the bag with dried slabs of Red Spore fungus. "I have had this shoulder pack since I was your age. My grandpar' helped me make it. It has never been to war though, not until now." He paused and counted under his breath. He packed a few more. "How many took the oath?"

"Thirteen."

"That many? I hate those phapping monarchists. Coming here, stealing our kids."

"We're adults, grandpar'."

"You're all kids to me. They're stripping our clan bare of a whole generation. Sybling's Pact, my dot! Drord's Guts, how are we supposed to manage now?"

The old fellow was right, the virtue of the Sybling's Pact seemed pointless now. It was the seniarch's duty to ensure that every sybling was bound by equality. As a kindom, everyone was family, conjugation ensured that. The pact of duty and protection held every sybling safely in their place. Service and reward, bestow and acquire. The principles of seniocracy still ran deep within the syblings of the nation, despite the tyranny of the monarchy. Once the people served each other, now they served the royal family.

"They tax our coffers to keep the peace. Now, they take our kids to make war," said Brokka. "They've already robbed me of two, now they want a third."

"Two? Who?"

His grandparent ignored him and recounted the extra slabs in the bag. Sadness smoothed the aged lines across his face. He stopped counting, his eyes blackened and he faced his grandchild.

"Near three decades ago, the press-gangers came. They took your uncles for a war that never was."

"I had uncles?" asked Drolla.

"Vlakka and Groffa. That kladger Guetono took them too. Hlammi was too young. Gone two years and we never heard from them again. Royalty sent their condolences with two engraved pebbles as token cairns. Lost at sea, they said."

"Where are the stones?" asked Drolla.

"I took them to the caves and threw them into the deepest pit I could find. I sang the funeral hymn, and they clattered down into the darkness long after I had finished. We remembered them for a while. Then you came along and the memory was all too painful. We vowed to keep that royal tragedy a secret, and we have despised the monarchy ever since."

"And now they take me."

"You want to go, don't you. I don't blame you. Hlammi has always been difficult. So please take this." He pressed the bulging satchel into Drolla's arms. "Trade it wisely, use it to make everything a little less uncomfortable."

Drolla's heart was so heavy he thought it might fall right through him. He reached for his grandpar'. The elder blinked away his tears and they hugged for the first time since childhood.

The entrance to the doyen's manor was unguarded.

"They've taken the sentries as well," scowled Brokka.

The doorway's architraves resembled arching brewberry vines, their branches reached and intertwined with each other. Carved from funglstone, it was centuries old. The entry was dressed with thick black leather drapes that hung stiff to the floor. Behind them the foyer was dark. Light bled up the ramped corridor from the reception room below. This was not an entry Drolla often used. The rear entrance by the kitchen garden was 'good enough for him'. The pantry was his reception room. Brokka led him down toward the light. Sobbing crept up the hall toward them as Brokka led the way down toward the light.

A chandelier of a dozen smolderstones lit the chamber. Frescoes of idyllic garden scenes adorned the walls. It looked ridiculous, walk out the back door and you could see the real thing. Tapestries of past doyens covered exits to corridors, they led deep into the labyrinth of the underground mansion. The black and white fur carpet pattern spiraled into the centre of the room. There sat Hlammi, on a barrel for a plynth. He was scribbling at a curved bench that arched half way around him. He finished one note, stamped it, slapped it on a pile and started on another.

Sroddi sat at his parent's feet. He toyed with Podium game pieces. He wasn't playing the game properly, he stacked the cubes, cones and pyramids on top of each other. It amused him to watch his little piles collapse. Perhaps it made it easier for him to cope with his parent's tears.

"Oh Drolla, it's just awful," bawled Kwinno. He pounced into Drolla's arms and sobbed on his shoulder. Hlammi paused his writing and sighed.

"Stop crying, or go do it somewhere else."

"What are you writing?" asked Brokka.

"Letters of introduction for our kin. Petitions, begging favour for their care."

"Don't be ridiculous. They will all be faceless martyrs the moment they leave the village."

"They'll be fine. They'll all return home safe."

"Like my uncles?" asked Drolla.

The colour ran from Kwinno's face. His mouth fell open and his lip quivered. His sodden eyes glared at Drolla.

"You told him?" scowled Hlammi.

"What uncles?" asked Kwinno.

"Par's elder siblings. They died long before we were born," said Drolla.

"How could you keep this from us for all these years?" Kwinno's tears had stopped.

"The tragedy was ours, not yours. We chose to rejoice your future, not mourn their past," said Hlammi.

"What other secrets have you kept from us?" asked Kwinno.

"None," said Hlammi. He stole a glance at Drolla.

"Well, they're not taking him," said Kwinno. "He'll be killed. We'll hide you in the caves."

"I can't. I won't," said Drolla. "I have to go. I want to go."

Kwinno ignored him. "There must be some deep pits hidden where no-one will find you."

"Stop this nonsense," snapped Hlammi. "He has been drafted. He must go."

"Yes, you would like him gone, wouldn't you? You have always hated him. Now someone else can get rid of him for you."

Hlammi stood and slapped Kwinno hard across the face. They fell into each others arms.

"I don't want him to die, par!" Kwinno whimpered through more tears.

"Neither do I. I have been harsh, and I am sorry for it. But..."

"They will kill us all if he hides," said Brokka. "Then they will kill him when they find him."

Hlammi turned to Drolla and took a hand in his.

"It was never your fault. I should never have held it against you."

"That's enough Hlammi," said Brokka. "It's too late for all that now."

"Too late for what?" asked Kwinno. His par' and grandpar' both ignored him.

"You are the clan doyen, Hlammi," said Brokka. "A seniocrat. You have an example to set. The monarchy is watching. You must host a brave farewell."

"I sometimes wish you had not retired par'," said Hlammi. His voice quivered like a nervous adolescent afraid to face an adult's task. Proof, even the most stolid and stern can lose their nerve. Drolla curbed his sympathy, one pitiful moment could not erase two decades of malice. Drolla picked up Sroddi and hugged him tight.

"Let's go find the others."

The plaza simmered with nervous gossip. The villagers filled the paved grounds and spilled past the outer ring of planters. Children climbed the edging trees for a better view while elders sat in their shade. They scolded the brats tossing unripe nuts at them. Protective families clustered around their recruited adults, all dressed in their finest robes. In the middle of it all, the doyen's podium was empty.

The war horn had not yet sounded, but no-one dared be late. The old two-armed conscripter had convinced them his threat was real. Through a long, vine choked arbour, Brokka led the doyen's procession. From the residence to the plaza, the tunnel of red translucent foliage cast a pink shade along the winding path. Cradling a woven grasswood basket, a somber Kwinno followed his doyen. Hlammi wore his official robe, it depicted the Perse Hills he ruled. A long dark purple poncho edged with a white hairy fringe hung around him like a closed umbrella. Mauve dyed furs draped his rounded shoulders. He marched with his rod of office, a funglstone stave as tall as himself. The long blunt bladestaff strode the ground like a fourth leg. Tense knuckles gripped the feathered hilt. Carved like a fang, the polished pommel glinted sunlight at every stride. Before Monofication, it was a weapon of war. Now it was merely a ceremonial relic.

The clan hushed as he arrived, and parted a wedge that allowed Hlammi to approach the podium. Without his circling guard of honour, the clanlord cut a lonely figure. He slowly moved with the dignity and nobility of a thespian, and his solemn face reflected the people's sober mood. As he mounted his little central stage, the folk closed the gap and reshuffled themselves so all could see him. A giggling child and an angry elder broke the austere silence. They were shushed by irate seniors nearby. When the clan had settled and paid him their attention, Hlammi struck an orator's pose and spoke.

"Fellow kinfolk, we gather to bid farewell. Today, the army takes our finest. To them a soldier, to us a loved one. The clan will be poorer for their absence, but we must always be ready for their return. They go to fight a noble cause and join thousands of our syblings across Drahn to repel an evil foe. Let them go with our blessings, let them return to our praise. Together we share..."

"Together?" yelled Zlodda.

Hlammi's eyes widened, then narrowed stern with his frown.

"My Drolla goes with your Zonna, and with all the recruits. I share your loss."

"You had private talks within a closed tent. A secret deal for special treatment, perhaps?"

"What? No!"

"Then why?"

"It was royal business. Nothing to do with....."

Skeptical groans arose from the disgruntled spectators.

"Royal business? What a loyal seniocrat you are," said Zlodda. "I think it's high time we had another seniorial bout."

As upset as the villagers were, Zlodda's suggestion stank of mutiny. Their silence expressed their support, or lack of it. An incredulous Hlammi looked to his parent. Brokka scowled back at him. Drolla leaped onto the podium.

"A ballot today? We are leaving today to go to war. None of us might return and rather than see us off, you would host another petty power grab. I have more reason than anyone to dislike our doyen, but he did not do this."

"He could have done something," cried an anonymous voice. Drolla snatched the basket of letters from Kwinno and tore the lid off. He sprayed handfuls of the scrolls down at his fellow recruits like a farmer scattering seeds.

"Here's what he did. They're your endorsements. Your doyen meant to bind the drafter to place you all in the monarch's care," said Drolla.

"I was supposed to hand them out," cried Kwinno. "Now you've ruined everything."

What a pathetic sight the scrambling recruits made. They snatched from each other and squabbled over the crumpled bits of paper. The parents were no better, they were frantic to secure their own child's note. The rest of the folk watched the pitiful performance of their peers with mild amusement. Drolla would not miss these people. He was glad to leave.

No one saw the herald arrive. The war horn blasted long, low, and loud. The tallest enforcer led the troop. Like a spearhead, they parted the crowd and lined the gap. The villagers were annoyed at this forgotten interruption, but their deference forced them to step aside. Through the wedge, old Quetono strode to the podium.

"Help me up."

Dandaron offered two hands and coaxed Drolla and Hlammi down from the podium, then he lifted the old drafter up onto it. Quetono scanned the faces gazing up at him. The warm smile of a loving uncle stretched across his face.

"Syblings," he said. "I have come to collect my recruits. Doyen Hlammi, you lead a true and honest clan. You should be proud, everyone eligible is here. We found no need to seek out shirkers."

"Of course you didn't," yelled Zlodda.

Nervous laughter cackled across the families. The sour faces of Drolla's family openly displayed their contempt toward their fellows. A sense of unease for their welfare crawled up his spine. The impulsive clan could not be trusted. This whole affair had once again revealed their true nature. The great seniors and noble elders were fickle, and an embarrassment. They were as toady as the southern thralls across the channel seas. One slight bit of praise and they were happy to curtsy away their children's lives. Hlammi, through Brokka, would reassert his seniority. The retired doyen knew how to govern these fools.

"I trust you have said your goodbyes. We are leaving. Recruits, follow me."

The finality of the situation hit everyone at last. Howls and sobbing filled the air. Nervous conscripts were torn from their brokenhearted parents. To others, shouts of encouragement chased them as the enforcers rounded up behind the recruits and pushed them ahead. As they trudged past the village outskirts, many threw up their hands and waved a final farewell. Drolla did not even look back.

I.6 - THE LONELY HORDE

The mood of the escort changed the moment the village was out of sight.

The old fellow threw his walking stick across his shoulders, and broke into a trot. The recruits swapped grins of disbelief, but their broad smiles soon vanished as strong insistent palms shoved them forward.

"Get moving."

Their shoulder packs bounced and slapped their sides at every step. Drolla spun his satchel around his neck and clutched it to him. He doubted his cousins' packs held treasure like his. The thought made him hug it even tighter, as tight as his grandpar's hug.

The first in a trilogy of assaults on their senses struck hard. The pong was ripe. It was muggy like moldy laundry and the smell was getting worse.

"Ugh, it stinks like you," said Zonna, as he backhanded Drolla's arm.

Drolla's fist pounded his shoulder. Zonna grunted and raised a hand ready to strike again.

"Enough," shouted Dandaron, smiling.

The second insult was the noise. Echoing from behind the last hill, the clamour confused their ears. It sounded like a motionless stampede, yet seemed it might gallop past any moment. They reached the crest and the view presented itself. That was the final insult.

A thousand grimy nudes milled about in an aimless, churning throng. Up close, the white cloud was disgusting. Armed soldiers patrolled the perimeter of the mob, herding them like animals. They were all kept a respectful distance from a small bright red pavilion. Resting officers casually gazed about from under the awning. Beyond the tent, a dozen or so little white narrow tee-pees stood together like a row of teeth. The troop of enforcers slowed their trot.

"Halt."

The unfit mushroom farmer was bent over with his palms on his knees, panting at his cousins. The enforcers encircled the group, and the old drafter walked on toward the awnings. Four beige clad officers left the shade and met him mid way. Out of earshot, Quetono spoke with one. The officer glanced at Drolla for a moment and nodded. The old fellow patted his shoulder and entered the pavilion.

"I am quartermaster Jandra."

"Hello," said Zonna.

"Shut up!" he spat. "You do not speak. Strip! Come on, hurry up. Off with those fancy rags, you won't need those."

The baffled recruits obeyed without question. Embroidered cloth fell from all except the doyen's child. His parent had never presented Drolla with his clanvex, the adult's robe. Three family crested pennants sewn into a star. The cornered joins laid over the head and hung off the shoulders. With a belted middle, each tapered flag hung down the chest and dangled between the thighs. Kwinno had earned his, Sroddi was born. Hlammi promised Drolla his own as soon as he birthed him a live grandchild. A promise he never had to keep.

Drolla rolled his shoulders. His old tunic slid to his feet and he stepped out it. Nudity suited him fine, his sweaty caves forbade clothes, he was used to it. He never wore them except whenever forced to attend official appearances. Clothes did not hide modesty, they boasted rank.

The cousins stuffed their silken ponchos into their shoulder packs.

"Hand them over. You were told to bring nothing. They are now confiscated."

Jandra stared hard at them, daring them to protest. The packs were their only possession. They were meant to remind them of home. Now they had nothing. Now they were nothing. The other quartermasters snatched the packs and returned to their awning. Jandra grunted his spiteful approval. If only grandpar' knew, he would have kept his gift. These fools had no idea of the fortune they had just taken. Jandra noticed the enforcers had quietly dismiss themselves. The fawner saluted them long after they had left before the newbies regained his attention.

"Here, wrap ya feet," he threw a bundle of thick bandages at Zonna. "Pass them out." Drolla unrolled three heavy linen strips like party streamers and bound each foot. "Make them last." The smirking quartermaster waved his upturned palm in a slow, broad arc and presented the seething horde. "Now, you may join your peers."

Without a second prompt, Drolla strode off into the crowd. Ten steps into it and his cousins would be lost forever. Alone at last. Surrounded by a thousand nobodies, it was the freest moment of his life. Right now, there was no expectation of him. No responsibility nagging at him to get back to work. There was nothing to do. Although, as good as it was, it did not sit quite right. It was difficult to suppress the guilt. He was like a naughty child skipping lessons, yet no-one cared. He shrugged it off. Give it time, the shame was bound to fade.

He turned his attention to those around him. The horde was fascinating. In his clan, everyone shared some resemblance. Here there were hundreds and hundreds of faces, and none alike. Strangers were weird. So many squatted and meditated, right out in the open. As if they were treading the waters of time, waiting to move on. Some gazed at him with vacant looks, others stared intently like they expected an urgent message. Everyone else ignored him. A noisy group of four sat and tossed little sticks, and one of them noticed Drolla's interest.

"Wanna play?" he asked.

"I don't know how."

"I'll show you."

"Are you gambling with pebbles?"

"Yep. When we tally up, the losers pay."

"I haven't any money."

The group fell about laughing. Two friendly smiles motioned for him to sit and join them.

"None of us do. We don't play for money. We play for food."

"Yeh, they don't feed us enough on this trek."

"So if I lose, I starve?" asked Drolla.

"Yup."

"What if I don't pay up?"

"Then ya won't ever eat again."

"Ya get ya phapping' teef shmashed right down ya phappin' froat," warned a toothless grin.

"Best of luck then," said Drolla. He jumped to his feet and walked away.

"Cheat!" Three pounced onto one and bashed him just short of unconscious. He sat up wobbly, spat some blood and resumed the game. Those nearby that cared to watch, lost interest, looked away and resumed their own indifference.

The horde sprawled around him in all directions. His eyes moved past the red tent and up the road. His beautiful mauve forest crept north, up and over the hills. The entrance to his cave was hidden somewhere up there. He wondered if it missed him yet.

"You from that village?" asked a stranger's voice. "Homesick already?"

"No, not really," said Drolla.

"Be grateful yours was the last. I got dragged from the first."

"How long has it been?" asked Drolla.

"From the Bevwood, I could have ran to the Pen in fifteen days. I've walked nearly a hundred. Now I have to walk all the way back across that damned yellow prairie."

"A hundred days? That is a long way."

"How many of you did they take?"

"Thirteen," said Drolla.

"Thirteen. Is that all? Hardly worth the trouble herding us all up the valley."

"Well, I'm glad they did."

48

"You're glad they did. He's glad they did," he said to no one, "shit, they must have wanted someone pretty special..." he wandered off mid-sentence, "...wasting our bloody time, trudging across the soggy countryside to no depot. Where's our rations? It'll be another day before we eat again. Could have been in a bath weeks ago." His grumbling faded into the din. Once again, Drolla stood alone.

A southerly blew up the yellow valley across the meadows. If only it would carry the stink up the hills and through the village. He yawned and smiled, one could hope. Waiting to depart had lost its charm. He had been here for an hour and was already fed up. Boredom explained the dejected faces everywhere. Except for the cluster moving toward him. They had determination on their faces. They had intent, malicious intent. As they circled him, his cousin scowled.

"Found you. Child," said Zonna.

Drolla could not decide which insult was worse. Tromma and Flutto snickered.

"Did you lose the rest of your cousins?" asked Drolla.

"They are your cousins too," bleated Tromma.

"Not anymore, none of you are. Not since we left the village."

"You don't escape us that easy," said Flutto.

"You don't choose when it ends," added Zonna.

"Yes I do. You are nothing to me now. So, drop the tough act, you impress no one."

"How about I press your phappin' eyeballs out."

"How about I lay a sickle's blade across your throat again?"

Drolla patted his side and went cold. He felt around his middle. Nothing. His little glass knife was gone. It was in the drying sheds, right where he left it.

Zonna smirked and raised his clenched fists. Drolla struck a pose and prepared to defend himself. The bully lunged at him. Drolla twisted aside and punched him in the head as he launched past.

He spun surprised, holding his stinging face. Flutto threw Zonna a broken stick, snapped sharp. His face stretched into a vicious grin.

"Whoa." Drolla showed his palms and stepped away.

"No one to save you this time," jeered Tromma.

Zonna moved toward him, and stabbed the air in front of Drolla's face. The two offsiders leaped at Drolla and bent his arms behind him. The bully laughed, a finger tapped the splintered tip.

"I am gonna stick this right up your kladger."

Screeching glass tore at their ears. A blade as black as oblivion stabbed the air between their faces. Crystalline bevels tapered to an invisible edge, sharp enough to slice through daylight itself. Anxious eyes followed the edge of the blade and met the warrior's scowl.

"Drop it and stand away," said Dandaron.

Whatever they held, everyone let go of it and backed off.

"Meant no harm, thyre," spluttered Zonna. "Only playing."

The giant trod and snapped the stick in half. He sheathed his shard. Any nearby winced at the squeal of the grating blade sliding back into its glass scabbard. His towering frame leaned in and cast a dire shadow over the nervous cousin.

"This one is mine." The words splintered through his gritted teeth. "Now run away."

Without a sound, the cowards nodded and scattered. Quartermaster Jandra stepped from behind the fateshield.

"Recruiter Quetono sends for you. Come with us now."

Dandaron spread a gentle arm around each of them. He moved them forward and set the pace from behind.

"How did you find me in this rabble?"

"He kept an eye on you," said Jandra, poking a thumb back at Dandaron. "You never left his sight."

Two enforcers either side of the entrance tore aside the red drapes. Dandaron winked at his obedient attendants. Their curious eyes trailed Drolla as he entered. The curtains fell together after him. Inside, it was brighter than day. A single dazzling orb hung from the ceiling's peak. Drolla's squinting eyes peered at his hard faced host.

"Are you an idiot?" asked Quetono. The question did not wait for an answer. "I would have thought, considering your parentage, there might have been some glimmer of intelligence."

Dandaron's eyes were fixed on Drolla, as if he was expecting an answer. The uneasy silence that followed unsettled him. Perhaps an answer was required. Perhaps he was an idiot if it meant he was to read minds now, and couldn't. A pile of shoulder packs lay on the floor staring at him, begging him to take the hint. The flap of Brokka's pack was unlatched.

"The fungus?" said Drolla.

"There Dandaron, see? I knew he'd guess."

"It was a farewell gift from my grandpar."

"A gift that could have cost you your life. Anyone out there would have wrung your neck for it."

"It's not mine now, it was confiscated."

"Of course it was confiscated, it's contraband. If that was shared about, we would never shift that lot."

"That's the point though isn't it? To relax and ponder the mysteries of life? Personally, I don't like the stuff. It's too euphoric, it makes me sick."

"You had a sack full," said Dandaron.

"Brokka gave it to me to sell off, for favours, you know. He does not trust the monarchy, or you."

"Oh. He has a grudge against me, does he?" said Quetono.

"He said you took my uncles and they drowned."

"When?"

"Decades ago. Before I was born."

"Oh them? They were Protorian Guards, they never left the palace."

"Then how did they die?"

"Perhaps defending your par's honour?"

"I doubt it. He doesn't have any," said Drolla. Dandaron burst into laughter.

Quetono grinned wide. "It seems they held a lot from you, jester."

"Probably..."

Their good humour stalled the conversation. An awkward quiet choked out the tent like a thick cloud of stale bog mist. Words had escaped them and would not be summoned back. History had too many holes in it and not enough details to fill them with. Perhaps it was best to side step them for now.

"A long held grudge," said Dandaron.

"What little I know, I found out yesterday," said Drolla. "All my life I have been treated like the mushrooms I harvest."

"One day soon, you may learn the full story."

"The past means little to me now. I am grateful you rescued me from that stinking bondage."

"You silly child," grinned Quetono. "You have merely swapped one yoke for another, and the army is a far more severe master."

"It offers freedom in the end, does it not?" said Drolla. "That is all I have ever wanted, and now I have a chance to fight for it."

"You might die for it," said Dandaron.

"A short life of adventure is better than long one imprisoned in the filthy dark."

"Very good. Do not mention your grandpar's gift to anyone. You may rejoin your comrades," said Quetono.

Outside the tent, the umber sunlight seemed dim as if overcast. Yet, there wasn't a cloud in the sky. The reality of the noise and the stink made the meeting seem like a dream. Now, with a clear conscious and lifted spirits, Drolla welcomed the crazy din and the stale pong of the grubby mob.

"So, where was I?"

1.7 - THE PENAL REWARD

The small hillock stood alone in the yellow field.

Its gentle rise was covered by some of the horde, the rest of them massed around it. It was a push, but Drolla managed to stand near its low peak. He had elbowed his way up for a better view of the surrounds. Without reason, he yearned for one last look at his village forest. Every step brought argument or complaint, anyone already there cherished their little spot. A heightened sense of security seemed to comfort them, even though they really were no better off than the rest.

Beads of sweat raced each other as they crisscrossed down his torso. The naked daylight stung his dull grey skin. It pined after his shaded forests and darkened caves. The raw hides of his new comrades were tanned bright white from a hundred days hiking in the relentless sunlight. They all milled about as if the sun had lost its heat.

Unless you went south, the orange sun never set. Here, it skimmed forever around the horizon once per day, every day, day after day. The further north you went, the higher the sun would climb, casting ever shorter shadows. Always traveling the sky in an endless daily round. Few ventured too far north, the barren flatlands of the Helatax deserts stretched for years, even fewer stayed there.

Now and then, daring pilgrims would trek to the sunburnt pole. Their mission was to stand on the tip of the northern axis. With the sun directly overhead and their shadow hidden underneath, they were convinced they would become ageless on the very spot where time itself stood still. But alas, the faithful never returned. The gullible say they are stuck forever, spinning in the twisting hub. The cynics scoff. They reckon the religious fools are baked as dry as powder, and scattered into oblivion by the wasteland zephyrs.

Life clung to the coasts and islands of the channel seas around the equator. Fed by tropical rains, the temperate belt was fertile and prolific. Drolla's shady forest was several days travel north of the Ocean Serene, and today an unclouded sun blazed without mercy. If only the red tent would summon him again. For now, he had joined the ranks of the exposed and would have to endure it with them. An age would pass before any of them might enjoy again the refreshing chill of a dark, underground bath.

Urgent war horns and impatient whistles tore through the air. Distracted for a moment, the walla hushed. During the lull, the yelling started. Armed soldiers ran amongst the horde and shouted orders. Spears corralled the rowdy and compliant alike off the little hill. Shepherded into wedges, they arranged themselves where the blades and lances pointed.

A hundred warriors directed a thousand recruits with taunts and praise. Lanes spread from the centre and led outwards between nine segments of formed-up conscripts, each spaced an arm's length apart. An officer in teal stood before Drolla and his peers, shouting at them to move back, shuffle down, sort yourselves out! He took the front position at the point of their wedge. When the soldiery were satisfied with the ordered formation, all were commanded to squat.

The empty inner core on the hill was soon filled with officials. At the very centre, sappers uncoiled ropes and dug a little hole. It was as slender as an arm, and just as deep. Dandaron laid a long sturdy lance beside it and resumed his place beside Quetono.

Heads soon followed the figures racing across the meadow. A lone nude sprinted toward the forest, but his green pursuers ran faster.

"Another runner," said a stranger nearby.

"The enforcers will catch him," said another.

"Only a fool would bother. We all know there is no escape," added a third. He pushed his forehead into his elbow and sighed. "Another skydancer."

"Must be a new one, from that purple village," guessed the first.

At the edge of the forest, the enforcers tackled their prey. They all tumbled into a cloud of grunting, screaming dust. The spectators within the horde exhaled a collective groan, as if they too had felt the ten bodies of enforcers' muscle pound them into the dirt. Quiet muttering rippled across the nine segments. Some watched the green troop parade their captive back to the main force while others relaxed without a care. Either way, the mumbling commentary continued uninterrupted.

They dragged the deserter to the central arena. Restrained by three powerful enforcers, the fool howled and struggled to escape their grip. His squirming only tightened their hold.

A tall crimson toga topped with a mantle of jet black feathers stepped forward. Despite his obvious presence, the drone of the horde continued. They did not seem much impressed by him. The officer snapped his fingers. A war horn blared three short bursts. That got their attention, but they chose to ignore it too and the low din still murmured. He turned and frowned at Quetono. He raised his arms above his head, as he dropped them he roared.

"Silence!"

Up and down the alleys, every soldier barked at the recruits. Threats of violence upheld their sharp commands. They were deadly serious and beat one defiant idiot unconscious because he was too stupid to shut up. It did not take long for the hubbub to die down. When all was quiet, the officer in red smirked and waited. He delayed for a little while, displaying his complete power over them and their total obedience to him. Oozing arrogance, he sniffed in satisfaction.

"Syblings of Drahn." Palm side up, his outstretched arm pointed to the cringing figure held by the enforcers. "Another deserter. Another shirker who would not stand with us. Fled before there was danger. Would such a coward face battle with you? Chosen to join the monarch's great campaign, he chose to abandon us. Now, we abandon him. The law is clear. Watch how the craven desert us for the last time. Hoist him up." He waved a hand and stepped aside.

Now sobbing, the terrified runaway peered into the crowd, his gaze darted from face to face. A hot anxious flush of disbelief blazed through Drolla as the deserter's desperate eyes met his.

"Help me," yelled Zonna.

They lifted the naked prisoner off his feet and laid him over. Their firm grip held him aloft. They spread his legs and exposed his hidden cloaca, clenched between his buttocks.

"Drolla, make them stop!" His pleading voice broke like an adolescent.

How? He couldn't save him even if he wanted to, and he wasn't sure he did. He had suffered a decade of persecution and torment at the hands of this nasty kladger. Hatred of his cousin quashed any compassion he might have had.

Besides, his own helplessness absolved himself of any guilt. He wasn't about to kill his cousin for bullying, the army was about to execute him for desertion. There were many times he had wished he was dead. He wanted him to deserve it. Zonna glanced back at his executioners and gasped in horror. Defeated eyes pierced Drolla's core, Zonna mouthed his final words, "I'm sorry."

Chills raced up his spine. An apology. Drolla could hardly believe it. That moment of regret evaporated ten years of resentment in an instant. With a sympathetic smile, he nodded his forgiveness. Now, all Zonna deserved was pity. Somewhere from the unknown depths of Drolla's heart, tears welled for his poor cousin. He dreaded what was about to happen.

The enforcers firmed their hold on the prisoner and braced themselves. Dandaron inserted the pointed tip. Zonna's screams tore across the plain as the thorn shoved deep into his body. It skewered him up to his middle in one smooth, agonizing thrust. Ropes hauled the pole up high with him on it. His mortal cries gurgled through the blood gushing up his throat. He coughed and spattered gore with each frantic breath. Sappers pushed the base of the thorn into the hole, it fell deep and stopped with a thud. The impetus caused Zonna to slide down the pole from the impact. The tip burst through his mouth and silenced him forever. White blood and black shit drained down the shaft and pooled beneath him. While his fisted arms trembled his life away, his legs flicked and jerked like a spastic doll. In that horrible moment, the world was silent and Drolla wept with muted sorrow while his dying bully danced in the sky.

PART TWO

MEZZINA

2.0 - THE EXPERT NOVICE

Outside Xendurbia, beyond the urban boundary and past the city orchards, the hectary had already assembled outside Sky Dance Crater.

The small amphitheater was the place of public execution. Palama's judgment had doomed many criminals to this lonely arena. He scoffed and remembered the frightened faces of the murderers facing death. Their proud bravado never failed to desert them. Courage and defiance tried to hide the fear silently screaming inside them. It was only fair the terror was let out. Justice insisted on it. Families of the condemned came to mourn, while the families of victims came to cheer. But today, the empty arena was silent.

Dandaron escorted Palama to the waiting soldiery. They were formed up in a three quarter disk, like a pie with a missing slice. In the gap, the staff loitered until they saw their new commander approach. They quickly took their positions ready to receive him. Quetono grinned at Palama's arrival and reached for his hands. He squeezed them with genuine affection and led him aside.

"Time to meet your crew, nephew," said Quetono. "They already know who you are. Best if you don't chat too much, just a nod of recognition will do for now. There will be plenty of time to know them later."

The hundred stood silent. It was eerie and unnatural. Palama was more used to noisy crowds in busy malls, and feisty observers in his rowdy hearings. Their level of self control was impressive. It was a wonder how so many gathered together could not make a single sound.

White silk togas bound their torsos and draped over their heads like shawls. It seemed a strange way for soldiers to dress.

Quetono led him to the three officers. They curtsied face up, then bent their necks and lowered their heads to face him. With an upturned palm, Quetono introduced a thick set brute wrapped in his dark blue toga. His back was straight and his fists were firmly mounted on his hips.

"Joltoro, khillionaire of the Black Legion," said Quetono. "Here by special appointment." The soldier's face stiffened then nodded.

"Tranna, his hectarion, master of the hundred around us."

"Tranna, that's an Orienna name. We are about to tour your province and enlist your kin. I trust you know the way," said Palama. His jovial tone fell flat.

"Yes, thyre. I do." The reply was bland and officious.

"Jandra, our quartermaster. Whatever you need, ask him," said Quetono.

"An Oxxian, you are a long way from home, westerner," said Palama.

"Drahn is my home, thyre."

His uncle was right to advise, silence and he was a fool to ignore it. These were proud warriors with little time for idle chat with a soft urbanite. His face flushed hot as he imagined them shrieking with mirth behind their silent, stone faces. His first step was a misstep.

"Yes, very good. It is time to go." said Quetono. "Commander Palama, give the order if you would."

"The order? Right, yes…" He looked to scan expectant faces, but only judgmental impatience stared back. Joltoro flicked an eyebrow in anticipation. Palama understood. Facial expressions and body composure spoke volumes in his trade. He judged more by how people acted than by what they said. He saw anticipation. He raised his voice and delivered his command.

"Khillionaire. Troops. Let us embark. Lead the way."

One hundred sober faces cracked wide open and burst into laughter. There was no malice in the merriment, it was obvious that it was genuine good humour. Palama smiled back at his uncle and shrugged.

"Move," roared Joltoro.

"Yo," the hectary boomed as one. Three hundred soft leather sandals slapped the pavement. Sounding like rain, the trek had begun.

Joltoro and Tranna saluted Palama and ran off to join their warriors as they crossed Old Wharf bridge into Orienna.

"Uncle, I feel a fraud. I have disappointed everyone already."

"No you haven't, we are all well aware you are not the right fit for this. But your par' and I agreed you needed the experience. We convinced the monarch to let you lead the expedition, so long as I watch over you."

"Is that the reason you resigned your presidency, to accompany me on the mission?"

"One of them, yes." He smiled at his nephew and turned to three hefty young soldiers. Each wore a steward's ribbon, blue checkered white, on one arm. "Look at these three beasts, would you? A gift from Vondaka."

"Patr', would it not be wiser to send them back?" asked Dandaron.

"With you as my fateshield, I have nothing to fear."

"Then why do we need them?"

"Watch this. Come on you three, let's go."

Quetono stripped off his toga and tossed it to them. Between them, they stretched it flat on the ground. The elder stepped onto it and squatted, the trio hoisted the cloth up and cradled Quetono in his new hammock. He giggled like a child as he lolled about until he was stable and snug. Half a dozen enforcers surrounded the proud stewards and the little group set out to catch up. They soon disappeared, swallowed up by the marching troops and ushered into the middle to join Joltoro. Dandaron looked down at Palama.

"Your army has left without you."

The pair walked for hours in silence. Palama soaked up the serene atmosphere of the empty countryside. Travelling through the rural tranquility, it was hard to imagine there was any discord in the world. But where there were people, there was always strife.

Dandaron too was forever lost in thought. He would run off, circle the corps, weave between the troops to check on Quetono only to arrive back by Palama's side without a hint of breathlessness. Dandaron was five years his junior, Palama secretly admired him. They had known each other for nearly two decades. Many times they shared childhood holidays at his uncle Quetono's country villa. He always treated him like a true cousin, but just as often, his parent Vondaka would quash that sentiment. 'He is not one of us.' He would spit the words out like bloody snot. It mattered not, there was nothing his parent could ever say or do to damage their friendship. Vondaka knew it and hated it.

"Holding up all right?" asked Dandaron. "There is a few more hours march yet before we rest."

"I'm fine," said Palama.

"I can arrange some bearers."

"No. Thank you."

"How was your farewell?" asked Dandaron.

"Hard. Tindara was as upright as ever, but Nolana was a wreck. I promised we would meet at Churon's Pen with their grandpar.'"

"As much as I dislike Vondaka, I am glad they are with him," said Dandaron.

"He vowed to care for them, but I doubt it."

"They are his own grandchildren."

"He is the chancellor, not a chaperon. They'll be at the Waif's Lodge by now."

Commissioned by the Consultorium and administered by the League of Barren Uncles, the royal boarding school cared for sponsored orphans and fostered children. They were raised strict. Amity, discipline and tuition educated the wards from child to adult.

Disciples of the Amber Creed tutored the youth from the teachings of the Nine Heroes. Many of the orphans were adopted once they matured, even uncles needed heirs. Others sought their own fortune, while those fostered returned to their clancestral estates. Palama and Dandaron shared their youth in that ancient lodge.

"At least it's better now since you renovated it," said Dandaron.

"Par' thought he forced me, but I did it for Uncle Quetono. If he was still the president I would not mind leaving the kids behind at all. But now Krantolo has taken his place, I worry for them."

Earlier, the sun was in their eyes when they left Xendurbia. Now it stung their backs. Their purple shadows stretched before them like the shade of dancing trees. Palama's thighs burned as he kept pace with the steady footfall of the soldiers' stride. Neither sprint nor stroll could maintain the endurance of their measured, even step.

Perhaps he should not have declined the ride in a hammock. Pride did nothing to ease his aching spine. His eyes searched for Dandaron. Was it better to quietly admit defeat and be carried like soft gentry, or collapse from exhaustion and be fussed over as if an invalid?

They must have thought him a weird thing. His place was in the centre with the officers, not straggling behind them like a peasant. The simple fact was, he preferred it. He mused and daydreamed as he strolled through the countryside, ever watching the impressive pace of his ordered force. He did not feel shunned or reclused, he just enjoyed the solitude for now.

Hours of crop and hedge began to make way for copse and grove. Trees and shrubs grew denser and merged into the edge of the woodlands. Grey foliage flittered like sunlight dancing off distant lakes. The wide road paved field and forest alike, and disappeared into the shaded canopy ahead. A war horn sounded and the troops slowed their pace. Startled by the unexpected blast, Palama tripped over his own feet and stumbled into the rear ranks.

"Careful, thyre," a deep voice consoled him. Its owner's grip helped Palama regain his balance.

"Thank you, umm..."

"Boohala." A huge grin beamed at Palama.

It was the loveliest face he had ever seen. Piercing light orange eyes smiled and a blissful grin stretched across his gorgeous face. His jet black teeth glinted pure charm. Time stopped as Palama studied the flawless beauty of the image that stood before him. Bordering on lechery, his prying eyes scanned the toned physique. Sweat ran the crevices of his perfect, thrawny body. Adoring the moment, he stared transfixed.

"Back on grid," barked Tranna. The spell was broken, his gaze averted. Until Boohala retook his place, the hectarion glared on with officious disapproval. His tone mellowed as he addressed Palama. "Thyre, Master Quetono begs you join him."

The host came to a complete stop and was ordered to squat at ease.

"Fine soldier, that Boohala," said Palama.

Tranna grunted an indifferent reply and led him into the centre of the resting army.

Old Quetono posed naked while his three stewards wrapped his toga about him. The old fellow ran his eye across their folds. He nodded his approval and they squatted at his feet. An uncle's hand rested on Palama's shoulder.

"Today, we recruit the first of the worthy from within that forest. We are expected, and they are to be conscripted. We shall impose the monarch's will and enforce the kindom's welcome. Those who choose not, we impale."

"Really?"

"It's legal and it's moral. If they will not die for the kindom, then they will not live in it," said Joltoro.

"This is our first call. Let us go do it."

Ten enforcers swarmed around Quetono, Palama and Dandaron and they entered the forest. The road led to the forest clanburg of Bevwood. Tranna and Boohala led covert squads ahead. Four dozen peeled off left and right and disappeared into the timbered maze.

"There is bound to be deserters," said Dandaron answering Palama's quizzing frown.

Palama tore off his black mantle and threw it at Quetono.

"That," he yelled. "Was the last one. Ever."

An arm draped in green reached out and plucked the garment from the air before it insulted its target. From end to end, Dandaron fondled the cloth and the plumage, feeling for anything sharper than a feather. Palama blushed. He snatched it back and tossed it aside.

Rage boiled up from deep down. He blinked hard. A lone tear escaped and fled down his cheek. It was not a tear of sorrow, a drop of sheer frustration had squeezed out.

"Palama," said Quetono. "He was a deserter. You saw him run. Everyone saw him run. They all had to see him punished."

"Since we began this mission, we have gathered a thousand recruits," he replied. "We have impaled at least one from every town. They have seen enough punishment. They all resent it. And what if they all run away, do we impale them all?"

"Don't be silly," said Quetono.

Palama slumped onto the plynth with his face in his a palm.

"They blame me," he whined. "Not the law, or the deserter. I gave the order, it's me they hate."

"They may hate you, but at least they obey you." Quetono paused. "If you wish to control their bodies, you must control their minds."

"They aren't soldiers," said Dandaron.

"Will they ever be?" bleated Palama.

"They must," said Quetono. "The kindom demands it."

"This is the monarch's war, yet everyone else is bound to fight it," said Palama.

"Nephew, your cousin was forced into this conflict like everyone else. That mob out there needs firm direction from the monarchy right now. They need us to keep them devoted to defeating their invaders."

"Do you really think they care?" asked Palama. "They have never seen the wealth from the sand. They never see the monarch, nor do they understand royalty. All they know is the old ways."

"The monarch enforces the peace between the seniocratic doyens."

"None of them know Soltoro, and he knows none of them. Yet he expects them to die for him," said Palama.

"He would die for them too. He is devoted to them, you know. It is the monarch's burden. He has a personal responsibility to every sybling of Drahn. Ever since Xendaka crowned himself, the monarch is committed to the welfare of all the clandoms."

"The Protorians make sure of that," smirked Dandaron.

"Each check the other," said Quetono. "Make no mistake Palama, your cousin will lead his syblings into battle himself. He will expect them to follow."

"We have all been pushed into this war, and we all have to fight our way out of it," said Dandaron.

"I cannot push them all the way to the Pen. I want them to follow me. They must want to do it."

"At last." Quetono whispered to himself.

"Where is Joltoro? He was meant to be here as well," said Palama.

"He prepares the assembly to move out," said Quetono. "He will be here."

The scarlet curtain pulled aside and Joltoro strutted into the red tent and curtsied. His indigo toga wove tight over one shoulder, across his torso and down one thigh. Wrapped in white linen like a bandage, his scabbard contrasted bright against his dark blue leg.

"Pardon my delay Commander. The troops are now ready to march."

"Good. The sooner we arrive the better," said Palama.

"Joltoro, could you explain to our commander what loyalty is?" asked Quetono. "No, no. How would you prove loyalty?"

Without a moment's hesitation, Joltoro replied to Quetono.

"We have a thousand recruits. I have one hundred soldiers. If you made the request, thyre, we would kill them all. It's only ten each, it'd be done in no time."

Palama's jaw dropped open. His gaze flew from one face to another, from an adamant Joltoro to a smug Quetono. Dandaron just smiled.

"Why would you do that?" asked Palama.

"Because he asked us to."

"And if the monarch demanded it?" asked Quetono.

"His demands mean nothing to us," said Joltoro.

"Uncle, how do you allow this treason?"

"I am surprised you do not appreciate their sentiment. Does it not align with your own pro-seniarch beliefs?"

"A few moments ago you were pushing the monarchy and obedience to it, down my throat."

"Oh, we expect it of the syblings. They have no choice but to serve. So now we ask, who will they serve?" asked Quetono.

"The monarchy demands total loyalty," said Palama.

"A loyalty it does not repay," said Joltoro. He paused embarrassed.

"Go on," insisted Palama.

"Soltoro doomed us. Quetono saved us and earned the soldiers' gratitude. He has our loyalty, not the monarch. But the monarch has his."

"Saved you, how?"

Joltoro hesitated again. A nod from Quetono urged him to continue.

"Under Commander Yontala, I led the attack on Ebon Shore. We finally caught the sand thieves, and we wiped them out."

It was a long deserved victory, but the expected honour soon became a disgrace. We were lured back to Xendurbia to what should have been a public triumph, but we were rewarded with a private condemnation. Yontala blamed a thousand disobedient warriors for the foreign inheritor's death. Soltoro exiled Yontala to parts unknown. Ten outraged hectaries quit the civic centres in every direction. They vowed revenge on their unfaithful ex-commander. Months later, they found his cairn. Yontala had stopped running. He preferred suicide by poison than the vengeant wrath of his jilted subordinates. Denounced for both fatalities, Vondaka disbanded the Black Legion and condemned nine dozen officers to Sky Dance Crater.

"Their prince was drowned," said Palama.

"And we were doomed," said Joltoro. "Quetono pardoned us and assigned us as his recruitment militia."

"Vondaka opposed the move," said Dandaron. "But Soltoro used his veto and favoured one uncle above the other."

Quetono winked a salute at Joltoro. "You brave kids saved our sand."

"These kids," said Palama. It was as if a muddy pond cleared in an instant. "We took them. I took them. These recruits are mine. They are my charge and yet they are all strangers to me." Palama exhaled an enlightened sigh.

A moment passed while a proud uncle admired his clever nephew.

"Excellent," smiled Quetono. "Perhaps a killionaire might explain your provincials."

"Drahn breeds a three headed beast," professed Joltoro. "The Oxxians are brutes. One must be constantly severe with westerners, if not they will challenge you on everything.

"Whereas, the Munikans and Mezzini are compliant and used to obedience. To them it is the natural order of things, and they expect to be led.

"But your recruits are from Orienna. Easterners are proud and stubborn. They will be neither be led nor driven. If they think you respect them, they will go anywhere alongside you."

"You mean we have handled them wrong since we left?" blurted Palama.

"They have been disciplined as per the monarch's law," said Quetono.

"The monarch's law. Well, Soltoro does not own them, I do. From now on, we manage them with encouragement, not punishment."

"That suits us, thyre. We are not shepherds," said Joltoro.

"They are still conscripts. I want them to become soldiers."

"As do we all," said Joltoro. "Soon, we shall fight alongside these recruits. We would prefer to fight alongside comrades."

"How do we start?" asked Palama.

"Routine," said Joltoro. "The marches have been staggered. It's all about the food. If we cannot reach the next ration depot in time, we shall send porters ahead to the depots. They can fetch the rations back."

"Rest and eat the same time every day? That does not sound too bad," smiled Quetono.

"Set a consistent pace and have regular stops."

"Yes, it has been a bit like droving a wild herd," said Palama.

"They must not feel like chattel, or prisoners," said Joltoro. "Allow the recruits to get used to the regimental structure. The soldiers will encourage them. I will see to that."

"Very well. Thank you Joltoro." Palama stiffened his back. "It is no secret, I am as naïve as that mob of yokels out there. But we must all become worthy peers to you and your warriors. I want my cousin to watch this Orienna horde march into Churon's Pen as one proud legion."

The red ceiling cloth peeled back and fell to the ground outside the pavilion. The open sky smiled down at the exposed gentry. The day seemed brighter. The sappers dismantled the tent around them. The discussion was over. It was time to march.

"By your leave, thyre," said Joltoro. "I wish to counsel my soldiers." He strode off and attended to his troops.

"Uncle?" said Palama. "Why was this discipline not already in force?"

"My dear nephew, we have been waiting for you."

2.1 - THE HASTY DAWDLE

Two days had passed since they left Zonna on his pole.

The compliant horde moved out with a solemn silence. The point was taken. Royal obedience was demanded by corporal consent or by capital punishment. Zonna learned that the hard way.

What an ironic tragedy for the village. The farewell was bad enough, but a funeral is unbearable. Especially this one. It was not difficult to imagine the seniors and elders gathered around his grave, sobbing like children into the pit. Drolla could see them mourning the poor cad they had lost and denouncing everything the monarchy represented, and everyone who represented it.

In their blatant grief, they would weep until their genuine tears turned fake. Then, the most virtuous of them will demand another senioral bout. The monarchy may retain sovereignty, but the clanfolk feuded still with bloodless battles to elect a new doyen. Each challenger would boast louder than the last, endorsing their own integrity. But as usual, any serious effort to campaign would end up lost amongst the squabbling cousins.

Brokka and his covert bribes had always quelled their lazy dissent and would do so again, no doubt. Hlammi would still smirk down at his fickle subjects gathered about the doyen's podium. Together, they would pretend the picket never happened, while they clutched their fat little purses. What an excellent time to not be there.

The army headed due west, across turf and meadow along the trough of the valley. Endless moorland acres wandered past at an impossibly slow pace. The circling sun traveled even slower. Long bygone days saw the Mauve Forest left far behind, and excited fewer days saw the mystical Blue Hills advance ever nearer.

The nine sections held form, driven true by their armed escort. Drolla struggled from the first day. He feigned stamina, but that was exhausting. The broken step of three thousand feet crunching the dry pastures often sounded like the tumbling waters of his hidden highland brooks. He was not aware of his daydreams until he jolted himself alert, and did not notice himself stare back into them either. Sometimes the mob seemed to synchronise, as if every breath panted in time and every heart beat the same rhythm. The endless measured gait became entrancing. Was he trudging forward across the field, or was it passing under him as he trod stationary on the spot? Often it was impossible to know.

A shrill war horn startled a sudden gasp of reality. The monotonous shadow lifted and the comrades shared grins of relief, proving that others heard it too. Sore joints and throbbing thighs welcomed the halt and a rest.

"At last," said a tubby fellow nearby. He dropped to the ground and began to unwrap his feet. "Fifty days so far, and twice more to go."

"Don't count the days, count the hours. Just make it to the next stop, then the next. It's far too daunting to imagine the whole trek at once," said another while he massaged the calves of his long skinny legs.

"I wonder why we have stopped here, we are nowhere near a ration depot. I'm starving."

"Yeh, look at you. You're wasting away."

"I haven't eaten at all yet," said Drolla.

"New 'cruit from the forest hills? Did you know who they skewered? These royals are phapping merciless."

"He deserved it. He did far worse before he ran away."

"Did he?" His lanky comrade held out a smiling hand. "Penno, fisher."

"Drolla, granger." Two new friends locked palms.

A shrill whistle blew from the cluster of officers. Soldiers ran up and down the section aisles calling for attention and roused at those not paying it fast enough.

"That's the caterers whistle," said Penno with a frown of wonder.

In the centre of the sectioned horde, sappers erected the official marquees. On the opposite side of the field a hungry section rose and filed past the tents, then resumed their original places in formation. One segment after the other took their turn, then those around Drolla rose without him.

"Come on," said Penno. "You'll miss out."

The shade of the marquee soothed his sun tired shoulders. An impatient caterer thrust a pie into Drolla's chest. His hungry hands clutched the large fat pastry.

Dandaron and his fellow enforcers kept watch as the hungry recruits took their daily meal. Quetono followed his fateshield's gaze and stopped at Drolla. He smiled wide and waved. Dandaron leaned in and whispered to the old recruiter. Quetono shook his head, he winked at Drolla and turned away. Dandaron let his gaze linger for a moment.

"Move on, you stupid kladger." The caterer stared impatient fury at Drolla. Penno pushed him along. With lunch in hand they returned to sit and eat.

Drolla watched in disgusted fascination as Penno's food disappeared. A blissful moan followed each bite.

"Oh, veev are goof a'day." Penno spat crumbs and gravy with every word.

"What is it?"

"Mmm, fiff." His bulging cheeks grinned.

Drolla was now too hungry to care. He bit deep. The air-dried seedmash pouch crunched and shattered like glass. Inside, the rich spicy gravy tingled his watering mouth. Herbs peppered the soft meat embedded in chunks of clear jelly. He uttered his own groan of delight as the fermented fish melted into a dozen flavours at once.

"Told you," smiled Penno, licking his fingers.

An after meal doze lasted an age before the horn blew. In a half unwoken dream, he imagined the distant bellow of a rancher's bugle. The obedient flock chased their herder across the paddocks and the tired fat beasts grunted at every hurried step.

"On your feet," barked a soldier. "Another day's trudge ahead," he grinned.

His comrades had already climbed onto their feet and brushed the dust from under themselves.

Thus, the daily regimen was set. Walk, eat, rest. Days bled into weeks and trudging slowly evolved into marching. Spurred on by the soldiers' encouragement, the recruits soon saw the wisdom in the forced routine. The steady, synchronised gait eased the effort of the march. Few were exhausted after six hours and felt the three hour rest was now excessive. The desire to end the trek, get to the barracks, and start training spread throughout the mob. Before long, the rest period reduced to an hour per day. Their growing self confidence accepted their fate. This new positive attitude toward becoming a united force impressed the warriors. With sun-kissed skin as white as valley fog and bodies fit from the daily march, their hearts were as light as bathing froth. So, when their morale was at its height, fate decided to test their grit.

"It's true," said Penno. The back of his hand shielded his words. "There is rebel talk everywhere."

"Really? I haven't been listening," said Drolla.

"Have you been eating?"

"The food hasn't been that bad."

"Not that bad? For the past ten days it's been either stale, moldy or soggy."

"You're exaggerating."

"People are getting really angry. Look."

Drolla scanned the morose faces around him and shrugged.

"Well, blame the local doyen. He is supposed to keep the depots stocked. It's the clan's tribute to the monarchy."

"Yes, but the storekeepers are quartermasters of the army. It is their job to make sure the food is good."

"So you're blaming the quartermasters?"

"No, I blame the army. If things don't get better, we will revolt."

"We?"

"You pair. On your feet. You're both on catering duty today." The shadow of Quartermaster Jandra covered Drolla and Penno. They squinted up into the sunlight behind him.

"Excellent," said Penno. He sighed with bland enthusiasm as he hauled his hungry bones onto his reluctant feet. "Finally, it's our turn to fetch more rancid slop."

"Aren't you lucky. You'll be doling it out to your hungry comrades, as well. Move," said Jandra.

A score of recruits waited with Hectarion Tranna and a single striking soldier. Tight clad in white silk, his perfect physique was a gaze magnet to any with an eye for beauty. To everyone else, he was a source of envy.

"Thank you Jandra, go to your station and prepare for our return. 'Cruits, form up around myself and Boohala here. The depot is an hour's trot away, so keep up."

They set off with a steady jog.

Heavy storm clouds hung halfway to the horizon. The low sun painted their bloated grey underbellies a painful pink. Like infected wounds, they threatened to burst at any moment. A steady sweet breeze forewarned the impending downfall. In the distance, a dirty brown shape rippled in the wind.

"Run," yelled Tranna. "Before the skies fall on us."

A trot broke into a dash. Spitting rain fell like frozen needles onto their sunburnt faces. The wind picked up and the beige awning flapped like an angry beast desperate to be free. The drizzle turned into a shower. At last, torn from its tethers, the twisting canopy smiled and frowned as it made its erratic escape across the gusty open plains.

Tranna leapt over the low stone turret that walled the entrance to the store. Without the awning, rainwater ran in ruts and poured into the depot.

"Where's the trapdoor? The place is flooding," said Tranna.

Drolla and Penno dove into the mud. They paddled sludge aside and stemmed the flow. Tranna stripped off his toga and tied it between the bare poles. The whole troop huddled under the makeshift awning. Tranna sneered in disgust at the lechers ogling Boohala tying off his toga. His naked body rippled and flexed as he pulled the shelter taut.

"You two, down," roused Tranna. "The rest of you stay up here. I will call you down when we are ready to load up."

Penno disappeared through the floor first. They ran down the spiral ramp into the gloom below.

Underground, it was hot and airless. The reek of stale mold stung their nostrils. Grey storm light filtered down the rampway and showed an unlit smolderstone. Drolla plucked it from its carrier and struck it against the stone wall. It glowed and revealed a daunting mess. Back in its sling, the pale light filled the dingy chamber. Empty jars littered the sodden floor. Crumbs, dried slops and other goop smeared the tall tables. Grimy utensils were scattered everywhere. Dirty empty jars filled the shelves that lined the round wall from the floor to the ceiling. A tattered curtain barely covered the only arched passageway. Beyond it, the darkness snored.

"This is bad," said Tranna. He yelled, "Glotta."

"You know him?" asked Drolla.

"A cousin's cousin. A strange one, never mixed well. He has been alone here for years."

"Perhaps that's why," said Drolla.

"It looks like the place was looted," said Penno.

"Glotta!"

"What?" An angry voice exploded from behind the curtain. A filthy hand ripped it aside and a fat, bad mood panted into the room.

"Wow," said Drolla.

The sweaty sheen of the swaggering storekeeper stank like stale shite. A nostril flared and his gut twinged at the unwelcome scent of home.

"You're late," said Glotta. "Hurry up and load the shelves. My store is near empty and the army will be here soon."

"Glotta. It's me Tranna. What do you mean, empty?"

"Tranna? Hello cousin. What are you doing here? I thought you were the suppliers."

"What happened here? What happened to you?"

"I think we know where the food went," said Penno.

"It's not my fault," said Glotta, scowling at the rude guest. "Doyen Flomma and the local clan keep bringing me too much. I have nowhere to put it. This is only a small depot. I have to eat it to make room." He burped and picked between his teeth.

"Boohala," called Tranna. The hunk slid down the ramp and stopped dead at the sight of the overweight storekeeper. His ragged, unwashed poncho looked like a child's filthy bib over his swollen belly. "Search the stores."

"So, how much inventory do you have, Glotta?"

"I don't know. I'm always hungry. I can't keep track. Flomma is very generous, he always brings me more food every visit."

"But, there is nothing here. Look at this place."

"I know! It's not my fault he's late."

Boohala's frown returned from beyond the curtain.

"Enough to feed a hundred. Maybe two," said Boohala.

"Glotta, we have a thousand hungry soldiers heading this way," said Tranna.

"Do they bring food?"

"No! They bring trouble." His calm demeanor began to desert him.

"Too soon. Too little. They cannot have mine," snapped Glotta.

"There is not enough anyway," yelled Penno. "This will do it."

"This is a phapping disaster. How close is the next depot?"

"A day and a half," said Glotta. "It's the last one in Orienna before the river crossing at the Zampont. They have plenty. Take their's and leave mine to me."

"It was never yours, you filthy glutton," said Penno.

"Enough!" Tranna put his face in his palms. After a moment of quiet, his eyes shot open and clapped his hands.

"Right. Boohala, you and the others empty the stores and bring all you can carry to the assembly. You two, we need to get back to warn the army. Glotta, you are coming with us to explain yourself."

"You can't take my food. I can't leave my depot," said Glotta.

Tranna drew his blade forward and pressed the pommel into the fat storekeeper's belly.

"Move," he growled.

Glotta waddled up the ramp. He strained at every step and paused to wipe the sweat from his eyes at every third. The rain had stopped and the recruited caterers were sunning themselves, oblivious to the drama below. Tranna tore down his toga and looped it over one shoulder.

"Come on."

He and the two recruits broke into a jog and left the bloated storekeeper dawdling behind. He grunted at every step, and his belly blubber rippled like a pond of pudding.

"Hurry up." Tranna yelled back to him. He ran back to his cousin and threatened to spur him on again at shardpoint.

"I can't," he puffed. "My ribs hurt."

He stopped and clutched his chest. A mournful bellow fled a face distorted with agony. Strained joints crackled under his bulk as he dropped to his knees. Dying eyes rolled back beneath their lids and he fell aside. His settling mass squeezed out his final gasp.

"He just dropped dead," said Drolla.

"He ate himself to death," said Penno. "Now we are gonna starve to death."

"Shutup! Come on, we have to get back fast." He broke into a trot behind them.

Across the plain, the wheeling mob advanced ever closer. Tranna bound one corner of his toga to the hilt of his shard. Held high, it unfurled like a serpent and signaled their premature approach. A body of enforcers soon met them and swirled about the anxious trio.

"Urgent report for Joltoro," said Tranna. "The depot is empty."

"You will report to Palama," said Dandaron. After a short glance toward Drolla, he turned his focus toward their destination. "Pick it up."

Legs burned and exhausted lungs stung and complained at the final sprint demanded of them.

Their arrival was met with an instinctive parting of the masses. The enforcers did not slow their pace until they reached the centre. Drolla dropped to his haunches. He panted so hard he thought he might faint. Quetono slid from his hammock and joined his commander and the officers.

Tranna swept about, someone was missing.

"Where is Penno?" he demanded.

Drolla shrugged. Still panting hard, he squinted and pretended to think.

"He pushed past me and disappeared into the crowd," said an enforcer.

"Fool!" Dandaron slapped him to the ground. Knocked out cold, he did not get back up.

"The news is out, we should act quickly, thyre," said Tranna turning to Palama.

"Why?"

"The depot is empty. The storekeeper is dead. The missing recruit is a hungry gripe."

Their faces darkened as they realised their predicament.

"Find him. Shut him down before..." Palama spoke too late.

Outrage flared up in pockets across the mob. Their shouts increased as the network of mutineers joined forces in their shared grievance. Opposing cries scolded the agitators, but this only hastened the violence. Scuffles broke out between the rebels and those loyal, and soon turned into serious conflict. Good defenders were bashed and kicked senseless. Those not so ardent pulled back from the vicious attackers. The turmoil slowly turned its attention towards the centre, towards their perceived oppressors. Unarmed, the frenzied rioters screamed 'death to the monarchy', 'kill the soldiers'. Without a rational thought between them, they scrambled like ants. Innocent recruits stumbled aside confused, and avoided the insane leap to violence.

Dandaron reached for Drolla, plucked an arm and hurled him toward Quetono. He tumbled in the dust and stopped at the elder's feet. He smiled down at Drolla holding his skinned knee, wincing like a child. The enforcers surrounded the officers. Joltoro's war horn summoned the hectary and the white soldiers formed a greater ring between the naked recruits and the gentry within.

The abandoned enforcer sat up semiconscious and groggy. He rubbed Dandaron's stinging palm print on the side of his face. In the midst of the brawl, he woke in time to watch his own shard stolen and slashed across his neck. Penno snatched it and hacked at him before he could rise. Emboldened with their new found weapon, his supporters rallied behind him as he cautiously advanced on the guards. At first, they laughed at this misplaced bravery. But after he managed to mortally wound a few more of their own, they took him seriously. His rebel peers cheered and several mobbed the dying soldiers, squabbling over their shards. Three warriors pounced at Penno and pierced a lung each. His craven comrades howled in horror and dropped the weapons before they melted back into the raging throng of recruits.

"Hold." Joltoro's voice boomed above the din. The disciplined force held their stead, but they frothed like starved beasts denied their quarry.

A few courageous royalists squeezed forward to meet the soldiers.

"Commander Palama, spare the loyal," bellowed one brave recruit.

"Spare the loyal, spare the loyal." First tens, then hundreds joined the chant.

Palama moved between the enforcers and the soldier's rings of protection. Dandaron loomed beside him. They all realised his intention as he raised his arms. They were silent when he dropped them.

"Spare the loyal?" roared Palama. "Who of you can I trust now? Look about." He spread his arms left and right. Blades and thorns promised death to them all. "These soldiers are ready to murder everyone of you, right now, right where you sit." Palama paused. "I cannot think why I should not let them." His voice climbed. "I would rather enter Churon's Pen alone than to slink in with a mob of cowards who would riot over grumbling bellies."

"Everyone is hungry. Yet you blame us all for the crimes of a few."

"A few? Who? Which few? I do not know who, do you?" said Palama.

Shouts and screams erupted near the outside edge. The screams stopped but the shouting continued and the disruption approached the centre.

A bloody mass of torn limbs and tangled entrails were dumped at the soldiers' feet.

"Here is one I know of, thyre," roared a buff recruit. His deep chest heaved at each breath. "Let us find the rest."

That one expression of loyalty seemed to melt Palama's stern resolve.

"Loyal syblings. Bring me the mutineers and cleanse our bond."

For over an hour, little groups peppered throughout the horde seized their traitorous peers. Adamant accusers swore witness to the defendant's guilt before they were thrown to the vengeful mob and torn limb from limb. With a face of stone, Palama watched on with professional disinterest. He allowed them to judge themselves. It was obvious a few innocent, yet despised bullies and outed felons were gotten rid of as well. Both the horde and Palama knew, through unspoken consent, all would be better off with out them. Eventually, a peaceful lull meant the carnage was over. Fidelity was restored. The mutilated body parts of one hundred and twenty-three spurned syblings laid in a jumbled heap.

Quetono stepped to the grisly pile as if it was an alter and thrust his royal baton high. A relieved crowd threw him their attention. Before them all stood experience and authority, worthy respect and solemn prestige. During that quiet, austere moment the dying intestines squirmed as bowel gas hissed and gurgled. The mighty elder was expected to speak sense to the unsettled mob. His ageless wisdom was needed now, more than ever. Before he could speak, he was interrupted. The corpses finally broke wind. Louder and longer than any crass old grandpar' might fart, it ripped through the venerable silence.

Laughter erupted like thunder. Hysterical faces darted from one to another, sharing the euphoria. Their fears and doubts lifted like rising shade mist and together, in that moment, they realised everything was now alright.

Whatever grand speech Quetono had intended was lost.

"Kids, let's go," his heart blurted. "It's only a day and a half away. The next depot is by the forest river. There, we shall wash, feast and relax."

"With brewberries," yelled Palama.

Laughter turned to cheering so intense and heartfelt, it might have echoed to the mountains. The happy mob formed up, and like rubbish, the pile of flesh and bone and guts were left behind without ceremony.

2.2 - THE HONEST DECEPTION

D rahn's Vein bled across the golden fields.

Weeping forests draped either bank as the mighty river slithered south. The black foliage glistened like scales and a constant lazy zephyr drifted north, cooling the shade beneath the vaulted canopies.

A smug horde smiled quietly to themselves. After two days of no food, no rest and no shade, they craved the cool, dark sanctuary. From commander to recruit, the order to break off and relax was passed down the ranks. The welcome news promised a recess from all duties, but insisted all must indulge in the revelry. To bathe, feast and rest was a relief, but the anticipation of the pledged brewberries cultivated gossip praising the generous, noble Palama. Their heartless commander seemed changed. Since the riot and the reprisals he was seen in a very different light. He trusted their judgment, a sentiment they could only repay in kind.

Moments after their dismissal, hundreds sprinted to the water. Hunger and fatigue deserted them as they dunked and splashed and washed away weeks of heartache. All their worries were swept away, sent downstream with a long beige cloud. By the time they had walked out of the river, their souls were as clean as their bodies.

The endless southerly breeze chilled Drolla's wet skin as he marveled at the underside of the canopy. The arboreal tunnel loomed as high as twenty people and spread twice as wide. Soft white moss carpeted every bit of the shaded ground. Crackled grey bark covered the buttressed trunks like muddy cloth stretched over bones and their roots clawed deep, holding the river on course. Now and then, tiny orange lizards darted among the high branches and disappeared into the dark ceiling. Scores of disturbed Aurora bugs then burst out of hiding. Spiraling down the trunk, their collective iridescent wings fluttered like a shattered rainbow. Their colourful tunnel swirled to the nearest tree, twirled up its trunk, and disappeared again into the black foliage. Drolla parted the draping fronds that kept the shade sealed inside. Outside, the sun smiled at his return.

The noise and colour arrived long before the caravan. Like a flock of desert birds, hundreds of caterers danced a rhythmic trot toward the horde's hidden stopover. There was not an adult among them. Children, seniors and a few agile elders were laden with overstuffed litters and shoulderpacks, each bore a thin pole topped with a little pennant. Their colour and icon advertised their contents. A vanguard of preserved flora and pickled fauna led a rearguard of fermented fruits. What a delicious sight for famished eyes.

Left, right and behind, the black leafy curtains flung aside. First brown garb, then green emerged and formed up to greet the visitors. The entourage was led by a huge beast of a person clad in a coat of shimmering silver furs. Behind him a naked child no older than Sroddi, struggled to keep his master in the shade of a tall flimsy parasol. Quetono strutted ahead with the royal baton held high. The frowning bat forced the gaudy convoy to a halt.

"A proud appearance, thyre," said Quetono.

"Proud to be here, your honour. Thank you for the escort Tranna. I trust we are not too late?"

"Governor Klovata," answered Quetono, "as usual, your timing is perfect. We could not have started without you."

"President Quetono. You are a long way from the Lodge."

"You are ill informed, governor. I am no longer President. Have we arrived before the couriers?"

"They seldom venture this far north lately."

"I see. Well, come into the shade and let me be your herald. You might show me your menu," said Quetono.

With the click of the governor's fingers, the entire loaded clan dispersed and ran forward, around and between their hosts and disappeared beyond the overhanging foliage. Palama moved to Tranna.

"Hectarion, I believe this was your doing?" said Palama.

"Not really, thyre," he smiled. "Lord Quetono asked me if I knew the way to Forgepyre. He preferred a governor's feast to the depot's rations."

"Uncle knows how to pamper his favourites. Nevertheless, I was rash to promise brewberries. But, your efforts made my foolish boast come true. I am very grateful."

"At your service, thyre." Tranna blushed at his commander's praise. He turned to Drolla. "With me. You are back on catering duty."

With an over flowing sense of virtuous altruism, the proud caterers unpacked the banquet. Scores of picnics surrounded the bases of the trees and boasted many tempting smorgasbords. It was a veritable wealth of staples and delicacies. Meats, vegetables, fruits and fungus in every combination of fresh, dried, pickled and fermented. Grains and nuts, honeys, nectars and flowers. Despite the recruits' hunger, their self restraint impressed even themselves. Their pride would not let them disappoint Palama again. They held back, content to ogle and leer at the lush buffet, until given leave to eat.

"So much food," said Drolla, "but, where's the..." From the corner of his eye he noticed the one thing he thought was missing. Glee erased his doubt as dozens of bloated skins filled with brewberry syrup were unloaded near the senior's festive quilt. Tranna thrust a tureen at Drolla. He clutched it close and sniffed the perfect aroma of the magical red slurry.

"Not a sip, or I will break your fingers with that ladle." Drolla was to wait on his betters.

Quetono and his guest joined Palama at the senior's quilt. After a few quiet words of greeting Palama nodded to his herald. The war horn blew and hushed the hungry rumble.

"Orienna, there is no time to stand on ceremony. Eat, and drink your fill. You deserve it."

A great cheer erupted and soon faded into groans of succulent contentment. Full bellies and light heads soon relaxed and started to mingle.

The brewberry syrup loosened many tongues and opened even more hearts. Stories of home were swapped and like folk gravitated into cliques and many formed heartfelt bonds. Drunken boasts promised to meet up next conjugation and vowed to fuck each other's gorgeous brains out. This binge bound the syblings of Orienna to each other even closer than any of them had expected.

Dejected, a sober Drolla filled bowl after bowl as Quetono and Klovata reminisced their past. Palama and Dandaron played some silly board game and drained their cup at every bad move while the other laughed and drank at their misfortune. Or good fortune, it was hard to tell. By habit, the enforcers sat in a ring around the officer's quilt. It gave some semblance of their usual duty, but as drunk as they were, they were not taking it serious. Joltoro smiled up at Drolla, and in his merry mood invited him to sit with him.

"Take this dish, pour yourself one."

Drolla doubted his khillionaire's sincerity and glanced at his half empty tureen.

"There are other waiters, take a break. Sit with me. Tranna tells me you were a great asset at the depot." Drolla appreciated the compliment, but he appreciated the syrup more. The tangy juice tingled down his throat and fell into his empty stomach like a rock into a pond. It was not the first time he had drank on an empty stomach. His seasoned innards hiccuped and prepared to welcome another swig. "We did think you were a mutineer too, like your friend."

Drolla spluttered into his bowl. His eyes peered over its rim and darted at the interrupted gentry now looking at him.

"Yes, we are so glad you weren't," said Quetono smiling.

"Friend?" said Drolla, shaking his head, "Not at all. He complained too much. I thought it was just the hunger talking."

"You knew beforehand and said nothing?" quizzed Dandaron. "We could have prevented the riot."

"I am glad how things turned out," said Quetono. "The dregs were culled."

"The recruits judged, and they condemned the guilty themselves," said Palama. "If he was spared, he was deemed innocent."

Quetono burped and tilted his head at the governor.

"I must thank you again for providing this excellent feast Klovata. But, where is Flomma and his share of recruits?"

"I sent the recruits months ago, when the first drafting call went out."

"And Flomma?" asked Quetono.

"He was stuck on a pole for failing his duty to the soldiery of the monarch," said Klovata.

"We understand he and his clan kept their depot well stocked..."

"Overshtocked," slurred Palama.

"... and that a member of your quartermaster staff mishandled the ration depot."

"He ate it all," said Palama.

"You are not using him as a scapegoat for your own failure to the monarch, are you?" finished Quetono.

"He was a servant to the monarch. The penalty was legal." Klovata blushed and swallowed hard. "Besides, he was a seniocrat and very difficult to deal with."

Palama unfolded his legs and rose onto his haunches. He stared ice at Klovata.

"On your return, you will supervise a seniorial bout and install their elected doyen immediately."

"Naturally," said Klovata. "It is one of my duties to ensure the commoners maintain their charade of the old seniocracy. If only they observed the same duty to the monarchy, then my job would be a lot easier."

"I think you underestimate them," said Palama.

"Oh no," Klovata smirked. "You see, the trouble with easterners is they are all from Orienna. They make the worst servants. They will be neither pushed nor pulled."

"Yes, I have heard that before," said Palama. "And yet, we have managed to induce them to work with us," said Palama.

"You might think you have wheedled some semblance of loyalty out of them. But beware, they simply cannot be relied upon."

"You have a very cynical view of the people you govern," said Quetono.

"It is the only way to manage them. I doubt you will get this lot to the Pen, let alone to the battle front. Frankly, I am surprised you got them this far."

"My Orienna Horde will win this war," boasted Palama.

He ignored the governor's laughter.

The Blue Hills were deserted and it was clear why. What an unforgiving ordeal. Sharp, fractured boulders laid stacked one upon the other half way to the clouds, and stretched north and south for days. The moment the mob entered the gorge, their formation fell apart. Angry rocks leaned into the pass and threatened to slash any who strayed too close. They trod where they could. The path was littered with splintered slate wafers, centuries deep. Such was the shared misery, while they struggled for hours through that hateful pass, all ranks dissolved.

The soft comfort of the shaded moss carpet where they lolled about, fat and drunk, was only a few days gone. It seemed an age ago. Now they faced this treacherous hike. One needed wary attention, and tread with care. A hasty misstep on a loose flat rock would skid sore feet out from under the reckless. Joltoro ordered togas to be torn into strips and doled out as extra foot wraps. The trek was beyond arduous. In the cold dark shadows of the jagged peaks, the air sang with clinking shingles and raging curses.

Despite the risk, only a few dozen were too injured to walk. They were either carried like shoulder packs or slung in toga hammocks. The disappointment in Drolla's heart ached more than his bruising feet. For years he dreamed of this place. He had always longed to visit the paradise he imagined. This wretched quarry and its mountains of shattered stone were nothing but pain and disillusion.

Beyond the broken canyon, the lands were lush. A vast emerald grassland, as fine as hair, spread waist deep across the slopes and plains. The prairie's fickle breath churned the endless Emerald Veldt like ocean swell. Silver crests waved down into the verdant valley and coaxed the exhausted travelers to the welcome comfort of their new home at Churon's Pen.

The distant army base sat proud beyond the grasslands. Surrounded by a wide moat, canals from the north and south connected to the great Bahlo River. Like the Vein, it too separated provinces and emptied into the equatorial channel. His happy peers boasted it was the largest cluster of buildings on land they had ever seen. Through the shimmering haze, Drolla could only see bands of blue, beige, green and orange with a black centre. A round city with blurry streets rippled like a pond.

There it was. Their trek was over. To some, at last! To others, so soon?

The air was thick with cheers of relief, glad to finally arrive and put the long journey behind them. Others quietly sighed their dread, saddened they might lose newfound comfort in their fellows' company. Everything was about to change.

A few short blasts of the war horns snapped the hectary to attention, but the horde did not need the soldiers to corral them this time. Like second nature the recruits formed up into a nine segmented marching disc. They surrounded Palama and the officers, and ensured they were in the dead centre. Despite the individual feeling of each one there, those emotions were put aside to become a body of one mind. The mind of a legion. With courageous pride they waded through the grassland sea to join the mighty army of their Drahni syblings.

Near the centre, Drolla strode with Tranna and Boohala at the peak of their wedge. Dandaron led the nine enforcers that ringed the commanding party. Quetono had dismounted his toga hammock and strutted beside Palama. His three stewards hung tight around him. They hung a little too tight. Quetono frowned a silent demand they seemed to either miss or ignore.

"Stand back you lot," said Quetono. "You have all become rather too clingy lately,"

The three swapped looks and stayed as they were.

"Thyre, Chancellor Vondaka appointed us to you."

"You were to carry me, not crowd me. Away. Further."

With a scowl they obeyed, but mumbled their discontent behind their palms to each other.

"When?" muttered one.

"Ssshh!" the other two hissed.

Dandaron broke ranks and quickly moved on the trio.

"Move out of the core, beyond the enforcers."

"Our orders come from the chancell..."

The glass blade shrieked as Dandaron half drew his shard.

"I am his fateshield, you are mere stewards. Heed me or die."

The enforcers laughed and jostled the shaken stewards as they fumbled to pass through their protective ring. Drolla blushed wide-eyed at Dandaron. He caught his onlooker's glare and winked a cheeky grin. Ever since their first chat back home, this brute loved to show off.

As his fateshield joined his side, Quetono reached and squeezed Dandaron's shoulder. Palama smiled at them both.

"I hope cousin appreciates his new legion," said Palama.

"I hope he appreciates that it is 'your' new legion," said Quetono.

Many hours later, dark blue streamers launched into the sky from within the camp. One long, forlorn deep blast of the war horn confirmed the signal and the entire host halted. Drolla stood in awed silence. A high mound hid the moat. Along its outer ridge, a high fence of stone columns carved like claws lined its entire length as it curved out of sight. Along the moat's inner bank the mighty walls hid the camp within. Palama's horde faced the only bridge, beyond it stood the towering entrance.

Sculptured from funglstone, vast decorated slabs lined the entire outer gate. In honour of the first monarch, the images were embossed battle scenes from the Monofication Wars with the victorious Xendaka at the centre. Master of the people, the military, the law and the land.

Drolla smiled, it was a welcome sight. He was glad to be there. The endless days of perpetual sun was an ordeal he was happy to forget. Now he could rest. Of all he left behind, he missed solitude the most. He craved the dark underground and a long cold bath.

Apart from the fluttering pennants atop the great wall, the place seemed deserted. A city this size should be noisy, bustling with crowds, markets, something. All he could hear was a thousand breaths panting in anticipation, waiting for something to happen. The officers seemed not bothered as they casually chatted amongst themselves. It was hard to imagine what they were waiting for. Drolla's impatience made his wait even more unbearable. To have come so far and simply stand outside was a frustration he could do without.

The monstrous gate creaked and began to move. Hinged halfway up, the top fell back and the bottom lurched outward. Groaning under its own weight, it slowly swiveled open and locked horizontal with a dull morbid thud. Frowns turned to grins as the excitement grew. Spirits began to soar and chatter began to buzz.

"Silence," roared Joltoro. The order and compliance rippled from the centre to outer rim in an instant.

The clamour of an army tramping on stone echoed from the open gate. Four thousand fully armed and dressed soldiers appeared, trotting over the arched mound between the stone claws. From across the moat, they approached, fifty abreast.

The legions split and surrounded Palama's horde like two hands cupping a bowl of brew. When the army had the horde surrounded, the lancers lowered a ring of thorns. Naturally, this circular phalanx caused the recruits to face outwards. It was a confronting and unexpected welcome. Overtired and hungry, a few scampy rascals at the outer rim taunted the spears by presenting their chests in jesting acts of defiance.

The lancers joined in on the joke, but warned them not to tempt their thirsty pikes too much.

From the outside edge closest to the bridge, two rows of resident enforcers brandished their unsheathed shards and penetrated the mob. Using their shields as buffers, they shouted.

"Make way!"

They parted the crowd and lined their tapered channel to the centre. The recruits had shuffled aside to accommodate them as if they had drilled it. Drolla's superiors stood clustered in the middle. The enforcer's prefect stepped forward and handed a message to Dandaron.

"Enforcer Dandaron, welcome to the Pen. By order of the Monarch Soltoro, this message is for Khillionaire Joltoro alone. Please inspect the seal."

Dandaron held the small translucent vial up to the sun. A tiny rainbow rolled across the pearl glass tube. The scroll slid back and forth as he shook it. He licked his fingers and ran them lightly around the rim.

"Enforcer Glendoro, this container and its contents are secure."

Joltoro snapped the royal seal and emptied the note into his palm. He discreetly unrolled as much as he needed to read.

"Commander Palama, I am to escort you to the monarch immediately," said Joltoro.

"We should not keep him waiting," said Quetono.

"Pardon thyre." Joltoro blushed. "The monarch summoned his cousin only."

"I see. Of course. You best hurry then nephew."

"I will find you later," said Palama.

Without another word, Joltoro and Palama strutted off toward the open gate.

"Enforcer Dandaron, you and your security team are to accompany me back to the constabulary at once. Your debrief is expected and marked urgent," said Glendoro.

Dandaron shot a worried frown at Quetono, it morphed into a snarl as he saw the trio of stewards nearby.

"Hectarion Tranna, my fateshield has a conflict of conscience," said Quetono. "His royal duty insists he abandons my personal protection."

"Boohala," called Tranna. The hunk stepped forward and curtsied. "You will escort Quetono to the gentry's marquee."

"That is our duty, thyre," complained his first steward.

"You are porters, not soldiers," snapped Quetono. "Your tenure has expired."

Boohala gripped his hilt and stepped between Quetono and the scowling stewards.

Quetono smiled and waved his fateshield on, motioning him not to worry. Dandaron stared hard but was forced to accept the situation.

"Off you go." Quetono was insistent.

He joined Glendoro and they led their troop of enforcers out of the horde. The two lines snapped into action and began to exit the gap exactly as they had entered it. The recruits retook their original positions and the open wedge closed behind them like two curtains falling across a doorway. The surrounding lancers hoisted their spears upward and rested them on a shoulder.

"March on!"

Lingering back beside Drolla, the three stewards began to fidget. They seemed restless and hissed at each other in a muted argument.

While the mass of recruits mounted the bridge and crossed the moat, a lithe young figure leaped from behind a stone talon. In a blur, he disappeared into the crowd. None nearby noticed. Their attention was drawn to the moat, and the heavily laden catamaran passing under them.

"It is stocked with rations and weapons," said Quetono. "One of many we will meet at the western border soon enough."

A purple clad marine watched over a few naked sailors crawling among the ropes. When it appeared from under the other side of the bridge, the masts were raised and the sails let out. They billowed and flapped before the rigging groaned and pulled taut. The breeze filled the canvas with a snap and the craft shot off towards the canal.

Through the great gate, the horde were funneled into columns and Drolla found himself in the immediate presence of Quetono and his guards. With the lancers leading and trailing the rank and file of the horde, they strode the broad highway into the guts of Churon's Pen.

"I have not been here for years. So much has changed," said Quetono walking down memory lane.

"For the better I hope, thyre," said Tranna.

"Good to be back, eh? Look at that," said Quetono. From either side of the broadway, against the inner wall, alleys lined with diners and taverns stretched to and beyond around the city.

"The brew-bars will be packed later on," said Quetono. His grin tore his face in half.

"Too posh for me thyre," said Boohala. "I prefer the cozy little berry-dens."

"Take Drolla, he is good with a tureen," laughed Tranna. Drolla squeezed a smile. He hoped the hectarion was kidding.

An avenue of hungry smells filled the still air that hung between the lanes of butchers, grocers and brewers. Vacant patios and empty sunken booths lined the wide forested greenway. The bushland was strewn with fields and fenced yards, gardens and orchards. Fruiting vines festooned the shaded groves. As they crossed Spoke Bridge, horned fauna grazed the patchy grasslands beside the viaduct. The small timid herd drank from the central brook. Spooked by the tramping soldiers, the beasts panicked and bolted into the undergrowth. Laughter erupted as the angry shepherd howled curses and chased after his scattering flock. Past the babbling waterway and mossy woodlands, open parklands flanked endless rows of barracks. Thousands of small marquees, permanent awnings and a small forest of teepees bled into row after row of military premises.

"The Quartermaster sections have grown," said Quetono.

"They house the med bays and shardsmiths forges too now," said Tranna.

"Shard-spalling Drolla," yelled Quetono. "Now there is something to look forward to."

"You won't be a soldier without it," said Boohala.

Without warning, a vast emptiness appeared. The inner edge of the city gave way to an enormous arena. In the distant centre, a black dome sat skirted by a green fringe. Between here and there, orange sand turfed the bare arena.

Within earshot of Drolla, tense whispers broke out again among those whining stewards.

"Are we doing this?"

"I am not sure we should."

"We've been paid." One noticed eyes on them, "Sshh." Dread carved deep into their hopeless faces.

The escort of lancers halted the horde half way out into the arena, and without a prompt the recruits herded themselves back into their disk formation. In military step, the lancers marched away fifty-odd paces, enlarging their surrounding ring. They broke the loop and either end doubled back on itself into a great semi-circle.

From either horizon, a dozen legions appeared from behind the central black dome. Horns and pennants filled the air above them. Chants and battle cries led their rapid advance.

"Behold. The might of Drahn," said Quetono. He posed proud and watched twelve thousand warriors march to welcome them.

Again, the trio began to argue under their breath. They ignored the spectacle drawing down on them.

"We should have done it by now."

"He might take his money back," one said.

"I have spent mine."

Each indigo khillionaire, clad brighter and smarter than his peer, led his circling legion from the centre. Teal hecatrions spiraled between the ranks from edge to centre and back again, herding their seasoned warriors.

The trio forgot themselves and their panic mounted. They also forgot to whisper.

"We'll be killed if we don't."

"I'm not having that."

"Better him than me."

The armies poured in to fill the void between the horde and the lancers. Once surrounded, whistles blew and squads sat, one after the other. The commotion settled like a rolling wave.

By the central Black Dome, a wedge cracked and widened. Royal arrogance draped in brown passed through the obedient gap. Three score black tunics, striped white like marble followed. They tromped a dutiful march as they escorted their regal master.

"Chancellor Vondaka," said Tranna in hushed awe.

"Backed by the monarch's Protorian Guard no less. What are you up to sibling?" said Quetono. "Boohala, stride forward and welcome the chancellor. Pass this baton to him and escort him to me." The soldier did as he was bid and left Quetono's side.

Shadowed by his fateshield, Vondaka strode an ominous gait toward his sibling. Like ancient foes, Drahn's mightiest elders mirrored a rival glare. A steward yelled.

"There he is. He has seen him."

"He has seen us."

"Then let him watch. Now!"

The assassins launched their attack.

"Wait!" roared Vondaka.

Anger, fear and risk pounced on unsuspecting trust. The stewards leaped onto their patron and Quetono fell beneath them. His eyes flared at their betrayal. Wheezed by the first blow, he coughed up bloody phlegm and spat it into the nearest face. But their pounding continued and each blow knocked a little more wind out of the elder.

At first their violence was mindless. They broke his ribs, but not his neck. One punched in his guts and kicked at his head. One held Quetono in a headlock while the second stomped his ankles. His frail fists pounded their midriffs, but the brutes did not feel Quetono's feeble defense. Kneecaps popped and arms were broken. Each snap brought screaming agony.

Drolla, awestruck at the speed of the violence, toe kicked one up the kladger. He yelped and dropped to his knees and clutched his screeching genital. His victim growled and lashed out a wild haymaker that struck Drolla's jaw, he dropped like a hot stone. His face throbbed and the sky spun. The clouds shrieked and yelled and roared as they squeezed together, stretching around the twisting sky. He looked away and faced the ground. It was the warriors who shrieked and yelled and roared as they crushed together, desperate to pull the melee apart. For fear of striking Quetono, no shard was drawn against the attackers.

Boohala ran back and bound into the fray, he spun Drolla aside by his ankle. The three traitors went beserk. These powerful beasts unleashed a violent fury, desperate to fight off the defenders. A dozen bawling recruits swarmed the tiring foes. They tore them away from Quetono and threw them into a sprawling heap. The Chancellor and his Protorians arrived too late, but just in time to seize control.

"Finish them. Now," roared Vondaka. Fontaza flashed his screeching blade thrice. The stewards' heads were struck off in an instant.

Drolla dropped to his knees and scooped up Quetono, he held him as gently as his long dead Bretto. Vondaka stood before the sun and frowned down at his beaten sibling. In his towering shade, bruising eyes squinted open and smiled painfully as they adored Drolla.

"Thank you. My dear young'n."

Just as quickly, they closed and his head lolled back. Drolla hugged him closer, there was breath still in the elder's broken body. Tears of relief soaked his blushing cheeks. Through narrowed eyes, Vondaka studied Drolla. Enforcers burst from the green awnings under the black dome. In a legal fury, Dandaron sped toward the scene of the crime.

2.3 - THE POLITE DISCOURTESY

S and sprayed as Dandaron skidded to a halt by Quetono's side.

He squat semi-prone, his stern glare melted at the image of the battered elder laying in Drolla's cradling embrace.

"Do not move, hold him still. Field-Surgeon Torono is on his way," said Dandaron.

He spun as he stood and faced Vondaka. The enforcer scowled at his chancellor like an angry fist threatening a smug mouth. The spectators held their breath.

"The culprits have been penalised," said Vondaka.

"They were your agents," roared Dandaron.

"They acted alone."

"They could have been questioned."

"I suppose we shall never know."

"We might guess," hissed Dandaron.

The doctor arrived and elbowed himself between the towering egos. He knelt and examined his patient. Half a dozen nurses swooped in and settled around him like birds and awaited their instructions.

Fingers felt a pulse, nostrils smelled the breath. Gentle hands fondled every bone and knuckle. After a moment of quiet consideration, Torono whispered his directives. The nurses sprang into action and splinted every limb and bound every joint.

"Blood on his breath, he has internal injuries," said Torono. "Broken bones and dislocated joints need to be reset. He must be hospitalised immediately."

The nurses moved Drolla aside. They slid a stiff mat under Quetono and lifted, ready to transport him to the royal clinic.

"Thank you Torono," said Vondaka. "Have your staff keep me informed."

"I shall keep you informed," said Dandaron. "I will never leave his side again."

"A fateshield never should," snarled Vondaka.

Mute with rage, Dandaron faced his enforcers. They encircled the ambulance and escorted them away.

"Hectarion," said Vondaka. "Send for a mortician's crew to clean up this mess," an open hand pointed to the beheaded corpses, "the flies have arrived already."

"Thyre." Tranna obeyed, and sent a soldier on his way.

Vondaka turned and smirked at the horde. He cleared his throat and raised his voice.

"Syblings. Hold your tongues and heed me now." The buzz of the crowd settled to hear. "Drahn's noble uncle, our Lord Quetono, was assaulted near to death by bladeless shardhires. Served instant justice, those three traitors lay dead at our feet. Despite the cowards' violence, the noble Quetono lives."

"As does his persecutor," shouted a righteous voice, hidden within the mob.

Vondaka sneered at the unwelcome comment.

"Fear not dear syblings. The conspirator will die for the misdeeds of the would-be murderers," said Vondaka. "Quetono lives only by the swift actions of his brave and loyal recruits. You saved his life, take solace in that. He will recover. But, the allocations must proceed. It is a Drafter's reward to see his recruits forged into warriors."

Vondaka called for a lance and tore a hemline strip off his toga. The frayed ribbon was a palm wide and an arm's length. He tied the brown silk off like a pennant and speared the shaft into the sand of the arena.

"Let this pole stay rooted here until we all gather again to witness our beloved Quetono remove it himself."

In the absence of Khillionaire Joltoro, Chancellor Vondaka handed over the allocations to Hectarion Tranna.

"At the monarch's behest, after allocation, the recruits are to receive two day's furlough. He vows an informal inspection of his newcomers later," said Vondaka. He turned to his fateshield and sneered behind the back of his hand. "If he can set his box of potions aside for one day."

Vondaka growled and flicked his jagged satin. He threw his head over to face the distant black dome and tromped away between his Protorians. They swirled around him like a draining bath and left, taking their royal vanity with them. Several war horns blew, each echoing the other around the arena. Every legion rose and roared and stamped like a wave. Then, as quickly as they arrived, the dismissed warriors dispersed to the edge of the arena and melted into every alley and lane of their military suburbia. Again, the horde stood alone.

Tranna addressed the hectary of soldiers he had led since the beginning of the mission. He thanked them for their loyal and proficient service to the monarchy thus far, but that task was just the beginning. Now, they were to be dissected into squads. A swarm of crisp orange kilts ran toward the assembled recruits.

"Your grexitors arrive."

Siblings and cousins insisted they not be separated, new found friends and comrades demanded the same. Each soldier peeled off seven favourites and gathered them around the squad leader that called his name. Drolla soon found himself part of a mob of surplus recruits. The friendless and those without kin hung back like leftover bruised fruit.

During the entire trek, Drolla was quietly pleased that he had never run into his cousins again. Yet, here on this last day, they passed him on their way to group into their own new squad. He ignored their calls to join him. His fake smile and phony wave soured their candid offer. They happily shrugged at each other and jogged off and followed their squadster to the barracks.

"It seems you too are a loner," said Tranna.

"Palama has missed all this. He was meant to be here. Now, the horde has disappeared without him."

"Drolla, we have trodden our own path for months. But now we are here, the monarchy will lead us down theirs. The royals made sure everyone was where they were meant to be."

The number of unallocated recruits began to dwindle, as did the quality of the squad leaders. They became scruffier and crankier. One hadn't even turned up.

"Down to the dregs now," said Tranna.

"Perhaps I should have joined my cousins," said Drolla.

"You think?" said Tranna. His smile looked about to see the last of the squads dawdling away to Brewers Avenue. Behind, he noticed the very last of the rejects clustered around his mark. He caught his eye and motioned him over.

"Boohala, I have another to add to your troop."

He scanned Drolla up and down and clicked his tongue.

"As you wish, thyre. But you should know, I was instructed to gather the roughest crew that needed the smoothest polish."

"Instructed, by who?" asked Tranna.

"We await the mighty Xindro," he replied with unmistakable sarcasm.

Tranna burst into a laugh that was both cruel and sympathetic. He patted Drolla's shoulder.

"You'll be fine. Really."

The palanquin bobbed to and fro and back again between three porters. Sour froth welled up at the back of his throat. The monarch clenched his teeth and swallowed. Sweet chalkjubes did nothing to ease his churning gut. The black velvet drapes were drawn tight and except for the narrow beam from a tiny skylight, he squat in total darkness.

He moved another Drafter's report into the swaying spot of light at his lap. The couriers delivered them every few days in bundles from across the kindom. The monarch quietly smiled to himself, his subjects really were efficient in their attempt to outdo each other and appease their benevolent sovereign. Their zeal in boasting the quantity and quality of their fresh recruits, while admirable, became pompous and dull. No matter, as long as his army grew.

He held a smudged letter from his uncle Quetono and skipped the standard regal waffle, head counts and the weather to study one particular paragraph.

'Joltoro is a worthy asset, you were most wise to grant his pardon. His loyal hectary drill the recruits as we travel. Once they receive weapons training, they will be a force the monarchy can rely on.

As to Palama, he has seized and perfected his command throughout the mission. He quashed a minor rebellion, then embraced their eastern loyalty. He is quite a different person.'

"So, the magistrate thinks he has an army now, does he?"

His cousin Palama. Different, how? Soltoro had not seen him in person since childhood. Soltoro never understood why his Chancellor would exclude his own regal child from a royal life, but he was always kept far too busy to ever wonder too much. Vondaka forever crooned that it was wiser to fill the palace with those adept at monarchy.

Still, Soltoro's curiosity always kept a distant eye on Palama and he often learned more than he liked. His lone cousin was not a monarchist. Seniocratic sentiment deserved the reclusive life of a local magistrate. He had long since decided his cousin was a fool. Now, he was a fool with a legion behind him. It was pointless to ponder over the paragraph, nothing new would emerge from its text. He threw the note aside and and rested his weary eyes.

Eleven days out from the palace, the royal entourage entered Churon's Pen and the dozy monarch did not even realise. The litter halted. Its abrupt drop tore Soltoro from his meditation. He believed if he dreamt often enough, the future might present itself. Yet, the sudden stop surprised him. Squinting sunlight burst past the curtain as Vondaka yanked it aside.

"We're here. Drink this."

A vial the size of a finger held a pale violet slime peppered with flecks of... something. He gulped it down whole. The liquid slid down his throat like coughed up phlegm. The bitter after taste was worse, but the euphoria and confidence that tingled into every extremity of his body was instant and amazing. He paused for a moment to wallow in that first flush of pure bliss before dropping the vial onto the floor. It rolled among the scattered reports and the empty message tubes.

Slapping his cheeks to compose himself, the monarch of Drahn stepped into the cold light of day. He was startled by the sudden roar of thousands of soldiers. The senior ranks were gathered closest to him and the rest spiralled out to the common soldier. Rings of indigo khillionaires, teal hectarions, orange grexitors and white soldiers seemed an endless curling loop. Their powerful and welcoming cheer echoed across the camp. Although, even in his foggy state of mild intoxication, the verbal salute did sound a tad forced.

Three Protorians helped him up the two steps of the podium. Despite this, he was still no taller than a head above the rest. Most of the vast crowd had never seen their monarch before. He cut a very mediocre figure.

The mighty sovereign wavered a little as he struck an orator's pose.

"Greetings, noble warriors of Dra..." He turned down and coughed into his elbow. Groans of disapproval rose here and there from the assembled troops like wisps of stale marsh fog. Soltoro broke into a coughing fit and dropped to one knee. Between gasping breaths, dry retching turned wet and he vomited down the steps of the podium. The stench of purple acid filled the air and the nearest officers recoiled in disgust.

The monarch's fateshield rushed to his side and scooped him up. The Protorians ushered them to the royal marquee. They were followed by a cohort of concerned khillionaires. Glendoro gently placed his charge onto the central plynth.

"I am fine," said Soltoro, forcing a whimpered smile.

"Even you do not believe that," replied Glendoro.

"Dismiss the syblings. I cannot return." A hiccup burped and stank like old fish.

"Relax thyre, the chancellor is with them."

"Of course he is."

Torono burst into the marquee. He neither curtsied nor spoke. He grabbed his monarch's arm and straightened it toward him. The doctor stabbed one hand into his armpit and wrapped another around his wrist.

"Temperature and pulse."

None dared to interrupt his whispered counting. Their physician's self imposed dominance was never to be questioned. He had saved far too many important lives, you prevented his work at your peril.

"High and fast," he said to his assistant. The doctor threw a dismissive glance at the mighty nobles, stiff as statues and frozen with respect. A wry smile betrayed his vanity as he handed the monarch his arm back. Torono leaned in close to whisper to Soltoro.

"Pardon thyre. I had to, before you relaxed..."

"You know your business Doctor," sighed Soltoro.

Torono smelled the monarch's words, and peered deep into exhausted eyes.

"You are too ill. No fit state..."

"Our syblings prepare for war, by my command. I will lead them. Thank you for your concern. Dose me up with your potions, medic. I have too much to do." He exhaled at the effort. Torono whispered to his assistant, who then rushed from the tent.

"Thyre, if I may, I speak for all," said Fandara. "Your health is of prime importance to the morale of the soldiers. We have the logistics in hand. As the new recruits arrive, we shall train them ready for battle."

"Which I will lead them into," reminded Soltoro.

"Not if you do not rest," said Torono.

Soltoro nodded between a renewed bout of coughing and held up a conceding palm. His loyal generals could not hide their concern. Even after the monarch composed himself, their frowns remained waiting for another spluttering fit.

"Fandara, convey my sentiments down the ranks. For now, I will obey the doctor. But I intend to inspect the camp as soon as I can escape my new jailer."

Fandara curtsied. He led the exit and cleared the tent. Torono's assistant elbowed his way through the soldier's midst.

"After they all left, Torono prescribed that box," said Soltoro. It lay open on a tall table beside him. The little trays lay folded out, filled with amber vials, some full, some empty. Palama wondered if his cousin had finished his monologue and would get to the point of this meeting. Their long journey had just ended. He was tired, hungry and needed to wash. Surely this summons could have waited. "Detoxifiers," he continued, "for prevention and cure."

"Surely you do not suspect us of poison." Joltoro was indignant.

"How can he? We have not been here," said Palama.

"Correspondence from our uncle has kept me informed of the events throughout your journey. I am surprised you are both worthy of his favour," said Soltoro.

"Who are we to question the wisdom of our elders?" said Joltoro.

"Quite." Soltoro paused. "Cousin Palama, I have read that you have become an accomplished commander. For that I praise you, but that commission is over. You are assigned to the martial magistracy here. We need someone who understands the lower class of criminal amongst our ranks."

"With respect thyre, the recruits and I have been through a lot together. We have a solemn bond that neither can break," said Palama.

"If the bond is that strong, perhaps we can bend it a little for a while. It is settled. You start tomorrow. Your legal staff will brief you. There is quite a case load, the dungeons are full."

Soltoro paused for a moment to ensure Palama understood.

"Joltoro. Your competence has done you credit. You will retain your rank and your new legion. I expect them to redeem you when we face the enemy."

"I will teach them how to kill foreigners, thyre."

"Yes. At that, you proved yourself more than capable."

A Protorian burst into the closed marquee. He dropped onto one knee and faced his monarch.

"Zakala, I said no interruptions," Soltoro roared at his breathless messenger.

"Quetono has been attacked. He is on his death bed."

Audacity swaggered toward the last squad in its own good time. The stiff orange cloth rolled across his shoulders as he shrugged off his indifference. He spat off to one side while he stared at the intimidated crew. One hand grasped a glass fist, the pommel of his shard. It lurched back and forth with every step. The sand squeaked underfoot as he circled the motley crew. With an incredulous smirk, he eyed them up and down and stopped at Boohala.

"Surely this can't be the phappin' worst of them."

"Nope, you missed those. But these are kinless, and raw."

"They are always phapping raw. I wanted to shatter their egos, not coddle them."

"Ha. Well, they are yours now." Boohala's smile fell from his face as the grexitor glared ice.

He faced his new unsuspecting crew and stared at Drolla.

"My name is Xindro, your squad leader. I am Oxxian and you are not. But you are all phappin' disgusting, except the little one. Why is that?"

Unwashed since the dusty Blue Hills, they were dirty with dark grey powder. It coated them like boots, gloves and masks with random smears here and there across their sun-bright hides.

"They have trudged a hard road," said Boohala.

"Yeh, we are tired..." said one.

"Ya filthy and ya stink," said Xindro, wide-eyed at the bravado.

"...and hungry," said another.

"Phap! Anything else you wanna complain about? Let's get the tears done with now."

"We are not complaining," said Drolla.

"Aren't ya? Well, that's all right then," said Xindro. "I would have thought the army had sorted you all out long before getting here."

"We sorted ourselves out," said Drolla.

"Yeh, we killed all those kladgers we could."

Xindro glared disbelief.

"It's true. There was a mutiny over food. The commander made them weed out and murder the guilty themselves," said Boohala.

"Killers already? That is a good start," said Xindro. "I can't wait to hear all about that." He unclipped the buckle around his middle and handed his shard and belt to Boohala. Pinching a corner that draped over his shoulder, Xindro lifted his arm and unspun his orange toga in circling loops till the cloth piled around his feet.

"Phap that itchy rag," he said stepping out of the coils, "who's up for a wash and a feed?"

Apart from the shard belt he strapped back around his middle, he was as nude as his recruits. His coaxing grin led them back to his digs.

The exhausted squad followed Xindro down alleys and along lanes, through a maze of awnings and marquees. Rows and rows of curved tents had already been settled by old and new recruits alike. Some were empty, some had bodies lazing about in the sun watching the shade creep past. They trotted by a rowdy group still toasting each other. His cousins saw Drolla and cheered at him and raised their cups. Their laughter faded sooner than the sting of their mockery. So what, he was well rid of them. An endless line of identical domes streamed by before they were called to a halt.

"This is us. In," said Xindro.

Before them, a translucent white dome stood on three low arches. All three door flaps were tied up. A beige flaxen mat lined the floor from wall to wall. In the centre of the marquee sat the central plynth, a simple funglstone post. There was room enough for at least two dozen recruits to squat around it, yet it was sparse and uninviting. After months on the road Drolla expected some sort of comfort, even a simple cushion. The groans from his peers hinted they agreed with him.

"Boohala, open the phappin' door."

He pushed past slumped shoulders and knelt by an arched strut. With a grunt, he pulled the handle of a trap door and threw it open.

"Follow me," said Boohala, peeling of his filthy tunic.

Drolla was the first to follow and led the recruits as they clambered down the spiral ramp into a large round chamber. The clack of a smolderstone lit the interior with a cool pearl glow. Its gentle light lit up tasseled cushions scattered about rippling furs and crumpled woolly quilts. They lined the floor like a cozy sea of shaggy luxury. In the middle, a low table was covered with bowls and jars of pickled treats.

"If ya hungry, take what ya like. But keep goin' down," yelled Xindro, over hungry groans of delight. The ravenous kids scooped up what they could and slid down the ramp to the next level. In the lower chamber, everyone melted at the sight of a huge cold water tub waiting for them. The bath was size enough for all, a communal spa. Drolla was taken aback at the speed the others climbed in. He was used to bathing alone, but the water was far too inviting to be a snob. He slowly eased in beside Boohala and laid back and let the cool water soothe his exhausted body. If he was alone, Drolla was sure he could slip into a deep meditation for days. As it was, the friendly sploshing and giggling chatter sounded like a kindergarten. A bowl was shoved in his face.

"Here, try this," said Boohala.

Drolla looked down at some nasty strips of jelly leather floating in a grey slurry. He would have preferred not to, but the bowl insisted. With thumb and forefinger, he gingerly plucked a short piece and nibbled the end. It was like rubbery fungus, soggy and flavourless.

"Pickled faun hide. So delicious," said Boohala, chomping on a piece whole. "After all the rich, fancy rations from the depots, I am glad to have normal army food again."

The thunderous silence of disbelief was deafening.

"This is army food?" asked Drolla. A closer look of the morsel pinched between his fingers only made the idea less appealing.

"There is plenty to get used to," said Xindro.

"Like this? Day one in the army and it's a group bath with strangers?" asked Drolla.

"Accept it, we won't be strangers for long. No privacy now and there's no phappin' secrets either. Us here, is all there is. You can't trust any of them up top. Only us. Till death or discharge." said Xindro.

"All I meant..." said Drolla.

"Did ya? I see," said Xindro. "Well, this is what I mean. You will all vow an oath of fidelity to this group, our new squad. Raise a hand to prove your intent to hold us in this bath loyal to each other before anyone else."

The hesitant group glanced about. They followed Boohala's lead and raised a hand to pledge their bond.

"I do," said Drolla. Unsure, the rest felt obliged to copy him.

"Good," said Xindro. "I am glad you did, otherwise I would have drowned you here and now."

A nodding Boohala thawed their frozen glares of disbelief.

"So," said Xindro looking at Drolla, "who the phap are you? What do they call ya?"

"Drolla."

"What were you before you left?"

"I was a mushroom grower, from Phuusha in the Perse Hills."

"Phappin' hate mushrooms. What sort?"

"Red Spore," said Drolla.

The spa exploded with whistles and whoops of admiration and jest.

"Whoa! We got a rich one here fellas," jeered Xindro.

"The heir of a doyen, no less," said Boohala.

"I was no heir," said Drolla.

"Well pardon us, your majesty..."

"If you must know, I was glad they took me away. I was less than a serf to my parent and despised by the whole clan on his behalf. I'd rather be here than there."

"You will return one day and claim that plynth from your par'," said Boohala.

"I did have some Red Spore. My grandpar' gave me a sack full, but it was confiscated."

"What a pity," said Xindro.

"Our birthdays would have been way better than everyone else's," laughed one.

"When does Pannatalia start here?" asked another.

"When did it start back home?" said Boohala.

"When the first baby is born," he replied.

"And how many phapping pregger folk do you think there are in an army camp?" said Xindro.

"We might get Midnth Day off, if the royals consider we deserve it," said Boohala.

"Well if I did have some, I would definitely share it with you all," said Drolla.

"We might hold you to that," said Xindro. "You," he said pointing to the next bath mate.

And so around the small group, soaking together in the bath, each one after the other said their bit.

Yanna was a fisher from the Oster Beach, solid build with a round face and huge arms. Klommo, a tall thin urbanite butcher from Blacktree. Grikka the builder hailed from the archipelago of villages that dawdled across the far eastern Wetland Plains. Stout Dwaxxi was a farmer from the western forests of the Bevwood. Finally, there was Flynx.

"Seventeen?" said Xindro. "Are they recruiting phappin' kids now?"

"Seventeen is adult," said Flynx.

"Only just. You should be home, pregnant."

"None of them are," said Flynx pointing to his mates.

"They are in the twenties, heading towards seniority. For phap sake."

"Where are you from?" asked Boohala.

"I ran away from the Lodge."

"What?"

"Kinless kids like me got punished with curfews and half meals when the new president took over. The posh lot, those with family or 'uncles', got well looked after. Except those poor twins. Locked in deep chambers first day there. Anyone who spoke about them, got the same. When they sent me south, I escaped."

"But, how did you get in? There was army everywhere," said Xindro.

"I waited outside and snuck in with you lot. I just mingled about like I belonged."

"Ha, fantastic. Your secret is our's now," smiled Xindro, "and none will forget our vow."

"Or the punishment," said Flynx.

"Dead right," said Xindro. "Now Boohala, tell me all about the riot."

After a few hours, their epic journey had caught up with them. Cleansed, and with full bellies, the soft fluffy luxury of the dark leisure chamber above the bathroom was impossible to ignore. His fellows chatted for a while, opening up more about their own lives. One by one, darkness and laxity drifted them into drowsy silence. Xindro's plight struck a chord with Drolla. His tale stirred a mix of envy and pity.

"I fell every phapping orgy," said Xindro. His dozy troop watched him dress. "Nine birthlings I've got, each one wilder than the other. I also have half a dozen siblings with just as many kids each. They are raisin' mine with theirs. We are a big clan, so they are used to it. They can have them. The unruly brats are like a feral herd." He straightened some pleats of his orange kilt. "Our family estate is a large fruit forest, a days trek north-west of the waterfall city." He strapped his shardbelt around his middle and rested one palm on its pommel. "The army is my only escape. I phapping love it. Here, I am a somebody amongst nobodies. At home, I'm anybody to everybody. I'm a warrior, not a baby-sitter."

"Until now," said Flynx.

"Rest up kids," snarled Xindro. "Soon, you start a month of training. I shall enjoy watching you lot broken into little pieces."

He trotted up the ramp and disappeared outside.

2.4 - THE UNIQUE SIMILARITY

The quartermaster's gazebo was understaffed and surrounded with impatience.

Five weeks training was over and everyone was keen to get their kit. Xindro promised to finish off the day's shopping with a few syrups at the Aurora Grey. They had lived on water, jerky and pickles for the past month. Now, they vowed to gorge themselves on brewberry syrup, sausage and jellied fruits.

The past month had tested even the most fittest of the recruits. If it was the monarch's wish to break them, he near succeeded. Smiths, farmers and scribes were torn down and rebuilt into warriors. Many would falter under the incessant grind of the pitiless training, but none were let fail. The torture was eased just long enough for the weary to be reminded that foreigners, the thieving Miokh, were to blame for their suffering. Dragged from home and forced into a war they did not understand, the draftees brooded at the injustice. But while their hatred festered, their bodies strengthened. They would be ready to battle whether they wanted to or not. Consent was not requested, it was mandatory. Their plight would be easier to endure if they accepted and embraced the fate they could not escape.

In the first week of training, severe physical exercise nearly broke their bodies. Constant sets of squats, pull-ups and other detested bouts of aerobic workouts were interspersed with endless jogging around the arena. Drolla knew every colour, every scent and every purpose of every awning and every tent that ringed the edge separating the sand from suburbia. As the days passed, his legs and lungs began to cease their painful complaints. His fierce dislike of physical activity was fading as his endurance and stamina increased. Each day he often thought, *it wasn't so bad once you got used to it.* He knew he was lying to himself, but an exhausted delusion soothed the aching truth.

The second week broke their individuality. Squads were pitted against each other in mass sporting competitions. The child's game of passball was upscaled with a polished marble sphere the size of a head. Many clumsy would-be athletes ended up with broken toes. Reset and bound by medics, they were pushed back into the contests. Grunting sweaty scrums rammed and pushed each other over lines in the sand. The same lines they hauled their rivals across in their roaring tug-o-wars. Relay races were sprinted to victory, and to loss. Teams fought their way along a leader board until one squad remained. A small clan of loud Oxxian loggers received the champion's garland. Made from plaited rings of bright green flowers from the spiny dandleherb. The weed sprouted its ugly blooms everywhere. Like a royal torkh, the wreaths rested on their shoulders around their necks. They were worn with a boastful pride for a single day. After that, their celebrity wilted and faded with the fragile petals and they were nobodies again.

"We was champions of the arena," complained one who felt spurned at his loss of notoriety.

"Was," snapped a hectarion. "Get back on grid." He raised a handwhip and coerced the complainant to comply, while heckling laughter from his peers kept his grumbling mouth shut.

Week three put them all back together. They marched around the arena for days until they trod as one. Squads curled into a hectary. Hectaries swirled into a khillion. Khillions spiraled into an army that spent even more days drilling the disk formation and its various manoeuvers.

On the last day, Palama visited his Orienna Horde. The chatter had supposed he sneaked out of the judicial compound. His scarlet robe squeezed its way through his happy troops into the middle to join Joltoro. Sixteen other legions saw the morale of this obscure mob rise way, way beyond their own as a thousand grins cheered their commander's return.

"Carry on," said Palama, smiling at Joltoro. Both strutted around each other as if in a dance, and led the horde from the centre. They marched with the same mobility in the final weeks of their trek to the Pen. With regimented precision the great gyre rotated like a cyclone in slow motion. At Joltoro's command the outer edge split and circled back inwards, the inner ranks moved out to take their place and refresh the outer lines. Then, like veterans, a wedge opened up and folded back upon itself pushing the central officers to the head of the legion.

Palama broke off and ran up rank and down file slapping palms and patting shoulders. He whooped up his warriors into an excited state, punching the air and inviting them to join in. It seemed eons ago, but on this day they were whole again. In that moment their hearts floated like clouds and in their minds the Orienna Horde was invincible.

But the joy was short lived. A score of drill-chanting Protorians trotted out from the black marquee and surrounded Palama. His loyal horde booed and hissed as he was escorted back to the regal dome. It was as though the monarch's guard had torn their heart out. His parting speech would mend them all and forge their resolve to make him proud and shame everyone else.

"Whatever my consequences," cried Palama, "they will seem nought compared to this past hour with you. Train well, my wild Oriennans. Soon, we will show them all how it is done."

Their roar and applause filled the arena and left the remainder of the army dumbfounded. No khillionaire led a legion like Joltoro, and he made no move to quell their euphoria. "Let them see," he boasted.

A day's furlough was granted to quiet yesterday's furor. No news had come of their dear commander's fate. Gossip presumed royalty punished him in some cruel way. Soltoro was a jealous sovereign and it was expected his wrath would impose a harsh recourse. Rumour vowed the storming of the monarch's dome if Palama was touched in any way at all. Clearer minds quashed the emotional talk of treason within the legion. There was no time to foment discord now. The slander subsided, but the sentiment did not die with the whispers.

Weapons came onto the arena in the fourth week. Heels dug into the sand as shoulders scrummaged behind shield walls. Hard tanned hides collided together like herds of rutting horny beasts. Companies of blunted thorns clashed as each phalanx faced off. Hour upon hour they wheeled about in formation. The uniform forest of spears undulated like a coat of hackling spines...

"Next," yelled a clerk.

Drolla's mind was ripped back to the scene at hand. But the call was not for him. Hundreds of recruits grouped in their own little squads, surrounding their orange leader waiting to be called. While others allowed idle chatter, Xindro demanded silence from his group. He knew eyes were on him and he scowled now and then when he caught their gaze.

"What are they staring at?" whispered Flynx.

"Nothin'. Shutup," barked Xindro.

Out on the orange sand, hundreds of new soldiers trained as flingers. They were separated during the month's training and forced into the corps of ballisters. Each were armed with a woomera and a quiver filled with long fletched darts. At fifty or so paces, pink ribbons stretched into rings around stakes that marked out their targets. On command, the novices fitted a shaft into their throwing stick. They leaned back for a moment, then lunged forward and flung their arrows into a high arc.

Whistles followed grunts as they watched the coloured shafts fly. Disappointed groans saw them fall short, far and wide.

Coaches roared and vented. They were useless. Again, nock, aim, launch, again. Volley after volley, they hurled their darts together until they began to pitch as one. At last, clustered shafts flew like wingless flocks and every beak stabbed the sand inside the rings at once. Sporadic cheers and applause rose up from onlookers along that side of the arena. The coaches barked at their trainees and sent them to pull their darts. The recruits bolted to the targets, before they collected and requivered their own arrows, they stood around and checked out the dartfall pattern. Whose landed where? How tight and uniform was the cluster? They regrouped around their instructor and reset themselves to continue their practice.

"See that?" said Xindro. "Those flingers will be great artillery, and will kill for us from a distance. But they are not so brave as us shardsters." He half-drew his shard and kissed its pommel. "We kill our foe face to face. We get to watch the life drain from their eyes. It's wonderful."

Xindro heard his name. His crew waited as he jogged to the gazebo.

"They have shards too," said Boohala. "Unlike us, they can strike near and far."

"He is a proud shardster," said Yanna.

"He is the best."

"Hold out your hands," said Xindro. Surrounded by upturned palms, he counted out little painted tokens into each one. Drolla inspected his own little white triangle, red square, green circle, grey oval, and a black rod the size of a finger. "Follow me." He walked off into the nearest alley.

The mercer's tent was a sea of coloured fabric. Bolts of fabric lay heaped about with samples draping the inside walls like confused curtains. It was as if a cloth rainbow had crashed through the roof and had not been tidied up yet. On the central table, rolls of white silk lay stacked high in precarious piles. It seemed the slightest bump could bring the whole lot tumbling down. The vendor swapped their white token for a rolled up bundle. Drolla held his own up and let it unfurl. The soldier's toga slid over his elbow like a waterfall. Light ran across the folds, and he rubbed the tight weave between thumb and forefinger. It was the lightest and yet the most densely woven thread he had ever seen. It was nothing like the rustic garb he was forced to wear back home.

He pinched two corners and spread his arms apart, the cloth's edge stretched from one hand to the other. The third corner touched the floor. Drolla bundled the garment and hardly felt the slick material as he draped it over a shoulder and loosely wrapped it around his middle. He smoothed out a wrinkle and nodded his approval to himself.

"What thread is this?" he asked.

"Bonewasp gossamer. Quadruple spun and battle ready," said the tailor. "Finest Drahni silk couture. Look at the edging. Beautiful."

"Yeh, yeh it's gorgeous," said Xindro. "One size fits all. Let's go." He was snarky and impatient already, and pushed his troop out ahead of him.

"Boor," the mercer grumbled.

The air in the tanner's pavilion reeked of leather, wool and fur. Rugs and mats were strewn across the floor and laid in lopsided piles by the opposite wall. Racks stood like trees and the branches were hung with sandals, belts and all sorts of little totes. The curved table between them was covered in bundles of thonged sandals inter-wrapped with a belted pouch. Standard army issue.

"Quick, throw ya red token in the bowl and take a bundle," said Xindro.

Drolla stood idle and admired a row of strange small satchels hanging from the ceiling behind the tanner. They were little handbags made of coloured hair and fur, or engraved bald leather with dainty braided straps.

"What are they?" he asked.

"A special purse," smirked the tanner, "for your... intimate things."

"They're disgusting," said Xindro, snarling his distaste.

"You like that one?" asked the tanner. "Nice choice."

He passed the bag to Drolla. He examined it front and back and gently stroked the silken white hair. After snapping the firm clasp open, he inserted his fingers. Drolla smiled as he gently fondled the plush woolly lining. It was soft, luxurious and sensual.

"That's enough," said Xindro. "They are not barren uncles yet." He snatched the purse from Drolla and threw it at the tanner. "How about you quit grooming, you pervert. No one wants to join your circle jerk."

"You don't know that. He don't know that," said the tanner, winking at Drolla.

"Really? Let's ask him then," said Xindro. "Drolla, do you know what a frigster is? No?"

Drolla stared back his ignorance. It was obviously some city foible plain country folk never encountered. Xindro faltered as if he couldn't explain, or wouldn't. Boohala raised a palm and blinked a nod at Xindro.

"They are masturbaters Drolla," said Boohala. "They don't join Conjugation."

"They don't fuck. They're phappin' deviants who skip the orgy and toss each other off." Xindro found the words.

"It's not illegal," the tanner protested.

"It's not normal," blurted Xindro. He turned and faced his recruits. "If you lot want to whack yourselves dry with these perverts, then buy ya filthy crotchbag for all to see. But you can phap off out of my squad, right now."

"Ew, no," said Drolla. "We have nothing to buy anything with anyway." His blank faced comrades shrugged in agreement.

"Come back when you have the money, or the urge. We could work something out." The tanner smirked a naughty smile. "You know where we are."

"We know what you are! You dirty phapping queer." Xindro corralled his squad from the tent. "Out. Move."

The tanner yelled after him, "Onanophobe!"

Xindro hollered back, "Wanker!"

The sign above the entrance of the saporist's den read; *'Properly seasoned, anything is edible.'*

Under it, a large brute with crossed arms posed like a tavern's bouncer. He straddled a tall spindly stool that complained when he shifted his bulk from one creaking leg to the next. His beige linen skirt was tucked and crumpled underneath him and the faded red leather vest hugged so tight, the black woolly lining squeezed out of it everywhere. Straining clasps threatened to snap and shoot off like a slinger's pellet at any moment.

"No exit till I say so," he said in a voice as deep as thunder.

"We're going in, you idiot," said Xindro.

"Show me your flavours."

Xindro moaned at the bother and thrust out a hip. A lone vial the size of a finger, filled with fine white crystals like powdered salt, sat in its holster next to his beltpouch.

"Is that it, only one? What is it?"

With a deluded self imposed authority, the stupid bouncer reached for the vial. Xindro spun on a heel and in an instant, his half drawn shard stood where the vial had been. The bouncer's hand halted just as fast. His fingers lightly wrapped the glass blade. A glint of light ran up its smirking edge.

"It is mine and I am keeping it," said Xindro. "Do you want to keep your fingers?"

The bouncer delicately uncurled his hand and placed it safely back in his lap. Xindro elbowed past and entered the den.

"You?"

"None," said Boohala. "Why spoil plain good food. I shall wait out here."

"They can leave their stuff with you," said the bouncer. He eyed the recruits with a contemptuous glare of distrust. "We be sick of you kladgers thieving our powders."

Racks of curved shelves stood head and shoulders above Drolla and his mates. Stacked side by side, countless jars and vials filled the loaded shelves. Like tall spice racks, they were filled with coloured powders, flecks and liquids arranged from black to white with every colour in between. They bled from one hue to the next.

"Wow, look at them all," said Klommo. He ran a finger along some dusty labels and read aloud a few of the names. "Citrus Tang, River Mint, Black Salt, Whitefire Breath, Ocean's Delight..."

"Shut up," yelled Xindro. "Touch nothing, and get in here."

The corridor of open cupboards spiraled into a central nook lit by a lone smolderstone hanging from the dark ceiling. It shone a spotlight onto a polished tall table. There was an assortment of little white bowls, each carved like a small cupping hand. In an open display box, ampules held samples of the spices, herbs, salts and sugars. Their host stood by the table. Pale yellow silk draped his torso. It hugged his armpits and fell back over the shoulders.

"Phap me. Sontro the caterer has been promoted."

"Yep, I out rank you now Xindro."

"Why do we need these?" asked Flynx.

"They're new. They know nothing" said Xindro.

"Should I give them the spiel?"

"They are all yours."

Sontro faced the innocent recruits. He smiled and puffed himself up like an orator.

"Right, listen carefully. Ever since the first day Xendaka built Churon's Pen and housed it with his new army, catering was a problem. Until the herds and fruit gardens were established, food was provided by the clans."

"Like the depots?" asked Yanna.

"Exactly." Sontro continued. "But the finicky tastes of the soldiers varied so much that food was wasted. East and west disliked either's cuisine and the middlens hated both. Regional palates were too different to please them all. The catering corps' solution was to produce the blandest food possible and let each flavour it to his own taste. Hence, this great sapory was created and has grown in variety ever since.

"From that, the sharing of flavours between comrades meant each only had to carry their own favourites. Usually four. It has since become an army tradition to swap and share flavours. It is considered very bad manners not to," he glared at Xindro. "So who would like to try a sample?"

"Got any Red Spore?" asked Flynx, with a bratty grin.

"You should know the army prohibits it," said Sontro.

"We do," said Grikka. "But, we would still like some for Pannatalia. Drolla used to grow it."

Sontro's eyes narrowed. "Did he?" He leaned toward Xindro and whispered behind the back of his hand. "I know dozens, if not more, who would gladly drown us all in cash if you could get some."

"Well I can't. We are here for ya spices. Hurry up and choose, you brats. We have spalling to do yet."

The heat of a cloudless sun blazed from inside the shardsmith's forge. It was a dome of stone with twin chimneys set atop, one inside the other. The taller inner flue exhausted the fumes of the smelter, the outer vented the chamber itself.

A screaming white hot haze licked the roaring air above the inner flue. When the fire died, the outer chimney coughed a thick cloud of blue-grey fog. A muffled cheer was heard from within, and soon, a proud recruit emerged hugging his brand new weapon. His grinning peers shuffled away chattering and comparing their brand new blades.

Xindro's squad was the next in line to enter the mysterious dome. Now it was their turn to perform the coveted shard spalling ceremony. They were told nothing of the ritual and waited with nervous impatience.

A chamois awning hugged the outside wall like a twirling skirt. Open pails of fragrant grease scented the shade with pine and citrus.

"Rub yourselves down, it will soothe the sunburn," said Boohala.

"Sunburn?" asked Drolla.

His skin shivered as he smeared himself with the icy lotion.

"Whitefire sunburn," said Xindro. "It will melt ya phappin' skin off. Hurry up, you're first."

He pushed Drolla ahead through the thick leather drapes. The room was hot and airless. The aura of the furnace bathed the room in a pure, crisp white light. Shaped like a stone igloo, the forge stood waist high and just as wide. In its hearth, the whitefire burned like silent lightning. Its flames were tiny blinding orbs that grew and popped like bubbles the size of fists. The steady random eruption of bursting spheres burped out its constant searing heat. From a large pile, the shardsmith fed another slab of funglstone into the forge, stoking the blistering froth. One step away from the fire, a tall narrow vase stood alone. The smithy topped it up with a light oil decanted from a nearby barrel. By its base, a scuffed tile sat beside a bucket of glistening black powder.

The shardsmith cocked a curious eye at Xindro.

"Oi, aren't you Pondra's kid?"

"Grandkid," said Xindro.

"He was here a day ago. Brought all these blank shanks up. We had a chat and sat in the sunshine for a while. Then, he was gone. No one saw him sneak back down under."

"He's not allowed up top."

"He is by most. He doesn't deserve his penance."

"Was he well? I have not seen him for a while."

"He was lonely."

In silent contemplation, Xindro scowled at the fire. The conversation was over.

"Grab a shank," the shardsmith's casual demeanor disappeared. "It is time to spall. Focus now, you will only get one stab at it."

Spoilt for choice, Drolla's eyes ran across the rack of dozens of long black batons. They were the size and length of an unbent arm and shaped like cudgels. All were pre-made, identical, and looked nothing like swords.

"Hurry up, just pick one. They are all the phapping same," said Xindro.

"What's your name?" The shardsmith pulled the novice's attention to him.

"Drolla."

"I am Vratto."

"Another phapping easterner," said Xindro.

"Ignore this Oxxian kladger," said Vratto. "Those shanks might be all the same now. But your heart, mind and soul will steer the spalling. Your efforts will make your own shard one of a kind."

Drolla gripped the narrow end of the club, his fist rested at the blunt pommel. He closed another hand above the hilt and ran it full length, rubbing off the faint coating of fine powdered ash. Apart from a shallow ring engraved half way along, the black glass was the smoothest thing he had ever felt. He smiled at his own warped reflection in the shiny rod.

"Grip the hilt with both hands and step over to the furnace," said Vratto. "On my mark, push the thick end into the fire. When I call, withdraw it."

Vratto stepped around Xindro and knelt. The bellows roared as he cranked the handle round. Faster and faster the breath of the spinning fan blew like wind into the fire. More and more flames lathered, swelled and burst hotter and brighter than the sun on the clearest day.

"Now."

Drolla plunged the thick shank into the blazing whitefire. The heat was impossible and the blinding glare slammed his eyes shut. He wanted to see, he needed to see. Time stood still as he waited for Vratto's call. The cold grease began to melt and the sticky oil ran down him like aromatic sweat. Every bit of skin that faced the fire began to sting, he was sure he was melting as well. Squinting through slitted eyelids, he saw the black glass rod glow as bright as the fire.

"Ready..." said Vratto. "Pull it out... now."

Drolla yanked it from the fire and held it up. The forge seemed lit by the light of a thousand smolderstones as the shaft glowed white hot, yet the handle was still black cold.

"Quickly now, quench it."

He spun to face the vase. He upended the rod and sank the blistering glass into the oil with a single thrust. In an instant, the liquid boiled and spat. A hissing fog filled the room. It smelled like fruit and tasted like acid. Just as quick, the outer chimney drew the oily mist and belched it into the sky outside. Vratto nodded. Drolla pulled the steaming rod from the oil and let the excess drip back into the vase.

"Don't phap this bit up," said Xindro grinning.

"Drolla, place the shank over that tile. As straight as you can, gently tap the end onto it," said Vratto.

The thud of glass on stone sounded hollow, and for a moment there was silence. The rod's innards began to splinter like crackling ice.

128

Both Xindro and Vratto stared at each other, their heads tilted listening to the fracturing glass, waiting for the final snap.

"Tis done," said Vratto. "Draw your shard Drolla."

With one hand he gripped the shaft below the ringed groove and with another above it, he pulled the naked hilt.

As the blade withdrew from its new formed scabbard, it screeched like a nightmare.

"Show us a look," said Xindro.

While Drolla vaguely eyed his brand new blade while the other two inspected its shape and edge.

"Not dead straight, it veers a bit," said Vratto.

"The edges are perfect though," said Xindro. "Well done Drolla."

Crackling silver veins ran like lightning from the spine to each razored edge. Three blades like fletching tapered from the hilt to the pointed tip. Forged harder than stone, they twisted a little and curved ever so slightly. But, the new born blade did not care for the opinions of mortal flesh, the wrought glass shard considered itself perfect.

"Upend the scabbard and pour out the powdered swarf. Otherwise it will screech every time."

Drolla did as he was bid and pushed the shard back into its sheath. The internal cavity was the exact same shape as the blade. They were a perfect match. Neither could mate with any other and its lethal form was as unique as himself.

"From you Drolla, your shard is made," said Vratto. "Now, let your shard make you a warrior."

2.5 - THE SCATTERED ASSEMBLY

T he toll of the fourth bell echoed solemn throughout the Pen.

It was the hour of Verdara, the fourth child of Protor. He proclaimed himself the first attorney, and took it upon himself to lay down the law. A fluffy mantle hid his slouching shoulders, a tradition honoured and maintained by all the lawyers who followed his doctrine. Verdara summoned any and all to either testify or be judged. With fluent logic, he convinced his noble siblings to agree upon the natural legal order of a civilized people. His canon doomed criminals and blessed those who abided by the laws. Thus, it was in everyone's best interest to exercise and preserve justice.

Every hour on the sundial were once reserved for self reflection. No one but the mystical Amber Creed took this devotion to the extreme. During the fourth hour, it was expected to question one's own criminality. Are you really as honest as you could be? These days, average folk left the study of the ancients' motives to the zealots. Professional jurists debated probity and inked their verdicts onto scraps of paperbark. The documents were stored deep in the subterranean archives. The laws applied equally to all, from the greatest sovereign to the lowest orphan. Circumstances seldom interfered with the rule of law. Guilt or innocence was never determined by emotive oratory, the facts of the case were always weighed against the written legal code.

Ten thousand crisp white tunics filled the great arena. Once recruits, now the kitted up warriors waited to learn their trade. Squatting a few paces apart, they clustered in their little squads around their orange clad sergeant. They spread out far enough apart so each could soon swing their proud new shard. A hundred hectarions draped in their teal garb wandered amongst their troops. Tranna skirted Xindro's squad and nodded a friendly greeting to Boohala and Drolla. For a moment, he blazed a cold stare at Xindro. He cocked his head as if to silently demand a reason for the ominous gaze. Tranna smirked his answer and turned his attention to the other squads under his charge.

"What the phap was that?" said Xindro.

"Maybe he likes you," replied Boohala.

"Maybe he hates you," added Flynx, grinning.

"Maybe you could shut up. He doesn't even know me."

"He knows of you," said Boohala. "Everyone does."

"On your feet. We start now," said Xindro.

Drolla was the first to stand. In that instant, he regretted it. His nervous heart pumped him full of doubt. A sea of curious faces slowly turned and frowned his way. Instinct demanded he sit back down. Coy and awkward, Drolla's knees bent a little trying to coax him back onto his haunches. His mates joined him at once and relief regained him his composure. Xindro smiled at his obedient warriors as they formed up around him. Following Boohala's lead, their arms reached out and they shuffled about, ensuring they were far enough apart. When satisfied, they looked inward to Xindro. Moments later, their immediate neighbours did the same. After them, adjacent squads began standing as well. More and more stood. Without any official order from their superiors, the army organically rose. A single ripple surged across the crowd from one side of the arena to the other. Tranna and his fellow hectarions simply shrugged and shared the moment. They heard no command to start and saw no reason to stop. A lone voice interrupted the moment of confusion and shouted.

"Look."

Soft white clouds chased the heavy grey blanket away to the eastern Blue Hills. The dreary sky cleared and revealed a fresh, bright day. A swift breeze swirled down from over the outer wall and sped around the arena through the standing troops. The warm wind brought a mild relief from the cold still air. A tremendous flight of little blue river birds caught in the draft circled over head. The countless swarm was packed so densely it shaded the soldiers below. Peals of laughter followed indignant curses, the bird shit fell like spitting rain from the squawking flock. Even so, their visit was a welcome sight. It cheered their indentured hearts knowing wildlife still thrived without help nor interference from people at all. The freedom of the natural world was a great source of envy. The eyes of every warrior followed the fluttering trail. Its streaming shadow chased itself around the arena a few times before it caught an updraft. As if one creature, they peeled off and flew into the clear orange-pink sky. A mighty cheer rose and chased the fleeing birds. Inspired, the eager warriors began their training.

"Today, you learn to kill," said Xindro. His excited kids glanced at each other. "To do that, you need to know the anatomy of the life you will take."

His voice rose over the ever increasing racket of a thousand other squad leaders lecturing their own little troops of warriors.

"Boohala, be my model."

He moved to the centre of the group and unclipped his shoulder clasp. His toga slid off and unveiled a brawny statue. Boohala posed like a naked tripod.

With a big toe either side of two middle toes, each foot perched on their paw and pointed away from the other. From heels and ankles up past solid calf and shin, behind each knee, three powerful thighs stood under a triple-hipped pelvis. Within it, intestines and his womb nestled above the intimate phalva hidden between three taut buttocks.

Inside his abdomen, offal and gut clustered around his central spine. His heart pumped deep within his chest, set amidst three huge lungs surrounded by a trefoil ribcage wrapped in bulging, shapely dorsals.

Twin collar bones extended across pectorals to each shoulder. An arm hung from above each armpit, inline with each leg. Tricep, bicep, elbow, and forearm reached to a wrist. On the hand, two forefingers were flanked by a thumb on either side of the palm.

From the shoulders, trapezian muscles stood like buttresses, supporting his long neck. Sitting atop, his oval head faced skyward. Three eyes, evenly spaced around the skull allowed him a panoramic view. By each eye, thin, crescent-shaped webbed gills hid internal ears. Between those, a tiny nostril flared at the stink of ten thousand peers. His elliptic face gently tapered to the mouth and the circular lip pouted like a poke drawn shut. Basking in the adoration, Boohala bent his flexible neck to face his admirers. His eyes rolled forward to focus on them.

"I know marble statues in the capital that would envy that body," said Flynx.

Boohala grinned wide, his lip stretched like a fleshy halo and revealed gleaming black teeth that lined his tercet jaws.

His smile was cute, his face was pretty, but his physique was beautiful. He had the classic sturdy form with unblemished skin, whiter than ocean surf, stretched across the perfectly muscled frame that posed the ideal stance.

"Are we finished admiring the pretty one?" jeered Xindro. "Let me show you how to kill him." As quick as he drew his shard, Boohala instinctively jumped a step back and rejoined the little circle of trainees.

From the middle, Xindro outstretched his blade and pointed it toward Drolla's neck. He slowly turned and the blade swept like the shadow of a sundial, and pointed from one gulping throat to the next.

"The monarchy would have me, like every other kladger here in orange, train you their way," said Xindro.

"They do need to learn the basics first," said Boohala as he dressed.

"The army will teach them defence. Textbook shit. I shall teach them them offense."

"Well, you are pretty offensive," said Klommo. The blade's tip stopped at the comedian.

"You are a funny little kladger, aren't ya? Tell me butcher, how do you dismember a carcass?"

Klommo lost his grin and bit his lip. The shard slowly moved and pointed to his shoulder.

"Come on smart mouth. Forgot ya trade already?"

"At the joints?"

"At the joints. We'll learn you amputation. After practice, there is a real treat coming."

Above the clamour of the assembled warriors, a remote booming voice of a lone khillionaire traveled like a cooee on the wind and silenced the arena. "Praaaa-ax."

"Now we drill," said Xindro. "Copy my moves and keep up. First draw your shard."

With the hilt in one hand, and the sheath in another, Drolla withdrew his blade. His heart melted at the sight of its dangerous beauty. In the bare sunlight, the silver veins glistened deep within the black glass like lightning that danced through thunderclouds. The colour faded clear as it bled to the invisible edge. He exhaled a hopeless sigh as he fell in love with something that was a part of his very soul. The shard was more than an object, his energy forged this weapon and their spirits were together bound. Xindro had forbidden them to bare even a hint of blade until today. Drolla now understood why. Xindro grinned wide and admired his crew adoring their own precious blades.

Hours passed while Xindro posed the specific stances. Drolla and the rest copied as best they could. Boohala wandered among them, correcting any errors in their stances and moves.

They drilled and they drilled and they drilled. Draw, present, thrust, block, deflect, slice, stab, sheath, again, again, again. With regular rests to recap their lessons, their fervour hardly waned in anticipation of the mysterious treat they were promised. Every so often, caterers mingled amongst the training recruits with clear glass firkins and offered fresh water to the thirsty warriors. Gossip boasted this was an act of altruism, a favour done off-duty. This generous deed earned them great admiration and gratitude. Although, some were rebuked in jest for not serving any brewberry slurry at all.

War horns tore through the air.

"At last," said Xindro. His toothy grin glinted like onyx.

From the judicial hub, scores of jade enforcers drove out hundreds of fettered strangers and filtered amongst the army. Squinting at the sunlight, the captives were naked but for a wide ring painted legal green around their middle. Arms were tied wrist to elbow and the ankles were hobbled by a heavy cord. Rope collars and tethers bound the poor wretches from one throat to the next. Four were delivered to Xindro and his crew. The enforcer cut them from a dozen others and handed the single rein to Boohala.

"Only four?" demanded Xindro.

"How about none?" The enforcer flashed indignant eyes at the stark insolence. "Move, you filthy felons," he roared, and yanked the lead binding the rest of his prisoners. Each stumbled after the other as their necks were jolted forward. He ignored their complaints and yanked again, even harder, and led them to the adjacent squad.

Boohala quietly held the leash. The four sorry prisoners huddled together like frightened children. They had good reason to.

"Who are they?" asked Klommo.

"The treat I promised," said Xindro. "You get to kill them. He clapped two hands and rubbed them together with glee.

"We cannot kill syblings," spluttered Grikka.

"You already have." Xindro's tone became indignant and his excitement waned.

"That was different. That was justice," said Yanna.

"So is this," said Xindro. "They're criminals. They're already sentenced to death, held over for soldier practice."

"Are we executioners now?" asked Grikka.

"No. You are phapping soldiers. I want you to feel glass hacking flesh."

"You cannot wait till the battlefield," said Boohala. "You need to be ready."

"It doesn't sit right, killing in cold blood," said Grikka.

"Someone has to die for his crime. Someone has to do the killing. You or him?"

"I'll do it," said Drolla.

There was no escape. These prisoners were going to die, and the soldiers were going to kill them, here and now. Drolla dreaded the thought of it. His face and fingers went numb. Thornbugs tornadoed in his guts. This war was the price of his freedom. Violent death was a natural part of the battle and he had to get used to it sooner or later.

Courage, he thought, *you wanted this.*

Boohala held the prisoners' leash and motioned the nearest to him. With nervous, hopeful trust he slowly hobbled forward. Boohala placed a tender hand on a shoulder and peered into trembling eyes.

"What's your name, sybling? Where are you from?" He asked with a calm and reassuring tone.

"Gindara. Near the Kithwall."

"And your crime?"

"I... I killed my parent, but it was an accident."

"Who cares," snapped Xindro. "Get on with it."

"You knew your death was postponed?" asked Boohala gently. Gindara squeezed his eyes shut with the slightest nod. "Then, be brave and prepare yourself."

"Push your blade here," said Xindro, pointing to Gindara's chest.

Drolla drew his shard and placed the tip over Gindara's heart. Between two pectorals, the tip sliced a tiny cut. Gindara flinched.

"Sorry," whispered Drolla.

His nerves made him clumsy. His squadmates frowned at him. He was embarrassing himself. He had to ignore Gindara's pleading stare. Memories of his childhood bullies helped harden his heart. He let a murderous gloom fall and shroud any virtue he had left. He shrugged off his compassion, and swallowed deep.

"Drive it deep with one smooth thrust. It is a bit of a push through the muscles and ribs, but carve his heart and he will die fast."

Terror gripped the prisoner's face. His breathing hastened and his welling eyes bulged in disbelief. Boohala held Gindara steady. Drolla grunted as he pushed the blade part way into the unwilling chest. The skin and flesh was tough. The guttural bellow startled Drolla. Gindara's knees faltered but Boohala held him on his feet. The poor thing still lived.

"Don't stop now," yelled Xindro. "Push."

Drolla shoved even harder to end this cruel torture. The blade plunged further. It sliced through sinew and scraped past bone. There was a slight pressure, then a muffled pop, and the blade pierced deep. Boohala let Gindara drop and the weapon arced through his internals. Blood gurgled up his throat and choked his final scream before it was uttered. As he fell to his knees, the blade withdrew and brought a bloody torrent that spilled onto the sand. His eyes rolled back and he fell aside. Dead.

Drolla's comrades looked on in stark horror. So near, so brutal, so final. Drolla was faint and queasy, his heart galloped like thunder. He swallowed his disgust and wore a phony face of hard grit. Glancing at his peers, he saw they too had trouble hiding their true feelings. Grey faces betrayed their nausea and fear. With hands on hips, Xindro grinned and sighed like a proud uncle.

The three remaining prisoners recoiled at the murder. They huddled each other for comfort. One seethed with anger and glared hatred at Drolla. Another stood aghast, his gaping mouth unable to voice a sound. The third hung his head and sobbed into his chest.

Two morticians arrived as fast as corpse-flies. One carried a hammock draped over a shoulder.

"Finished with this one?"

"Can't ya wait?" said Xindro. "We have more yet."

"We're phappin' busy mate. If we don't clean them up as soon as they drop, there will be a hell of a mess later on. Look." Their gaze followed his pointing palm.

The nearest grexitor cheered on his crew. They stabbed and chopped their poor wretch to pieces. When they looked back, the morticians had bundled Gindara into the hammock and were trotting away. Everywhere they looked, the condemned were being killed by trainee warriors.

Moments ago, an intense silence veiled their private tragic scene. Now, the howl of a hundred screaming atrocities filled the arena.

"Well done Drolla," said Xindro. "Now you have all seen the hard way." His eyes smiled wide and cocked a daunting glare. "Let me show you a better way."

Boohala motioned for the next prisoner. His fearful peers shuffled back a few steps from the whimpering sook. He stood apart unawares, alone and closest to the slaughterers. Xindro grabbed the dangling leash and cut the taut tether between their necks.

"They got you there," laughed Xindro. "If your eyes weren't shut bawlin'..."

The tears disappeared. He stiffened his back and jerked the leash in Xindro's hand.

"Hold your arms out," said Xindro. His anger yanked hard on the lead.

"Why? Just make it quick. Take my head off."

"We will. But we're gonna chop bits off you first. Wrist, elbow, shoulder. Ankle, knee and hip. Then, we'll do ya neck. Hold ya phappin' arms out."

"No." He squinted away his brave tears.

"Your crime doomed your life to these young warriors. You chose your fate, you will not deny them theirs." Xindro's voice rose from yelling to a screech. "Hold ya phapping arms out."

Above the din, pandemonium broke out two squads over. Squealing whistles, barking orders, and defiant howls stole the attention of anyone within earshot. Every eye nearby turned on the sight of eight unfettered prisoners, all armed with a stolen shard. Some seized from naïve recruits, others taken from the soldiers bleeding out at their feet.

They cut their tethers and formed a protective ring. With nervous caution, their circle edged away from the nearest warriors challenging them. In the momentary standoff, one gained a little courage.

"We would rather die fighting, than be slaughtered like animals," he boasted.

In the silence of his daunted peers, a furious Xindro accepted their challenge.

"You'll get both."

He ran full speed towards the rebels. With barely enough time to react, the nearest two stood unready to face his attack.

As they met, two hands relaxed their grip as they left their wrists. With a circling swipe, Xindro sliced one off each without warning or hesitation. Blood arced through the air as their shards hit the sand. Stunned, they froze wide-eyed.

As he stepped between them, he brought his blade down on their other elbows and removed a forearm each. The victims dropped to their knees and tried to grab at their bloody stumps with hands they no longer had. Giddy from blood loss, they offered no resistance as spectators dragged them clear. Both chests swallowed vengeant blades deep.

Xindro plucked their shards from the sand and stepped into the centre of their frightened circle. He eyed his foes and readied himself to begin his lethal dance.

The crowd surrounding the circus increased. Many had quit their training and crushed together, all keen to witness Xindro's reputation. He was hated by some and loved by others, yet respected by any who knew of him. He stretched out his arms and curtsied like Throthm. Each hand held a shard, the blade tips pointed skyward. One dripping white, two still dry and thirsty.

Three braves took turns lunging at him, yet he deflected them with ease. They tried to attack together, it made no difference, he fended them off as if he fought only one. They all thrust and parried in turn, desperate to land a strike. Xindro made it look as if they were merely sparring. His wild eyes flashed and his grin rose and fell as he toyed with his amateur foes. Again and again, he would lower his guard simply to encourage them to slash at him. Xindro allowed a near miss now and then, just to wow the crowd. He kept both actors and audience in play as long as he could.

"He is such a show-off," Boohala muttered.

"I am glad he is our show-off," said Drolla.

As Xindro crouched to duck under a wild swipe, he took the third foe's leg off at the knee. He fell onto his side, screaming and clutching his wounded thigh. The grey meat trembled for a moment before it squirted his life out.

Xindro stood with upward strokes. The fourth and fifth had their armed limbs struck off at the elbow. In a frozen moment, he spun a graceful turn, his weapons arced low and sliced open two bellies at once. Their pink guts tumbled onto the ground in front of them. The spectators moaned with delighted horror.

Swooning at the gore, the sixth and seventh panicked. The cowards dropped their weapons at Xindro's feet, and squatted in submission. They screamed their apologies. They blamed their dead friends and begged for mercy. Xindro hung his head for a moment. With a slight nod he threw his head over and faced his eyes away from them, but not his ears. The cheats dove for their weapons. Xindro spun and drove a shard each down through their collars, deep into their chests. His comrades gasped then cheered with awe and relief. He played the crowd well. He withdrew both blades at once from their necks. They toppled forward and watched their own blood pool out in front of them, but they didn't watch for long.

The cleverest waited till last. He had seen his comrades get hacked down one by one, and seemed to assess Xindro's style. Facing off, they stepped around each other. Cautious, with shards en guard, each looked for a chance to strike.

Xindro threw his two extra weapons out of reach and pointed the fisted pommel of his own shard at his opponent's head.

Seeing that as an opening, the fool leapt toward Xindro. His aim was to bring his blade down on him so hard it might chop him in half.

He missed. Xindro stepped aside and his opponent lost his balance from the impetus of his strike. Xindro spun his shard handle backwards, facing the blade toward himself.

A black glass fist arced from behind and smashed the side of his skull. Bone crunched, a socket shattered and the eyeball popped. Its clear jelly spattered across Xindro's face. The foe was stunned, and his underbelly hit the ground with a plop. Splayed legs held him in an upright daze. He did not see the final strike coming. Silently, his head left its shoulders and fell into his lap.

Drolla ignored the roar of the jubilant mob. They were insane with joy, they had just borne witness to the exploits of the greatest shardster in Drahn. He had proved his reputation. Drolla quietly watched Xindro leave the scene. He carefully stepped through the gory corpses, trying not to slip on the bloody sand that squelched between his toes. As he sauntered back to his squad, he wiped the optic slime from his grinning face and spoke.

"See? Just like that."

2.6 - THE MODEST PRIDE

Glum black tulle curtains hung idle in the breathless shade.

It had been a long day and the tavern seemed bored. The entrance arch frowned at passer's-by and totally ignored the drunk patrons stumbling down the exit ramp. When Xindro came into view, the arch smiled wide at his approach. A breeze inhaled and the curtains danced, glad at his arrival. The small troupe stopped outside. With fists on his hips, Xindro quietly coaxed his team to admire the old structure with him. Sheets of grey funglstone, carved soft and riveted together, dried into a gruesome polylithic dome. Faded paint peeled like mange and the broken ramp was missing a tile or two. From within, the mellow hubbub exhaled a warm greeting.

Exhausted from the day's training, the old tavern was a welcome sight. Drolla needed to cleanse his mind from the exertion of endless coaching and the distress of the prisoners' slaughter. The morticians plied their craft well and removed the bloody corpses as they fell. By day's end, the warriors had learned their trade and left a deserted arena of orange sand mottled with blackening bloody stains.

Xindro's exhibition of butchery was hours ago. The aftermath was mayhem. His celebrity elevated as adoring fans crowded the mighty shardster. At first his ego welcomed the attention. But things soured when he realized each were all mere sycophants. He soon tired of their shallow esteem and said so.

"Phap off!" The throng crushed even tighter, trying to hear the great shardster speak. "Back the phap off. You're all nothing but a pack of filthy kladger-tongues." His adoring fans roared with laughter. Xindro glared about, his furious fingers wrapped his hilt. His snarl looked as if he might erupt at any moment. If he did, there would be a lot fewer admirers. Tranna elbowed through the mob and demanded his grexitors call their squads to order.

"Get back on grid. Move," he yelled.

Like disappointed children, they moaned and dispersed back to their training. Xindro nodded his appreciation to Tranna. Again, he stared a long silence at Xindro.

"A fine display, thyre. Your talent is wasted among the ranks," said Tranna.

"It is where I prefer. I am no officer."

"Often, a soldier has no choice where he serves."

Tranna offered his palm to Xindro. Neither gaze left the other's and they clasped hands. Tranna stepped in close to Xindro.

"A force higher than us both has set malicious eyes on you. Tread carefully."

"How do you know that, easterner?" demanded the Oxxian.

"The gentry is at war with itself, and plots to ruin any heroes."

"I'm no hero."

"Not yet, but a covert western bloc intends to laud you. Train your Oriennans well, you will need them." Tranna released his grip and disappeared into the bustling mob.

Xindro scowled at Drolla as an eavesdropper. He was cranky from then on during training. He ordered Boohala to take over the rest of the day's exercise and snapped at anyone who fumbled their moves. At long last, the war horn sounded and signaled day's end.

"We done? Right, let's go get drunk. My shout," said Xindro.

Drolla was the first to sheath his shard and nodded to the rest to hurry. Xindro had already walked off without them.

"Our place is the other way," called Yanna, running to catch up.

Xindro led them on a winding tour deep into unfamiliar back streets. Over the woodland stream, past the finer brew-bars and fancy diners. Through alleys of stinking slaughterer's pits that led into the dingier lanes by the outer wall. In a permanent shade, they stood out front of Xindro's favourite tavern.

"This... is your berry-den?" asked Boohala.

"It looks like a swill joint," said Dwaxxi.

"It's the Aurora Grey," said Xindro from half way up the ramp.

Rather than storming into the room and wiping the drapes aside, he sneaked in. He gently pushed one arm between the tattered black tulle and slid through the gap. Once in, the curtains hung as if undisturbed.

"I shmelled you comin' down the lane," yelled a voice from an open trapdoor.

"You heard the cheerin'. You knew I'd slink back here," said Xindro.

"Of courshe. Every boozhey showoff needzh shomewhere to boasht."

"Tales of the bold deserve a toast."

"Toasht yashelf, that'sh your shpot over there."

Drolla threw him a sly glance. He wondered who this jesting, well spoken person was. He certainly wasn't the angry, foul-mouthed ruffian they had spent the whole day with. Xindro and his crew gathered around a floor table. The waiting platter was covered with little dishes of fermented sweet meats and fruits. Beside it, a tottering stack of empty bowls leaned against a large tureen.

"Thank you uncle," yelled Xindro.

He passed out the bowls and ladled the bright scarlet brewberry syrup.

"Uncle?" said Flynx. "You should have seen him today," he shouted.

"I heard. The gosship ran through the camp hourzh ago," replied the trapdoor.

The kids' excitement was renewed. They relived Xindro's exploits blow by blow. This admiration he did not mind at all. He reveled in the chatter about him by his intimates and grinned at every comment. Their praise was genuine, they had nothing to gain from it.

"How bad was it when he sliced open their bellies..." said Yanna.

"How good was it when their guts fell out all over the place?" said Dwaxxi.

"I learned that move from a zealot of the Amber Creed."

"No way. I thought they were a secret society," said Klommo.

"Alright, he didn't 'teach me', I saw it once and copied it." Xindro laughed.

Boohala raised his bowl and proposed a toast.

"Here's to Xindro, and here's to us. The best little squad in the hectary."

"Cheers." They all yelled with gusto, toasting themselves.

The small table went quiet for a moment while they drained their cups. A collective gasp brought smiles all round. The warmth of the brewberry syrup mirrored the warmth these comrades shared. Drolla grabbed the ladle and offered them all a refill. Klommo rolled his vials from the sapory onto the table. He picked up a tube of tiny blue crystals.

"Ocean's Delight, anyone?" he asked. He sprinkled some onto his bowl of silvered meat. "It makes everything taste like seafood."

"Krantolo's poison," Flynx grunted in disgust.

"What do you mean, poison?" frowned Klommo, licking his worried fingers.

"I hate him and his clan," said Flynx. "He is a filthy slave-driver. He thinks he owns the Fenn Delta. Everything from Old Wharf to Salford is choked out with his shellfish farms and salting flats."

"He is the new President of the Consultorium. Be careful what you say," said Boohala.

"It's true," added Yanna. "His estates creep across the estuary into Orienna and he bullies all the other fishing families half way to Oster Beach. His crooked shardhires and the local clanguards often come to blows."

"As soon as that old kladger took over the Lodge, some of us older orphans were sent on an 'excursion' to his estate to learn how to farm his waterways. We soon found we would never return. That's the place I ran from. So, I'll not touch that shit."

"What a principled young thing you are," said Boohala, with a dab of pride.

"No worries," said Dwaxxi. "I'll have yours." He showered his pickled fruit slices.

"Hey, Xindro. What's that flavour you keep by your side?" asked Flynx.

"Nothing you'd like." The smile dropped from his face.

"Come on," said Klommo grinning, "share the wealth."

"Anyone who touches my vial, will lose their phapping fingers. Got it?"

The conversation stalled. *Ah, he's back,* thought Drolla. Amused eyes flashed around the table. Xindro scowled into his empty bowl.

"Hey, Xindro's uncle," yelled Flynx, "could we have another tureen?"

"His name is Klordra, you phapwit," said Xindro. He turned and yelled. "Make it the purple stuff this time."

"Pleazhe!" the barkeep roused.

"Please," answered the scolded nephew.

Klordra limped over to their little table. An apron wrapped him like a kilt. One leg was off at the knee, with a black glass stump that tapered to a pointed tip. Spiraling vines and fruiting brewberry flowers decorated the opaque shaft. He was tall and thick set. Once heavily muscled arms were now chunky and sweaty. Battle scars crisscrossed his body like a badly drawn map. His mouth had been slashed years ago and healed into a taper that trailed across his face. He noticed Dwaxxi looking at his stump and cocked a threatening eye at him.

"That's a fine mould, thyre," said Dwaxxi. "Army shardsmith?"

Klordra flicked a tiny smirk. It seemed he decided this upstart had a genuine interest and his mood mellowed.

"Yup, finest Drahn glass. Losht me leg in the Battle of Ebon Shore. Crushed between hullsh when we boarded the enemy'zh yacht," he tapped the glass stump, "a gift from the commander, 'outshtanding bravery' he shed."

"You were a fine soldier uncle, but you are a far better bar tender," said Xindro.

"Forever the shmartash, aren't ya Kshindro?" said Klordra. "You're a fine shardshter, but you've not yet fought a foreign war. None of you have."

"I don't even know what we're fighting for," said Flynx.

"You poor buggersh. Pour me a shlurry and throw me that cushion. I'll tell you why the monarchy marchesh you all to the edge of the nation to die."

Xindro rolled his eyes and poured him a brew. The rest sat up straight, keen to hear Klordra's tale.

The Battle of Ebon Shore

Three orderlies massaged an arm each. The fragrant lotion rubbed heat into the commander's aging muscles. A cool breeze floated through the shade of the domed marquee and chilled his burning limbs. On the table nearby, his fateshield placed a fist on a corner of the map.

His finger stabbed the page. "They should be here."

"Now the legs." An outstretched palm reached for the map.

The commander narrowed his eyes and studied the spot. It was the obvious place. From the flat seaside, the diggers had easy access to the high dunes. The same dunes that hid his inland approach. He led over a thousand soldiers, itching to end this campaign. If there was a confrontation, he could rely on them to prevail. The warriors craved a furlough, and eliminating this enemy would give it to them. If, that is, the thieves were beyond the mound.

A scout ran towards the commander's tent. He curtsied outside and panted between his broken words.

"Catch your breath first. Are they there?"

The scout nodded, and a grin spread across everyone's face. They would all be home for Conjugation.

The commander peered over the crest of the black dunes. The ocean's breath stank of foreign ships. A dozen barges had beached themselves onto the foreshore. Hundreds of diggers shoveled dry sand into cloth buckets, and hundreds more passed the endless chain that filled the dredgers' bins. Moored alongside them, scores of empty skiffs bobbed over the breaking waves. Out beyond the rolling swell, three transports escorted a commodore's catamaran. Its fluttering red pennant bore the emblem of the hated enemy. Each vessel crawled with valiant marines, proudly strutting about their polished decks. None guarded the unarmed workers on land.

"At last."

After a three-year hunt, back and forth along the coast, their foes would not elude them this time. They would suffer the fury of a frustrated legion of Drahn. Their impatient monarch ordered his warriors to protect his precious black sand. His vengeful chancellor ordered the raiders be annihilated. Today, the commander would do both.

On the tufted plateau, the Black Legion calmly formed up. There was no new lofty speech. Neither chatter nor cheers. Silence forged their resolve. It was time for battle, a surprise attack. With their shard by their leg and a shaft under an arm, the front ranks lined the crest of the dunes. As one, they knelt on their shields and launched themselves over the edge. Row after row, fifty wide, they skimmed down the sandy banks.

The bucketeers soon howled at the assault descending upon them. The diggers were too busy to notice and when they did, it was far too late. A speeding phalanx of thirsty spears skewered the scattering workers.

As their shields bogged into the level sand, the warriors bounded to their feet. They threw their lances aside and unsheathed their weapons. In a vengeful frenzy, their glass blades slashed and hacked at any still standing. Those escapees who had reached the waves frantically splashed toward the nearest barge. The crews aboard did nothing to help their fellows, nor did they mount any defense. In a selfish panic, they tried to set their barges adrift. The flingers nocked their woomeras as they arrived at the water's edge. Their long darts showered the surf and the barges. Few escaped the death that rained down, those who did were soon dispatched.

Keen to engage the transports, the warriors commandeered the abandoned skiffs and rowed like maniacs. They swarmed onto the defended escorts and began their carnage afresh. The marine's bravado was no match for the ferocity of the soldiers. Once they had slaughtered all the resistance on one vessel, they hopped to the next. Meanwhile, sappers chopped at the hulls and the transports began to sink.

The catamaran's mainsail crackled and snapped as the wind filled it out. It was a tardy attempt to flee. The best fighters clambered aboard, but they faced a mighty defense. The gentry's bodyguards bravely held their stead. Reinforcements joined their comrades and they hacked at the masts. Like a felled trees, they twisted off their stumps and crashed across both decks. The tangled mess crushed the howling defenders. The catamaran then heaved and dropped to one side. It too was taking on water fast. The sappers had scuttled the stately yacht as well. The jubilant warriors quit the floundering cat' and left it to its fate. Victorious, they returned cheering to the shore. Butchered corpses tumbled back and forth with the crashing surf. When the last of the skiffs skid onto the bloody beach, by malice or for sport, all the yielding survivors were killed on the spot. All but one.

Three guards held a short loud official ranting in his own tongue. His sodden velvet garb hung off him like wet laundry. He glared a furious hatred as the commander approached.

"He says he is valet to the prince, thyre. He says he has a message."

The valet babbled his alien gibberish. It sounded like he spat out a mouthful of poisoned splinters.

"He says, 'Foolish Drahni. You have drowned the Premier's Heir. All the kin of Miokh will avenge him. Expect war.'"

The commander sniffed at the threat and waved him aside. The guards led the valet away and the fool continued his vitriolic tirade until a blade took his head.

The wind had changed, and the sweet smell of rain blew toward the coast. Out across the stormy ocean, lightning danced between the heavy blue clouds. Advancing grey curtains pelted the distant waves, and far off shore a tiny pink sail fled into the looming tempest. Commander Yontala licked the salt from his lips and sighed at the weather.

"Today's breeze blows forth tomorrow's storm."

"You forgot the bit about your award," said Xindro.

"It wasn't about that," snapped Klordra.

"You were the first onto the premier's yacht?" asked Klommo. Klordra glowed proud.

"Wow, and did..."

A wild commotion stumbled up the ramp. Three clumsy boozers tore down the dainty curtains with them as they fell in across the threshold. The idiots laughed and flailed about, swaddling themselves like babies.

"There's an entrance," said Boohala.

Klordra launched to his feet and scurried as quick as an insect. He pushed the point of his stump into the throat of one of the revelers.

"That'sh azh much fun ash you're gonna have in here."

Xindro appeared beside Klordra and grinned down at his helpless friend.

"Jandra, you little stain," said Xindro. "Drord's Guts, you are hopeless." He tore aside the fragile netting and freed the squirming quarry. "He is with me uncle, I'll vouch for him."

"On your oath then, but thish pair can phap right off out!" roared the landlord.

He stomped after them and pushed them down the ramp. They ran stumbling along the lane, laughing all the way. When Klordra was satisfied they were gone, he marched back to his galley.

Xindro escorted his shaken friend to the table. Drolla ladled a bowl and passed it over. Jandra swigged it down and burped a wide grin.

"Cheers." His wrist wiped his mouth.

Jandra stared at Drolla for moment before he turned his attention to Xindro.

"So, grexitor, how goes the promotion?" Jandra laughed.

"You tell me." An open palm presented his crew.

Their chat became old news. Neither had seen each other since before the eastern draft set out. Xindro's antics in the Pen were outdone by Jandra's tales from the trek. Drolla's attention wandered. Unlike his peers, who paid a keen interest and weighed in on events here and there. The drone of tavern's blather resumed as if there was never an interruption.

The mellow buzz of the brewberries began to settle nicely, and Drolla took the time to survey the interior of the tavern. Broken weapons decorated the walls. Fractured shards, splintered lances, and torn shields were mounted from the floor half way up the curved ceiling. Each carried a little note from the boastful donor. Avid patrons keen to add to the tavern's theme, no doubt. The ceiling was painted in a dozen grey hues, twisting like streaming clouds, from the entrance to the galley. *A grey aurora*, thought Drolla. With a bit of imagination, the ceiling nearly represented the sky during the seasonal conjugation in a dreary monotone kind of way.

All the conversations began to meld and purr nonsense. Now and then a shout or a burst of laughter interjected, but Drolla was getting dopey. A solitary doze in the dark was way overdue, it had been a long day. He was slowly drifting into a meditative state. His surroundings strayed further and further away. The ruckus of the inn faded.

Images of the trek and the drills and the butchery were all painted over with memories of distant home. The muddled chatter sounded like the babbling rapids of his village brook. The air was fresh and the sun sparkled off the tumbling streams. Underwater fronds of blue and yellow moss swam like ribbons in the pristine currents. He thought he heard his grandpar' calling for him through the forest, but the muffled shout was momentary and distant. If he could see, he might be sure. He tried to peer into the dappled shade but the erratic breeze shifted the purple foliage back and forth, constantly blocking his view.

Little Sroddi ran past in a blur, giggling and flinging starburrs at him.

'Can't catch me', his cheeky voice sang.

It echoed in every direction and Drolla could not tell where from. Off to the side, footsteps splashed across the creek. With a grin of excitement he turned and took a step to chase his playful nephew.

Stop.

The scowling face of Hlammi appeared. It burned with fury at the basket of fresh Red Spore Drolla had spilled. He looked down, the fruit was scattered in the mud at his feet.

Once.

Only once did he do that years ago as a child. Never forgiven, and never forgotten, yet forever forsaken.

"Sometimes I wish I had never..." said Hlammi.

"Do you hate me so much par'?"

"I don't hate you..."

"You don't love me."

Kwinno appeared from nowhere and stood between them with a stiff back and fists on hips. With his face in the air, he was adamant and defiant, forever defending Drolla against the tyrant. He turned and winked at Drolla. His confident smile was always a comfort. His darling little sibling could always distract and melt their parent's fury. Kwinno was adored as much as Drolla was despised.

The only way to escape the intolerance was to hide alone in the fungal caves. He ran. The familiar track stretched ahead and the purple forest closed in behind him, cloaking his escape. The soft green moss was welcoming, but the snide maw of the black cave beckoned him to endure another bitter reprieve. "Come on, slink in here little coward. It's safe from the nasty world out there. You belong in here. Servant." The stale warmth wafted from the entrance like bad breath. One step out of the sunlight and the rancid mist of the sodden darkness flared his nostrils. His guts churned and his mouth watered. He retched. Not again. He was going to vomit. He snapped awake. The nausea eased a little as he placed a hand over his gut and another over his mouth. Bleary eyes blinked and cleared. He was back in the tavern with his comrades, and they were all staring at him.

Xindro leaned in close and whispered. "We know where your Red Spore is."

"My what?" blurted Drolla. A burst of laughter from his mates woke him further.

"He's back," said Xindro. "While you have been off floating along your brewberry cloud, we have been talking about you."

Drolla was surrounded by a wall of smiles.

"What did you say?"

"I said, we know where your Red Spore is, and you are going to get it."

"But, I don't know where it is. It was confiscated."

"Phap me, you're thick," said Xindro. "Wake up."

Boohala sighed, cleared his throat and stared hard into Drolla's eyes.

"Do you remember Jandra? He took your shoulderpack?"

Drolla turned his gaze to the quartermaster.

"Yes," he frowned.

"Then listen," barked Xindro.

"Your bag was not left behind," said Jandra. "I brought it to the Pen. It's in the underground store with the other equipment and valuables from the journey."

"So?"

"We want you to get it," said Xindro.

"You want me to steal it?" asked Drolla, looking at Xindro.

"It won't be stealing," said Xindro. "It was yours."

"But it's not mine now. The army owns it now?"

"Not really," said Jandra. "None of the stuff has been inventoried yet. But, once it's recorded, it is lost forever."

"So technically, it doesn't even exist yet," said Boohala.

"But it will soon," said Jandra. "There is a thin sliver of time, maybe a day or two, for someone to sneak in and pinch it."

"Before anyone knows it's there," said Xindro.

"Why me?"

"Well, we had a bit of a chat about that, and we decided you are the best one to do it," said Boohala.

"How?"

"It's your shoulderpack," said Xindro. "You know what the phapping thing looks like."

"But mainly because you were asleep," said Flynx.

"You're all crazy. I don't even know where the it is."

"Here," said Xindro. He snatched a scrap of paperbark from Jandra. "He drew a map."

"Why can't he go? He knows what the pack looks like, and where it is."

"I can't, I will be on duty," said Jandra.

"When?" asked Drolla.

"Whenever you do this," smiled Jandra. "I'll make sure my crew is nowhere near you. The place will be deserted."

"No one knows it's there." said Xindro. "Just stroll in and take it. It's foolproof."

"Why are you all so keen on the fungus. It's horrible stuff," said Drolla.

"We all wanna get high for Pannatalia. You promised," said Klommo.

"Folk like us will never get to taste it. It's far too expensive," said Dwaxxi.

"He won't do it," said Yanna.

"Phapping oath he will," said Xindro.

"Don't force him. It's his choice," said Boohala.

"You won't get caught," said Flynx. "No one else will know, and you will do us all a great favour."

Drolla sighed. "All right, show me the map."

2.7 - THE CLEVER DOLT

D rolla hid within the fronds of a featherbush grove.

Cold sweat ran from his worried forehead to his aching haunches. An anxious hour passed while he squat at the edge of the forest gardens outside an overgrown slaughterer's pit. For ages, nothing happened. Then danger appeared from nowhere. He held his breath as a dozen enforcers tramped down Butcher's Lane. Their eyes scanned everything as they passed. Nothing escaped their notice. With a lingering glare of mistrust, one stared right where Drolla hid. His thundering heart dared to betray him. Long, soft fluffy fronds swayed about him, iridescent pink shimmered mauve along the shiny foliage. Everyone admired the gorgeous featherbush. It was the worst place to hide. After an eternity, the enforcer's suspicion moved on. Drolla swallowed dry and sighed with relief. His eyes closed and relished a moment of calm.

The distant war horn called all within earshot to attention. It was time. Through the whispering orchards and across the bellowing paddocks, the muffled roar of ten thousand warriors marked the start of another day's training. While his comrades drilled en mass, he skulked here alone. *I should be there with them*, he thought. He wondered if he was missed already? Would his squadmates vouch for him? What if he was caught? Could he be condemned for desertion? Might he end up on a pole? Why didn't he think of these questions yesterday?

Jandra vowed the disused exit was unguarded. It was cut into a mound overgrown with strangle vines. Yellow wandermoths fluttered amongst the red blooms that lines the choking runners. Drolla stood at the tunnel entrance. The gate itself was carved from funglstone.

A sculptured, artistic spider's web. The crafter's blade shaped the mushroom flesh while raw and soft. Once dried, it was as hard as stone and as light as air. The unlocked gate was hinged at the top, he raised it high and peered into the darkened tunnel. Drolla stood poised on the uncertain brink of this dangerous quest.

An unwelcome sense of coercion began to niggle. He was imposed upon to do this great favour, one with no reward for him and perhaps only penalty. He had no use for the fungus, it disgusted him. Is this what friendship is? Is this what friends do? He never knew real friends. He had cousins, but they were like enemies. Now he had friends, squadmates, sworn by each to protect the other. Yet here he stands, ready to risk all for them. So they might enjoy a few days in a blissful stupor. They owed him for this.

It occurred to Drolla, he could not name a time when anyone did him a favour. Kwinno often tried, but Hlammi would stifle any kindness by praising him, "save your noble efforts for something worthwhile." Should not friendships be mutual? Doubt began to convince him this was a bad idea. How was this little jaunt meant to benefit him? From the depths of his memory, Brokka emerged and reminded him with a smile, "...trade this wisely. Use it to make everything a little less uncomfortable."

"Oh grandpar'," whispered Drolla. "How could I have forgotten you."

He now hoped the satchel was still intact. He hoped it was as full as Brokka had packed it.

They'll not get the lot, he thought, *I'll share a morsel and sell the rest*.

The idea of becoming cashed up was appealing. After all, what was so bad about a fat purse? It was Brokka's intent all along. His wise grandpar' would make him rich. New questions arose. How much could he earn? Where would he hide a cache of glowing Tamzi rods? Might he find a secret nook somewhere below?

Stop. Sense tore open its stark curtain and his fanciful ideas vanished. Get the fungus first.

He peered into the darkened tunnel. It was just another black hole in the ground, but, it was not his cave. One wrong turn down a long tunnel of promise might drop into a pit of despair. He studied the map again, burning its image into his mind. He sighed at his pathetic little smolderstone, then tempered his nerve and stepped across the threshold. The gate slipped his grip and fell closed behind him. The clang of the gate raced ahead down the tunnel. Its echoes faded throughout the labyrinth beyond and announced his stealthy entrance.

The slippery ramp stretched down forever. The reaching sunlight faded fast. Beyond the darkness the path leveled out. His ears rang in the silence, and his eyes bulged wide. His anxious senses strained to detect the slightest hint he wasn't alone. He had not walked a dozen steps when he froze.

His foot was wet. His face grimaced at the thought of what rancid slime he might be standing in. He sniffed the air and smelled a fresh breeze. He knelt to touch the liquid. It was only water. Not some stagnant pool of fetid runny guano. These were not his filthy caves. It was a military store, clean and ventilated. He had to snap out of it and get moving. His jitters were wasting time. Drolla struck his smolderstone, its pearl glow pushed the dark away. The broken floor tiles were grouted with damp black moss. The tunnel itself was lined with endless funglstone arches one pace apart and bound together with cleated hand rails. It was as wide, and as high as he could reach. He glanced down at the puddle, his rippling reflection sighed at his own stupidity.

After a good while, and a little way head, a dark billowy movement crumpled. Marked as a circle, the map showed the first intersection was due. As he carefully approached, the thick drape lit up. It was loosely drawn across the archway and danced a little whenever the inner breeze tickled it. He gently wiped it aside and stepped into a small vaulted dome. A single unlit smolderstone hung from the centre. His light scanned the walls, the curtains across the doorways were tapestries. One of an ancient battle, the next was a portrait of some long dead noble. Two others were dull landscapes that must have meant something to someone sometime. Drolla shone his light on the map, it advised he take the left exit.

He crept along the passage way, it veered slightly down and to the right. His simple map was a mere a guide. Shining the light back, the room he had left was out of sight beyond the ramping curve. He moved on. His bubble of light floated along the corridor. The unexpected glow startled lazy spiders and they scurried away in a panic to hide again in the dark.

The next hub had naked doorways, arched with cold stone and filled with ankle-deep water. Three exits faced him. Left was scrubbed out as a mistake. The exit ahead wasn't drawn, yet sickly vapours wafted from the unmarked portal. From beyond the locked gateway, an all too familiar stench insulted his nostrils. He recognised that hateful smell of home. Perhaps the darkened halls brought the memories back. But even so, real or imagined, the stink of sprouting fungus made him gag. Someone was growing their own contraband deep beneath the same authority that banned it. His smolderstone turned away and peered into the exit to the right. He crossed the room, sliding his feet to avoid any splashing. The silent corridors and chambers seem to amplify the slightest whisper into a deafening shudder. The hallway's ramp slowly rose and led him on the longest trail yet. The map was not to scale either. A square was his next checkpoint.

An age had passed as he crept along the lonely tunnel. Then without warning, it opened up into a huge store room. Row after row of shelving held thousands of glass jars. He approached for a closer look. This was an immense pantry of preserved food. Dried, pickled and fermented. Meat from the land, sea and sky. All manner of fruits, vegetables and mushrooms. Jellies and jams, grains and herbs and spices. The variety was endless. His empty belly twinged. Drolla snapped the seal from a jar of jerky and stole a few pieces. He examined the map while he nibbled tasteless scallops. They needed some of Flynx's hated blue salt. Even dried clams should taste like seafood.

His spirits lifted. There was only one more intersection before his destination. Soon, he would find his treasure. A black dot marked the Storeroom of Unallocated Sundries.

"The pile of bags are in the middle," said Jandra.

"You can't miss it," promised Xindro.

It was easy for them to say hours ago, drunk in a tavern. The exit arch was much wider and taller than the previous tunnels. It was large enough for a garrison of quartermasters to pass through. He was in the belly of the great store room proper now. Far behind him lay the narrower access tunnels. The light of his smolderstone slowly crept before him and plunged the great larder back into its lonely darkness.

Drolla glanced at his little map. Next hub, turn right. His light was fading fast. He shuffled faster as the stone grew dimmer. It winked out. Drolla stood surrounded by pure and utter darkness. A memory lit in his mind. Once, he dropped a smolderstone down a narrow crevasse. It was lost in his caves forever, but he determined he would not be. In the blackness, he closed his eyes and relied on recall. Fingertips never left the walls and he blindly felt his way out to the welcome sunshine. Surely he could glide a finger along a straight corridor to the next junction. He grinned at the idea. Before he took a step, his smile fell.

Hurried whispers bounced through the tunnels. He listened like a statue. His heart galloped so hard he could hardly hear. Were they voices? He wasn't sure. There they were again. They were getting louder. They were getting closer. They were coming this way.

His heart jumped into his throat. His numbing fingers fumbled his grip of the smolderstone. He nearly dropped it. Thornbugs cycloned in his guts at the thought of the disaster that might have followed the clack of stone and the flash of light. At all costs, he had to remain hidden from whoever owned those advancing voices.

He knew the junction was just ahead and reckoned he could reach it before they did. The stone walls were as smooth as they were cold, his blood was colder still. His fingers curled and traced the dull edge of the arched doorway. As he stepped into the room, he could see their lights crawling along the walls toward him. He had to exit the crossroad hub before they got there. He did not want to go back. They were coming from the left. As they advanced, their lights danced in and out of the room. The closer they got, the right exit began to catch some light as well. It was the corridor he was meant to take. Time was running out. His indecision would get him caught.

In a moment of darkness, Drolla jumped into the passageway straight ahead. He shuffled a short way along to hide where their lights could not reach. He held his breath and peered from the gloom. Moments later, two quartermasters entered the room. The same two drunks that fell into the tavern with Jandra yesterday.

A royal coup! Who told you that?"

"My uncle."

"How does he know?"

"He is a palace bureaucrat. He is up to his neck in it and does not like it one bit."

"That brat has not got the spine for it."

"Listen. That old new president...?"

"Krantolo?"

"Yeh, him. He is plotting to enthrone the prince, whether Soltoro survives the war or not. They mean to usurp the monarchy."

"The prince is a fool. He's the heir, he only needs to wait."

"Seems he can't."

"Why doesn't anyone speak out?"

"The palace isn't safe anymore. Whistle-blowers might well sky dance along side the conspirators."

The anger of an erupting volcano roared into the chamber.

"What the phap! Are you two doing down here?" yelled Jandra.

He appeared from nowhere and scared the life out of them. Drolla slapped a hand over his own mouth to stifle a yelp of surprise.

"We were going to sort out the confiscated stuff."

"That chore was postponed."

"We weren't told."

"Well you're told now. Is there anyone else down here?"

"No. We've not seen Pondra."

"Good. Get to the common room. Now. Move."

The shaken pair ran back down the corridor they came from. Jandra waited a moment and peered into the gloom of the entrance passage. He shrugged, turned, and ran after them. His verbal barrage faded as it chased them into the darkness.

Undiscovered and relieved, Drolla blindly continued down the dark passage. He was keen to increase the distance between himself and the quartermasters as fast as possible. A fresh, cool draught stopped him in his tracks. He struck his stone and stood marveled at the sight before him.

A vast basement presented itself, stretching further than his light could reach. Heaped from floor to ceiling, wall to wall, black glass ingots were stacked like bullion. He wandered in awe along the vaulted alcoves and lost count of the piles, let alone the ingots. Maybe tens of thousands of them. They glinted and dimmed as his dull crystal glow passed over them. He looked to his map. It was gone. He looked back. He looked ahead. He was lost. Like stepping into a shaded waterfall, an icy panic drenched him.

"Impressive, ain't it?" A voice creaked from the shadows.

Drolla jumped so hard from the sudden scare, he nearly reached the ceiling while his skin stayed right where he stood. He landed clutching his gasping chest. Wide eyes rounded on his frightener and beheld an ancient stooping figure. A crazy gap-toothed grin perching on a dull grey frame beamed up at him. Old watery eyes were friendly pools of welcome. In an instant, fear dissolved and morphed into wonder. The old person wore a scarlet sash over one shoulder. The other end lay by a hip. A little stone mallet hung from a woven grasswood holster, and black linen twisted like rope around his waist. It looped under his groin and tucked back into itself. Drolla stared blank. The old timer answered the unasked question.

"All that lovely black glass. Soltoro hoarded more and more every year. Just as well too, it might be all we shall ever have."

"Who are you?" gasped Drolla.

"Someone who is meant to be down here. Why are you not training, soldier?"

He pulled a lamp line toward him and lowered a smolderstone within reach. His little mallet sang as he struck light back into the geode. Squinting at its glow, he released the bungee and raised the lamp back into position. The vast chamber revealed itself as the brightness chased the dark into the hidden corners.

"You scared the life out of me," said Drolla.

"You should not be sneaking around down here. What are you up to?"

"I... I got lost..."

"Prank is it?" he grinned. "Some dare your squad sent you on, I'll bet."

"Not quite."

"Well, I found you. I always do. You brats cannot sneak down here without me knowing."

"You got me. I was told there was no one down here. He was wrong twice, so far."

"Who told you that?"

"My squad leader."

"Oh. My grandkid wears the orange now. He was promoted for this war. Do you know him?"

"Maybe, what's his name?"

"Leeporp."

"No, mine is called Xindro."

"That's him. Leeporp."

"Leeporp?"

"It's a family nickname."

The shardsmith. *Grandkid,* thought Drolla. "You're Pondra."

"I am." For a moment he smiled wide at being recognised before his face dropped. "Did he send you down here?"

"Well, yes, sort of..."

"That rogue. He could have come himself, I have not seen him for ages. What trouble is he getting into this time?"

"Ah... You see, I am vowed to secrecy," said Drolla.

"Are you? Oh, good. Tell me everything. If Leeporp trusts me, you should too." This old fellow was his only hope to find his bag, and his way out. The map was lost. Without help, he too could be lost forever. It was strange that Xindro had not recruited his grandpar' to steal the Red Spore. It was even stranger he never mentioned him. The old fellow splayed his arms and looked about. "Who would I tell?"

"I have to find my shoulderpack. They say it's in the sundries store."

"Is that all? I know where that is. Let's go," said Pondra.

"Don't you want to know why?"

"You can tell me on the way."

Drolla followed Pondra as he wandered through the great cavern. He stopped now and then to relight stones along the way.

"Hungry?" asked Pondra. "We should get some snacks, they are on the way."

"Is there time?"

There's always time for snacks."

Pondra led Drolla through a maze of narrow corridors. He had not noticed the smolderstones embedded in the walls until Pondra tapped them into life as he hurried along. He stopped outside a doorway. It too was draped with a heavy black leather curtain.

"First, a couple of quaffs, I think," said Pondra.

He ushered Drolla into the hidden alcove. It was Pondra's lair. The interior walls were lined with shelving from floor to ceiling. Half was a well stocked larder of gourmet meats and fruits with glass kegs of sweet waters and purple brewberry syrups. There was a dozen open baskets laden with a fortune of Tamzi glash rods and drops. On the floor, black ingots stacked high by a pile of funglestone slabs. A red striped yellow fur quilt hung like a hammock and was weighed down by grey wooly cushions. Pondra unrolled and spread a grasswood mat. He threw a cushion on each corner and placed a low floor table in its centre. From a bloated skin, he poured some syrup into a small tureen and handed Drolla a crystal goblet.

A sweet rich tang danced across Drolla's tingling tongue. His throat moaned with pleasure as the warm velvet liquid slid down without any effort at all. Candied vapours exhaled like a mirage and his cheeks flushed with a cozy afterglow.

"I have never tasted anything like it," said Drolla.

"Not many have. It's a royal brew, fit only for a monarch. Another?"

"Yes please," drooled Drolla.

"A toast. To Leeporp and our secret meeting," said Pondra.

"To Leeporp," grinned Drolla. He threw back another glass of liquid pleasure.

"It's probably best you don't call him that, and please don't tell him I told you. It's a family nickname. He likes it kept secret, very secret."

"I would not dare, I'd lose my tongue," said Drolla.

"Yes, and your hands," he laughed. "Then you couldn't write it down." His smile frowned and his cheer sobered. "He can be a bit too violent sometimes."

"Everyone is violent here. Death means nothing. We had to kill prisoners for practice. It was horrible. I am forever expecting to be arrested for murder, even though I know I won't."

"This is the military, killing is what they do. If you dwell on the lives you take, you will become weak and the fret of it will get you killed."

"Yes, I need to harden up, I suppose."

"Not too hard, not like Leeporp. I mean Xindro."

"How did he get that name?" asked Drolla.

"I shouldn't say."

"Why not?" grinned Drolla. "If Leeporp trusts me, you should too."

"All right. I had a friend once. A royal friend. When I lived at our family estate outside Xylla, he visited often. They were always social visits, our home was his secret getaway. This one time, we shared a cold tub after a drunken picnic feast. Bantering, having a laugh, you know. Little Lee... Xindro climbed in with us. Not yet even two seasons old, and already bold and boisterous. He splashed about and climbed onto my friend's lap and farted under the water. The sound of the bubbles breaking the surface was hilarious. The name stuck."

"Bath fart? Ha! That is fantastic," laughed Drolla. "No wonder he wants that kept quiet."

"The only ones here who know are me, him, that friend-as-was, and now you."

Drolla copied Pondra as he winked and placed a finger over his shushed lips. They clinked glasses and gulped another round.

"He is not your friend anymore?"

"No," said Pondra. His eyes grew black and his lip curled into a hateful snarl. "He betrayed me. Exiled me down here for the rest of my life."

"It's not much of a life."

"It's better than no life."

"But you are not locked in, can you not just escape home?"

"I am my own gaoler. If I escape and the caverns are found dark, he vowed to send shardhires to murder my entire clan.

"Wow. What did you do?"

"I did him a favour."

Pondra was involved in a royal disgrace. Near two and a half decades ago, a baby was stolen from the birthing pillow. To all the world it was pronounced stillborn. It wasn't. The kidnapper, the friend, begged Pondra to foster the child in secret and hide it amongst his own huge clan. 'For the sake of the monarchy, he bleated.'

In the spirit of good and loyal friendship, Pondra kept faith for five years and the child was treated as one of their own. Then one day, Protorians arrived. They took both Pondra and the child into custody. He was under arrest and neither ever saw home, or anyone ever again.

"And this was my reward," scowled Pondra.

"That's a terrible story," said Drolla.

"The kid's grown now and doesn't even know who he is. Few do."

"Who is it?" asked Drolla.

"I will not tell you that, I would fear for your life if you knew. But I will tell you this, if his birth certificate ever came to light, there would be royal chaos."

"Where is it?"

"I couldn't say. That's another thing keeping me alive. While the secret is safe, so am I."

"Oh, Pondra. It's too cruel."

"It's not so bad, I'm used to it now. I sneak up now and then and get some sun. But it's all becoming far too busy and far too noisy. I get visitors sometimes, soldiers who lose their way or kids larking about."

"Well, now I know you are here, you can count on more visits from me."

"Good, you would be welcome any time," said Pondra. "For now, let us go get your pack."

"I should get out of here, before I am missed."

"What's so special about it that Leeporp would risk sending you down here for it?" asked Pondra.

"It's full of Red Spore fungus."

"Drord's Guts, it gets worse. That kid is such a troublemaker."

"Would you like some too, for Pannatalia?"

"You are too kind young Drolla. I would rather be home for it. To see the new babies born, and celebrate all our birthdays together, that is all I ever wanted."

"Maybe one day soon, things will change," said Drolla.

Neither of them believed it.

2.8 - THE CALLOUS MERCY

Through the purple shade, the last streamer fluttered across the village plaza.

The party was over. A few cranky elders oversaw the children sweeping and raking five weeks worth of scattered party rubbish. Duty was a commodity traded for privilege, even the old folk earned their keep. Every now and then, a little one would squeal with delight when they found a lost sweet or toy, still wrapped, hidden amongst the trash. Teens pulled down faded streamers from the surrounding trees and dismantled the plaza canopy. The month of Pannatalia had come and gone. Every birthday had been celebrated. Every birthling had been welcomed. All but one.

Seven months since Conjugation, those who had conceived now went into labour. A hasty child of stone was the first born this season, and the celebrations began. Once the canvas awning was stretched across the plaza, the banquets never ceased. As the newborns arrived, they were officially presented by proud families to the clan. Meanwhile, everyone else's birthday was toasted for the day. Throughout Pannatalia, every day was someone's birthday. More often than not, many on the same day. Those who shared a birthday also shared an empathy with each other, typecast by traits of the zodiak. While few took the predictions seriously, others professed the accuracy of the day's symbolism. The character of a person was ordained at the moment of their first breath. Unfortunately, the flaw of all superstitions is such that the foreseen foibles are so widely spread.

It was easy to justify anyone's personality to the date of their birth. Another favoured whim was to hope the child was born on the parent's birthday, or perhaps on the grandparent's. Some even gambled on it. Others cheated, and foolishly induced themselves into a forced delivery to ensure it, despite the mortal risk to both parent and baby. To the deluded proselytes, such was the importance of the natal date.

The plaza awning now always shaded someone. Hosts and guests came and went but the party never ended, loiterers waited for the next inevitable batch of revelers. Refreshed daily, an abundance of raw fruits and vegetables adorned the picnic tables. For months, mudbeasts and tablebirds were fattened up and now slaughtered as needed. Warm, quivering flesh was sliced from the dangling carcass and savoured raw. Under it, fresh blood dripped and soaked into spice and herbs. The mix cooled and congealed into a delicious dipping jelly. A true delicacy of the season.

All manner of drinking vessels, goblets, bowls and horns, were constantly and generously refilled. Nectar waters and brewberry syrups were ladled from great glass tureens that never seemed to empty. While the children served, the adults fussed, the seniors doted, and the elders relaxed admiring all their offspring. The measure of success was the one's own lineage and the proliferation of the family and the clan. Families blessed with newborns ridiculed those without them. Taunting boasts spat back, vowing to outbreed them all next year. Then, they would all laugh and toast each other's good health.

Each hour of the day brought a new round of jokes and tales, poems and songs. It was all cheerful practice for the serious recitals on the 13th, Midnth Day. The programme had evolved over centuries during the seniorcracy. After monofication, the schedule was extended. First, the children sang the family songs, and the seniors caroled their clan's hymn. Then all the subjects were required by a sovereign's edict to sing the national anthem and toast the Monarch's health. What followed was borderline treason, yet wholly unenforced. An organic reaction of the clansfolk desire for better times prompted the people to chant the Paladin's Bode. The tale proposed a mystical saviour who would one day rise up and free the clans of the monarchy itself. A faint hope of the return to the seniocratic order. This was an especially seditious act ignored by all as a mournful fantasy, never to actually be achieved. The retired Protorian Guards made sure of that when they returned home.

At twenty years old, the doyens' first-born were inducted into the Protorian Guard for a decade. While they served the monarch as his royal protectors, they served their doyens as loyal informants. Discharged at thirty, they returned home a senior and succeeded their previous doyen. Ten years of service to, and indoctrination by, the regal order ensured the seniocratic clans remained loyal to the monarchy. Brokka was the last doyen's heir of this clan conscripted into the guard. Before Hlammi was of age to be summoned, his tragedy and scandal struck the family. The consequences rendered he and future heirs of his clan exempt from that particular royal duty.

At day's end, Hlammi, the solemn clan leader, mounted the podium to lead the final chant. He struck his usual pose, took a breath and paused.

"Paladin's Bode," he voiced alone. The audience repeated his words in a respectful whisper. Together, they recited the ballad in tune.

The Paladin's Bode

"Came one day, the lord of none,
the unknown child was serf to one.
Set free of bonds and cast away,
his own liberty, he would betray.
Entrapped again, bound by desires,
his passion burnt like bubbling fires.
Forced into war, he mastered death,
he fought for kin with every breath.
And when the monarchs died at last,
he buried the tyranny into the past.
The folk rejoiced their mending bane,
the seniorial way will never wane.
Shared by all and owned by none,
never again, ruled by one."

A dozen days later, both young and old hated the cleanup duty. The grumbling workers paused as a lone pregnant figure slowly waddled past. Drolla had finished yet another walk around the village. He had taken a brisk plunge in the icy creek, anything to bring on labour. He clutched his poncho tight, ignoring the wall of eyes. The young ones stared with curiosity while the elders frowned concern. He should have birthed by now.

As doyen, Hlammi had extended the celebrations, hoping against hope that Drolla might deliver him, at worst, a tardy water baby on the last day of the month. That was four days ago, no-one ever birthed this late. The doyen could wait no longer. The patience of the clanfolk ended when the new month started. People began to grumble, they were sick of partying and wanted to get back to normal. They had babies to tend. If the doyen's heir had not birthed yet, something must be amiss. Rumours spread. He was not pregnant, just fat. The baby knew better than to be born of the doyen's brat. It was lust-spawn, not conceived at Conjugation, and the slut would bear the bastard in secret later. None were true.

Drolla made his way through the garden into the doyen's mansion. Kwinno rose and ran to his side. With a sibling's tenderness, he helped Drolla straddle an old pouffe covered with long black hair. It was matted and it was itchy. Of course it was.

"Par' is in a frightful mood," said Kwinno. "The elders virtually ordered him to tear down the party things."

"I saw," said Drolla.

"The whole village are tired of waiting for you. They say it is an insult to Pannatalia."

"It's not my fault. I want this baby out of me more than anyone."

"You have missed every birthday, even your own."

"And no one even noticed," sighed Drolla.

Hlammi swept into the room. His purple toga twirled around him as he squatted on the chamber's plynth.

"I noticed," said Hlammi. "You should have been here."

"I am sorry. The lack of any attention has kept me far too busy."

"You were appointed birthing aides," said Hlammi.

"Them? Those three old duffers looked like grandpar's great-uncles. Were they all you could afford?"

"Oh, you are impossible. No wonder the villagers have been gossiping about you."

"Following your lead, no doubt," said Drolla.

Hlammi shot to his feet, stiff with rage.

"Kwinno, fetch the nurses. I shall summon a doctor. It is time to induce this baby out." Kwinno threw Drolla a sad and helpless look. "Now!" the doyen insisted.

It was true, the expectant excitement faded with the month and any would-be well-wishers had slowly distanced themselves by the end. Hlammi's mood darkened with every passing day. He too had abandoned hope of a timely birth. Drolla's desperation festered as he was deserted by his own parent on the eve of his first grandchild's birth. Solitude was his new companion. Hlammi dragged Kwinno from the room. The ancient doulas saw nothing, and cared less. While Drolla sat alone, his pains began.

Hours of taxing labour followed. He suffered in uncomfortable silence for as long as he could, while his three aides watched on with a bored indifference. Hlammi instructed them to call for him after the child was delivered, he said nothing about caring for Drolla. His proud parent had also forbidden everyone else from the birthing chamber. The noble doyen set a fine example for the rest of the clan. Stay away. 'Decorum,' he dribbled, and the toadies gladly complied.

Alerted by Drolla's howls of agony echoing through the halls of the sunken mansion, Brokka and Kwinno ignored their doyen's command. They forced their way in to help Drolla bear his first child.

"Pardon thyre, you are not permitted..." said one aide with a false sense of authority.

"I will deal with the doyen, you deal with Drolla. Your lives depend on his," said Brokka. They all three promptly turned to Drolla's welfare.

"They. Gave me. A potion," panted Drolla. "Even though. I started."

"Doyen Hlammi ordered it, thyre." The aide's voice creaked with fear.

Brokka scowled a murderous glare, it fueled terror into the hopeless elders. The induction drugs made Drolla violently ill. With nothing left to vomit, he spewed stringy bile. He was almost to weak to deliver. For the last hour, he would pass out for a while and jolt awake not knowing where he was. Realisation stabbed his womb and the desperation flooded back. The agony was not over.

"Make it stop grandpar'," pleaded Drolla.

Kwinno tenderly kissed a clenching hand while Brokka mopped his sodden brow and stroked a defeated shoulder. Whether by a sense of duty or heartfelt care, Hlammi relented and arrived in time to witness the birth. As he entered, Drolla bore down. With a final screaming push, a dead grandchild splashed onto the birthing pillow. Hlammi's face twisted with horror and disappointment.

"Stillborn offspring from jilted spawn," he whispered with disgust. For a moment Hlammi glared contempt at Brokka, then he turned and fled.

Instinctively, Drolla scooped up his grey newborn and tenderly blew air into his little face. It neither breathed nor blinked. A kindly elder with welling eyes gently took the corpse and wrapped it in yellow silk. Drolla was exhausted and heartbroken. Kwinno drove his sobbing face into Drolla's chest. Embracing them both, Brokka wept his stoic tears.

The old natal aides cleaned and examined Drolla. Their frowns nodded in agreement.

"Broken," they whispered.

Pondra's hug squeezed tight and would not let go.

"I shall return soon," said Drolla, breaking the embrace.

"Bring Leeporp. We shall picnic like royalty," said Pondra.

"I will."

Pondra pinched away some joyful tears.

"I won't follow you out. There'll be lights fading somewhere down here. I should get back and keep them lit."

Drolla stepped out of the tunnel and gently lowered the cobweb gate. Behind it, Pondra looked like a prisoner after all.

"Stay safe," he said, moving back into the dark.

"See you soon." He need not have bothered, Pondra was already gone.

Drolla tucked the fat shoulderpack under an armpit and headed for the sapory.

Through a forest thicket and across a furtive bridge, the lazy manicured parklands led into the familiar streets between the barracks. Drolla sought the intersecting shaded lanes and kept a wary eye for roaming sentries. Across the alley, the same brute dozed outside the spice shop. He nodded too far and fell off his wobbly stool. He jolted awake and stood as if nothing happened. One hand scratched his groin and he farted, another hand hid a muffled shout before he trotted toward a distant shit pit. Drolla bolted to the unguarded doorway and slipped inside.

"Sontro?" called Drolla, far too softly. He crept in further. A lone voice muttered to itself and glass clinked. Creeping past the winding cupboards, he called again.

"Who's that?" came a startled reply. Drolla stepped into the ring of light around the saporist's table. "What do you want?" he hissed.

"I was here a while ago, with Xindro," said Drolla.

"Xindro? Oh yes, I remember. Look, if he has sent you here for Red Spore, I still don't have any."

"He didn't send me."

"Well, I would not sell you any either."

"Would you buy some?"

Sontro's eyes narrowed. "Maybe," he said with a doubtful tone.

Drolla plonked his pack on the table. The flap fell open and revealed dozens of dried slabs, packed tight against each other. Pure white palms contrasted the bright red gilled rows. Sontro gasped. His eyes bulged. He snapped his jaw shut and stared disbelief at Drolla. After an thoughtful moment, he left his sample table and disappeared between the spiral shelves.

"Go home. We're closed," yelled Sontro. His bouncer grunted and the front door slammed shut. The bolt slid home and pattering feet returned to the central nook.

"I expected a little powder. Where did you get all this from?" asked the saporist.

"A parting gift from my grandpar'."

"A most excellent grandpar'. Do you have any idea what this haul is worth?" said Sontro. He really did have a hard time not grinning like an idiot.

"Of course I do. I have sold this stuff to Tamzi traders for years. A dozen rods a slab."

"That's wholesale. Here, it is worth so much more."

"I am happy to sell it for that. You can on sell it for what ever you want."

"Oh wow. You are too kind. Theres so much. Do you want to sell it all?"

"Yep. Except for this piece, and that one. These are for my friends."

"You will be everyone's friend once this gets out," said Sontro.

"What?" Drolla blurted. "No. I only want the cash, not the fame. Keep my name to yourself."

"Of course. It was a figure of speech. Look, I can't buy all this off you at once. Who keeps that sort of money handy?"

"Oh, I see," said Drolla, crestfallen.

He closed the flap of the pack. Sontro reached and reopened it. He leaned over and sniffed the fungus with a connoisseur's delight.

"But I will hold it here and sell it off for you. Once the whisper gets out, it will go in no time. Come by after Midnth Day, and collect the proceeds. How about that?"

"Alright. But remember you are doing business with a friend of Xindro."

"You said he didn't send you," said Sontro.

"He didn't, but he will make sure you deal fair."

"How dare you." Sontro stiffened his back and straightened his face. "I am Oxxian. I have no intention of cheating anyone."

"Alright. I shall see you then."

Sontro extended a palm, they shook hands and sealed the deal.

Excitement and impatience hung in the air like dust in a sunbeam. The low floor table was set among the fluffy rugs. After a long while, almost too long, Flynx had returned from his errand with everything Drolla asked for. A pestle and mortar, a small glass flip-lid stein and a few spare jars for left-overs. Seven faces squatted in silence and watched every move he made. Drolla unwrapped a hidden piece of dried mushroom from his robe. It was as brittle as old jerky.

"Is that all there is?" asked Flynx.

"It's more than you've got," snapped Xindro. "You came through Drolla. Well done."

He snapped the red from the white and placed it in the mortar. Once ground to a rich crimson, he gently poured the powder into a spare jar. He took extra care to ensure it flowed as smooth as liquid. He repeated the procedure and placed a palmfull of the pure white powder into the stein. Drolla was ready, he sat back on his haunches and looked at his mates. He treated them with faux deference, as was the lapster's duty, and politely awaited the indulgers' request.

It amused him that they had no idea how to do red spore. Whereas Drolla had been surrounded by it for years. He was the elder's favourite sporetender, but he was never invited to join in. The rest of the kindom might have legalised sporewhoofing only on Midnth Day, but Drolla's elders were forever high, and more, on the stuff.

"Who's first?" he asked. No one volunteered.

"How strong is it?" asked Klommo.

"As strong as you like. The red is the potency and the white is the dilution. The pinker the mix, the stronger it is."

"How strong do you have it?" asked Xindro.

"I told you, I don't like this shit. Years ago I indulged too much. I was alone far too often. Now it just makes me sick. Besides, someone needs to stay alert."

"Well, that's no help," said Grikka. "I don't want to be sick from it."

"You wont get sick. I'll do a nice mellow mix for a first timer."

"Then blend me one up barkeep, as strong as you see fit," said Boohala.

Drolla grinned wide. They don't know what they're in for, he thought.

He gently scooped a thumbnail of red powder into the stein. With the spoon, he lightly folded red and white together. He was careful not to disturb the mix too much. Easy does it, we don't want it cloudy yet. He let the lid fall shut and handed the stein to Boohala. The mix shimmered the palest pink. It was better to err on the side of caution, and begin with a weaker mix. A tyro's mind might burst.

"Now what?" asked Boohala.

"Shake it a few times, flip the lid and inhale the dust," said Drolla.

He took the vessel and glanced around his peers. They glared back keen encouragement. Boohala shook the stein hard. The powder fell to the bottom and the swirling dust filled the vessel to the brim. He flipped the lid open, and in one mighty whoof, Boohala inhaled the lot. Drolla knew the strength he mixed. He knew how it would affect him.

The weight of the world crushed into his head from every direction. The pressure bore down into an icy central point of his consciousness until it was almost unbearable. There was a distant flash from beyond the endless dark and the pressure began to reverse. As he exhaled, a sphere of inebriating vertigo grew faster than the mind might catch. One's very psyche expanded without limit to the edge of everything. The body relaxed and sighed as if wrapped in the sunny warmth of a spectrum's mirage caught in the mist of a waterfall. The mind would race and random memories and thoughts would arc and dance like lightning. If your thoughts weren't kept in check, they might stray away a million years in an instant. Eventually, the font of imagination would subside and gently throb in a delightful woken trance, only to settle and stare into infinity and question every forgotten moment of it.

The stein went round the table. By now, Boohala and the rest had been there and back, and seen the end of time itself. They compared notes as if they were gods squabbling over creation. They blathered and quarreled like a thirsty flock at a shrinking oasis. The stein went round twice more, a little pinker each time. After a good long while, the frenetic banter waned.

Soon they began to lay aside like the petals of a wilting flower. Convinced they knew better, they nestled into their own private thoughts. Drolla had no idea what awesome travels his friends were taking now, but he could imagine. It was best he left them to it. He needed to be alone. Pannatalia sucked, it always had.

He slowly packed the utensils onto a tray. He thought of Pondra and considered paying him a visit, but decided against it. The old loner would wonder why Leeporp had not come as well. His intoxicated peers quietly mumbled their own new found understandings, yet would not remember a glimmer of their brilliance by tomorrow.

In the mumbling silence, Drolla's name thundered down the ramp. Shouts and calls for attention burst into the chamber. Xindro and Boohala blinked and shook their heads. They leapt to their unsteady feet to counter the intruders. The rest gazed on, indifferent to the bedlam. Flynx crawled into a dark corner and hid under a crumpled quilt.

"Who is Drolla?" demanded Fontaza. The fateshield stank of malice. He was there the day Quetono was attacked. He dealt out the summary justice, and seemed even more dangerous today. Groggy and surprised, the squad all looked at Drolla. Two Protorians seized him, bound him and pushed him up the ramp. Xindro and Boohala ran up after them. Up top under the marquee, Fontaza spun and faced them ready to answer their unspoken complaints.

"He is to be escorted directly to the legal panel for immediate judgment."

"On whose order?" asked Boohala.

"By legal warrant," said Fontaza. He smirked at Xindro. "Your grandpar' Pondra is already there. It does not look good."

"Get out of my way," said Xindro.

"You are barred. It is a closed court," said Fontaza.

"You won't stop me." He took one step too many. Fontaza and his Protorians pounced into a defensive stance with blades half drawn. It was a restrained warning of the imminent violence they were ready to commit. Xindro slowly drew his shard and smiled at their stern, worried faces. "You think your phapping rank will save you?"

"You think your clan will survive you? You know the threat that hangs over them."

"Xindro," said Boohala. "Step back, I have a better idea."

After a moment, Xindro conceded. He slumped his shoulders and pushed his half-sheathed weapon home.

"Take him away," said Fontaza. The Protorians pushed Drolla ahead of them. As they frogmarched him down the lane, he looked back to his friends and saw their muted argument with Fontaza.

An hour passed while Pondra and Drolla waited under the legal pavilion. Still bound, they stood before the judicial panel. A door curtain was wrenched aside and two royal officials took their places at the bench. A slick brown robe sat beside a scarlet toga, topped with a black feather mantle.

"Greetings Pondra. Old friend," said Vondaka.

"Old, yes. Friends, no."

"This is not how I imagined we would meet again."

"This is precisely how you intended it. I know why I am here, and I know why he is here." Pondra nodded to Fontaza.

The brute's breathing was heavy and unnatural, every panting breath he exhaled seemed a mortal threat. Outside, around the pavilion, a dozen Protorians kept an obedient yet disinterested guard. Inside, Drolla and Pondra stood quite alone against their prosecutors.

"Shall we begin," asked Palama.

"Yes. Pondra, aided and abetted this criminal to steal from the military store," said Vondaka.

"That must be established first," said Palama. The red commander's gaze rounded onto Drolla. "Chancellor Vondaka, please read the list of charges against the recruit."

"As you wish. Item one; contrary to recruitment directions the accused brought an illegal substance, namely Red Spore fungus, into the military company."

"That charge was stricken by Quetono," said Palama. "The penalty was confiscation."

"Him and his damned pets," said Vondaka. "The second charge; the accused was absent without leave from military training. Three; the accused enacted an illegal entry into the military stores. Four; he stole confiscated property, the same Red Spore fungus, from the monarchy. And five; he onsold said property for personal financial gain."

"Drolla, how do you answer these charges?" asked Palama.

"Well, with respect thyre, the gate was unlocked and my shoulderpack had not yet been logged as royal property. So technically, I didn't actually break in and I only took my own stuff back."

"Don't be clever," roused Vondaka. "Red Spore fungus is a banned commodity within the confines of Churon's Pen."

"Not on Midnth Day," said Palama. Vondaka grunted and cleared his throat.

"It is the responsibility of the military to provide recreation to the troops. Not him," yelled Vondaka. "And where is the money? It belongs to the Treasury."

"I don't have it. I only kept a small bit of shroom to share," said Drolla.

"The whole camp shared a bit and they didn't get it for free," said Palama.

"No wonder it's so overcast with all those torpid minds floating about in the sky," said Pondra, smiling.

"Silence," roared Vondaka. "This is no place for your flippancy. Who did you sell it to?"

"No-one. There is no money," said Drolla.

"Are you trying to tell me you donated the fungus? Who received it?"

"It seems everyone has," said Palama.

"You all fail to see the seriousness of this crime. Hundreds of soldiers are out of commission today, stupefied, under the influence of that dangerous drug," said Vondaka.

An attendant ran forward and interrupted the proceedings. He whispered his message to Vondaka. His face fell and his eyes went black.

"Anything relevant to this case, Chancellor?" asked Palama.

"Our witness has been found dead. Drowned, it seems."

"We have his signed statement on file. Stamped and sealed as authentic." Palama passed the parchment to Vondaka.

"I have read it." He faced Drolla, "It is attested, you boasted to your squadmates about the parting gift from your grandparent. You vowed to share it one day. In that squalid little berry-den, you and your group conspired to steal the contraband. You were aided by a quartermaster," said Vondaka, he turned to inform Palama. "We await his confession. He drew you a map and left a gate unlocked, didn't he? You sneaked in and your fellow defendant here helped you commit your crime."

"Pondra had nothing to do with it. He found me wandering around lost down there. I forced him to help me. I vowed to kill him if he didn't."

Pondra closed his eyes and slowly shook his head.

"No you didn't," said Palama. "It's his maze, he could have lost you at anytime."

"Or reported it later," added Vondaka.

"Instead, he willingly helped and concealed the theft," said Palama.

"Clearly, neither are innocent," said Vondaka.

"I think the verdict is irrefutable," said Palama.

"What have you judged it to be?"

"From the evidence and their admissions, they shall be logged as guilty."

Pondra stared disgust at Vondaka's grinning eyes.

"Wait," blurted Drolla. "Before Pondra found me, I overheard some soldiers gossiping about treason."

"How is this relative to your case?" said Palama.

"Not sure," confessed Drolla. "But they said the prince is plotting a coup against the monarch."

Palama burst out laughing. "Irrelevant and false."

"You mean President Krantolo is conspiring with Prince Diltoro to usurp the royal plynth. That plot?" said Vondaka.

Palama's smile disappeared. "You know of this, par'? Soltoro must be informed."

"He does not want to know," said Vondaka. "He has left the matter in my hands. The fools shall incriminate themselves soon enough. With my guidance, of course."

"Ooo, politics and intrigue. It's been twenty-five years since we were in this much trouble, eh?" laughed Pondra.

"You just cannot keep your mouth shut, can you?" said Vondaka. "You never could be trusted."

"I was trusted with a stolen child for four years. He became one of our clan, everyone loved him."

"You loved him too much. You forgot who he was."

"Was that not the point? You hid him with us, everyone was meant to forget who he was. He was meant to live an anonymous life."

"Yes, but not as an Oxxian," Vonkaka's lip curled in disgust. "We shall soon be rid of them as well."

"And yet no one knows who he is, even he doesn't know himself. He is more anonymous than ever."

"And it has to stay that way. The fewer who know, the better."

"You cannot make me forget him. Vondaka, you know I vowed never to name him."

"I cannot take that risk. I simply cannot trust you."

"You never have. You locked me underground for two and a half decades. I kept your secret."

"What secret? Which child?" demanded Palama.

"Never you mind," snapped Vondaka. "The arbiter has judged you guilty. As the monarch's proxy, it is my role to pass sentence. Pondra, only under duress have you endured your commission. That term has expired. Your sentence of death is reinstated. Fontaza, to your duty."

Drolla choked. Pondra's knees bent under him. He groaned a cry of despair and the colour drained from him. Their fatal predicament had escalated all too soon. Fontaza hoisted the old fellow up with a palm under one armpit.

"Point of Order, Chancellor," said Palama. "You have condemned him for an offense outside the scope of this tribunal. More than that, we are in the midst of Pannatalia. There should be no death during the month of birth."

The chancellor hissed at the constant unwelcome corrections.

"Spare me your superstitions," seethed Vondaka. He nodded to Fontaza.

The wheezing beast hauled Pondra beyond the rear awnings and pushed him onto the sand. As he drew his shard, it screeched its fatal terror.

"Fontaza, hold your blade," yelled Palama. "Par', you know this warrant is invalid."

Xindro burst through the front of the pavilion surrounded by nine jade enforcers. In one hand, he held up Quetono's winged baton. In another, he flapped a single page and moved to speak.

"With what right do you burst in here unannounced?" shouted Vondaka. "This is a private tribunal."

"Regal trumps legal," said Xindro. His smirk dropped. "I bear the rod of Drahn in lieu of its royal owner. The noble Quetono bids me to adjourn this session immediately and escort the prisoners directly to him." With a nod to Palama, he handed over the writ. "He requests you attend as well, thyre. He insists it is most urgent."

"Leeporp, they're killing Pondra," bawled Drolla.

Every eye under the pavilion turned to Fontaza. He grinned and let his blade fall across Pondra's neck. Glass slicked through flesh and bone and his head fell with a dull thud. It rocked a little and settled to stare at Drolla. One eye winked shut and his old blood pooled about him.

"No..." In a howling fury, Xindro pulled his shard and bounded toward Fontaza. The fatesheild backed up, eyes wide, his face blushed raw fear.

"Stop him," roared Vondaka.

A Protorian stepped from behind the pavilion. He stabbed his pommel at Xindro's head. Blindsided, the glass knob struck him hard and he dropped in a senseless heap.

2.9 - THE HIDDEN EXPOSURE

"**P**rotorians! Gird hither," roared Vondaka.

A dozen marbled tunics stormed into the pavilion. They surrounded Vondaka and Palama with weapons half-drawn. There was no passion, the indentured first born simply did their duty. Not so the enforcers, their fury seized Drolla and pulled him within their defensive circle around Xindro. He lay motionless at their feet. Fontaza regained his bold composure and bravely edged his way around the wary enforcers. His arrogance thrust two Protorians aside and he joined Vondaka. The proud fateshield stood fearless behind his royal protectors. A pensive standoff took root.

"Send for a mortician. Xindro needs a medic," commanded Palama.

It was foolish to expect the Protorians might carry out his requests. They stood like trees. They obeyed royal commands. To acknowledge his legal authority would be beneath their dignity. Messengers, they were not.

"Chancellor, pull your guard back," demanded Palama. Vondaka nodded and the Protorians pushed their hilts home and stepped aside. One enforcer ran off to the mortuary while two others carried Xindro away to the hospital. "Report his condition to Dandaron immediately." With both baton and document in hand, Palama ordered the remaining enforcers to carry out their charge. "You will escort myself and Drolla to Quetono."

"I shall accompany you, child," said Vondaka, as smooth as glass.

"You have already exceeded your authority here today. You were not invited. You will not attend." Palama turned and left. He sent a runner ahead to inform Dandaron of their impending arrival.

Anger and sorrow blended like shadow and fog, and the world was a nauseous blur. Urgent and determined, the enforcers drove Drolla and Palama across the orange sand with a courteous insistence. As they approached the infirmary, their allies came into view. Boohala paced loops above Quetono's chamber. Ever statuesque, Dandaron welcomed the escort's approach. On arrival, the enforcers widened their open circle and halted around the four consorts.

Drolla's heart was in his guts and his tears had run out. Boohala curtsied Palama, and placed a consoling hand on Drolla's shoulder.

"This was unforeseen," said Palama. "The chancellor duped me."

"How?" said Drolla. "You sat beside him."

"It was an inquest, not a trial. He has shed illegal blood," said Palama.

"What happened?" asked Dandaron.

"Pondra was killed, Xindro too maybe."

"What?"

"How did Vondaka know so much?" asked Drolla.

"After your arrest, Fontaza blabbed," said Boohala. "We had a spy amongst us. Xindro drove the squad downramp. He pushed them into the spa and promised to drown them all. Their protests and denials swayed him, he deemed them innocent. Except Flynx. He begged Leeporp to believe him."

"Leeporp?" asked Dandaron.

"How did he know that nickname?" quizzed Drolla.

"Vondaka planted Flynx to watch you," said Boohala. Their eyes turned on Drolla. He shrugged a clueless reply. "The coward confessed his treachery and pleaded forgiveness. So we held his head underwater. The filthy kladger thrashed about and shat the spa. Klommo and Grikka dumped the body in the creek. We came and told Dandaron and Quetono. He sent Xindro."

A lone enforcer sprinted across the arena toward them. He skid to a halt and curtsied.

"Enforcer Dandaron," he panted. He looked to Palama. "Triage report as ordered."

"That was quick," said Drolla.

"A medic saw to him at once," said the enforcer. "His skull is cracked. He has been drugged, but he is expected to heal through his coma."

"Good news. Thank you," said Palama.

"He won't be happy when he comes to," said Drolla.

"If he does," said Dandaron. He turned to the enforcer. "Gandra, place some sentries to protect Xindro. Ensure they are are only Oxxian guards. We shall send the surgeon soon."

The enforcer nodded, and ran off down Sentry Row.

"Especially Fontaza," Drolla yelled after him.

"Boohala," said Dandaron. "I ask you to stand guard here while we visit Quetono. We too must have no interruptions."

"With pleasure, thyre." Boohala curtsied deep, his adamant grip throttled his hilt.

"Why has uncle summoned us?" asked Palama.

"Drolla would have joined Pondra," said Dandaron.

"Why? He has no cause."

"That did not save Pondra. Quetono fears Vondaka is out to cull any he deems an enemy, including himself."

"Surely Quetono does not think the chancellor was behind his attack," said Palama.

"We believe he assigned those stewards to assassinate Quetono somewhere in Orienna. Fate or cowardice held their hands until they saw their master in the arena."

"What evidence do you have?" asked Palama.

"None. Fontaza slew them before they could be interrogated."

"Then perhaps your accusations are premature," said Palama.

"I think you are right," said Drolla. "They were arguing about something. One yelled, 'Let him watch', and then they pounced."

"I knew it," said Dandaron through clenched teeth. Palama was silent.

Torono emerged up from the hospice rampway.

"Quetono can see you now. He took a tonic, but I cannot say how long it will last."

Drolla and Palama shared a worried frown.

"An urgent patient awaits you in the triage tent," said Palama. "Xindro is badly wounded."

"Drord's Guts, not him too." Torono ran off across the sand.

"Alright," said Dandaron. His voice quavered. "Before we go in, I must warn you Quetono is very weak. His condition may be confronting. Be brave for him."

Drolla followed Dandaron and Palama down the ramp. The light in the chamber was dull and the room smelled of sweet potpourri. Garlands of herbs festooned the walls.

Drolla stood back a for a moment, he did not recognise the person swaddled before him. Sensing his reluctance, Dandaron moved him into the light, closer to Quetono. He was clutching his shoulderpack tight to his chest like some cherished thing. They had him propped up on his bunk with pillows and cushions, but he did not look comfortable at all. The splints and bandages were wrapped far too tight. A purple and yellow face cracked open a toothless smile at Drolla.

"You look sad young one," said Quetono to Drolla. "Am I so repellent?"

"Oh no thyre, I am very glad to see you alive."

"Then why?"

"Someone innocent died just now."

"Sweet child," said Quetono. "No one is innocent, and we all must die."

He wheezed and coughed. Dandaron gently dabbed a spot of blood from his chin.

"Why did you summon us uncle?" asked Palama.

"You three kids are the dearest of all things to me," said Quetono. Palama's eye quizzed Dandaron. He winked his reply before they glanced at Drolla. A frail smirk continued, "I know I wont survive this, so I must tell all three of you."

"Tell us what uncle?" asked Palama.

"The past and the present. So you might survive the future."

"Patr', please do not over exert yourself," said Dandaron.

Quetono flashed him a smile, then motioned them closer.

"I was sixteen when I bore my first child. Drabana was the best thing to ever happen to me. As he grew up, we became more like siblings than parent and child. He was tall, strong and wise beyond his years. He had a great future. He could have been monarch, if Soltoro was not already named first heir.

"He was fifteen. We traveled to The Kataraxs for his first conjugation. The new governor erected a mating platform out over the waterfall. It was to be the event of the decade. But we never arrived. Trail bandits attacked us on the way, just past Zephth. They murdered half our escort and drove off the rest. They forced us into a clearing by the forest road. We fought as best we could, but there were too many. Drabana wounded two of the cowards before a third killed him, then another took my arm. Some were spooked when their masks fell. One stood over me, "Doomed," he whispered. They all ran off and left me for dead. I crawled to my child's corpse before I passed out. I wish I had died then as well. But, my escort returned and tended us till the rescuers arrived.

"As I recovered, I mourned the unbearable loss of my dearest Drabana. He did not deserve the violence brought down on him. I had plenty of time to ponder the reasons behind it, but Vondaka assured me it was a random attack. His agents quickly traced and caught every one of them. The fugitives were taken to the very clearing in the forest where they had ambushed us. Around Drabana's cairn, he impaled all seven of them. Their corpses honoured Drabana's memory long after they drained and dried. Justice was served.

"As soon I was fit enough to travel, I went to his grave. I wept again as I said my final goodbye and fixed a little plaque to his funeral stone. It was both an explanation and a warning to any who might read it. No one dared interfere with the shrine. The criminals hung there until their rotten bodies slid to the ground. The wild beasts of the forest eventually ate what little skin and bone was left of them. Around his cairn, the seven poles still stand. My dear noble sibling Vondaka boasted he did it as a favour to me, to bring me some closure. I was very grateful, but am sure there were eight."

"It was so long ago uncle," said Palama.

"It's like yesterday," said Quetono. He faced Drolla. "The very next conjugation, I was in Xendurbia. The monarch summoned me to his court and commanded me to forget my tragedy. Bontoro was such a callous idiot. He stumbled through life without a drop of empathy. He did his best to console me in his own clumsy way, but a field of banquets and an ocean of brewberries did nothing to distract my heartache. But then, a certain someone did. Their natural beauty wove a spell of desire around me I could not resist. Oh Drolla, the auroras were extra beautiful that season, but not as beautiful as him.

"Bontoro held an audience for the heirs of the provincial doyens. Brokka presented Hlammi. Drord's Guts, he was gorgeous. I don't know if the comet's tail was more intense that season, but the urges definitely were. Afterwards, I tried to charm him, but at twice his age, I doubt he found me at all appealing. But my eyes never left him. During the feast his nerves forced him to drink far too much. He staggered alone and unnoticed from the banquet. I followed him out, and soon found him being sick into a vase. To spare him any shame, I snuck him to my chambers to clean him up. Well, one thing led to another and we mated."

"What?" blurted Drolla. Without a sound, Palama gawped wide-eyed and Dandaron calmly stared at his fingernails.

"Afterwards, he passed out, and neither of us joined the orgy. I watched over him while he slept. When he sobered, he regretted our drunken fling. He withdrew his consent, and accused me of rape."

"But how could he?" asked Palama. "It was conjugation. Everyone mates with anyone, it does not matter who. There is no such thing as conjugational rape. No one ever says no."

"Tell Hlammi that," said Quetono. "He has never forgiven me, and I have never forgotten him. He traveled home as soon as he could. I had hoped to see him again when he was drafted into the Protorians, but Vondaka was sure to veto that forever.

"In the end, I was probably too old to carry. I went full term. But, after the birthing, I fainted when I held my newborn. He smiled at me, or perhaps I dreamed it. It was such a blur. When I awoke he was gone. Vondaka told me it was deformed and stillborn. He decided it was far too gruesome for me to see. Besides, it had already been disposed of. I was lost to my heartache again for months. Until my agents brought me some wonderful news.

"While my birthling died, Hlammi's did not. He was pregnant by me and his first child lived. He still does... and he stands here before me." The eyes of a loving parent burnt deep into Drolla. His knees went weak, frost ants crawled across his skin in a wave.

A child should only knew their birth-parent. Mass fornication during the conjugational orgies ensured the seeding parents remained anonymous. Unknowingly seeding someone else was a pleasant enough chore, but the real reward was to become pregnant oneself. The singular lineage of the family pedigree was paramount. There was no need to complicate things with two parents bickering over control of the family. Only one parental senior sits the ancestral plynth at a time. Domestic power was not shared. Nor were family secrets, until now.

"Me?" Drolla pointed to his own heart. Reality splashed cold like a forest shower.

"Yes," beamed Quetono. Drolla's frown slowly lifted with the corner of his smile. The confession continued. "Hlammi insisted I was never allowed in your life. He vowed to expose our affair. To avoid a royal scandal, Vondaka convinced me to comply. But, I have silently watched you from afar, and hoped to one day meet you. At last, my chance came."

"This is why you resigned your presidency," said Palama.

"I had to face Hlammi again," smirked Quetono.

"The marquee," said Drolla.

Both parents waited in deathly silence while Dandaron tied the door flap shut outside. They listened as he herded the nosy villagers out of earshot.

"You are not taking Drolla," said Hlammi. "So, you need not have come."

"My dear Hlammi, aren't you even a little happy to see me after all these years?"

"No, I wish I had never met you. I know why you're here."

"I am here by royal command."

"Liar. Anyone could have done this. You came to gloat."

"It's true, I did want to see you again. I also wanted to assure you..."

"He is not going." Hlammi was adamant. Quetono dropped his friendly tone.

"The kindom goes to war. The monarch needs soldiers. Drolla is eligible, he must go."

"He knows nothing of the world outside this village. He doesn't even know who he is..."

"Yes, you have sheltered him rather well, haven't you."

"He's my child to raise."

"He is my child as well" pled Quetono.

"Don't be disgusting, you should be unknown."

"Well, I am not. He has been mine ever since..."

"Ever since you raped me," spat Hlammi.

"You know that's not true. You have used that lie against me all these years."

"And you have always denied it."

"I admit it, I adored you the moment I saw you. But you got drunk and I merely nursed you while you were sick and passed out."

"Then you raped me."

"Hlammi, enough. Think back, remember what really happened. You woke aroused. Your eyes glowed and your gorgeous cyan flash was as soft as fur. It shone like a blue sun. You were hot with lust and you nuzzled into me. I tried to move you aside, but you held me even tighter."

"You should have left me alone."

"What was I supposed to do, climb out from under you?"

"Yes."

"I couldn't. You wouldn't let me, and besides I didn't want to. You know the passion took us both. We are as guilty as the other." Quetono's heart melted. "You were so beautiful..."

"I see your face in Drolla everyday. He is a constant reminder of what you did to me and I will never forgive you. He stays here."

"He cannot," yelled Quetono.

"He is still a child," pleaded Hlammi.

"He is an adult. He grew up and you didn't notice."

"I've kept him safe."

"You've kept him imprisoned."

"He is needed here. This is just your excuse to take him from me."

"You are the one making excuses. I am not taking him. The army is, and if they cannot take him they will leave him here. Dead. That I cannot prevent. I came in person to convince you to let him go."

"It was never his fault. I have been so cruel. I cannot lose him now." Hlammi's voice began to break.

"I am here to save his life. He must come with me."

"He can't..."

"Hlammi, listen. Do you know why he so dear to me?"

"Why?"

"I fell pregnant too. He was your sporling, like Drolla is mine. I named him Halama after you, but he died at birth."

"I. I never..." Hlammi's stature drooped like warm wax. "Oh, poor Drolla."

"He must leave with me or die by execution," said Quetono. The compassion had left his voice. He was tired of being nice. "And if he does, be sure that every single living thing in this shitty little village will die after him. I promise you that."

Hlammi composed himself back into his rigid stature and glared pure venom at Quetono.

"His life is in your hands then."

"He will be in my care and guarded by royalty. He won't even know."

"He must never know," insisted Hlammi.

"So Drolla, I broke my vow. You deserve to know," wheezed Quetono. His breathing laboured. How was this secret kept all this time? How had Quetono endured till now? How cruel. Twice he mourned a tragic loss. Joyous fate found his secret sporling from afar. When at last they met, fate again tore them apart. Would it not be better, if neither had ever known?

"Let him rest now, he is exhausted," said Dandaron. He moved to usher them out.

"Not yet," creaked Quetono. "Palama, the table. Those scrolls. One for you to archive and one for Drolla. Not those, they are my funeral arrangements."

"Surely it is too soon for that, uncle," said Palama.

"Shush. The scrolls."

Palama passed one to Drolla and unrolled his own. It was Quetono's Bequeath. Palama read his copy aloud. It attested that Drolla was Quetono's sole beneficiary. His city villa at Xendurbia, and his entire country estate by Zephth, along with ownership of all other properties, assets and personnel would be transferred into his name. In addition, if he accepted the offer of legal adoption, he would inherit his clan name, his titles of nobility and his position as last heir within the royal family. Quetono grinned at Drolla with contented adoration.

"I hope you do," he whispered.

Drolla sighed. He knelt beside him and took his hand. This noble heart was the parent he never had. He was the parent he should have had. Every moment now counted.

"It's too much," he whispered. A tear ran down his cheek.

The smile fell from Quetono. "Please," his saddened eyes begged Drolla.

"I will."

The smile returned to Quetono, and he faced his fateshield.

"Dandaron, my orphan pride. You are now grown, and your life is now your own." He winked and whispered. "I have left you a mighty fat purse as well."

"Patr', you have already given me everything you ever could. I want nothing more than your good opinion."

"Oh, my dear Krodangan, forever selfless. Your grooming is complete."

Quetono threw an open palm, and a worried eye, to each of them. They clasped his hands, and he pulled them in close. His voice was now urgent.

"Kids. Heed me now. We are all surrounded by treachery. Kith plot against kin. This sham war might well tear royalty apart. Palama, without cause you are now a prince's rival. Dandaron, a false uncle holds an unnatural grudge on you. Drolla, you are now empowered to guard your newfound cousins. They will need it. You three must ally, and pledge to each your fidelity, for good or ill. Vow now before me."

While their young eyes left him and searched each others, the elder quietly closed his. Without a sound, Quetono softly exhaled a smile and passed away.

2.10 - THE ENSLAVED LIBERTY

The wind had settled and the bay was calm once again.

In the permanent dusk, ten thousand smolderstones festooned the length of the esplanade. They sparkled like a ring of stars and shone over many victory celebrations. The Tamzi were defeated. Zintrix would retain its economic independence.

The ships of the Tamzi Kith were at the same time both war craft and merchant vessels. Each member of the crew was a soldier and a trader. Greed and force were their tools of trade. Where one failed the other succeeded. While they preferred to trade, it was far more cost effective, but as a last resort they did not shy away from violent combat. Most of the known world traded with the Tamzi, whether they wanted to or not. The Zintrix did neither.

The nation sat on the north eastern coast of the Krodangan continent and laid due south across the channel from Drahn. They were a proud and self sufficient country, blessed with many natural resources. They mined marble, gems and a strange orange metal found nowhere else. They grew their foods in forests and raised their beasts across the plains. Seafood was harvested from the vast Krodangan Sea. Grasswood and funglstone plantations fed construction. They boasted the only things they imported were foreign bad habits, and they were few.

The Tamzi Kith coveted this independent wealth and they had to have it. Drark vowed to destroy any foreigner who dared to take his possessions. Yes, he deemed all of Zintrix as his own. He was related to every major clan. The cunning fornicator carefully targeted his prosperous allegiances. At each conjugation, he ensured only those who suited his needs seeded him. Drark denied his seeders any natural anonymity, he coerced their obligation to their sporlings. Through his child by them, he wielded his influence over the leaders in every industry across the nation.

The captains of finance, farming, craftsmiths, fishers and ranchers; the soldiery and lawmakers; even the arts and scholars, all paid homage to him. His arrogance modeled himself a modern day Protor. He and his nine children ruled as an executive board. Drark's Tribe was self made, and the self appointed directorship of a nepocratic corporation.

Uncles, nephews and cousins joined by blood and cash. His capital was the city that lined the waterfront of Thoft Bay. His palace, the company headquarters, mounted Drark Island. Linked by guarded ferry, it sat inside the starboard headland of the bay itself. Three great towers hugged the taller, inner tower. From his lofty spire, he supervised his domain. Under his isolationist management, the good people of Zintrix enjoyed a unique freedom and personal prosperity.

The banquet hall was packed to the rafters. Director Drark and his exalted tribe huddled around the central podium. Benches and stools radiated, shoulder to shoulder, out to the walls of the enormous chamber. Polished like mirrors, gleaming copper tablets hung like shields. They were engraved birth certificates merging clans and wealth, and displayed like trophies and admired as such. Coloured banners hung from columns, hallmarked with embroidered emblems of proud clandoms. They reminded those present of Drark's superiority over them. He was not a sovereign, he was the boss.

Course after course of the most exquisite delicacies were laid upon the tables. They were quickly gobbled down by his grateful guests. Not every warrior of the day enjoyed the privilege of Drark's generosity, so those present made the most of it while they could. Endless kegs of sparkling mashwater rolled in, were emptied and rolled back out again. It was the largest and rowdiest berry-den Quetono had ever seen.

The local dancers took turns and entertained the festive masses. Impromtu groups jumped into their own jigs, and often ended in friendly scuffles. Dirty songs and quarrels broke out here and there. Each mob tried to outdo the other. Quetono and his retinue watched the merry ruckus with an uncomfortable awe, but enjoyed it none the less.

As the last of the feathered dancers strutted off to fading drums, a herald called for the orator. The speaker of high renown hushed the audience without a word. He stalled a moment and rounded his gaze on the eager faces. They waited to hear him tell their tale.

"Thrice..." he bellowed, startling the inattentive, "...did the Tamzi tempt our merchants." The orator scowled at his audience. "Corruption was thwarted, bribes were exposed, as were the traitors' innards. No foreign brokers would tax our coffers. Zintrix would be no subsidiary." He paused to allow the grunts of agreement and table slapping die down. "Fortune settled on Zintrix when Drark himself welcomed the Drahni Quetono. An exclusive pact between sovereign friends was struck. We would trade black glass direct, without fee to any Tamzi trader. Forewarned by spies, this insult inflamed the greedy wrath of the islands' Panarch. Thus, the emperor of the Kith recalled his fruitless envoys and assembled his martial navy. Thoft Bay would be his. In this very hall, Drark the magnate consulted Quetono the warrior. Aloof and independent, the gracious Drahni feared no Tamzi penalty and sided with Zintrix. Then he drew his plans to expunge the looming peril."

"Drark's favour knows no bounds," whispered Paraxa under the orator's booming voice. "He treats you like their saviour."

"His people do, but Drark envies my celebrity. Stay close, fateshield. We are safe once home, not before," replied Quetono.

"I cannot leave this rabble soon enough."

"We shall leave once he stamps the damn papers. Bontoro expects a resolution."

"The monarch should have come himself," snarled Paraxa.

"Every light that ringed the bay was put out. Every mouth was hushed, every noise made quiet. Only the sounds of gentle waters lapping at the hulls, and the lazy pennants fluttering in the breeze, broke the cautious silence. Moored sterns of trawlers and ferries and yachts hugged the coastal docks. In hidden silence, their vengeance waited. It was the very image of a barren city, as if all had deserted inland. But the people had not fled, their clemency had.

"Beyond the mouth of the bay, a bright red buoy bobbed alone. A long yellow banner with words scrawled in black greeted the unwelcome invaders. The message it bore floated the heavy hearts of the cautious enemy. *'Zintrix bows down the Tamzi might.'* Relieved, their arrogant folly sank the buoy and into the empty bay they sailed, already triumphant.

"A hundred Tamzi craft teemed about their Panarch's flagship. Two thousand Zintrix boats lit their bow lights. By oar and sail, they sped to the centre of the bay. The ever sparkling shoreline invited a conceited awe. As the lights advanced, their speed did not slow. And while the dupes admired the looming lights, unawares, the enemy corralled themselves. Alarm soon stole their hubris as they madly crowded together. Our local flotilla tightened around them like a trawler's net. All too late, they realised the reception was a trap.

"Mighty prows, lined with copper tusks rammed and smashed the hulls of the outer ships. As they sank, panic crushed the scrambling vessels ever closer. Splintering decks were lashed together into a great undulating pontoon. Juveniles, adults, seniors and elders alike gladly rode Drark's boats into the fray. Forty thousand free citizens stormed the floating battlefield and overwhelmed the desperate Tamzi raiders."

He paused. The listeners were allowed a moment of quiet to reflect on their own participation. The hall was silent. From a whisper, the orator's voice rose to a bellowing crescendo.

"Every hour, twenty rival crews were slaughtered. Cut free, their scuttled ships took them, dead or alive, to the bottom of the bay. In the end, from atop a lone sinking mast, the Panarch of the Tamzi Kith saw his merchant armada was lost. As his flagship too finally sank, he cried foul and shook a cursing fist at Drark's victorious tower. It was over. The merciless depths had swallowed them all."

"If only they had read the message on the buoy properly," roared Drark. The house erupted in hilarious triumph. The old orator curtsied the applause as if it was his, and the riotous party resumed. Drark bounded over to him and pulled him aside. His attendant thrust a jar of mashwater in one hand and a fat, bright copper rod in another.

"Director, you are far too generous."

"I know. But it *was* a wonderful telling. Although, I do think I played a greater part than you portrayed."

"The audience already knows the part you played. They wanted to hear about the Drahni Quetono, and his clever idea."

"Yes. I suppose it was his idea," said Drark. "But, when an oppian bloom stands too tall, it must be pruned."

"Then I shall leave you to your gardening, thyre."

He watched the orator led away and turned to Quetono.

"I have a gift for you."

"Have you stamped the contracts?"

"My secretaries prepare them as we speak. This is something else, something special."

Drark bid his herald call for attention. He pounded his metal sceptre on the marble floor. Three sharp pings echoed throughout the chamber and pierced every conversation.

"The Director calls for silence," he bellowed.

Drark stepped up onto his podium and for a moment, smirked down at Quetono and his staff, before he addressed his people.

"Today, we vanquished our enemy," said Drark. "We owe that victory to our sly friend Quetono." The audience cheered and patted their tables in mutual agreement. "And so, to honour his great favour, Zintrix tradition demands he is rewarded with an even greater boon. A gift-child."

A sporadic round of applause seemed to doubt it was a good idea.

Swaddled in jade silk, a grey babe just four months old was presented to Quetono. He stood like stone in disbelief. When he refused take the bundle, the childminder laid the little thing at his feet.

"What cruel joke is this?" spat Paraxa. "You well know Lord Quetono has lately lost two children. One murdered, the other stillborn."

"Two tragic losses in as many years. I trust this gift-child fares better."

"You what?"

"This babe is my own. My last born. The one you denied me last conjugation, remember?"

"You lecher," growled Quetono. "All you craved was sway with our monarchy. You wished to add Drahn your depraved portfolio. I told you then, we are a pedigree nation. We do not breed with foreigners."

"He still mourns those lost kids," roared Paraxa. "Have you no compassion?"

"So I fucked a cripple instead," yelled Drark. He steadied the contempt in his voice. "A filthy beggar from Gutters Row. It was disgusting, but I got through it. I thought of you, and how you dared spurn me. Me! Your reward for that insult Quetono, is this peasant runt."

The audience hushed like mountains watching a volcano erupting in their midst.

"Director Drark," said Paraxa. "Our presence here during the invasion was a mere coincidence. At the monarch's pleasure, we assisted Zintrix. But we are here to settle our trade accord. We have no use of a child. We thank you for your kind gesture, but we must respectfully decline."

"A gift-child is a sacred Zintrix custom. It is a selfless act, a blessing from the fertile to the barren. It cannot be declined," crooned Drark.

"We don't want the damned thing," snapped Paraxa.

Half a dozen long green velvet cloaks trailed into the chamber, shadowed by an armed security escort of deep maroon ponchos. Tall poleaxes ringed the secretaries and Drark's podium like a picket fence.

One placed a tall table in front of Quetono. Another laid out scribbling utensils, while a third placed parchments onto the table.

"Oh, how opportune," said Drark. "My clerks."

He stepped from the podium and grasped his legal seal. His mark, three circles clustered around a middle fourth, embossed the butt of a copper stamp. The lid of an inkpad flipped open and he pressed the seal onto it. He paused with his fist in the air, red ink dripped like blood. His brazen eyes burnt into Quetono's scowling face. He was unmoved by the threat. Paraxa fell to his knees, scooped up the sleeping babe, and passed it to the nearest shardhand.

"Vindra, take this. And do not drop it."

The soldier held the bundle like an overripe spikemelon. The awkward Drahni soldier drew childish giggles from a few of the tipsy onlookers. Drark still stared at Quetono. Without taking his eyes off him, he pounded each page as the secretary ripped them away, one after the other. Once done, they collected their effects and the secretaries vanished as fast as they had appeared.

"Excellent," said Drark. "Business is always a pleasure. Enjoy your gift. His name is Dandaron."

The maroon security team formed up to escort Drahn out. As his small group left the silent hall, the crowd slowly stood and applauded Quetono. Sad faces empathised with him. They too, had all felt his humiliation. They too, had suffered the inescapable coercion of their mighty Director. Their applause admired the noble Drahni. They cheered how he dared to snub their Director's familial influence. No one else had ever done so before. Drark held no blood ties over Drahn and the gift-child prank was an insult to a solemn tradition. Their praise was genuine and lasted long after their guests had left. Drark screamed at this unexpected display of sedition from his disloyal ingrates.

"The feast is over. Everybody out."

Four days had passed since Quetono exhaled his last. In utter darkness, Drolla soaked alone. His squad mates were gone and the chambers were empty. The janitors had already been through the rooms. Every mat, rug and quilt was rolled and stacked aside. The tub had been cleaned and the bathwater refreshed. All the food was gone, except for a lone jar of spicy nutclusters. There was nowhere he could think his mates might be, they were just not here. He decided he was glad of it, time was needed to ponder his tragic losses, and his opulent gains.

Dandaron sent a courier with news of Pondra. The morticians had embalmed him, and Klordra had shut up shop. He had begun his trek to return his uncle Pondra to his forest home in Xylla. He would get his wish too late. Xindro was still comatose, luckily. Across the Pen, dread and excitement awaited his recovery. His fury and lust for revenge was expected to be epic. Especially since Vondaka had declared Fontaza a person inviolate. It was presumed such an edict would be completely ignored by the grieving grandchild.

Drolla mourned both elders. But he was now all cried out. He could not farewell Pondra, so he focused his attention on Quetono. Today he would farewell his benefactor, his seed-parent, his liberator. He could not comprehend the wealth and status he had been granted. He could not appreciate how this could have come to him. Not too long ago, he owned nothing. Now he possessed more wealth than his own clan, and he outranked his own par' as well.

Quetono was two years younger than his own grandpar'. Brokka always brought him firm comfort and Drolla wished he was here. *What would he think of me now?* he wondered. Wait. Realisation blazed like a sun bursting from behind a rolling cloud. They had known all along. His par' had kept this secret from him all his life. Drolla now understood why Hlammi hated him so much. His gritted teeth seethed with fury at the cruel injustice inflicted upon him by his own birth-parent.

"That slut punished me!" His wrath slapped the spa water. As he blinked away the splash from his eyes, he vowed they were the last tears he would ever shed.

"Thank you, officers," said Dandaron. He dismissed the enforcers sent to escort Drolla to the funeral pavilion. Every alley buzzed with throngs of mourners heading to the arena, he was glad of the official company. Every shop and outlet were closed. The streets around the edge of the arena were packed with the camp's civilians. Without the enforcers clearing a path, Drolla may not have been able to push his way through. The arena itself was filled to overflow with soldiers of every rank. Everyone of them squatted with silent respect.

"So many mourners," whispered Drolla.

"By Vondaka's command," Dandaron muttered just as quietly. "Any found absent would find themselves buried alive outside the Pen. The enforcers are scouring the suburbia as we speak."

Only Fontaza heard them.

"There is one still missing," he snarled from the back of his hand.

"Laugh while you can, coward. You know you are doomed," said Dandaron.

"Quiet," spat Vondaka. "Nephew, must these peasants stand with us?" The monarch ignored him and nodded to Glendoro.

"Quetono's instructions demanded it," the fateshield answered.

Soltoro smiled quietly to himself as Vondaka swallowed his indignant pride. The monarch admired the weather. The sun stained the underside of the overcast sky like orange wool. It threatened rain, and the air was alive and fresh.

"It looks as though it might drizzle soon," said Soltoro.

"I hope it hails," said Vondaka. His sour eyes darted to Fontaza's agreeable smirk.

The short stout Soltoro sighed and stepped back from the edge of the awning. He flapped the folds of his teal velvet robe until they hung just right. Tied around his middle was a sash of fine woven glass fibre. Waves of different hues rippled across it when he moved. The electric air of the impending storm bristled up his mohair mantle. The fine, white hairs danced in the air like gossamer. The more he tried to smooth them down, the more the static frizzed them up.

Vondaka cast a glare of disdain at his mighty leader's unmanageable clothes. He wore a stone grey tunic that wrapped his torso and left his legs bare. Loin flaps with edges embroidered in red and gold silk hung between his thighs. He calmly petted his grizzled blue fur stole. Palama stood apart from his cousin and par', as was his custom from years past. The black feathers of his mantle sagged over his shoulders, and his damp, scarlet toga clung to him like a second skin.

Before them, a crater of sand surrounded the grave. A deep circular hole, bricked like a well, awaited its permanent resident. A hexagon slab, as wide as one could reach, stood by the shrouded crane. The stone was embossed with Quetono's cartouche.

Vondaka signaled to the herald. The war horn blew long and forlorn. Quiet mutterings shushed like passing drizzle across the multitude. He stepped forward and held the spear up high. It's faded, tattered strip of cloth hung still in the breathless arena.

"Not long ago," said Vondaka, "we vowed once recovered, the noble Quetono would pull this lance himself. To our endless sorrow, that will never be. Today, he is farewelled and will rest forever on this spot." He yanked the dull grey cloth aside. It slid off the crane and revealed Quetono's coffin, a huge glass jar. Bound and squatting, his arms held his knees to his chest. He floated in the translucent emerald fluid, preserved forever. A buoyant ruff held his head in place face up.

A sad queasiness overcame Drolla. Despite his vow, his welling eyes threatened to spill. He dabbed them dry inside his elbow, collected himself and stood as a proud heir might. Dandaron however, could not hide his sodden face.

Soltoro mounted his regal podium and gave his eulogy. He congratulated the syblings on their affection of the noble Quetono. Only true admiration and respect could drive so many to attend his mortal farewell. He extoled Quetono's great history in less detail than expected. Royal sibling. Uncle to the nation, drafter to the royal army, foreign trade master, hero of the Zintrix war. President of the Consultorium. Today he joins his peers, those martial heroes who predeceased him. Under the orange sand, their noble tombs honeycomb the arena. He will squat here, forever looking up to his beloved warriors. Like croaking toads across a swamp, the army grunted their approval. The monarch puffed out his chest, proud of his speech and glad they had all concurred.

Glendoro held a hand to Soltoro to steady himself as he stepped down from the podium. Palama took his place and paused to scan the ocean of tired faces. He saw his target audience and turned to them alone. He slowly raised his arms, when they dropped, he slapped his thighs.

"Horde of Orienna," he bellowed. A thousand deep voices chanted their reply.

"Behold the horde."

"The grandest Drahni ever known, rests eternal here today," he said. "Great was he, who pulled us all from our very homes and set us on our path. He tore us from our clans and formed us into his own. He led us together, and dragged us across plains and mountains and rivers. He tired with us, he hungered with us. He laughed with us. He rolled fat and drunk with us in the shade of the mighty Vein. He suffered with us and he rejoiced with us. He brought us here to become warriors of Drahn. To fight for our lands and for our wealth. While he cannot finish his noble task, in his name, we will honour our pledge and go to war under his banner." Every body of the Orienna Horde stood at once. The audacity of their cheers and applause surprised all around them. They cared little for decorum, a thousand loyals cheered their Commander Palama and saluted their Uncle Quetono. He let them rail for a time before he raised his arms to quiet them. The toll of the glass tubular bell echoed its solemn knell around the arena. The morticians' crane set about lowering Quetono into his tomb.

Palama led the mourners in the Funereal Hymn.

The way of life, is we all must die.
From lust we're born, from our parents torn.
Then bid to thrive, not just survive.
We pass each age, from fool to sage.

Spawn from within, the desire for kin.
Brings children forth, from south to north.
The clans doth grow, above and below.
From young to old, let our lives be told.

And when death nears, hold your grieving tears.
For time is short, fate's cord pulls taut.
Recall the cheer, that was shared each year.
Those gone before, remembered ever more.

As the headstone slab laid and sealed Quetono forever, Vondaka mounted the podium. He thanked the warriors and civilians for their attendance. To toast his memory, the brew-bars and berry-dens would offer free rounds till the end of the third hour. The clouds finally fell. Without a word of thanks, the babbling crowd quickly disappeared into the rain and filtered back into suburbia.

"Open bars? Very generous," said Soltoro.

"Quetono's new heir will pay the bill," hissed Vondaka.

The gentry left the funeral awning under a canopy of umbrellas. Their attendants escorted them back to the monarch's pavilion. Heavy rain began to fall on the deserted arena. Soon, the funeral marquee was cloaked with pouring rain.

"Your family has left without you, prince," said Dandaron.

"They are not my family."

Right now, on this sodden day, he would have preferred his lonely stink to this crowded woe. This was not the pace of life he expected. He squatted on his haunches, and put his face in his palms.

Dandaron broke his statuesque stance and sat beside Drolla.

"Alone, at last."

"Yes," smiled Drolla. "Poor Quetono." Dandaron frowned sideways at Drolla. There was a long faraway pause before Dandaron broke the awkward silence.

"Before Paraxa retired, he transferred his vow and oathbound me to Quetono. I became his fateshield." Dandaron stared at the sand. Lightning flashed and lit the thundering rain. A lone tear ran down his face. "Some fateshield I am. Paraxa would never have left him unguarded." He drooped his head and his shoulders bobbed a little. He sighed deep. "He has watched over me since I can remember, and I was not there when it mattered most."

"Don't damn yourself. Quetono knew what happened. You are blameless. The assassins took him from us."

The grief fell from Dandaron's face. There was a tone of futility in his shaking voice.

"Pat'r waited years for you. You were to be his hero. His Paladin's Bode."

"How did he know about me?" asked Drolla. "Half my clan don't even know about me."

"Quetono received welfare reports about you for years. How you were, what you were like. That Tamzi trader Vrune was a good merchant, but he was a better spy."

"Vrune?"

"When I was about twelve, I found his hidden letters. Patr' caught me reading them. He told me who you were and why you mattered. From then on we read them together, in secret."

"I never knew a thing."

"He hated the life you had and vowed to do right by you."

"How did you come to him?" asked Drolla.

"Adopted from Krodanga, they said. But, I don't remember. I was too little. I do remember he wept and vowed to never desert me again. I didn't know he had. I grew up in the Waif's Lodge. Palama was there, and he was my only friend. After that, patr' sponsored me through the Enforcer's College. He paid for everything. Every Conjugation and Pannatalia was spent at his country estate, away from everyone."

"Why?"

"Vondaka insisted, 'I'll not have that alien polluting our sacred celebrations.' Paraxa was always with us. His training groomed me to one day take his place. I owe everything to Quetono."

"I think he did a fine job raising you. He was proud of you. You heard him, you are free to live your own life now."

"Don't be ridiculous."

"Why? You can do whatever you like now. You have earned your freedom."

"Freedom? There is no such thing. No one is free," said Dandaron.

"Not even the monarch? He has more freedom than anyone."

"He has none. He serves everyone else. His life is not his own, you know. No one's life is their own. Parent, child. Thyre, thrall. Monarch, subject. We all serve someone."

"Master, slave," added Drolla. "Once I thought so too. But after this war, when I am rid of the army, I will never serve anyone ever again. I won't have to, Quetono's inheritance has promised that."

"You have no idea, do you granger?" said Dandaron.

"What do you mean?"

"You might have his titles, his wealth and his property, but you have all his reliants as well."

"His what?"

"His staff. There is over a hundred of them, all on ageless contracts."

"What are they for?"

"They manage the estates. Domestics, gardeners, craftsmen, clerks and the like," said Dandaron. "You might think twice about surviving this war now." He laughed at Drolla staring into a blinding insight. He had been blessed with a great prize with a greater cost.

"I wouldn't know how. You deserve his inheritance more than I do."

"I can't. I'm a foreigner. He was my patron not my parent."

"Dandaron, I know Quetono released you, but I need your guidance. Please, pledge yourself as my agent. I need you, the reliants need you. Name your price."

"I am no shardhire, Drolla. Old Paraxa oversees the estate for now. In honour of patr', I pledge you my protection and vow to shield your fate as Quetono's heir."

"Until either releases the other," added Drolla. Dandaron frowned and shook his head smiling.

They clasped each other's hands, cementing their new pact. The comfort of a sunny breeze settled over Drolla. This was good. He had never feared for his life before, yet now he had his own fateshield forever guarding his wellbeing. This is how the elite are so arrogant, there is always someone else to fight their battles for them. Drolla was now one of them, one of those he despised. This world was still too big for him, he needed Dandaron more than anyone.

Thick fingers curled gently around his skinny hand as it rested lightly in the giant's palm. Dandaron gave it a tender squeeze. Not a firm handshake that greeting soldiers would share, nor how merchants closed a sale. Drolla knew what this meant. He looked up and saw the gaze you should only see at Conjugation. Yet Dandaron had never been to one, and they were not at one now. He saw feelings that were natural, innocent and forbidden. For a moment, there was a glimmer of mutual affection. Dandaron snapped his hand back and shot to his feet. He smoothed imaginary wrinkles in his toga and paused as if to speak. He didn't. The rain had stopped and sunbeams streaked from behind the broken clouds. Dandaron nodded an awkward farewell and trotted off across the sodden sand.

PART THREE
OXXIA

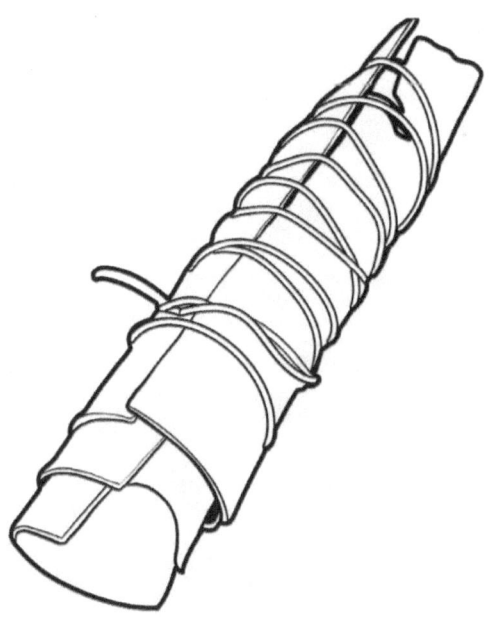

3.0 - THE AVID LETHARGY

A gentle rapping on the chamber dintel broke Palama from his shallow meditation.

It was a welcome interruption. Again, his mind had wandered again down an ugly path. Lately, whenever he sought the serenity of solitude, or respite from his tiresome duties, all manner of fears and worries rose from his subconscious to torment him. His soul forever fretted for the well-being of his twin children, Tindara and Nolana. He hoped they were well cared for at the Lodge, but had heard nothing from them. No letters or reports awaited him on his return from Orienna. Even during the frenetic times of a nation preparing for war, not all the couriers were commandeered by the military. In his half-woken dream, he scolded himself. Even though his court martial caseload kept him overworked, he had not written either.

He struck a stone to light the room as the curtain to his chamber slowly swept open. A small frame politely stepped in and let it fall gently behind him. He hid his dimming smolderstone within the folds of his gown. The uninvited guest was draped in plain travel clothes that seem to hide him in plain sight. After a curtsied greeting, he introduced himself in a soft tone.

"Pardon my intrusion, thyre. My name is Honkro, I am a personal messenger from Paraxa."

"Paraxa? Estate manager for Quetono?" asked Palama.

"The same. He sends his most deepest condolences and mourns the tragic loss of your noble uncle. He trusts the great Commander Palama is well. He asks after Dandaron and requests you might offer him his sympathies as well. He hopes to see him safe home after the conflict."

"Perhaps you should address him yourself. He may feel slighted," said Palama.

"Alas, that is not my errand, thyre. I am only permitted to contact you. He begs you receive Quetono's documents. He is confident you will execute his probate and lodge them into the Consultorium Archives at your earliest convenience."

"Why is he not present himself?"

"His official reason not to attend the funeral in person, is that he is too infirmed to travel."

"His real reason?"

"He fears he would be intercepted and remanded."

"By whom?"

"The chancellor."

"Ridiculous."

"It is a opinion he holds with deep conviction. He sent me incognito to avoid any suspicion. I am to deliver, to you personally, a small cache of private correspondence. You are advised to read them alone."

"Why?"

"He trusts you may find meaning in them, thyre. He believes they may hold answers to some mystery around Vondaka."

"How so?"

"I have no idea, thyre. That is your task to decipher, I'm afraid."

Palama scratched ink onto a small paperbark scroll.

"Take this coupon and enjoy some leisure in the civic sector. A tavern's bath and a meal."

"Thank you thyre, but no. I must not dally. I cannot be seen here. I shall sneak away directly."

"Well then, tell Paraxa I thank him for the papers. I will give them my immediate attention." The courier curtsied with a hand over his heart and rose to leave. "By the way, how did you get past all the sentries?" asked Palama.

"Everyone is celebrating Quetono's memory," he grinned. "The halls are as empty as the taverns are full. No one noticed this old beige-fellow stealing through the shadows."

He then departed as silently as he arrived.

Palama placed Quetono's bequeath aside. The satchel was a white leather barrel, a forearm high and a palm wide. The finest sheets of grasswood pulp stood scrolled and packed like pickled snakefish. There was no immediate hurry to settle the probate. He clipped the lid shut and looked to the bundle of secret correspondence. He untied a thin leather thong that bound the fine chamois wrap. Swathed within the little parcel, paperback scrolls were rolled each within another. He peeled them apart and perused the titles. Each laid in chronological order, across four years.

"These are twenty-odd years old, and all addressed to uncle," he muttered.

For: Commander Quetono.

By: Dean Tikolo.

May I congratulate you on your successful recent venture in Zintrix.

Your mighty exploits preceded your return. While some may call you the accidental war lord, I know the only fluke involved was your presence there. Your brilliant military mind conceived the winning strategy that mere shopkeepers carried out.

"I remember you Dean Tikolo," growled Palama. "Ever the shameless flatterer."

Your mercantile mastery has seen the royal subsidy to the Lodge increase more than we could have ever hoped. For that alone the League of Barren Uncles are eternally grateful. I am happy to inform you that Drark's gift-child sent here under your patronage, has been formally enrolled. Being five months old he has joined the baby's creche under the attentive care of the nursing staff.

Every effort will be made to comfort and educate the child. It has been made clear to all involved that even though he is a foreigner, he must be treated as a native and a ward of the state. You can expect future reports on his progress.

Palama took the second letter in Paraxa's list.

For: Commander Quetono.
By: Dean Tikolo.
Please accept the following reports on the progress of your Zintrix child.

At fourteen months old, the infant is of a sickly nature. His body is weak, he is developing slowly. He cannot feed himself properly and has not yet grasped toiletry. Often he has acute attacks of shyness and during his bouts of endless sobbing, he is completely inconsolable. His language skills are wanting and it is very difficult to communicate with him. We have him in the best of care with a dedicated nurse to act as surrogate sole parent, but there is just no bond forming at all. We cannot understand such severe alienation, unless it is his Krodangan nature. Despite this, we shall persevere with tenderness in the hopes Dandaron can be encouraged to grow.

"Dandaron?" said Palama.
He took the third letter with a piqued interest.

For: Commander Quetono.
By: Dean Tikolo.
Despite our best efforts, Dandaron refuses to interact with the other children.

He is now two and a half years old and just started talking. Nothing more than monosyllables. The child is far behind his fellows of the same age. He is defiant and refuses to participate in any other activities. He spends most days bedridden as his body is weak and under developed. We suspect he is smarter than he acts, but he is happy to let us think him an idiot so he might be excused from any normal interaction. To this end, we fear his health is declining. The medics have him on various tonics and elixirs. While we are doing everything in our power to keep him healthy, his condition continually deteriorates. I will notify you of any changes in the future.

For: Commander Quetono.
By: Dean Tikolo.
It is with profound distress that I am obliged to inform you that Dandaron has taken a turn for the worse.

Despite excellent care for the past year and a half since my last report, he has continually regressed and finally lapsed into a coma. It seems Drark's gift-child has given up on life itself. The medics expect him to die within days.

Counselor Vondaka is due tomorrow and insists there is no need for you to attend. It would be a wasted journey. We have couriers on standby for any urgent messages we may need to send. Please await further correspondence.

"What?"

For: Governor Quetono.
By: Dean Bomaka.
Congratulations on your elevation to Governor of Munika Province.

We are most relieved that the Lodge is now within your personal jurisdiction. Thank you for my appointment as Dean after the execution of Tikolo. It was gratifying that his crimes of corruption and neglect did not go unpunished. Counselor Vondaka's response was rapid and firm. All of the relevant staff involved in the fiasco of Dandaron's supposed death, have either been suicided or disappeared.

Rest assured, Dandaron is still as healthy and sensible as we found him on your arrival. The relief and joy finding him alive and well was in stark contrast to the expectation of bidding his corpse farewell. I have studied his file in detail. The records of his health and deathly decline are quite perplexing. His instant recovery seems miraculous and his demeanor is almost as if he were a different person.

"You know, you really should get your own fateshield. They are extremely handy."

Vondaka handed a smolderstone to Fontaza. Within the long narrow corridor, his voice was stifled into a harsh whisper, like an echo that never returned. His friendly mood was unsettling. Vondaka seldom made small talk. Nothing he ever said was without cause or rehearsal. Perhaps he still gloated over the death of Pondra, or his grief for Quetono had faded, if he ever had any. Either way, his cheery demeanor meant he considered himself in total control.

In single file, Fontaza led the shuffling parade. He held the smolderstone high and lit the narrow tunnel ahead. He wheezed and rasped like a corpsefly buzzing back and forth through the pool of light. The fool strutted as if his altruism was like some enticing perfume. In truth, his obedience stank like an unwashed servant. Palama trailed a few steps behind, just beyond the slavish pong.

"I do not need security," said Palama.

He never socialised, and seldom appeared in public. The only free time he enjoyed was spent with his kids. His twins were the only joy worth living for. When he wasn't in the justice halls, he was with them. Every day between chores they picnicked together in the shaded maze of their private gardens. Sitting on grass at leisure was always better than squatting on marble in judgement.

"Surely some defendants have threatened violence now and then?"

"More often from their relatives, vowing revenge. It never mattered, anonymity has been my best protector."

"And the courtroom constables," said Fontaza with a sneer.

"See? Everyone needs a guardian." Vondaka chuckled with a hint scorn.

"If you are suggesting I oathbind a fateshield like Fontaza, I would rather do without," said Palama. Fontaza sniggered and shrugged.

"It is fitting for a person of your rank," said Vondaka. "You are a public figure now. A Commander of the Draft. Military magistrate. Cousin to the monarch. A royal successor."

"Par', stop. Your exaggeration stinks of ambition."

"Does it? Better than the stench of sloth. When you return to the city, you will need a fateshield beside you. Master Glendoro will assign you an enforcer. Someone suitable, someone robust."

"Dandaron is now free," said Fontaza.

Palama stopped dead in his tracks. "What. Return?"

"I have Miokhi ambassadors secreted throughout the capital, I need you to ensure the prince does not discover them."

"We are on the eve of war and you harbour enemy spies?"

"They are my spies. I have already secured you a position within the palace. Prince Diltoro suspects nothing."

"I will not be a spy," Palama hissed.

"Shush now. We shall discuss it later. We are there."

At the end of the corridor, the funglstone door was closed. Fontaza slid a bolt and pulled the top toward them. Light from the chamber poured in under the door as it swung open. Palama followed Vondaka as he quietly stooped under it. They were in the monarch's hall.

The skylight shone a narrow spot onto the central podium. The black sandstone shell of the dome was lined with smolderstones clustered into chandeliers. Dainty chains of Zintrix copper hung from each. Glendoro, fateshield to the monarch and master of the enforcers watched a striker wander the hall. Each chain he pulled, threw down pools of light and lit the place bit by bit.

"Ow. Must you prod there?" said the monarch. His doctor ignored the complaint.

"I am happy with your recovery," said Torono pressing his fingers into Soltoro's groin.

"Your elixirs are as potent as they are delicious."

"The toxins are now flushed from you, but you must keep to the diet. No more potions, they will only do you harm."

"Shame. My guts are boiling like whitefire." He burped.

"A scar from the poison, I cannot heal that. Try this shalewater, it will soothe the burn." The monarch snatched the vessel and swigged it down. Vondaka stepped from the shadowed wall that skirted the hall beyond the light's reach. Torono handed him another, "Gargle and spit. Freshen your breath."

Soltoro did as he was bid. He turned his head aside and spat into a cloth. He spied his hidden audience.

"How long have you been there, eavesdroppers?"

"I do apologise thyre. I was not aware this meeting was double booked," said Vondaka.

Torono huffed and packed away his satchel. Soltoro flared at his chancellor's impudence. After his wrist wiped his mouth, the monarch roared.

"You are early. And unannounced. Why did you sneak in through the toilet door?"

"Palama accompanied me, thyre. His rooms are on the way here."

"You housed him near the shitpits?" He scowled down at Vondaka.

"Not so near."

"I should not be surprised. It is in keeping with his treatment over the past two decades."

"Thank you, thyre." The crooning Vondaka again inflamed Soltoro.

"That was not a compliment!"

The thundering monarch took a moment to calm himself. During the pause, their attention was stolen as another attendee entered the hall.

With head held high and a straightened back, an old soldier strode into the hall like a statue. Sinewy knuckles wrapped his pommel and held it ever forward. The shimmering deep blue folds of his toga rippled

224

like water as he floated across the white glass floor. He approached the plynth and curtsied Throthm's salute.

"Welcome Lord Zonara. I don't suppose you have met my cousin Palama," said the monarch. "He is our royal magistrate."

The old soldier was second in command of the military, only the monarch ranked above him. As such, he was lord of Churon's Pen. Zonara was in his mid-fifties and should have retired a decade ago. It was his well-known opinion that he had not yet found a suitable successor. Until then, he determined to remain supervisor of the national army. His tall solid physique was as intimidating as his demeanor. He commanded with a marble fist, yet charmed with a feathered palm.

"General Zonara, your reputation is a credit to you. It is an honour to meet you in person," said Palama.

"And you arbiter," said Zonara. "If only it were in better, peaceful times."

"If it were, none of us would be here," said Soltoro.

"Are there any others to attend this surprise meeting?" asked Vondaka.

"No. Who were you expecting?" Soltoro did not wait for an answer and moved his attention to his cousin. "Palama, I have misjudged you. Despite your seniocratic sympathies, your fidelity to the realm is proved. You emptied my prisons and filled the arena. I see now why they kept you hid away in the city courts. I have read the writs, your craft served us well cousin. You have my gratitude."

Palama curtsied and craned his neck. His eyes glistened and his heart hammered. It was incredible. At last, the tingling sense of final acknowledgment crawled up his spine. It pushed his head even higher. He welcomed the royal favour from his humbled kin.

"Stand up cousin," said Soltoro. "You do not curtsey today."

"The soldiery thank you as well," said Zonara.

"Palama," said Soltoro. "I visited our uncle before he died. He enlightened me regarding your virtues. Your actions have proved him right. So, as amends to our past animosity, I wish to reward you. Name your prize."

"I would ask you reinstate me as commander of the Orienna Horde."

"Thyre," interrupted Vondaka. "Quetono holds no sway now. Palama is to return to the palace. Do you forget our agreement?"

"I did not forget, nor did I agree. You did all that."

"Cousin," said Palama. "You said once we might bend the bond I had with my recruits. Do you now mean to break it?"

"Would you not prefer the comforts of the city?" asked Zonara.

"Once I might have, but I will not desert my recruits now they are soldiers. I wish to fight this war with them."

"Well said. Quetono's legion is yours," said Soltoro.

He and Zonara shared a nodding grin.

"Poh, this is intolerable," said Vondaka. "So much cannot be undone."

"Would you prefer to return to the palace and take his place?" asked Soltoro.

"My place is by your side," said Vondaka.

"Aren't I blessed," said Soltoro. "Sort the details, will you?" He paused and sighed. "I do miss uncle Quetono. His advice was always clear and unbiased." He cast a dour glance at his uncle.

"He deserted everything to chase some long lost slut-spawn bastard," said Vondaka. "He was a fool to name that village idiot his heir."

"Spare us your malice, Chancellor. By rights, Drolla should be here in his pater's stead. He is now his legal heir. Zonara, where is the recruit now?" said Soltoro.

"I do not know, thyre. After his arrest, his squad was disbanded. He has not been seen since the funeral. Fret not, he shall be found."

"Perhaps he is with Dandaron," said Palama.

"Another bastard," Vondaka spat through gritted teeth.

"How soon before the army marches?" asked Soltoro, ignoring his uncle's spite.

"They are ready now," said Zonara.

"Good. Palama go to your legion. Vondaka, find Dandaron and Quetono's Heir. They will accompany us on the Monarch's Yacht. I wish to become acquainted with my new cousin."

"Soltoro, I strongly advise against it," said Vondaka.

"Do you?" roared Soltoro. "In that case, I am even more willing to meet him. Make the arrangements, we sail forthwith."

Palama stared at a lifeless Xindro. His brow was bruised black and swollen still. Spread flat, his body laid awkward. His head lay in a sling like a netted melon. He was perched on two slumped shoulders behind, his front arm rested in his lap. From his bony hips, useless legs tapered to three limp feet. His limbs lay alongside him, not under him. The pose was unnatural. Only the dead fell prone. Alert or resting, standing or squatting, one is always upright. Yet here before him, Drahn's mightiest shardster lay sideways.

Draped white, Palama blended incognito on the arena that day. Quietly mingling with his horde, he was caught in the crush of spectators scrambling to witness Xindro dance his murderous waltz. Palama remembered condemning those criminals weeks earlier. They were vile, unrepentant and got what they deserved. The bloody performance was a pleasure to watch. Afterwards, while he received his secret visitor and the cryptic letters, the crowded berry-dens cheered Xindro for hours. He heard later of the drunken tales, the shardster's prowess rendered him near immortal. Yet here he lay, as still as a corpse. Palama called his name and shook a shoulder, but there was no response. Had Pondra's secret cost Xindro his life as well?

"He has not moved since we laid him here," said a shadowed voice. Its owner stepped into the light and dipped a shallow curtsy. His jade kilt hung around him as rigid as his tone.

"You've been here all along?" asked Palama.

"We share the watch. Dandaron assigned his most trusted officers."

"He looks dead."

"He may as well be," the enforcer grunted. "We talk to him non-stop. The nurses feed him broth and take his shit, but nothing changes. It has been so long, we doubt he will ever recover."

"An hour ago, one of your peers sent me here. 'Imperative', he insisted. Would you know why?" asked Palama.

"I could not guess." The guard shrugged off his feeble fib.

Torono slapped the drapes aside and strode into the room. The enforcer snapped to attention at the doctor's sudden arrival. An elder followed at a milder pace. Light grey, the fine woolen cloth loosely coiled his elderly stature. His tired frame mismatched the life in his eyes. They widened and smiled at the sight of Palama. With a tilt of the doctor's head, the enforcer shuffled to the doorway.

He paused to advise Palama. "I am just outside Commander, if you need me."

"Good," spat Torono, "and keep everyone else out while you're at it."

"Your service is appreciated," said the elder.

The enforcer nodded his regard to the elder's kind words before he slipped through the doorway.

"I was sent to see Xindro, but I think I am too late," said Palama.

"Nonsense, he's not dead," said Torono, "are you butcher?"

He gently patted a thigh. The skin flinched at his touch. The elder pointed a palm at the patient, inviting Palama to inspect him closer. He leaned in and smelled Xindro's breath. It was stale and it was shallow, but it was there. He was alive.

"Does he doze?" asked Palama.

"I doubt he is even dreaming," said Torono.

"Then, where is he?"

"Who knows. I have not used Vraxroot Oil before, it's a potent sedative. This is the first time I have ever had to fake a death."

"You mean he is drugged?"

"Of course he is. By order of Vondaka. In fact, he demanded Xindro should never recover."

Palama stared in disbelief. The elder nodded his agreement with Torono.

" 'Be sure the Oxxian never wakes.' I was forbidden to revive him. Well, Xindro does not sleep and you are going to rouse him, not me."

"My colleagues insist Xindro lives. Drahn is in great need of him," said the elder.

"I cannot believe this. Par' wouldn't..."

"Spare us your pretended outrage," spat Torono. "Your parent has you fooled."

"Torono, Palama really has no idea. His lifetime of isolation has left him ignorant of politics and intrigue. That is why he is perfect."

"As you say. I have no time to debate the matter. Now look," he held up an empty phial, "this will render Xindro conscious again. Pop the lid between his lips. Make sure he inhales the gas. After a few moments, he will be quite sensible but still unable to move." Torono handed Palama a second ampule, tinted pale green and filled with a fizzy liquid. "Once he drinks this, the paralysis will wane within the hour."

"Thank you, Doctor. Your efforts are well appreciated," said the elder.

"Glad to play my small part. I wish the elders every success."

The elder and the doctor clasped palms and nodded their mutual esteem. Torono disappeared through the drapes. Fading along the corridor, his loud haughty voice scolded the enforcer.

"Do not interrupt the commander, and let no one else enter."

"Hoh!" The enforcer barked his compliance.

A faint, throaty grunt came from Xindro. Palama turned to face him, but he was motionless. He looked at the vials in his palm.

"Wait," said the elder. "Not yet."

"Why not?"

"It is imperative we talk."

"You called me here. Who are you?"

"My name is Bendro. I am Vice-President of the Consultorium. I was elected after Krantolo's promotion. Quetono's resignation sparked a series of events that could well ruin Drahn."

"My uncle had nothing to do with it. War was already declared."

"You misunderstand me, young thyre. The war itself is the very distraction the usurpers are exploiting."

"If you mean the conspiracy of Prince Diltoro, the monarch and chancellor already know."

"They think they do."

"Explain yourself," said Palama.

"Thank you. While the monarch prepares his army at Churon's Pen, the prince and President Krantolo began their campaign of coercion within the capital. In the name of funding Soltoro's war, tax increases penalised their opponents while exemptions rewarded their supporters. Now the promise of stricter policies concern many of the Doyen Assembly. Their kin within the Protorian Guard have kept the clan leaders well informed."

"As they should," said Palama.

"True. But, the prince has formed a City Marshalry. The ranks of this new regal militia is filled with bought traitors, petty felons and the idle. All the worst sort. As soon as the army departs for Oxxia, the prince will impose his personal police force. The Protorian Guard are already confined to the palace surrounds. Soon, they will be disbanded."

"Without the clan's firstborn embedded within the palace, the doyens would lose their leverage with the monarchy," said Palama.

"Royal power would shift into the sole hands of Diltoro. He is weak, and without any allies the prince will succumb to Krantolo's ambitions. He has already deserted his presidential duties and plays mock-regent. He means to make himself tyrant."

"This is all very serious, but it is a matter for the senior citizenry. You do realise the monarch's army is on the eve of war?"

"Of course, nothing can be done till after that. But if the east and west rise together they will thrust all of Drahn into a civil conflict. The noble folk of the capital states need to suffer tyranny firsthand before they would even entertain the idea of an uprising. There is a groundswell of support that favours a return to the seniocracy, and it grows each day.

"The Oxxian provincials are tired of the Munikans' regality. They are sick of being lorded over by royal entitlement. The Mezzini Province tags along like a groveling younger sibling, desperate to be part of the loyal entourage. In the east, they watch Krantolo's salt farms stretch along their coast. Orienna has not yet openly pledged any allegiance, except to itself."

"Vice-President, this stinks of sedition," said Palama.

"It does," said Bendro. "That's why we need a member of the royal family who supports our cause." The elder paused and his glassy eyes cut right through Palama and stabbed at his very soul.

"Me? You cannot be serious."

"Young thyre, you are not as anonymous as you might think. You are a very well respected arbiter and your seniocratic sympathies are known to those who care to notice."

"Soltoro is the monarch. When he returns ahead of his army, he will exert his royal power and quell any usurpers." Palama stared his meaning into Bendro.

"If he returns. If he doesn't, we must be ready. Diltoro and his marshals will be. My colleagues have chosen you as sovereign."

"You old fools have gone senile."

"Perhaps. But, we are not wrong. The stability of the monarchy must be maintained. Diltoro intends to upend it. You are royal blood and we are sure you are no tyrant."

"You have the wrong person," said Palama.

"No we don't. There is no one else. Revive Xindro and oathbind him as your fateshield. He is the champion of Oxxia. With me as President and Xindro as commander of the provincial armies, we would aid you as monarch."

"This sounds like a western takeover. It has to be the most insane and treasonous plot I have ever heard. I cannot be a party to this."

"Yes," Bendro sighed, "some said you might decline. I am disappointed, but it will not slow our mission. Please think on it. For now, revive Xindro, he will see you true."

"I would welcome Xindro as my fateshield. By his desire, not yours."

Palama flipped the lid as Xindro inhaled. His eyes popped open and his lungs gurgled. He coughed and spat.

"Phap me, at last." He blurted so loud his voice broke. He coughed and spat again. Through heaving breaths he yelled. "I have been awake. The whole, phapping time."

Palama and Bendro burst in to laughter.

"Have you heard everything we said?" asked Bendro.

"I have heard every phapping word said since they laid me here. Palama, pour that fizz into me now. Please. Drord's Guts, what a nightmare. The guards never, ever shut up." He swigged the antidote in one gulp. "Water."

Bendro gently held the carafe and Xindro chugged the vessel dry. Slowly, the pace of his breath evened.

"Welcome back, young champion," said the elder.

Xindro eyed Bendro.

"Thank you, thyre. I am sorry to tell you, but you stay-at-homes will have to play your politics without us. We shall kill our foreigners first, you can wreath your monarch later."

"We look forward to your victorious return."

"Palama, I will oathbind as your fateshield."

"Xindro, I gladly welcome you by my side."

"But know this," added Xindro. "I will use my new position to get to Fontaza. He will not die so quickly as Pondra."

"You are welcome to try," Palama smiled. "He is persona inviolate now. He is untouchable while Vondaka lives."

"Then he will not live a moment longer."

3.1 - THE IDLE VOYAGE

The old jetty creaked in pain as Dandaron shifted his nervous weight from one impatient foot to the other.

Stagnant water squelched from the yellow moss and the grey slats bowed in protest beneath him.

"I hope those planks hold," said Drolla. This was not the royal pier.

The chancellor's words still stung. 'You will not be seen at the monarch's departure,' Vondaka hissed, 'you will board the royal yacht at the Trawler's Jetty.' He made it quite clear, it was impossible that anyone should see Drolla in the company of the monarch.

Set amongst the bobbing moldering boats, these two lone figures waited for their betters. The intent was not lost on them. Dolla's inheritance of Quetono's estate was not yet common knowledge. Vondaka did all he could to hush it up. Royalty was embarrassed by him. It was deemed shameful, bordering on scandalous that a peasant farmer be elevated to such a high position within the royal family. Vondaka was livid and did nothing to hide his contempt of Drolla. Dandaron's empathy whispered, 'You'll get used to it.'

Neither had ever stepped off land before and the thought of it was daunting. Together they peered up the canal. The view took them out to the frothing torrents of the wild Bahlo river. The raging current would take them out to the rolling swell of the Northern Channel, then west to the edge of the nation.

Dandaron shot Drolla an anxious look. His eyes bled dread. Drolla agreed, the same nervous thornbugs buzzed inside his guts as well.

"It's so deep," moaned Dandaron.

"What is?"

"The ocean. We could fall overboard. We could drown."

"We could stay indoors. But those waves, they will churn your guts inside out. You will vomit for days, they said..."

"Who said?"

"...even with nothing left. I have not spewed since I left my caves. This is bound to be even worse."

It was obvious, they were not the same thornbugs at all.

They promised an eleven day voyage. The mighty catamaran would brave the journey and sail against the mightier tide. The easterly winds would drive them into the westerly waves. The Zonolith orbited the world each month. The belt of stones hung high in the sky, a thousand times higher than the loftiest clouds. Like the jewel of a lover's ring, the broken moon Petramon led the trailing belt of captive lunar gravel and dragged the great ocean tides along the equatorial channel. Today, in their ultimate wisdom, royalty saw fit to sail against the towering tides.

"We should hug the coast," said Dandaron.

"Close enough to swim to shore? We should have marched with Palama," said Drolla.

Drahn's Great Army departed Churon's Pen yesterday. Endless ferries convoyed the soldiers across the river into the Mezzini province. Their trek would take them through the endless forests and past the waterfall city into Oxxia, then south to march west by the coastal road. He had escaped his royal minders and perched himself atop the outer wall, hidden inside a shadowed rampwell of the elderkin's apartments. There he witnessed his comrades' parade.

Seventeen thousand restless soldiers assembled and cheered their monarch. The proud arena was filled with the chanting of oaths of allegiance. Enthusiastic cheers for war sung in his ears afresh. His eyes saw again their pride as they strode in formation out of the arena under the coloured streamers of their own khillionaire. He could smell the fellowship still, and missed it terribly. He wished he was among them. He yearned to be a simple soldier again. He wanted to be with his squad, with Xindro and Boohala.

"I just don't belong here..."

"You most certainly do," said Dandaron. "You are gentry now. The monarch himself made you his personal guest. He wishes to meet Quetono's heir and wants to hear your tale."

"Even more reason not to board. Surely, if we left now, we could catch up to the army?" said Drolla.

"Yes, we could. We could runaway and defy a royal command. We could incriminate our innocent friends. Vondaka would have us all on poles the moment he landed. That'd be clever." Dandaron grinned like a witty jester, while Drolla scowled like a berated child.

From the horizon of the curved moat, the monarch's yacht appeared. It was baffling how anything so large could float. It was at least five times larger than the small logistics catamaran that passed under the bridge when the horde first entered the Pen.

Three layers of cabins connected the twin hulls. Seemingly without end, they were carved from dark grey funglstone. Each sported a pair of thick tall masts. From those, black wingsails twisted and steered the vessel toward the pier.

The main cross-deck was crawling with sailors tuning the rigging as the mighty boat pulled up alongside their sad little jetty. A boarding plank arched through the air and slapped the boards at their feet. They were motioned aboard by an impatient marine. The nervous pair spurred each other on, bound to share their fates. The cleats of the plank dug into their soft feet and bounced with every step. As soon as they had stepped on deck, the plank was hauled in and the great mainsail was let out. Stretched between the foremasts, the great, white sail was emblazoned with the emblem of the black Trohr bat, the national badge. The wind filled it with a sudden thud.

The ship groaned. The bows leapt into the air and launched out into the centre of the canal. The sudden jolt startled the landlubbers and they lost their footing. With wobbly legs spread wide, their arms flailed about trying to grab anything stable. Roaring with laughter, the sailors did nothing to help. This was going to be far worse than they thought.

For three wretched days, Drolla confined his sorry self to his cabin. The room was dark and airless. He perched on a round bed, hung by ropes from the ceiling. Like a hammock, it seemed motionless while everything else pitched and yawed about him. The angry ocean ensured Drolla would not soon forget his virgin cruise. With his eyes slammed shut it almost helped keep the vomit down. But he knew better. In his mind's eye he saw the world spin and tumble and his guts churned in time with it, like courting lakebirds synchronised in a perfect nauseous harmony. He clutched the bucket closer.

"I think I'd rather drown."

He spat the watery bile that gathered under his tongue. Gritting his teeth, he swallowed nothing.

The floor lurched like a see-saw. Anything not tied down, slid between one wall and the other. Waiting for the perfect moment, he stood for the umpteenth time. Unsteady on his feet, he ran downhill and slammed into the porthole. One hand grasped a wall rail tight, another unclipped the stiff red curtain. The foggy little window flew open and the cold sea air burst into the hot, stale room. He gasped. His face flushed and his limbs tingled as the fresh air flooded his body. He closed his eyes and put his face to the open window and inhaled another long sweet lung full. As he exhaled he opened his eyes to see alternating walls of grey water and pink sky. His heart launched into his throat, but the nausea halted in a sudden moment of distraction. He could not believe his eyes. He blinked away the sea mist and groaned at an incredible sight. It defied logic.

A rope around Dandaron's middle tied him to the far side bow rail. He leaned forward, out past the hull and rode it up the inner wall of the climbing waves. Crashing through the frothing crest, he hooted with childish joy as the sea spray drenched him again, and he roared as the prow plunged down into the trough of the heaving swell. Wave after wave, Dandaron cheered and never tired.

A sailor sidled along the deckrail toward the sodden thrill-seeker. He called out to him and threw him a line. Dandaron caught the rope, heaved on it and tied it off. The sailor motioned to him to leave the bow and follow him. He smiled wide, waved and declined the summons, but the sailor was insistent. Crestfallen, Dandaron complied and untied himself. He strode proud with his new found sea legs along the hull, out of sight, and back to the main deck.

Drolla faced his familiar cell. He mounted his pendent berth and steadied himself within its centre. With a bucket clamped between his calves, he readied himself. Through the open porthole, an oval spot of sunlight ran back and forth across the cabin floor. He spent a good while watching it before drifting into a dozy state of meditation. His nausea had exhausted him. If he could rest a while, he might recover sooner. Weariness blurred time. Moments could have been hours. How ever long it was, his solitude was over.

The cabin door swung open. Orange sunlight blazed down the rampwell and lit up Dandaron's silhouette in the doorway. The room's sickly air rushed out past him.

"Ugh, this room reeks." He lobbed something toward Drolla. "Medicine from Torono, that will settle you. Catch."

Blinded by the back light of the doorway, his arms groped at the blur tumbling toward him. He snapped his legs shut as something small hit his lap. A phial. Without question, Drolla popped the cap and drained the sweet, slimy syrup. Vitality rippled through his body to the very tips of every limb. His stomach had settled. It was as still as... Drolla bounded to the porthole.

"We have passed the waves." At last, the ocean was calm.

"Get dressed, the monarch beckons," said Dandaron.

"Now?"

"He awaits Quetono's heir."

Drolla poked his thumb at the porthole. "I saw you face your fear." Dandaron spied the bucket. "I see you have been facing yours."

A broad sentry stood vigil outside the monarch's door. Clad as green as Dandaron, this brute stood mightier. They were old friends. They were Lodge-mates and they were fellow enforcers.

His was a military clan. The parents and grandparents had been khillionaires of the regal army, and friends to the royal family. A jealous neighbour, a lesser doyen in both status and ethics, coveted their lush and fertile clandom. After years of animosity, a crop water feud intensified and soon brought ambush and bloodshed. Heir, and lone survivor of the murdered family, the toddler was secreted away by a forewarned childminder. How he knew or why he warned no one else, was never known. The saviour disappeared forever after leaving the child with a note in the palace gardens. Monarch Bontoro himself sponsored the child's protection and ordered the vengeance for his slaughtered friends. There were no survivors after the massacre. Staff was disbanded and both estates were seized and sold off. The proceeds bloated the young inheritor's personal coffers. Raised by the Barren Uncles and tutored by the Amber Creed, he studied Rythene, Kyana, and Churon so he might heal injustice through force. And thus, here he stood. A wealthy orphan of an extinct clan. Master of the enforcers. Fateshield to the monarch.

Dandaron had spoken of him with an admirer's perfection. But, in the flesh the good life had been too kind to his friend. The bluestones that studded his white leather shardbelt bulged like frightened eyeballs and struggled to contain his proud paunch.

"Dandaron." He nodded. "Is this him?"

"Yes Glendoro, it is. He has been hiding away, unwell since we left."

"It is a pleasure to finally meet you, young thyre. I knew and admired Quetono."

"Thank you. It seems everyone did."

"Did Torono fix you up?"

"Yes. His tonic worked wonders," said Drolla.

"Good. He is a clever fellow. Without the doctor's potions, we might have lost Soltoro."

"How is he now?" asked Dandaron.

"Better, but he is on a special diet, so do not expect any food." He leaned in to Dandaron and whispered. "If I were you, I would not eat anything already unsealed."

Glendoro pounded on the wide door thrice, pulled down the top handle and tilted the panel open. A broad ramp led down into the cabin. The place was a mess. Scrolls laid scattered everywhere. Some were curled flat on side tables, others were still rolled up and tossed onto chaotic piles. Their leather barrels were strewn about with lids left open in a silent yawn. An open credenza had spewed its contents of reports, maps and letters. Many documents were defaced with red ink and others were crumpled into balls.

Tasseled plump cushions heaped themselves by the walls, almost hiding a fallen tall table underneath them. Crumpled fabrics crawled their way across the floor. Soft wool, silken fur and crisp linen carpeted everything.

Dozens of fist sized smolderstones hung from the ceiling. The round geodes, broken in half, were secured by little string nets. They dangled like vine-fruit under an afternoon pergola and swayed in disarray with the gentle rocking of the cruising catamaran. Most glowed, some didn't. Two unlit stones swung into each other's path, they collided with a clack and lit up again. The ensemble lit the floor in random roving waves. Deep blue velvet drapes covered the walls from the ceiling to the floor. They were almost invisible except for the pearl glow highlighting the sheen of their folds. A vase of potpourri scented the thick air. In the middle of it all, on an oversize pouffe, squat the monarch of Drahn. Soltoro beamed at his welcome guests.

"Thank you Glendoro. Please ensure we are not disturbed," said Soltoro. The fateshield nodded. Dandaron rolled coaxing eyes at Drolla, urging him to enter alone. Glendoro reached for the door handle.

"You too Krodangan," said Soltoro.

"Move," whispered Glendoro. He shouldered Dandaron through the portal and pulled the door shut behind them. Soltoro stared at Drolla. An elbow stabbed his ribs. He flashed a look of surprised agony at Dandaron. He was curtsying and the elbow still aimed at him. Dandaron glared back, threatening him to either curtsy or get another. Drolla dropped to his haunches and stretched his neck high.

"Apologies, thyre. He has had no time to learn any proper manners," grinned Dandaron.

"Precisely what I wanted to see." Soltoro turned his gaze to Drolla. "Haven't you been been a well kept secret?" Drolla could neither move nor answer. "Stand up. Drop your head child. Come to me, both of you." Standing at the base of the ramp, Soltoro pulled at a dangling lamp and lit Drollas face. "You do look like Quetono you know, but so does Dandaron, a bit. And yet, he's a foreigner, so what do I know." He shrugged and laughed at himself. His smile disappeared as he looked hard at each of them, shining the light from face to face. "While we're here," he said, letting the stone swing, "let us not be formal. There is no one to impress. We shall talk like family. As we should be." Soltoro scooped up a bundle of scrolls and kicked a few more aside to clear a space on the floor. "I have known Dandaron since he was little." Too distracted to notice, he placed an armful of curled paper on a floor table and covered a tray of laden crockery. "But, I know nothing of you." At his invitation, they squatted on cushions in the centre of the cabin. Drolla reached down and ran his fingers through the folds of the luxurious grey fleece. "So now Drolla, tell me all about Quetono's heir."

Without a second prompt, Drolla launched onto a journey of nostalgia. With true fondness, he recalled and described in detail the timeless beauty and tranquility of his forest village. He embellished the tales of his labours in his filthy caves, relishing in the disgusting details for pure entertainment sake. He boasted of the great wealth the fungus had brought his clan, a wealth he never shared in. He told how their undue fortune had brought unfettered disdain from neighbouring clans, he had a share in that.

Soltoro listened in captivated silence. While his wide constant grin remained unchanged, his eyes danced and flashed over every word. Drolla spoke of the drudgery of his daily life, his oppressive family life and how he had been treated worse than a child-servant by everyone. All except his darling sibling Kwinno. If not for him, he might have run away years ago. If there was anywhere to run to.

"...and then, out of nowhere, Quetono appeared and rescued me from it all," said Drolla, "and here I am."

"And here you are," said Soltoro. "From the bottom of the realm to the top. Yet, as glad as you seemed to leave home, you do sound like you miss it."

"I think everyone does after a while," said Drolla. "I saw an army of the homesick march even further away."

"They march for Drahn, for our sand, for our wealth."

"They march for Drahn, otherwise they're killed," said Dandaron.

"The brave may die in battle, but the cowards will die at home. That is the law. If the Miokh take our black beaches, Drahn is ruined."

"Fear not thyre, they are all keen. As adults, it is their job, they must impress the seniors. Old folk do love to admire their obedient youth. I doubt there is a single shirker marching west," said Drolla.

"My poor syblings," said Soltoro. "Somehow, we are all being pushed into a battle we cannot avoid. I tried to avoid it, but failed."

"How?" asked Dandaron.

Soltoro had summoned his consultorium. Without explanation, the advisory guild of elders sent only one. Their wisdom was far more robust than their persons. Old age and comfort forbade them leave their cozy nooks amongst the sacred conference halls of Elderville. Newly elected, spry and shrewd, Vice President Bendro was sent to attend the monarch at his military court. He would gladly report on the results of the negotiations with the Tamzi Kith.

The Soltoro's plan to thwart the war was met with ridicule and doubt from his own advisors. Nevertheless, correspondence was sent. He threatened to boycott the Tamzi Kith, and impose sanctions against their traders within his borders. He demanded they immediately ceased all purchase of any stolen black sands. In return they would be given special concessions and price negotiations would return to their agreement. Soltoro hoped the Tamzi would refuse to procure the sand from the thieving Miokh. He reckoned if the Miokhi had no buyers, they would cease dredging and the battle could be avoided. The Consultorium conveyed their appreciation for the benevolent attempt to save the lives of the Drahni syblings. The Doyen Assembly praised the monarch's sentiments, but admitted that without the subsidies the sand brought their clandoms, war was inevitable. Despite the emotional and intellectual reasoning, his offer was declined.

The Tamzi did not care from whom they bought and sold, it was business. Business they would not see interrupted by personal grudges, and particularly shallow threats from a second class nation. The Kith had entered into many violent conflicts to ensure the cash continued to flow. Experience taught the wise merchants it was safer, easier and far cheaper to trade commodities than to wage war. Bitter vassals of conquered kindoms were seldom reliable. Bought politicians and profiteering brokers were far more compliant. Yet in truth, if not for Drark and Quetono's counsel, the Tamzi would hold no grudge. A generation later, the once defeated empire still spurned their victor's aide.

"Now, there is no way to avoid it. War it is," said Soltoro.

"Quetono thought it was worth the fight," said Dandaron.

"Did he? I thought he only went east to fetch this one."

"Both, I think." Dandaron laughed.

Soltoro shifted his gaze to Drolla.

"And he has made you his heir," said Soltoro. "It is all very unconventional, but I suppose we must trust uncle's judgment. Dandaron has, haven't you?" The Krodangan did not reply, his fingernails stole his attention. "You were his fateshield for years, surely he confided in you?"

"More than it is safe to say, thyre," he agreed.

"I thought so. Tell me, what interesting secrets do you keep?" asked Soltoro. His eyes flared with interest piqued. Dandaron sighed. "Oh come on. Just between us, Quetono wouldn't mind now."

"He thwarted three attempts on your life."

"Only three?"

"Two separate occasions, assassins were intercepted and executed in secret."

"The third?" asked Soltoro.

"While in the Orienna, Quetono deduced who your poisoner was. He planned to expose him on his return. But his own assassins prevented that."

"They did. In the arena. Who was it?"

The cabin door flew open and a gusty breeze scattered the documents around the room. The stone lamps swung erratic and clacked a newer brighter rippling sea of light. Beams flashed light around the room in waves and lit up the intruder's entrance. Vondaka slammed the door behind him and stood stern with hands on hips. His critical frown scanned the room. Vondaka stepped past the host and his guests and brushed the parchments off the picnic tray.

"Why is this food untouched?"

He was annoyed and did not care to hide it. He moved the platter to a small floor table nearby and towered over them, waiting for their compliance. Drolla ogled the delicious spread. Nine white alabaster bowls sat full, each as big as two handfuls.

Whole dried fingerfish curled intertwined and stared everywhere. Supple brown slivers of corned flesh swam in their own briny juice. Grey fermented mushrooms floated in a translucent golden jelly. Green squash, sliced and pickled, were covered in a shiny oil and sprinkled with dried yellow herbs. A sweet gooey syrup drowned a chunky fruit salad. Hot, spicy nutclusters sprinkled with red sand salt. Blue and white root vegetables, cubed and tossed in a light cream gravy. Small raw meatballs were smothered with a curdled russet sauce. And best till last, fit for a monarch, deep dark purple brewberries wallowed in a vapourous pond of their own fine puree.

Until he saw the food, Drolla was not hungry. But now, his grumbling guts leered a famished grin at Dandaron. His eyes said, 'No!'

"None of us are hungry," said Soltoro.

Vondaka snatched a fish. Before he crunched on its crispy carcass, he bit the head off and spat it back into the bowl.

"Uncle, could you please show some courtesy to my guests?"

"Who, these two? Quetono's pet and his new brat?"

"You know they are both legitimate."

Vondaka flicked an eyebrow. It was a truth he could not defy. He faced Drolla.

"I do congratulate you, young thyre. Few are so fortunate. Many envy royalty, while others hate it and some would do us harm. Even our beloved Quetono could not be protected from assassins. I trust his former fateshield will serve you better."

Dandaron fumed and rose onto one knee. "Do you dare?"

With a soothing palm, Soltoro motioned him to remain on his haunches.

"Royal duty separated the fateshield from his charge, everyone knows that. They also know too well, your animosity towards Dandaron. I insist you cease beating him with Quetono's memory."

Vondaka smirked.

"As you wish. I have a far more important matter to address and it cannot..."

"Cannot wait, yes I know. Nothing with you ever can. Thus our informality ends." Soltoro sighed, exhausted already.

"You pair can get out," said Vondaka.

"No," snapped Soltoro. Instant anger stiffened his back. "They stay. You chose to interrupt us. You insist to raise some urgent issue, here and now. Let us all hear it. Out with it."

Dandaron sat quietly, staring at his fingernails. Wide-eyed, Drolla shifted his astonished gaze from one titan to the other. Vondaka squatted on his haunches. His tone changed in a moment. With a mild sincerity, he addressed Soltoro.

"Nephew. It is vitally important this matter is settled. Is your Final Word sealed in glass?"

"Of course it is," said Soltoro.

"I only ask in my capacity as chancellor."

"Really? How dutiful you are. I lodged my bequeath with the Consultorium before we left the capital."

"Who did you name your successor?"

"Diltoro," said Soltoro. "Obviously."

"What? Why?" There was a hint of distress in Vondaka's voice.

"You know very well why. His bloodline assures him his rule. It will put an end to all the plots that have poisoned the palace. To be honest, I am glad to be rid of it."

244

"He hasn't even reached seniority yet. Why is he not here to defend the kindom with his syblings?"

"By my order, Diltoro holds Drahn while we fight for it. If I lose this battle, the succession will be inherent."

"Last Pannatalia, Palama turned senior. Drahn needs the wisdom of a parental arbiter, not a childless prince."

"Palama is no monarchist, and seniocrats are unfit to rule." His stern royal face broke a smile. "I would sooner endorse Drolla."

Vondaka shot to his feet and thundered.

"No! The royal line must be kept pure by birthlings. I'll not watch some filthy lust-spawn don the regal torkh. Quetono was both a fool, and a filthy degenerate."

Dandaron stood in a fury. His grinding teeth sounded like breaking ice, his clenching fists creaked like twisting rope. He glared hateful disrespect deep into Vondaka then calmly spoke.

"You will not defame your sibling's noble nature again, or I will silence you forever."

"Dandaron!" Soltoro roused. "You forget yourself."

"Quetono knew you, I know you. Soon, everyone else will too," said Dandaron.

"Fontaza! Glendoro! Attend!" Vondaka screeched like a victim.

Two concerned fateshields burst into the cabin.

"Confine Dandaron to his quarters for the duration of the voyage."

They hesitated and their concern morphed into confusion.

"Enforcers do not arrest enforcers, thyre," said Glendoro.

They looked to Dandaron, then to Soltoro. He nodded gravely.

"This one we do," said Fontaza, snarling with glee.

He moved to arrest Dandaron. A screeching shard was pulled from its scabbard. Unarmed, Dandaron grabbed the pommel of Fontaza's half drawn blade. His struggling frown bared his gritting teeth while Dandaron wore a calm and impassive face. He slowly pulled on the weapon. Fontaza realised his intent and fought hard to keep hold.

"Fontaza, sheath your weapon," roared Glendoro.

Dandaron released his grip and the blade screamed home with a jolt.

"Someone else has a claim to your life," smiled Dandaron. "I'll not cheat him of that pleasure."

Fontaza grunted and stood aside, and cleared the path to the exit. In his own good time, Dandaron calmly smoothed down the wrinkles in his tunic and flicked away an imaginary hair. He curtsied his monarch and strutted up the ramp in front of his peers. Neither dared to manhandle him. Vondaka followed them out. He stopped in the doorway and looked back at Drolla. He snarled with amused contempt.

"Safe for now, peasant."

"Out," roared Soltoro. The monarch and the bastard stood alone. The cabin was silent and awkward. Soltoro winced a smile and he turned to Drolla and said, "Welcome to the family."

3.2 - THE FORBIDDEN SANCTION

A wedge of stinging sunlight stabbed into the cabin's gloom.

The sharp orange glare dazzled a naked, squinting Dandaron. Drolla stepped in quickly and closed the door behind him. The room plunged back into total darkness.

"Where's the light?" cried Drolla. "Strike a stone."

He blindly groped for the handrail by the ramp.

"Wait."

A small glass sphere began to glow in Dandaron's hand. The more he shook the ball the brighter it became. It was only the size of an eyeball, yet shone more white light than a score of crystal smolderstones.

"That's a Zharkhonian Star," blurted Drolla. Held out to him at arm's length, his fascination shone just as bright as the beautiful thing. The glass was as clear as air and floating within the transparent fluid, untold grains of fine smolderstone dust swirled and trembled together. The energetic friction arced and sizzled like searing whitefire without the heat of the blistering flame. Drolla had only ever seen that kind of light in glowing cash rods. The same glash Vrune traded for his magic mushrooms. The rich yet meagre dust sparkled a little wealth within the glass bars, but compared to this blistering orb, the amount of powder was like a pinch compared to a palmful.

"A gift from patr'," said Dandaron, "to make amends for my fifteenth birthday."

"Amends?"

"I missed my first Conjugation."

"Why?"

"Drolla, I am a foreigner. When I came of age Vondaka banned me, and then barred me for life."

"And Quetono complied?"

Dandaron nodded and sighed.

"It didn't really matter though. We always spent the holiday at his country estate, long before and ever since."

"That is a shame."

"I didn't know any different. We always had a fun time picnicking for days on end under the auroras and lolling around his gardens. They were always beautiful that time of year."

For untold billennia the auroras came. They marked the end of one year and the beginning of the next. Pharina, our lonely frozen stone, returned again from her far flung orbit and cruised between the sun and the world.

For a few fleeting days she spewed her prolific fumes across the sky. From north to south the coloured plasma ran high above, like cloudy rivers. Bathing in the spectrum's shade, life sprang fertile. Oceans spawned and flora bloomed. While beasts mated, the people fucked and the natural realm was sown afresh for another year. But that event was months away.

On a floor table, a polished forearm carved from scarlet jasper, with white quartz and gold arterial inlay, stood upright on its elbow. Four fingers stood like bent columns topped with fractured glass spires. Dandaron squinted as he set the blinding orb between the crystal talons. The small chamber was floodlit brighter than day. Three clear glass bowls huddled around the lamp holder. One was a third full of purple brewberry syrup with all the fruit already eaten. Brown flakes of jerky were all that remained in another and the spicy nutclusters were not even touched.

Among the scattered furs and wrinkled fleeces, Dandaron reclined on soft fat velvet cushions. Golden fish were embroidered into the white fabric. A line of mauve drips ran across them from the table to his chin. Two legs folded under him with the third outstretched onto an old misshapen pouffe. The green pimpled suede was faded and worn.

"Are we close?" asked Dandaron. "I have lost track of time in here."

"It's been three days," said Drolla. Dandaron grunted and scowled at the door. "I am sorry you are locked in here alone, but Soltoro likes my company."

"Fallen in love with you too, has he?"

"I think he loves everyone. He admires his syblings. He praises the senior's generosity and he adores his warriors."

"Paff," said Dandaron.

"He trusts you, you know."

"I know. I am his little Krodangan cousin."

"I think he put you in here to protect you from Fontaza."

"Ha! To protect him from me, more like. No, it was to appease Vondaka. He despises my foreign blood."

Drolla paused. His frown was drawn to faint speckles that flickered across Dandaron's chest.

"I met a Krodangan once," said Drolla. "He was full term pregnant, three months early."

"Really?"

"His flash was bright green. Across the channel, everyone in the southlands are green. The Fronst. The Zintrix, the Krodangans, all of them. They are different to us, because they are foreigners."

"Like me?"

"No, not like you."

Dandaron eyed himself. His chest blazed smalt upon his blank skin.

"It's blue," he gushed. He ran his fingers across his flash and felt a lawn of minute prickly scales standing erect. His skin turned white as he smoothed them down, but they flicked back over like tiny little sequins and shone blue again. The erotic rash ran over his shoulders and across his chests like a monarch's torkh.

"I've never seen that before." His eyes were wider than his grin.

Drolla squat for a closer look. "It's the wrong colour, and the wrong time. How?" he whispered. He clutched at the soft furry quilt rippled around him and reached for the bowl. He gulped down the leftover brewberry syrup. The vapour stung his eyes, the liquid burnt his throat and his lungs exhaled invisible fire. It was delicious. But, there was an odd aftertaste. It was like vomit, a sickly sweet vomit. Drolla retched a little and swallowed a failed burp. He knew that stink. A gooey russet sludge hugged the rim.

"What's this?" Drolla fingered the scum and licked it off. The flavour was unmistakable. "Oh no, you haven't?" Dandaron grinned and held up a half empty vial of pure magenta. It was Red Spore powder.

"Where did you get that?"

"Your stolen swag," said Dandaron. "I thought it was high time I had a taste."

"You have no idea what you have done?" Drolla shook his head and Dandaron's smile morphed into a confused frown.

"Well, I can't feel anything yet."

"You will."

Red Spore whoophing was revered for its tasteless and sensational euphoria. But the fungus had another, far less known effect. It was a mystery the elders kept to themselves, the dirty old lechers. As their indentured lapster, Drolla was privy to the clandestine debauchery of the old folk's private gatherings. No one, but the savvy, dared eat the powder. Its flavour was so revolting the idea was absurd and beyond unthinkable. Thus their naughty secret was kept. For when eaten, the Red Spore was a rapid and potent aphrodisiac.

Dandaron was horny and did not know it. A tingling flush ran through Drolla. A smidgen of carnal desire peeked from behind his celibate virtue. It was a pang he had not felt for a long while and one he should not be feeling now. But it was too late, they had swallowed the drug and now there was no escape. In his mind's eye, a smiling Vrune winked and reminded him, 'When urge too strong, must act on it'.

"It's warm," said Dandaron. "Feel."

Without warning, he pulled Drolla's hand to him and pressed it to his scalding chest. The heat was magnetic. He could not pull away, he did not want to. This was too naughty, this should not happen. It was out of season. There was no comet, no auroras, no conjugation. There was only them. They locked eyes and both saw passion staring back.

"I have never," said Dandaron.

"I know."

"I want to..." His chaste eyes glistened. Drolla nodded. He peeled off his toga and threw it aside. Together, they squatted with their legs interwoven. Drolla caressed Dandaron's thighs and watched him melt. His head drooped with his eyes closed, wallowing in the erotic sensations. His skin quivered as waves of pleasure cascaded along his body trailing the gentle touch of Drolla's finger tips.

Dandaron reached to do the same, but he grabbed Drolla's knees and squeezed them a little too hard. Drolla flinched and Dandaron looked apologetically with so much desire in his gaze, it was obvious the novice had fumbled. He tenderly guided Dandaron's hands along his thighs, allowing him to explore as far as he wished.

His smooth caresses tingled Drolla, he too let the excitement take him and softly moaned. The red slurry began to take effect. His urges were building and passion was fast morphing into raw lust. His own flash now burned hot and shone blue. His libido ached and begged to throb.

Dandaron slid a gentle finger down Drolla's inner thigh. He touched the warm, puckered lip. They locked eyes again, but now both saw raw sex. The tipping point had arrived, mutual consent was granted. Soon they would lose themselves within each other. Drolla ran his hand into Dandaron's groin, his eyes flashed with surprise. Never before had the fingers of another probed down there. He was swollen and his sopping halo flinched to the touch. Dandaron nudged his groin onto Drolla's hand. He was ready.

Drolla took the lead. They repositioned and got more comfortable. Their genitals pressed together. Each straddled the other, end to end, with ankles locked over their shoulders. For a moment they paused while their phalvas nuzzled and kissed. Dandaron soon became erect first.

Drolla's own organ twinged and began to retreat and pouch to accommodate an ever increasing insertion. Drord's Guts. Too big, too dry. Drolla clawed the floor and panted at the ceiling. A virgin's love probed deep. Soon enough, Dandaron's organ began to recede. Drolla himself became engorged and pushed Dandaron's deflating genital out. His erection plunged into Dandaron as he pouched. A cry of unexpected joy escaped him. Virgin no more. His breathing deepened, he engorged again and plunged hard back into Drolla. He thrust back too soon.

"Oh." Their sexy eyes smirked.

Their rhythm was now in motion. Back and forth their organs ground and pleasured each in turn. Plunging and pouching, giving and taking. Faster and harder. Time meant nothing. Both were lost in their mutual rapture and did not want it to end. Apart from the squelching tempo and measured panting, they laid silent and motionless while their organs fucked each other senseless.

At last, the pressure increased and their sex burst into climax. They both grunted and shuddered. Pure bliss waved through their sweating bodies. Dandaron let out a guttural groan and passed out, taken by la petit mort. Drolla laid still and exhausted. As the passion waned, their flash faded white. Their quivering loins were sodden with shared milt. Drolla nestled his groin into Dandaron to stem any spillage. The warm mingling goo embodied their utter satisfaction.

The cabin darkened as the little star dimmed and winked out. Drolla groped for the fur quilt and threw it over them both. Under the shared warmth, relaxation began to take him. Drowsy eyes stared into the darkness, and he wondered who he laid with.

3.3 - THE SEPARATED REUNION

D andaron stepped his jade cube into position.

It was not a good move, but it was the best he could do. It may have protected the central space, but merely postponed an inevitable loss. His column was too far away. Drolla slid his last onyx cone from across the board. Safe within the central cluster, it blocked the reach of Dandaron's cube. There was no move Dandaron could make to prevent Drolla from placing his column onto the central hex.

The playboard was a honeycomb grid, marked out on a fine pale chamois poke stretched flat. The outer edge of the round hide hemmed a blue braided silken drawstring. In the middle, six hexagons inked black surrounded the white central hex. The goal of play was to mount the centre place first. Fateshields, clanguards and thyres were cubes, pyramids and cones. As in life and on the board, the doyen's column commanded his clan. His support pieces would attack and defend his path to the plynth.

Drolla was an inexperienced player. Not so Dandaron, and he had won every game so far. But this time Drolla was about to beat him. Next move, his column would mount the podium. He had battled through move and counter move and was now poised to win the game. At last, he would sit the plynth.

The players checked the other's glance, and wondered if they had heard it too. Their faces were not quite sure. In its carafe, the nectar water now lay still. The boat was motionless, and everything was silent. Dandaron put his chin in his palm and frowned at the game board.

"How did you... ?" he said.

The roar was as sudden as a heavy downpour, as if the belly of a raincloud burst.

"A storm?" Drolla jumped to the porthole. The roar rose again. A jubilant army cheered the arrival of the monarch. "We're here."

Hefty pounding on the cabin door rattled its latch. An impatient foot kicked it off one hinge. Fontaza filled the frame and fresh orange sunlight streamed past his dark, ominous outline.

"Out!" His angry silhouette bellowed. "We have landed. Everyone else is already ashore." He pointed a scathing finger. "You, are due at the Enforcer's pavilion."

Dandaron gathered the pieces together and pulled the drawstring tight. Drolla gawped in utter disbelief. Dandaron grinned, "Shame. You would have won."

The tardy voyagers stepped up onto the deserted deck. Peeking from the horizon, between ocean and cloud, the smiling southern sun beamed at Drolla. He stretched his cold bones and embraced the orange warmth.

The fresh sea air had deserted them. It was chased off by a rank and exhausted army. But, in the spirit of unhealthy competition, the local fisher's outpost would not be bested. The stink of ocean's blood and guts, and the pong of army's sweat and shit took turns to assault the nostrils. It all depended which way the breeze blew.

The royal vessel dwarfed the hundreds of utility catamarans that flanked it. Their hulls were lashed together side by side and formed a long pontoon bridge. It ran parallel up the estuary along the Drahni shoreside. Gangways reached between them, creating an unbroken boardwalk from the first to the last. From every stern, a gangplank reached to the bank. Not one mast wore a sail.

Up on the high bank overlooking the river, the monarch's field marquee viewed the enemy territory beyond the opposite shore. The dull pale green prairie was flat, it was empty, and it was endless.

On this side, a broken kaleidoscope of awnings and open tents fanned out across the grounds. Beneath the arcades of coloured cloth, people were everywhere. Crawling up the low hills beyond the linen mall, thousands of little white teepees clustered like a forest of fangs. Under each one, a naked lone soldier rested.

"The sappers have been busy," said Drolla.

"The monarch has been generous," said Dandaron. "One last splurge before the battle." He pointed to a dark green canopy nestled behind a cluster of indigo marquees. "There's me."

"And me?"

"Explore?" shrugged Dandaron. "Find me later."

He strode off without another word and disappeared into the throng mingling throughout the coloured shade.

"How?" Drolla called after him, but his voice was smothered by the clamour of the crowd.

Not since that first day, when the horde of recruits swallowed him up, had Drolla been lonely. Once he relished solitude. Since then he had embraced good company. Now, the seclusion ached. He did not belong anywhere. He was too good for the soldiery and not good enough for royalty. Even his fateshield had abandoned him. Drolla stood unguarded and vulnerable. Now truly alone, he remembered Vondaka's snarling threat. 'Safe for now, peasant.'

He scanned the bustling view and saw not one friendly face. Perhaps his assassin was stalking him now. It was best to move on and blend in.

Navigating his way through the crowd was easier thought than done. Camp followers and merchants buzzed about like corpseflies, pandering to the warriors every whim. Comrades sat and posed while artists captured memento sketches. Bootleggers ladled out brewberry sly, and some had it spat back at them. Hawkers coaxed any who would listen into makeshift sponge-bath houses. Couriers ran errands. Mailbearers took down letters to be posted home. There were tinkers who would fix anything, tailors who would mend anything, and caterers who would feed you anything. Funded from the monarch's purse, everything was provided free to the soldiers.

The bustling mob became very tedious, very fast. They were either pushing something onto him or pushing him out of the way. His meanderings brought him to the lower outskirts of the bivouac. As luck would have it, right next to the shit pits. Perhaps he should return to his cabin. If solitude was being forced on him, he may as well enjoy it in quiet comfort. It might even be safer. The breeze shifted and blew north from the ocean. Drolla turned his face south. The air was fresh, and cool, and salty.

"Let us go see this precious black sand we are all expected to die for."

He left the noise behind and climbed up onto an elevated walkway. The slabs were grey and warped with age, the path led over a mossy hillock and down to the distant beach. An arbour stood over the start of the path, it read 'Gronnix Docks'. A mighty name for a feeble pier. Maybe it was a grand wharf once, but now it was a single stone landing.

'Both time and neglect doth rot,' his grandpar' used to say.

The stroll was pleasant enough. Without the stinging sun, the sea breeze chilled his face. An occasional seabird swooped at him in a territorial effort to spook the intruder away. One hovered nearby. It cocked its head and rolled and eye over him. After a squawk of complaint, a shifted wing let the wind take it. It shot straight up and out of sight.

With the end of the walkway in sight, Drolla began to run. He was galloping by the time he reached it, and launched himself off the end. Five steps passed below him in a blur and the black beach came up at him fast. He could not help but howl at the thrill of the air rushing past him as he arced through it. The sand crunched with a squeak as his feet drove into it. He landed a little too hard, and rolled a few times. His arms and legs flailed about like a broken tumbleshrub. He took a breath. Nothing hurt. Then the pure joy of this simple pleasure erupted out of him in a burst of rowdy laughter. He sat up and looked about. He sighed a happy smiling contented sigh.

"This is freedom."

The rushing cold foam washed his feet. As it withdrew, they sunk into the sodden sand. He wiggled his toes to bury them deeper and waited for another broken wave to crawl up the shore. This beach lay on the most south-western tip of Drahn. Drolla could not have been further from his home in the far north-east. He stood on the southern edge of his nation, facing the Great Channel. The very waters he had just sailed upon were now licking at his toes. To the west lay the Oxxian River, bordering their enemy. North would take him back along the wooden path to the camp. East along the coast, the black beach stretched before him. In the distance stood the Great Western Tusks, a range of stony hills, jutted up between the sea and inland. Its shattered peaks shredded the clouds that dawdled past. He reckoned they were about an days walk from here. Beyond them, the black sand ran east for weeks to the waterfall city.

In the eastern sky, the smiling orange sun appeared from behind the northern end of the stony hills. The scattered clouds around it glowed pink and mauve. Misty white fog hugged one jagged peak like a fluffy collar. Angry blue and grey stormclouds choked the southern skies that stretched out across the channel. The gentle surf sent white lines of froth racing up along the beach, only to disappear into the dark sand as the water receded. Drolla scooped up a handful of wet sand. Its sheen evaporated as it dried and the dull grit turned a dark hidden matte. The opaque grains reflected nothing, as though he held a shadow in his palm.

Above the crashing waves and the hissing shore, footsteps squeaked in the sand behind. Drolla spied a stranger advancing. His white toga was dyed mottled pale blue, like a fine cloudy sky. One corner draped about his head and hid his face. Spotted, he halted for a moment. With measured steps he strutted sideways in a wide arc. Slowly, he drew his shard. Had his assassin finally arrived?

"I warn you shardhire, I have expected you," said Drolla.

Perhaps feigned bravado might deter a confrontation, if he was lucky. His challenger spun his weapon from one hand to the next.

Its tip pointed to Drolla's throat. Dread tingled to every finger and toe. A nervous hand wrapped his handle and he tore the blade from its sheath. He flashed his shiny black sword and curtsied Throthm's pose. The lofty gesture was ignored. The silent brooding adversary seemed bent on intimidating his lonely victim.

The anonymous foe threw a lazy cross-body swipe, it easily glanced off Drolla's defensive blade. Another slash followed in an instant. His handle rang, and it jarred his hands. Too close. Drolla leapt back. He flicked the tangled brown toga from between his thighs and unclipped his belt. The toga fell around him and he stepped out of the puddle of cloth. Free of all restraints, nudity was his ally. He brought a second hand into play, this was to be a two handed fight. One palm gripped the hilt, the other held the pommel.

A black blur arced toward his shoulder. Drolla's blade cut the air and deflected the blow. Just as fast, the enemy's weapon returned and swooshed past his face. A miss, or a taunt? Drolla lowered his blade and with a swift rounded swipe he aimed to detach a knee. The foe grunted, he barely blocked in time before leaping back two paces. Drolla pointed his blade to elbow and wrist. Unfazed, his opponent rolled his shoulders.

An onslaught of repeated thrusts was launched onto Drolla. He wheeled his blade back and forth barely countering each blow. They broke apart. Drolla went on the offensive. Their shards clashed in three short bursts. Each strike rang along his blade ever closer to his numbing hands. They separated again. Drolla's breath began to desert him. Soon, fatigue would be his second foe.

He dug his toes deep into the sand. By fair or foul, he would not die today. A fatal cloud of resolve cloaked his heart, even though it pounded like a hammer. Twin dueling shadows stretched sideways along the black shore. With measured lateral steps, Drolla put the sun behind himself and coaxed his foe into the shade.

The tireless assailant stretched his back and with a nod, signaled another assault. With his blade over his head, he jumped at Drolla. The face covering fell and their eyes met.

Drolla knew him. Surprised, he staggered and fell back and his shadow fell with him. The sun blazed into squinting eyes. Drolla swung his shard in an upward arc with all the force his mortal terror could muster. War glass sang, and the attacker's blade spun from a startled grip and tumbled through the air. The weapon stabbed the sand nearby, planting itself out of reach. On his way down, Drolla kicked up hard and sprayed sand over the unarmed foe. He slapped his blinded face and quickly backed away a dozen paces, splashing into the shallow surf. He yelped as the salty water washed the black crystals from his stinging eyes.

"Cheat," yelled Xindro. "I never phapping taught you that."

"Leeporp!" Drolla panted with disbelief and pushed his blade into the beach. "I thought you meant to kill me!"

"Never..." A striding grin reached out two defeated palms and offered a friendly truce. "...I would not stand a chance."

Xindro smiled. The spirit of the exhausted soldiers lifted as more and more scattered trees congested the open plains. The edge of the dense woodlands was now in sight. The shade ran from the northern mountains to the channel coast. Within the hour they would march through the dark forest westward and breathe in the cool blue shade.

The wide paved highway wound deep into arboreal chill and led to Grax's Stream. It was a petty name for such a mighty river. The vast blue-green expanse flowed smooth in relentless silence. The best slinger could not cast a pellet anywhere near halfway across. Many tried, some competed, all failed. Where the road and the river met, an ancient bridge of moss and stone linked the middle province with the west. Two dozen immense piers, twelve a side linked either bank. The statues stood carved in glorious memory of long forgotten heroes. Waist deep between the arches, the outstretched arms of the sculptured figures grasped their neighbours' elbows. Together, their robust shoulders shared the burden as they supported the mighty crossing.

Great city plazas sat at the foot of the landings on either bank. Beneath them was the old capital. The Kataraxs was the famous border city between Oxxia and Mezzina. Old money resided there. The proud and noble descendants of the ancient seniarchs ruled from the waterfall city. During the Monofication, their clans had lost the sovereign plynth, yet kept the cash. The Customs House was wealthier than the monarchy, but royalty held the power. Now, it sat as the trading capital of Drahn.

The welcoming forest crept ever closer. Soon this march would end. The army had seldom rested since their departure from Churon's Pen. The khillionaires set a relentless yet steady pace. Hundreds from the catering corps ran amongst the rank and file of the great swirling mob. It was as if their battle had already begun. They doled out food each day and water each hour while the troops trudged their endless trek. River crossings and forest glades brought occasional relief, but never more than an hour or so. The waterfall promised a whole day's rest. And it was not far away at all.

War horns blasted south. The confused army were turned off their path and headed away from the city. Hectarions shouted down the grumbling disappointment. A crew of heralds soon circulated new orders from General Zonara.

"March south to the shore, bathe and rest. Await further directions."

The tramp of sandaled feet soon fell silent over the rolling dunes. Their spiral ranks dismantled across the shifting sands. One hectary after another peeled away and scrambled down the final ridge. Once on the beach front, the squads reformed in rows and layered along the shore like honeycomb. The salty sea breeze cooled their sweating bodies. Ocean fresh was not as welcome as jungle fresh, but it would do.

As the last of the seventeen thousand joined the first on the beach, the herald's horns blew their dismissal. Each squad built a pile of rolled tunics and stacked weapons. When given leave, they ran naked into the bracing surf like fettered beasts set free.

260

Under the officer's awning, Palama answered Zonara's summons. He sat astride his little folding stool. Sixteen khillionaires squat on the sand around him. His only companion was a secretary. Of all the nobility, Zonara had no fateshield. Staunch self confidence prevented his pride accepting that any could defend him better than himself. His potent aura had prevented any challenge to his personal authority, let alone an attempt on his life. But for his profound respect for Soltoro and the monarchy, he might easily make himself sovereign.

"Commander Palama, couriers from the city have relayed an invitation from the Civic Senate. The Kataraxs have opened their hearts to our weary soldiers. The generous residents have offered their homes and they would billet any who wished it."

"A noble gesture, thyre," said Palama.

"A pandering folly," said Fandara. "We cannot spare the time for this idle stopover."

"Aye," said Potono. "To welcome the monarch, we must arrive before he lands."

Joltoro perched himself on one knee.

"Soltoro cares more for his troops than their praise. He would take offense if his warriors were robbed of such a generous offer," he said.

Palama blinked at Joltoro's words.

"None doubt honesty, even when it's false," he whispered to Xindro. He knew Joltoro cared not what the monarch thought, not since the purge of Ebon Shore. Palama understood his sentiment, the soldiers deserved a furlough.

"Agreed," said Zonara. He snapped his fingers. The secretary nodded and handed out small tight scrolls to all present. "Here is a bill of etiquette, ensure your troops are well versed. Impropriety will not be tolerated."

Two hours later, the army was back in formation and trudged west along the beach. The sandy path curved sharp north, turning into the bay. With the great expanse of water on their left, the narrow beach

261

skirted the ever rising cliffs on their right. Soon they were shaded from the northern sun. It was hidden behind their towering destination.

An ivory column, as high as three hundred people, poured from the cliff top jungle river. The white water sparkled against the dull black sandstone cliff face, its base hidden within the roaring fog. Behind the waterfall, the underground city was carved into the stone beneath the river. Either side of the falls, the cliff face was checkered with hundreds of balconies. Each one led into a residence and all hung long coloured streaming pennants. They flicked and fluttered as if to motion their welcome like waving arms, whipped about by the wild updrafts and breezes caused by the rolling mists of the thundering waterfall. Such was the pride and appreciation of the citizens towards their brave syblings. Each banner signified an open house. Food, drink, bath and rest for any tired warrior who wished to lodge with them and be pampered for the day.

They marched toward The Kataraxs cavern. To the left of the falls, the cavernous opening let in the shipping through the deep waters of the black harbour. This side, a great portcullis yawned wide open. The army marched from the sand onto the mighty underground wharves. From there, they were welcomed by the city officials and cheering crowds. After Zonara dismissed the troops, the jubilant folk ran giggling amongst the rank and file. They pulled their willing adoptees aside, and led them up the ramped corridor, into the city proper.

Drolla listened in fascination.

"After they told us how to behave, they gave us the whole day off. Those phappin' Kataraxsians know how to party. They spoiled us rotten. More food and booze than I have ever seen in a single sitting. Best break ever. Nine hours later, we mustered to depart. Anyone not up top on the western plaza by the herald's third call were rounded up and sent over the falls," said Leeporp.

"Harsh. Were you late?"

Leeporp blinked and sighed. Drolla blushed.

The herald's first call was long and deep. It roused a few hundred white teepees camped around the plaza at the edge of the forest. They would not miss muster. The low tone echoed down the darkened rampways into the city. The second call was two tones higher, each half as long as the first. They were followed by thousands of soldiers. They emerged like ants and gathered into hectaries upon the open plaza. A vast crowd of civilians emerged with them, keen to cheer their departure. The third call blarped in short bursts of three. It was shrill and it was urgent. A few hundred emerged from suburbia on the eastern side, and stood confused on the Golden Plaza. They realised their mistake, and ran in a mad panic west across the great bridge. Execution awaited those who did not hurry.

The dutiful army finally assembled on the western Rivertop Plaza. After a day underground, they squinted in the orange sunlight. Hundreds of grexitors chanted their roll calls in a confused fracas. Any missing names were reported to their hectarions. Local vigilantes soon arrived with a group of military enforcers. They escorted twenty-seven deserters and fifteen still too drunk to even walk. The citizenry were disgusted with their disgraced guests.

"Cowards and the drunkards," they shouted.

Those angrier than others hurled their abuse and spat their curses at the ungrateful freeloaders. Blithe arrogance amongst the accused tarnished any with modest remorse. The offenders were unreliable. As the people proclaimed, so it breached the law, thus the laggers were doomed. While the outrage was not aimed at the guiltless, the shared disappointment stung. Their fellows had embarrassed them all. Zonara allowed the folk to vent a while, then commanded Palama and his Orienna Horde to close off the city entries and surround the urbanites. He insisted the great city folk witnessed the punishment of those they had vilified. They were advised not to avert their eyes, lest the joined them. Wisely, they complied.

The sappers had assembled frames from curved vines and three poles tied together in the middle. The condemned had a hand and foot lashed to the end of each pole, stretched into a star wheel. Then, without ceremony, the howling cowards were sent rolling down the paved banks. Tufts of grey tile moss flicked up behind them as they tumbled toward the river.

One after the other, they plunged deep before bobbing to the surface. Some floated head side down, some rolled face up and spluttered and swore. They gulped and gagged and shrieked. A few made a pathetic attempt to paddle wheel themselves back to shore, but the current took them all screaming to the edge. It took longer than expected, it was further than it seemed. But, when the last of them went over, the civilians stood silent and stared en masse at their departing visitors. Without a farewell, the dejected army left the noble folk of The Kataraxs and tromped into the dark Oxxian jungle. The cool blue shade closed in behind them and led them westward, to war.

"Those phapping 'cruits ruined everything," said Leeporp. "The folk loved us till then. We force marched ten days non-stop. It took that long for Zonara's shame to fade. He is a proud kladger."

Leeporp flapped his wet toga and wrung a corner dry.

"Wait. Why are you not orange?"

"Well, that's your phapping fault."

"How?"

"You stole into the stores. Your phapping fungus brought the Protorians down on us. They split the squad and Vondaka nearly got rid of me."

"Nearly?"

"Palama rescued me. He vowed me as his fateshield. He commands the Orienna Horde again, and named his first hundred, the Cyan Corps. This is their new toga."

"It looks like a dead body turning blue, splashed bloody white," said Drolla.

"Good, it is meant to."

3.4 - THE LOYAL TREASON

Deep within the canvas village, past the ripening throng and away from the noisy throughways, a small white domed tent glowed pale in the shade of a dark marquee.

Grey shapes blurred behind the curved translucent panels. Xindro loosened the laces of the entry flap.

"At last." A muffled voice grumbled from within.

"In," said Xindro.

An adamant palm pushed Drolla between the taut folds. He fell inside and landed at the feet of their host.

"Where have you been?" demanded Dandaron.

Drolla took his time to stand. "Exploring."

"I found him down on the beach."

"Where were you, fateshield?" asked Drolla.

"I was on duty." Dandaron frowned and bit his cheeks.

"I doubt you need one," said Xindro.

"I was fighting for my life."

"What, who attacked you?" frowned Dandron.

"This kladger." Drolla poked a thumb at Leeporp.

"I was only sparring. Testing his mettle."

"Your face was covered. I thought you were Vondaka's assassin."

"They would not stand a chance. You were lucky my shroud fell and the sun dazzled me."

"Really?" scoffed Drolla. "There was no luck in that."

"He defeated you?" asked Palama.

"Bested by a mushroom farmer?" Dandaron quizzled, and stared dismayed at Drolla.

Xindro grinned and shrugged. "I taught him too well, I suppose." He turned to Palama. "I will leave you to your business thyre, I have my own with Joltoro."

Palama nodded, and Xindro left without a word.

Another wandering fateshield, thought Drolla.

Palama's tent was empty, bar the meagre furniture. A worn yellow grasswood mat spread across the black sand floor. Its unfolded creases had not flattened out yet, and little piles of sand kept the corners down. A green tweed shoulderpack lay open off to one side, and a trio of ruddy leather sandals poked halfway out of it. Long since dried, his washed crimson toga draped half the inner wall. The black feather mantle hung at one end of it.

In the centre of the floormat, a wide, round kerchief spread where the plynth should have stood. Two half-sphere smolderstone geodes the size of fists laid upon it. Their pale beams reflected off the white ceiling and lit the room with a scattered pearl glow. By the stones stood a red leather flask, stiff with sealing wax. The contents could not have been more welcoming. The pong of strong brewberry sauce filled the tent. The thick juice was as black as the sandy floor and glistening soft white berries floated on a thin layer of creamy beige froth. Drolla gulped and swallowed his own mouth water. Four small empty saucers of polished amber stood stacked like shells, begging to be filled.

"I would prefer it if none of us sat in centre..." said Palama.

"Weird," said Dandaron.

In every other event, from kids in a playroom to the monarch in the palace, the seniority took pride of place on the central plynth, surrounded by subordinates. Palama was ignoring an ancient tradition. He was also inviting scorn.

"... and before we squat together, we have unfinished business. An oath was pressed upon us."

"Yet unvowed," said Dandaron.

Palama's eyes smiled at him. "Uncle Quetono begged we three should band together. To form our own personal triumvirate as a defense against dangers we could not then imagine. I have since been made aware of those dangers."

"What dangers are those?" asked Dandaron.

"Swear Quetono's vow and I will tell you everything," said Palama.

"Alright," said Drolla.

They squatted around the tablecloth. Palama leant in and filled three saucers and handed one to each of them. Drolla earnt a judgmental sideways glance from Dandaron as he licked syrup off a dipped finger. It was spicy hot.

"In honour of the wisdom of Quetono, we three here oath now to pledge our fidelity. Before all others, I vow loyalty to us and this our faithful trio," said Palama.

"As do I," said Dandaron.

"Me too," said Drolla.

They drained their bowls. Palama gasped, Dandaron coughed and Drolla held the burning goop in his mouth. His tongue swelled numb and he gagged as he swallowed the black acid sauce. Too strong a drink for the feeble. Too sweet for a monarch, too sour for a yokel. But perfect for Drolla. He grinned through glistening eyes, and whistled cold air from his burning mouth.

Palama outstretched a hand, encouraging them to do likewise. The knuckles of three fists kissed and cemented their bond. Their mutual fates were now sealed. A comforting ambiance settled within the tent. The air was warm with a heartfelt trust. For a moment, all the dread of the past and future had vanished.

"Soltoro speaks well of you Drolla, much to the chancellor's distaste," said Palama.

"Vondaka hates everything," grunted Dandaron.

"He is going to hate a whole lot more soon," said Palama.

"Do tell," replied Dandaron.

"While you pair cruised the channel, the army rested for a day at The Kataraxs," said Palama.

"Yeh, Leeporp mentioned it," said Drolla.

Palama shot him a quizzical frown.

"Xindro," explained Dandaron.

"Of course. Did he also mention that he sat with me during a parley with Prince Diltoro and the President of the Consultorium?"

"No." said Drolla.

"Good," said Palama.

The marble tiles were slippery. The clouding mist of the roaring waterfall settled like dew across everything on the balcony. Hidden within the forest at the end of a winding path, a sunburnt platform perched out from the edge of the cliff. The view of the bay below was both awesome and terrifying. It was as if the balcony defied gravity and might dislodge and plummet at any moment. By the end of the rear balcony, the river was close enough to spit into the rumbling water as it poured over the rim, turning from blue to white. The freshened air of the churning fog was invigorating. Far down on the water's surface tiny trawlers crawled home. They disappeared into the raging froth and entered the underground harbour.

Palama could not fathom why Prince Diltoro invited him to parley. They had not spoken since childhood. Diltoro had ignored him as much as the monarch, he refused to acknowledge Palama even existed. Their eyes had never met. The cousins were strangers. The scarlet arbiter guessed that his new found military command could well be reason enough for an arrogant whelp to recognise his peer. And yet, as he and Xindro approached the cluster of officials, intimidation churned Palama's guts.

"Only seven marshals," said Xindro, forever undaunted.

Yellow tunics stood between the invitees and the expectant party. Krantolo, squatted on his little perch. Neck bent forward, watching their approach. He was flanked by two mauve clad bureaucrats. Both were unknown and irrelevant. Diltoro sat ahead of them. His eyes were small and his shoulders slouched. Soltoro's royal black gown flowed over him like a thick blanket, as if the cloth was far too heavy.

The encrusted smolderstone powder failed to glimmer in the open sunlight. The little prince presented himself as a pale copy of the monarch's stout authority.

"Let them through, thank you Vrandala," said Diltoro.

The tallest of them joined Diltoro and took the deferent position of a fateshield behind the prince. The yellow guards lined the banister behind them. Two low stools waited for the guests. Obedient attendants scurried to place a short side table next to them. A fine doily was placed under clear glass flutes of fizzy nectar water and a bowl spicy nut-clusters were sat by. Xindro sneered at the tangy sticky seeds.

"Greetings Palama. Thank you for your attendance," said Diltoro. His posh accent sounded fake and as though he had a pebble under his tongue.

"Your messenger insisted it was urgent," said Palama.

"This meeting is vital and your attendance was mandatory," said Krantolo.

Palama frowned at the impudence of this flunky placing himself equal to members of the royal family. He was astounded that a public servant even dared to address a military commander so.

"I would like to know why your presence in The Kataraxs, and this meeting, is secret?" said Palama.

"Very suspicious," added Xindro.

"Mind your insolence soldier. Your duty is to serve nobility, not comment on it," said Krantolo.

"There is nothing noble about you, salt miner," said Xindro. "We know all about your orphan excursions to the seaside."

"Lies." Krantolo spluttered and blushed at Diltoro. His darting eyes pleaded for help to silence his accuser.

"Cousin," said Palama, "shall we skip the banter? Rescue poor Krantolo and tell me why we are here."

"As you wish," said Diltoro. "After par'... the monarch... left for Churon's Pen, I convened the Doyen Assembly with Krantolo and the Consultorium. I ensured the kindom operated as usual. We met daily and discussed the issues at hand."

"Well done you."

The prince ignored Xindro.

"During one divisive debate," he continued, "we joined together in the hilarity of an interruption. Foreign shardhires bearing seals of the Amber Creed presented themselves and their demands. They flapped their receipt at us and insisted on payment."

"Payment for what?" asked Palama.

"The league was hired to assassinate Soltoro," said Diltoro.

Palama and Xindro burst into laughter.

"You cannot be serious," said Palama.

"Hired by who?" asked Xindro.

Krantolo ignored the question and usurped the tale.

"The agents were immediately arrested. When questioned about the contract. They were more than happy to name their patron. And it is no one insignificant either."

"Many doubt the truth of it," said Diltoro. "Others scream treason. Either way, it was agreed the culprit must attend the assembly and answer for himself."

"Who do they want?" asked Palama. He sensed they were stalling, perhaps trying to guess what his reaction might be.

"Vondaka." Krantolo spat the name as if it was phlegm.

With the sound of a sudden deep breath, the balcony and everyone else on it shot away faster than anyone could run. It seemed to hover out over the middle of the bay. Palama could not believe his ears and wanted no more of it. He knew his parent was ruthless, but this was excessive. Was this just another rumoured crime he was to pretend to ignore? How long could he have faith in his parent's grace? He had to exit this patio.

"You have proof?" asked Xindro.

"Of course," said Krantolo. He held out his evidence.

"We detained the informants and seized this document. It is stamped with Vondaka's seal. We intend to interrogate him on his return," said Diltoro.

"You must ensure he does return," said Krantolo. "We trust you see the gravity of this situation and will support us.

"The City Marshalry will be stationed here on your departure. You are to arrest Vondaka and return him here for trial," said Diltoro.

"To guarantee your compliance, we hold your children as our honoured guests. You understand," said Krantolo.

Palama's mind snapped back to reality, he grasped his hilt. The marshals leaped to attention. Xindro reached an arm across Palama, and gestured calm. His eyes swept over the marshals.

"Stand easy you lot. There is only seven of you," smiled Xindro.

Diltoro held up a palm. Vrandala grunted like an indignant child, but he obeyed his prince.

Xindro turned to Krantolo.

"You have won no friends here today. We shall bring you the chancellor. But if any harm is done, I will hack you into a dozen pieces."

"How dare you," cried Krantolo.

"Cousin, bring me Vondaka," said Diltoro. "The twins will not be harmed. I promise you that."

Palama slowly rose. His legs were weak and his fingers trembled. Xindro stood and they both left without another word. As they climbed the winding path into the cold forest, Palama spoke.

"Blast the horns, we are leaving."

Leeporp poked his grinning head into the tent. He elbowed through and tossed a bundled cloth at Drolla. It bounced off his chest and fell open. He held the material up like an open window, soft white clouds drifted across a pale blue sky. Colours of the Cyan Corps.

"That is yours. You have been re-recruited."

Drolla draped the hem along his forearm. He fondled the weave, as smooth as glass, and squinted at Leeporp.

"Bonewasp gossamer?"

"Quadruple spun and battle ready," smiled Leeporp.

"Finest Drahni silk couture. Look at the edging." Drolla grinned.

"Beautiful," they laughed together.

Dandaron broke his silence and quenched the levity.

"No mention of actually preventing the assassination?"

"Nope," said Xindro.

"Well, his poisonings failed," said Dandaron.

"I have always heard the rumours of his crimes, but he is my par'. It was easier to ignore them than to press them," said Palama.

"Family demands loyalty. We must obey our only par', even if we hate them," said Drolla.

"He is the chancellor," said Dandaron. "He is powerful, and he guards Soltoro's sovereignty."

"And now the prince wants it," said Xindro.

"It's true. I told you, I overheard those quartermasters in the stores," said Drolla.

"Dandaron, you know Diltoro better than I. Do you think he is capable?" said Palama.

"The prince is a promise unkept and a boast never upheld. The child is stupid and Krantolo is his pilot. I expect he wants the torkh for himself."

"They can have it, they hold my twins," said Palama. "I want them back safe. Par's crimes have now endangered even his own grandchildren. I have to give him up."

"Easy said. You would have to kill Fontaza first," said Dandaron.

"That task is mine," said Xindro. He stroked his pommel with an evil smirk.

"I should lead a troop from the Corps to escort Vondaka back to face trial," said Palama.

"Palama, is Vondaka's summons a military matter?" asked Drolla. Palama did not answer. Dandaron flicked an eyebrow at Drolla. "We are at the war front. You would be labeled a deserter. Do you want yourself and your loyal escort impaled?"

"Of course not. What do you suggest?" said Palama.

"We should tell Soltoro everything and let him decide," said Drolla.

"Don't be ridiculous," said Dandaron. "He would condemn us all as petty provocateurs. His mind is focused only on the upcoming battle. He would resent the distraction."

"But if he knew, he might halt the war to save himself and the lives of thousands," said Drolla.

"And the Miokh might be kind enough to retreat and go home too?" scoffed Dandaron. "This conflict is unavoidable."

"We are in an impossible position," said Palama.

"No we're not," said Xindro. Three bewildered glares of disbelief turned on him. "The kids are quite safe where they are. We swapped out their guards yonks ago. The twins are protected by our own Oxxian agents. Their captors do not know it, but they are in more danger than their hostages."

"Is this Bendro's doing?" asked Palama. Xindro nodded. "Thank you fateshield, you have eased my mind. I can turn my worries elsewhere now."

"Then turn them to war, Commander," said Xindro. "There is glory in murder when you are forced to kill. None escape the fear, but some escape death. Let us be the butchers, and not the beasts."

"We should say nothing about this," said Dandaron, "and pretend we know less."

"We shall kill our enemies and march home victorious," said Xindro.

"Hand over Vondaka and rescue the kids," said Drolla.

"Oust my treacherous cousin and set Soltoro back on his throne," said Palama.

"Sky Dance the rest of the traitors," said Dandaron.

"What an excellent plan," said Drolla. He dropped to his knees and filled four saucers. "To victory," he toasted, "and to the monarch."

"Soltoro." They chanted and chugged back their biting brews.

Fontaza tore a doorflap from its stitching, it flopped aside like a dismembered tongue. Xindro scooped up his shard and and pushed the glass fist of his pommel into the Fontaza's chest. The beast grunted. His breath stank like compost. Dandaron leapt to his feet and stood by Xindro. Three furious hearts smoldered like volcanoes, each daring the other to erupt first.

"What is the meaning of this?" roared Palama.

Vondaka stepped in with a face of stone.

"How cozy," he said. "Stand aside, I wish to speak with your commander."

"You phapping sure he wants to talk to you?" blurted Xindro. He grinned at Fontaza. Any attempt at intimidation from him now was laughable. "Go on," said Xindro.

Flaring with hatred, Dandaron cocked his head, silently pressing the question.

A static wave flashed through Drolla. Without a thought, he scooped up the crockery and stepped aside. Time slowed, and violence loomed. While no shard had yet been drawn, angry hands gripped both hilt and sheath ready to unleash instant savagery.

"Enough!" said Palama. "Par', say your piece and leave. I am in no mood to entertain you."

It actually appeared that Vondaka's feelings were hurt. For a moment his face frowned with dispirited confusion. He soon curled his lip and composed himself. He spoke like an impassive courier repeating some cryptic message.

"The monarch has summoned the khillionaires to the war tent. Your immediate attendance is also obligatory." His tone changed direction like a chilling ocean breeze. "You will leave your peasant cronies here."

"My staff will accompany me anywhere I wish it," said Palama.

"Your staff?" Vondaka laughed. "You will suffer the contempt of their betters. This is no time to show off your new pets."

"Xindro, assemble the horde. Ready them to march with the main force," said Palama. His fateshield was reluctant and hesitated. A nod from Dandaron reassured him, Leeporp stepped through the torn entrance and vanished.

"You need not bother," said Vondaka. "I have advised Soltoro on this matter and he consented. Neither you nor your legion will cross the river. Zonara boasted of your efficiency at guarding the rabble at the waterfall city. You will order your forces to secure our vessels and the camp perimeter. We shall watch the battle together from under the royal tent. Do not dally."

He turned and swept to the exit. Amused, Fontaza took his wheezing grin and followed his master out.

"It cannot be true. Soltoro promised," said Palama. He dropped his shoulders, Dandaron sniffed unsurprised and Drolla stared at the flask. He watched his own hopes of glory run off with the chancellor and his fateshield. His chance to do battle for the kindom was thwarted on its very eve.

The war was all he came for. His very core demanded to know if he truly was a coward. Pride insisted he put his courage to the ultimate test. Death comes to everyone, but a life of shame is far worse a fate.

His selfish family would have hid him away for his own good, then hid their own disgrace with him in the deepest caverns, never to be seen again. A craven prisoner enthralled forever.

Ordinary syblings from across Drahn encouraged each other, they trained together and were resigned to battle together. He was denied the right to fight beside his peers and feared he would face the humiliation of being labelled a skulk. No amount of titles and wealth could erase the sting of your peers' disdain.

3.5 - THE GULLIBLE SKEPTIC

The monarch stood like an easel with a fist on each hip.

His royal black toga draped a shoulder and wrapped about his waist. Let out as a kilt, it hung off his hips like an uneven tablecloth. His shard slung from a belt of plaited white hair. Its handle was still swathed with the forgemaster's grey leather fold, the oil of the virgin blade soaked the hide like sweat. The thongs of his sandals crisscrossed up his shins and tied off behind the knees. Podgey welts poked between the laces that ran up his calves.

Under an open awning of the marquee, Vondaka leaned on a spindly tall table. A black leather satchel laid open. Curls of paperbark laid like fallen trees. His brown office robe shimmered like wet clay. Pinned under his armpits, it wrapped him like a curtain. A panting courier arrived and curtsied Vondaka. Fontaza grunted, his outstretch palm snapped open and closed, demanding the message. The fateshield passed the capsule to his master and scowled at the messenger. His eyes flashed dread, he rose quickly and disappeared. Vondaka snapped the seal and read the sliver of thin supple bark. He adjusted his toga and fondled its grasswood clasp. Gloating eyes left the table, he pinched a smile and peered into the distance of the Verdant Prairie.

Palama had braided his red toga battle style. Vondaka sniffed at his effort, it was a wasted display of childish defiance. Palama would not cross the river today. He wore a face like thunder and had difficulty disguising his disappointment.

"I trust your rabble has the hind perimeter sealed?" said Vondaka. Palama grunted a nod. "Good." His smirk enjoyed Palama's disgruntled obedience.

The fight was now out of their hands. Palama's mighty Orienna Horde was now a mere security detail. Being royal fateshields, Glendoro, Fontaza and Dandaron were the only enforcers present. The rest of the jade brigade scoured the surrounds beyond the horde's boundary. They chased off loitering merchants and searched for any last-minute deserters hiding away.

The military elite gathered around their monarch in a semi-circle. The khillionaires were all stiff clad in their indigo silk. They were wrapped tight, proud and petty. Stern learned minds quietly discussed the best plans of attack. Some were open to sensible suggestions, others adamant in their considered opinions. All struggled with a rational solution. Soltoro brooded in silence and ignored his wittering generals. He held his stance and his face searched the distant battlefield alone.

Palama stepped apart from the polite disagreements, and sidled next to his monarch.

"Soltoro," he muttered. "Unbroken and unbent, yet my bond now seems knotted. Am I fettered from battle after all?"

"Palama. Before any of them, I now rely on you," said the monarch. "If you see my signal, come to my rescue."

Two stone faces agreed.

Drolla peeped through a gap between the tent wall and the draping roof. He longed to be with the rest of the ordinary warriors. Even holding guard with his peers would be better than standing idly by in this awkward royal shade. He scanned the cluster of his betters in their bright blue garb. More than one cast a critical eye in his direction. He knew what they were thinking. He heard their whispers. They silently doubted the wisdom of Quetono, and the suitability of his new inheritor. This wide-eyed yokel from the far northeast, a backward corner of the nation, had the cheek to stand amongst the best and bravest in the whole kindom. Battle masters who rose through merit were forced to breathe the same air as this coddled adoptee.

Drolla understood their sentiment. He agreed with them. This time last year he was hawking up brown snot and sweating rivers within his putrid caverns. He had been nowhere and had done nothing to earn his new privilege. Even if he dared to explain that he understood them, these vain snoots would most probably scoff. Despite their mute objections, his presence was both legally and politically correct. He was a sporling of the royal family, and welcomed by the monarch. So, it really did not matter what these arrogant snobs thought. This time tomorrow, most might be too dead to jeer at their inferior.

The rear of the tent was closed on three sides. The open three out front each framed a different view. To the left, the monarch's yacht led the flotilla of rearranged catamarans. Lashed bow to stern, they ran north along the river and side by side from bank to bank. Boardwalks were laid across the cabin roofs. Gangplanks ramped from either bank and formed a long pontoon bridge. Atop the masts, long thin black streamers fluttered downwind like snakefish swimming upstream.

To the right, the white forest of fangs left no trace on the hillside. Their silken teepees, now unfurled, wrapped thousands upon thousands of rested Drahni warriors. Tent poles were lances again, and their shields were no longer squat mats. Now they sat clustered together within their fellow legions. As thick as grass, their numbers stretched from the mount to the river bank. Yesterday, the dismantled tented village and all its stores were packed onto the floating convoy by the sappers and the quartermasters. Today, they too stood in reserve.

Ahead, the opposite shore stretched across the open range. Over the river, the black sandstone bank gently rose to meet the dry, scaly prairie. Pale green lichen carpeted the enemy territory to the horizon. Past the mouth of the estuary, the black beach turned dirty brown and hazed into the distance. To the north, the faraway Dead Mountains seemed tiny mounds, joining the land to the clouds. Out across the prairie, a good way off, a small blurry force had assembled. They had been there for hours and the figures danced as a shimmering mirage.

"Do we at least know how many they are?" asked Soltoro. He could not mask his impatience.

"We reckon around three thousand," said Vondaka, looking up from his message.

"So few?" He threw his head over to face the khillionaires behind him. He took a step toward them. "Does anyone suggest a plan of attack?" His glare questioned each in turn.

279

"There is a difference of opinion, thyre," said Fandara.

"They are only three thousand, and we have seventeen," shouted Soltoro. "Surely, you can agree that we outnumber them?"

"I doubt it is their complete army," said Zonara. "I think it is a trick."

"How? Look, there is nowhere to hide," said Soltoro. He pointed an upturned palm toward the vast, empty field. The nearest ambush sites were thrice farther away from the enemy than the Drahn army was. "They could never be reinforced in time."

"I say we march at them," said Fandara. "Let my flingers bring them down and the rest of you can enjoy some sport dispatching the survivors." He grinned at his own brilliance. A few of his colleagues nodded in eager agreement. Zonara's stone face reflected his disapproval.

"We know the Miokh army is in excess of twenty-thousand," said Zonara. "Why do they only field three? Something is amiss. Without precise intelligence, I am not confident we should risk the lives of our syblings just yet."

"I have a note," said Vondaka, holding up a coiled strip of paperbark. "Just now delivered from my Tamzi merchant. He informs me that my shipment of Sparon herbs will be delayed."

"Drord's Guts!" Soltoro roared at his uncle. "How is that relevant?"

"His vessel was impounded," Vondaka continued, "during their stopover at Ghephokh. The Miokh capital has plunged into lock down. A federal coup has sparked a civil war within the state. Their main army is currently preoccupied fighting with itself."

"They have abandoned their vanguard," said Fandara. Every eye chased his gaze to the forsaken blurred enemy. All except Zonara, he stared doubt at Vondaka. The relief under the marquee spread like a splash of cold water. They cheered like gamblers who had seen the result before placing their bet. The doubters cleared their throats while the rest puffed out their chests. All dissent had disappeared.

Soltoro turned to Zonara. "We march en masse. We shall compel them to parley their surrender."

"And if they refuse?" asked Zonara.

"Then the fools will die," said Soltoro. "Let us go end this farce."

The jolly flock herded out behind their smug monarch and headed for the expectant kin waiting by the river. Palama and Dandaron stepped out in front of the tent and turned their faces toward the troops. Out of earshot, they chatted, pointed and nodded at the army. Vondaka sneered and scrunched up the merchant's message and dropped it onto the sandy floor. With gentle swipe, his foot half buried the note. He left his table of scrolls and joined Palama and Dandaron. Unnoticed by all, Drolla knelt and scooped up the small discarded scroll.

He smoothed it out and read, 'When you see our host assembled, send your monarch to his doom.'

Fontaza watched him read the message and smirked. He watched the rear tent flap squeeze shut after Drolla slid through it. He hated the grinning face of that animal, but the fateshield said nothing. Perhaps he did not care that Drolla had escaped, perhaps he preferred Quetono's brat be lost in battle. It did not matter, he had escaped unnoticed by those who mattered. With his heart in his throat, he sprinted towards the troops. He had to disappear among them before Dandaron realised he was gone. He had to get to Soltoro. He had to warn him.

The flingers lined the nearest outer edge of the swarm. They were the tallest of them all. Deep chests hugged pliant spines, their bodies were built to hurl death from afar. Woomeras were strapped to a quiver slung over one shoulder. Their darts stood proud, taller than them all. One rascal left his squad and with a welcoming palm Drolla was drawn into the throng. The flinger's mates then pushed him on. They misunderstood his mission and jeered him as a late-comer. He was shoved through lancers and he squeezed between the slingers. Ducking and weaving through each legion, he trod on toes and was pushed to the ground. Others picked him up and jostled him from one impatient crew to the next. He belonged to no squad and no hectarion called him into line.

Relief lifted his heart when his feet found a ramp. He was almost there. Soon he could warn Soltoro of the doom he faced. A firm grip held Drolla's shoulder and halted him mid step. Another pushy sybling shoving him about, no doubt. Drolla shrugged it off, yet the hand would not let go. His heart stopped stone cold as he glanced at large, strong fingers wrapping his shoulder and digging into his armpit. He dare not face their owner. He could not bear to see another disappointed frown from Dandaron.

"What are you doing here?" The insistent voice boomed. Drolla's face broke into a searing grin at the gorgeous sight of his old friend. "Palama's legion was forbidden to join the battle," said Boohala. He was dressed white like a recruit.

"Yet, here you are," said Drolla.

"I am incognito." Boohala grinned and patted a ribbon launcher hanging by his shard.

"I have to warn Soltoro. He has been fooled." The shift in the mass of bodies pulled them apart. As Drolla was dragged forward he yelled back. "See you after." Boohala nodded a smile. "Don't die," said Drolla.

Boohala frowned, shook his head and mouthed a grin. "No way."

Bustling soldiers closed off that farewell view. Drolla threw his head up and climbed the ramp, squeezing between the Protorians huddled atop the catamaran.

Soltoro left his forces and strutted down the ramp to the opposite bank. His royal guard and General Zonara watched the monarch carefully step sideways, arms akimbo, down the cleated ramp. He strode fifty paces up the sandstone shore and halted at the top edge of the pale green lichen. The vast expanse of the Verdant Prairie stretched flat behind him. Soltoro stood alone. He paused for a moment as if in quiet reflection, his restless army bore witness in silence.

Elders of Drolla's mauve forests often recanted this ceremony during their euphoric recollections. They boasted they had seen it from battles past, more often they were someone else's tales retold. The stoned old farts always outboasted each other, and quibbled over details that none could ever remember with any definitive accuracy. But the truth said it was an ancient seniocratic custom adopted by Xendaka during the Monofication Wars and used by every monarch since.

The warlord was going to war. Wisdom advised that kin should not be taken for granted. Expect them not to follow, nor force them. A free people would decide for themselves. Once, the gesture had meaning, now it was a farcical formality. Under the monarchy, the people had no choice. Now they were pressganged. Now they were expected to obey.

Zonara peered down at the lowly soldier that had appeared beside him. Drolla looked up at the towering old general and smiled. He then broke loose and ran toward the monarch with all the speed he could muster.

"Wha..." Zonara blasted. "Protorians, the monarch."

A dozen firstborn guards took chase. Drolla glanced back to see them almost upon him. If they caught him, they would kill him. His legs screamed as he forced them into a final burst and sprinted toward Soltoro. The monarch watched Drolla and the Protorians approaching fast and was taken aback at the fray bearing down on him. Drolla slowed at five paces and Soltoro reached for an arm. He plucked Drolla off balance and spun his panting cousin behind himself. The monarch splayed out his arms.

"Hold!" he commanded.

The Protorians encircled a defiant Soltoro and a cringing Drolla. Like stalking predators they slowly paced around them, ready to pounce if Drolla made the slightest wrong move.

"What fools are you?" roared Soltoro. "Do you not recognise Quetono's heir?" The Protorians sheathed their shards and curtsied their monarch.

"Forgive us thyre, we had no time to question his motives," said Zakala.

"Sometimes I doubt your devotion to your commitment. But I see you act when you must. Well done. Return to the ranks, I have an army to beseech." They did not move, Zakala stared at Drolla and flicked a curious eyebrow at his monarch. "My cousin will stay here with me. Advise the general."

The marbled tunics reassembled and ran back to retake their position atop the catamaran. Zakala reported to Zonara and he stiffened his back at the news. The distance and the northern breeze carried their words beyond Drolla's hearing. Every face now turned on the monarch and his attendant.

"What are you doing here, should you not be with the others?" asked Soltoro.

"Vondaka has betrayed you."

"Has he?"

"His merchant's note, it was a lie."

"Of course it was," grinned Soltoro.

"You knew?"

"Once I was naïve. Forever kept ignorant of everything around me. I was completely unaware Quetono had protected me for decades. But, since his death, many have quietly briefed me of Vondaka's crimes."

"He should be arrested. Diltoro is blackmailing Palama to do just that."

"Yes. What a folly, but it is all too late for that now. Look at the army."

"I know, they want to fight. They want victory and glory," said Drolla.

"More than that, they want their clan's pride. Everything will be straightened out after this battle."

"You could avoid it all. There is a price on your head."

"I know, but that does not matter now. Nothing that corralled us all here today can be undone. Victory will enthrone me a martial sovereign, or defeat will eulogize me as a warrior king. Win or lose, we shall all be heroes. But the battle must be fought first, and fought today. Will you fight with me Drolla?"

"Of course thyre, it is why I am here. It is why they are here."

"I am very happy to hear you say that. I often doubt the verity of my subjects."

"Set your doubts aside today, thyre. History awaits."

"Yes." The monarch faced his army. "I should make my plea, I suppose, and beg them to honour their vow. It is tradition, you know."

"I wouldn't. Let us two march alone toward battle together."

"We cannot take all the glory," joked Soltoro.

"Point your baton skyward," said Drolla. He threw an arm around Soltoro. A free arm pulled an arc and invited the army to join them. "Don't look back. Let them follow." Drolla grinned at Soltoro and with arm in arm, they trotted west.

"You are as sly as old Quetono," said Soltoro.

Not twenty paces in, hurried war horns blared. Hectarions bellowed and the soldiers roared. The brave Drahni Army swarmed over the river and entered into enemy territory.

When the indignant Protorians caught up and surrounded Soltoro, they elbowed Drolla aside.

"He might be firstborn, but he ain't no Protorian," grumbled Zakala.

The jealous troop worked in accord and shuffled him beyond the monarch and his immediate company. Soltoro shot his palm above his party.

"Rejoin your soldiery, cousin." The monarch shouted and beamed a salute to Drolla, then the delighted warlord welcomed his crowding army. Thousands ran to catchup and poured into position around the swirling core. By rank and file, they laid on outer layers and joined their jubilant kin. Their exhilaration would carry them to their fate. As they advanced to their outnumbered foe, the circular assemblage settled and began to rotate across the plain like a dawdling cyclone.

Pushed further out and dragged along to the outer arm, Drolla saw the lone warriors stand vulnerable in a desert sea of dried moss. The body of the spinning mass wheeled before Drolla and guided him and his fellows back to the furthermost lines from the front. The army settled into a steady jog and the half hour trot began.

Each time the swirling army drew him to the front again, Drolla saw it. A little way from the enemy, on the field either side, white spots appeared for a moment then disappeared.

"Did you see that?" asked Drolla.

No one answered. The ignorant mob pushed on their relentless pace, deafened by the crunching roar of the dry, emerald lichen they trampled underfoot.

The distant hazy enemy slowly came into focus. The oval cluster was naked and had painted their torsos black. If camouflage was their intent, they had failed miserably. They carried neither spear nor shield, but brandished their long spearaxes. The polished metal flashed like orange lightning in the morning sun. At one hundred paces out Drolla was outside the middle of great army, clustered among the shield bearing shardsters. War horns blasted their commands before the hectarions bellowed theirs'. The army slowed its jog and the outer edge closest to the painted nudes stepped apart and opened a wedge that tapered to the royal core. The Protorians mobbed Soltoro as he advanced into the opening and the inner ranks filed out and took their place around the outer edge.

Soltoro halted twenty paces out. The confident monarch curtsied. He stood proud and brave against his foes. He surveyed the small force opposing him. He turned his head and scanned his mighty army behind. Fandara winked and smiled while Zonara scowled at them all. Mistrust was still carved onto his stony face. Soltoro shrugged. This was his moment. His chance to parley and broker a surrender. If the outnumbered saw reason they could avoid a senseless slaughter. He would save thousands. He would be hailed Saviour of the Field and Hero of Drahn.

"Well?" roared Soltoro.

Unseen vitriolic trumpets split the air like screeching birds. White orbs appeared again out from the green carpet. From the left and right flanks, grinning heads rose up on bodies marching out of twin invisible gullies. The unseen dry riverbed was now obvious.

Their banks were carpeted by the same prairie lichen and their hidden depths snaked away to the distant hills. The entire Miokh army was concealed within. They clanked in formation from either side, up and out of the forked ravine, fifty abreast. Their torsos too were black, but they were not painted. They wore plate glass armour and chanted murder as they advanced. The Drahni reeled back in horror as reality struck them. They were duped and outnumbered. The cheating enemy used their own stolen black sand against them.

"Close the wedge," screamed Zonara.

3.6 - THE ORDERED CHAOS

The hidden enemy appeared like a parent's slap, sudden and unexpected.

The battle fell upon them in an instant. A shocked howl rippled across the ambushed mob. From the exposed forward centre to the defiant fringing rear, it surged like rolling surf. As the sonic wave rushed toward Drolla, a deep instinctive urge to yell welled up in him like a fountain. By then, the startled cry had become a conceded bellow. A groan of realisation. A grunt of contempt. In response, a determined air of bravado reflected back throughout the shaken army. By the time the war cry returned, it was a defiant roar. The Drahni soldiers were enraged, and they were indignant. All fear was smothered by the fury they held against the hidden frauds.

Two fronts of the emerging on-comers swarmed toward either flank. Hurling bitter insults, the lancers lowered their long thorns at the advancing enemy. The black vested lurkers boldly rushed, and their hateful smug grins ran directly into the phalanx. With their arms held overhead, they slung glass pellets at the faces of the defending lancers. The thorns harmlessly deflected off the glass armour, while the whizzing pellets seldom missed their mark. The thorns dropped away with their fallen lancers. The brave first line were killed instantly as the bullets burst through eyeballs and shattered skulls.

Spun from behind and arcing around in front of them, their pelt shields cascaded along the ranks into an interlocking fence of hard dried skin. Drahni leather stood against Miokh glass. The spooked survivors soon raised their pikes and joined their fellows behind the protective leather barrier. The enemy slingers now drew their shards and slashed at the hide wall. The brave siblings stood bolstered behind the shields and pushed hard to keep the hectic throng from smashing through. Blades flashed over and under in a wild attempt to stab and hack. Shards sang, flesh screamed and the lichen soaked up blood like cloth and ink. Above the pressing din, black and red streamers silently climbed high into the sky. Boohala had sent his summons.

"The Amber Creed. Shardhires."

Zonara pointed to the painted nudes and screamed above the impossible noise. The assassins were outed. Drolla gasped as the crush around him squeezed like a clenching fist. The stink of sweat and fear was unbreathable. He had put himself in a dangerous position. For a moment, he regretted his enthusiasm. But it did not matter now, death threatened from all sides. He had to keep upright and stay alert. There were hundreds of his peers between him and the enemy. If he paid attention, he would not be taken by surprise.

The Protorians that lined the open wedge hacked at the spearaxes like maniacs. They battled bravely to protect Soltoro. His fateshield Glendoro fought by his side, but most of the soft palace guards were out of their depth. As they attempted to closed the gap, they were themselves hacked down by the zealous nudes. Many of the firstborn watched their own guts spill out around them. They dropped to their haunches and howled in horror at the injustice. Some reached to bundle up their entrails while others thrashed about, and in their panic they entangled themselves within their own innards. The assassins casually stepped over the hopeless souls crawling away, their pink and grey intestines trailed behind them like the streamers of a kite.

Zonara barked his commands at Fandara and the other khillionaires. They in turn ordered their hectarions into position. Moving en masse to surround their monarch, the gaping open wedge began to close and entrap the boldest of the Creed's disciples. The shardhires may have taken the Protorians by surprise, but not the officers. They attacked with a ferocity that spooked the zealots. These teachers of the martial arts could not fight for shit. They had spent too long sparring amongst themselves and preaching to the untrained. Today the academics faced veterans. Vicious, merciless veterans who were, at last, able to unleash their pent up violence. And they did not hold back. Their blind ferocity struck panic into the stoic hearts of the faithful. And as they fell, the rampant Drahni trampled their butchered corpses.

"Lord Phrorph," roared Zonara.

The faithful minions nearby looked on confused. Who dared to challenge the leader of the Amber Creed? The lord threw his head over and scowled at his challenger. He tromped a few angry steps toward the old general and cried, "Zonara, you filthy apostate."

Phrorph fixed his cruel gaze on Zonara, then oddly spun his whole body with his spearaxe extended. Zonara shrugged in disbelief at the silly yet deadly pirouette. The blade whooshed past as it cut the air faster and faster, closer and closer. His intent was to slice deep across the belly and empty Zonara out in front of himself. It was said, for the Amber Creed, disembowelment was the only honourable way to dispatch an enemy. It was a slow death, time enough to ponder the end of a pitiful life.

Admired by his nearby flock, Lord Phrorph smirked, confident that he was about to impose his fatal blessing. Then, in an instant, Zonara pulled his shield from behind and deflected the racing hatchet into the ground. It flicked up a tuft of lichen as it bit into the black sandstone. Lord Phrorph lost his balance and stumbled forward, toward Zonara's awaiting shard. The blade pierced him at the base of his neck and drove hilt deep into his chest. Lord Phrorph exhaled in shock and blood spattered from his grimace. With a gentle push, he slid off Zonara's blade, collapsed, and gurgled his last.

This spectacle spurred on his colleagues to strike at the painted nude zealots even harder. Fandara cheered in sheer delight after he severed an arm with third of a chest of one fanatic and plunged his shard through the belly of another. Fandara danced in mockery at the wretch as he quivered on the end of his blade. He was far too engrossed to notice an attack from behind. A slashing copper axe hacked open his distracted midriff, and his guts tumbled out around him. It sounded like an emptied bucket of fish. Before he knew what had happened, he was squatting amongst his trembling gizzards. When he realised, he clutched at his open belly and screamed at the sky.

Twin mottled shadows sped silent across the jostling throng like flocks of hunting bats. From the Drahni rearguard, the flingers emptied their quivers. Hundreds of darts flew overhead left and right toward the Miokh attackers surging from the gullies. Keen to join their comrades up top, they fell in droves as arrows rained death onto the crowded ramps. Others saw the imminent threat and attempted to sidestep the arrows, carelessly pushing their neighbours under an arrow that might have missed. Fate soon rewarded them in kind, when they too were elbowed aside and caught their own dart and were impaled from mouth to cunt.

Those who had already fallen reflected fresh peril at their fellows. Striking the battle armour of the prone dead and dying, the brittle glass missiles shattered on impact. Splinters exploded and tore into any unprotected enemy flesh nearby. Death for them was not instant, but the injuries bled out fast. The wounded stumbled a little before they finally fell.

Repeated frantic orders pierced through the clamour, "Re-nock! Pitch!". Volley after volley, the shadows rushed overhead as the darts showered the enemy and skewered all they struck. The advancing numbers were kept in check for a while. Soon, all the arrows were spent, but the enemy kept coming scrambling over their own dead.

Drolla was a mere ten deep from the fighting front. A fellow pulled a shield from a dead comrade and pushed it onto him. The slow spiral of the battling formation gradually forced Drolla with the fresh troops to the outer edge while the weary were drawn into the middle to rest. But there was no rest there either. The naked fanatics were holding their own against the veterans. Zonara was the only khillionaire still standing with several hectarions, desperately defending their monarch. Soltoro was covered in blood and not a single drop of it was his own. The lethal agility of the stout little podge amazed any who cared to see. He was as vicious as his comrades, delighting in the danger and doling out his share of death to the wretched mercenaries.

Pushed to the outer edge of the mob, Drolla spun and pushed his shield in front of him in sequence with his adjacent peers. The wave clattered along the line as the shields' underprods stabbed the lichen sandstone. The syblings protected the next, left over right. The fear of the impending assault was gouged into the faces of his peers. His legs were numb, his shield weighed like stone and his shard, still sheathed, rattled in his grip.

Through the deafening violence, a foreign squawking trumpet announced another entrance. The armoured violators obediently ceased their fighting and stepped away. Everyone behind the shield wall grunted in approval of the unexpected respite, yet thousands of worried eyes followed their ringing ears.

During the lull of the changeover, a distant roar approached from the river. Like rippling scales, a thousand braided cloudy blue togas slithered as one across the patina field. The eye of the cyan serpent was a scarlet toga. Half unfurled, it flapped like the petals of an angry starflame blossom. Palama and his Orienna Horde sprinted toward rescue.

Fresh enemy troops clanked down the inner slope of the crescent crater of the dead. Leading the second wave, a large proud brute ambled ahead of his troops. His gaudy mantle drew every eye to him. Fluffy bright yellow feathers fluttered around his neck and spilled over his shoulders.

"Behold! Imperator Vrerth." His soldiers heralded his arrogant arrival.

The nervous recruits peeked between the cracks in their hide-wall. Taller than his comrades, he held an unsheathed shard in each hand, his third tucked a shield behind him. He pointed each blade in either direction. His subordinates grunted their salute and two lines forked apart to surround the exhausted Drahni. Now encircled like a scaly wreath, the new black armour pushed with an overwhelming power. Glinting glass rattled as it forced forward, white silk and grey leather bent at the pressure. There was nothing to dig their heels into.

There was no firm hold to push back with, the once dry moss was now a soggy mire.

The crush was unbearable. The heat was sapping all their strength. Lungs ached as they inhaled the stifling air and laboured as they exhaled their spent breath. Drolla's energy was draining like warm honey from a cracked vase. His fellows were swooning, some had fainted. With all his might he could barely hold himself up.

He did not feel the rigid grip in his armpit pull him back. Staunch fingers dug deep into his groin and he was hoisted aloft. The battle blurred beneath and surprised eyes followed him as he vaulted over them. The ground rose fast and took the skin off his knees and elbows. Drolla glanced at the rift in his syblings his exit had caused. He was thrown back six deep and where he once stood, was Boohala. He waved back with one hand as he slashed at the enemy with the other two. Four opponents pounced onto the hunk and after a momentary struggled pause, all were flung off flipping end over end. Several of their comrades were taken out as they crashed through them. More pounced again and the gap crashed shut. Drolla lost sight of his saviour within the bloody scrum.

A whistle squealed like a startled child and the attackers abruptly halted their push. The outer edge of warriors stumbled forward, hundreds were shoved to the ground by the unimpeded thrust of their supporters behind. In a sudden disarray, the Drahni fell about fumbling and yelling. The struggling warriors were too exhausted to pick themselves up.

This was the opening the Miokh intended. They leapt over the bumbling sprawling front and breached the outer ring of defense. A new attack started in earnest. Fighting on two fronts, the sly attackers began to spiral in through the Drahni ranks. Lines of syblings were peeled off like the skin of a fruit, and the fresh juice flowed just as freely. The enemy curled inwards and repelled the panicking lines toward the centre like a slow ocean rip. The sweaty mass moved like whirlpool and drew Drolla with it.

The middle was far less crowded than when he had left it, the medics saw to that. Bloody white stains began greying to black across the jaded war ground. Crescent shaped craters of the dead ringed each other like crests of a rippling pond. Between the peaks, the fields were cleared for more battle. Each as inviting as a freshly lined coffin. Neutral foes shared the gruesome burden and cleared the battlefield together. Surgeons and morticians armed only with potions and utensils were shielded by a nurse's charity. Protected by pink neckerchiefs, they were ignored and unharmed. They dispensed Rythene's care with impunity. Triage treated the wounded, doomed the critical and stacked the dead. Still, as sombre as they appeared, they laughed at the corpses. Some disjointed poses and dead faces were far too hilarious to ignore. They argued that brevity mellowed their morbid task and despite that, no corpse was laid without due reverence, no wounded was treated without due care. Unlike the Amber Creed who brought no medics and abandoned their fallen without a thought.

The elder zealots and juniors encouraged each other. Yet, they were worried. The bulk of their adults and seniors were dead. Lord Phrorph had set a futile example and the virtuous attempted to best his fatal effort. These disciples were crazy. Their ranks might take two or more generations to replenish the order. Now, they weighed the merit of each fight. Their bravado had deserted them.

From the tight web of young and old, they knitted a defensive line of attack. The elders had surrounded Soltoro while the juniors kept Zonara and his peers in play. A child ran at Drolla, flashing his golden spearaxe left and right, screaming like childbirth. Surprised, Drolla took unexpected and hurried steps back away from his juvenile assailant. He was not keen on killing someone so young. The brat looked no more than fifteen. Yet the kid's fury was as vicious as any adult there today. Confusion and alarm tripped Drolla backwards. One foot snagged another, and the ground rose fast and hit his shoulders hard. Clumsy feet kicked the air for a moment then pain screeched across his torso. Layers of his tight-wrapped toga burst open like petals followed by a splash of hot blood. His blood. The screaming child warrior lifted his shiny cleaver over his head and leaped towards Drolla. Despite his stinging chest, instinct pulled his shield over him in time to take the brunt of the crashing strike. The leathered shield crackled and chipped as the frenzied brat hacked at it, blow after blow.

Out on the open prairie, the stampeding legion was nearly upon them. A lone figure sprinted forward from the head of the serpent horde as if it had spat a drop of venom before striking. But it was the mighty Xindro. Cheers from within the embattled ranks rose up. The showoff shardster ran ahead of his horde grinning at his adoring fans. He wielded three glass blades and burst into the ranks of the oblivious enemy. His wheeling shards sang doom as they danced the mortician's ballet.

Following him, arms, hands and weapons spun through the air like a disturbed swarm of jumpbugs. Blood splashed like garden fountains. Xindro laughed at every stroke and yelled abuse at his wretched victims as he blazed a trail of mayhem for his ensuing comrades. The horde pressed through the gap of the recoiling amputees. Now it was the enemies' turn for a surprise. They howled in terror as their secret weapon was rendered useless. Their arms and legs were not armoured, and they were easy targets.

Led by the Oxxian champion, the Orienna horde put his martial techniques into deadly action. The serpent speared inwards and sideways. In their wake, they left trails of limbless bodies bleeding out all over their mighty glass armour. Hundreds fell howling at their quivering stumps. Their comrades recoiled in horror at this new and immediate carnage. If not for the spurring commands from their superiors, they may have routed there and then.

The horde penetrated the outer rings of the front line combatants and walled out the enemy. The spent syblings were protected by the fresh scales of the cyan serpent. Dashing through the carnage, Palama called for surviving hectarions to round up their wounded and fatigued. He commanded they escort them back to the river. Those able, were to prepare the boats for immediate departure. Many exhausted warriors found their second wind and refused to abandon their rescuer.

Reinvigorated by the presence of Palama and his legion, they threw themselves back into the fray.

The raging brat had soon tired and stood panting at his quarry cringing under its shield. Drolla took his chance, and kicked the young ones legs out from under him. The poor kid squealed, and fell onto himself. Drolla pounced and pushed his shield onto the squirming brat and sat on both. The breathless child lay gasping for air under the weight of Drolla and his shield. The belly wound was shallow and the bleeding slowed, but it still stung like mad. He tore strips from his toga and bound the wound tight. His resting gaze panned the arena. The place looked like a slaughterer's pit, and it stank even worse. The monarch battled within earshot. Glendoro fought by his side, but did not see the broken lance coming. It cracked over his head, and he dropped like a felled tree. In response, Soltoro carved open the chest of the attacker. The monarch stood in triumph over the screeching martyr. He took a moment to catch his breath and stretched his short back.

Without warning, death struck Soltoro from his blindside. The last senior of the Amber Creed broke with tradition and took his head off. From halfway behind his back, the tall assassin arced his metallic blade. The level slice was so swift, Soltoro's severed head spun on its neck. Blood seeped, then splurted like a ruffled collar before his noble head tipped and fell. His body dropped to its haunches and slumped aside. The nearby elder zealots rushed to the corpse and pruned off all his limbs.

"Curse your rescuers," one screamed.

Some juniors had scavenged a lance and ran to the rabble abusing the royal corpse. The grey thorn was impaled into the gaping neck. They pushed the pole until the tip burst out between his buttocks. Blood and shit sprayed over the jeering defilers. More kids joined the melee and helped raise the fatal message into the sky. Mingled roars erupted at the sight. The victors' ecstatic cheers drowned the despairing howls of the defeated. The battle was over. If not for the rescuing horde, the Drahni would have been slaughtered as they routed. High above the battlefield,

Soltoro's toga unraveled from his bluing corpse. In the casual breeze of the prairie, it billowed out like a plume of black smoke. In a distracted moment, the squirming brat under Drolla wriggled himself free from beneath the shield.

"'tis done," his broken voice squeaked.

The teen sprang to his feet. He paused to glance back at Drolla and with a hateful sneer, he slashed his axe. He laughed as he ran to join his mates and help them hold their prize skyward.

It was as if Drolla ran through a low door and forgot to duck. The stun was blinding. His face ran wet and the heavy ache pulled his head to the ground with a thud. Multiple blurry monarchs bobbed about above the herd of screeching adolescents.

The noise of the battle lulled and whispered like the gentle rumble of distant thunder. The sun faded into the clouds. The golden disk turned silver against the darkening sky. Maybe soon, as black as the skies beyond the southern horizon. As dark as the endless starry night. The folk there say, 'each star is a soul, and every soul becomes a star.' Perhaps, they might shine here too. Warmth bled from his throbbing head. Icy bites of imaginary frost ants swarmed up his numbing legs. Feeble hands failed to wipe away the tingling chills, and his eyelids grew heavier as the endless shadow hastened toward him.

Within the darkening mist, memories swirled and drained like leaves in a whirlpool until only one image remained. Alone in the drifting cabin, the last faint glimmer of Dandaron's lamp blinked out. He laid quiet in the unlit gloom and groped for the furry quilt. It wasn't there, nothing was. His dream dissolved and the deathly silence whispered, "Dan..."

3.7 - THE TRIUMPHANT DEFEAT

The armistice was tense.

The Drahni were forbidden to assist in the clearing of the dead, not even their own. The altruistic victors welcomed the dire undertaking. The fallen were stacked into the pit at the end of the hidden gorge. Sutlers accompanied the supply train and brought their fermented fruit oil. Umpteen dozen barrels of liquid fire sat ready. Drahni and Miokhi dead laid prone together, stacked into a tall round pyramid. The morticians flooded the hollow gully. Nostrils flared at the stinging vapours, the volatile fluid was far too ripe for a mortal nose. At a diplomatic distance, Palama and his forces squatted in solemn respect. The Imperator hosted the short funeral. His eulogy was concise and heartfelt. He bid all the fallen warriors of either nation an heroic farewell in his own splintered foreign tongue. Military silence replaced the civilian hymn. The cremation pyre was then struck alight. Invisible flames incinerated the corpses. The unseen fire shimmered hot like a mirage and slowly turned meat and bone into smoke and ash. For hours, the blue fumes spewed skyward like a geyser. The inferno roared like a waterfall and stank like a sewer. Hours later, the last of the embers smoldered still. An occasional slender white wisp would hiss and dance here and there. Soon the desert winds would scatter their honoured ash, with their glorious memories, across the lichen desert.

Palama's bare feet adored the plush carpet. Green veins streaked the fleecy white fur and squeezed between his toes like soft fluffy marble. It laid wall to wall under the silken awning, a tiny slice of luxury amid the tear-stained aftermath of battle. A bowl of rank pot potpourri hung from a ceiling hook. The sickly sweet fragrance did nothing to mask the ripening pong of the dead. It somehow made it worse. A short funglstone plynth carved like a mini volcano awaited Imperator Vrerth. Like dripping lava, orange tassels hung from the crimson cushion. The attending scribe shuffled papers about on his tall table. At first he cast a gloating glare, from then on his smug smirk ignored the conquered guests.

Nerves were frayed. The victors would soon present their terms. The sand was lost, the defeated knew this. They also knew, as delegates, they were persons inviolate. Still, the foreigners could not be trusted beyond the shade. Despite the Vrerth's security team surrounding the parley awning, Boohala captained a small detail of Cyan Corps, and kept their own rigid perimeter around Palama, Xindro and Dandaron.

Echoing into earshot, barking orders and shouting assent preceded the measured tramping footsteps. Parched moss crunched underfoot and announced the arrival of Imperator Vrerth. Proud generals strutted in behind Vrerth's shadow. His bright yellow feathered mantle had stiffened with spattered dried blood. Three thick curved glass plates were stitched together with copper twine and wrapped his chest. Rivers of smolderstone powder sparkled deep within the glazed cuirass. Grey leather pleats separated as he sat. Split to the waist, the studded kilt dangled between his thighs. The audience curtsied as he took the plynth.

"Not you," said Vrerth to Palama, motioning him to remain standing. The imperator's accent was heavy, but he spoke Drahni well enough. They looked silently into each other, the same as they had yesterday.

Across the battlefield, two commanders stood motionless. Their gazes locked as the mayhem raged around them. Neither were keen to advance a new attack. Vrerth's superior numbers held back, unwilling to re-engage Palama's horde of cleaving butchers. The Miokhi witnessed the orderly retreat and the silent truce began. Xindro and his boisterous followers ran back and forth between the lines that separated the idle armies. They wildly brandished their weapons and chanted in concert.

Their hoarse proclamation echoed throughout the mass of combatants. Xindro led the chant.

"Seniarch Palama! Seniarch Palama!"

The horde cheered after them, and inspired their surviving comrades to join then, cementing their support. The enemy pulled themselves back into a guarded formation, some even curtsied with mock homage.

"I salute you, warlord. It is a fine thing to be endorsed sovereign-of-the-field by your own army," said Vrerth.

"The elders' league might beg to differ," said Palama, serious and unflattered.

"Paf!" laughed Vrerth. "Would the craven stay-behinds dare defy your mighty legions? Your sturdy force commands respect, young master."

"I appreciate your praise, but with all due respect, may we begin the conference," said Palama.

"As you wish. There is much to be done yet. The terms are thus; your defeat forfeits the entire western province you call Oxxia and everything contained within it."

"Drord's phapping Guts," sprayed Xindro.

The imperator flashed him a sober glare. A frown from Dandaron halted any tirade Xindro may have considered.

"And what of the Drahni civilians living on those lands?" Palama closed his eyes and sighed.

"Any who wish to migrate east, may. Any who stay, will live under the Premiership of the Miokhi Republic," said Vrerth. "There will be no violence to your people, if you take your army and leave."

"We fought to protect our black beaches," said Dandaron. "We did not think the whole province was at stake."

"Of course you did," said Vrerth. "That was the deal."

Insults and profanities burst into the tent. Three guards failed to restrain the unwelcome visitor. He slipped their hold and stood before the imperator. Vrerth shot to his feet and roared at the fracas.

"Disarm the fanatic."

Three blades flashed and rested on the zealot's shoulders. He craned his neck as the edges nicked his flesh, as still as stone he hissed through gritted teeth.

"Do not hinder Creed business."

The guards tore his copper blade from his grip and hurled it from the tent. They looked to Vrerth for direction, with a scowl he waved them off. The guards moved to the fringe of the carpet, yet stood poised and alert. One false move and they would gladly hack the intruder down. The naked zealot was short and skinny and his eyes flared like a maniac. Half the black paint had worn off his torso and the other half was caked in dried blood. With outstretched arms, he held a bundled black cloth. It was Soltoro's battle toga.

"Thlarsh," yelled Vrerth. "You were promised time. Show some decorum." As he sat, the proud commander flashed embarrassed eyes at Palama.

"I am entitled to be here," snapped Thlarsh. "I want but a moment, and I will take it now." His wild eyes turned to Palama. "The contract is fulfilled."

He dropped the bundle and it squelched at their feet. The cloth fell open and revealed his cousin's head. The eyes were closed, but the mouth gaped like a cave. Soltoro's dying scream, silent forever. Xindro growled and his shard's hilt leather creaked in pain, throttled by his furious grip. Dandaron blinked away his welling tears and knelt. He covered the dead face and gently scooped up the precious bundle. The colour ran from Palama's face.

"If only we arrived sooner," he muttered.

"Your monarch fought like a beast," said Vrerth. "These deluded shardhires paid a high price. A few thousand lives for one. Pathetic."

"They died for free, in worship of the war hero Churon," replied Thlarsh. He pointed at the grieving trio. "Their traitor is yet to pay his fee."

"Not my concern. You have done your bit, now get out," said Vrerth.

The waiting guards sprang at Thlarsh. With cruel delight, they twisted each arm back on itself and frog-marched the struggling martyr to the edge of the smoldering pyre. He screamed foul terror as they hurled him in.

"Those fanatics are detestable," spat Vrerth. "Never again. Vondaka was a fool to hire them as well."

The Drahni trio were ripped from their grief. Confusion danced between their arching eyebrows before they all fell on Vrerth.

"As well?" asked Dandaron.

"But, he only hired the Amber Creed to kill Soltoro..." said Palama.

"He did, but they could never strike. Forever protected by an uncle, they said." Vrerth grinned a little. "So, he arranged this battle. It has been planned for years."

"Since you started stealing our sand?" said Dandaron.

"It was his idea. We should dredge the sand and so provoke a war," said Vrerth. "He wanted your monarch dead and arranged everything he could to ensure it."

"What prize is worth so much?" gasped Palama.

"Your Vondaka is a treacherous one," said Vrerth. "I was surprised he had not been outed before now. But, your reactions here prove his mastery of deceit."

"It does not make sense," said Dandaron.

"Not my concern," continued Vrerth. "Pack up your survivors and go home. I have an army that wants to bathe in your," he paused to wink a grin, "*our* black beach. Goodbye."

The conference was over. Vrerth stood. His minions followed him from the marquee and were swallowed by his protective wardens. The elitist guard ushered the proud imperator to his cheering battalions. Their victory celebrations had now begun. The scribe handed over the Declaration of Peace.

"Stamp here. And there. Thank you. Your copy. Ours. Please note," he pointed to a clause on the parchment, "failure to abide by these terms would result in a punitive response, one without mercy."

The arrogant scribe baled his papers and ran to catch up to Vrerth's entourage.

Palama, Xindro and Dandaron remained motionless and dazed. How did that happen? They had lost everything, their monarch, their sand and a whole province. The enemy sappers began dismantling the marquee.

"Move," a sergeant blasted.

The carpet was rolled from under them. Without the impatient command, jolting them back to reality, they might have stood there all day. With nothing else to be done, they began their solemn walk back to the river in silence. Glendoro took the black bundle from Dandaron. A detachment of the Cyan Corps ran ahead to proceed with the immediate departure. The catamarans were already overloaded with defeated soldiers ready to go home. In their hearts, most had already left.

"Well, it all turned out alright then," said Drolla.

"Are you still delirious?" Dandaron squinted his disbelief.

"No, no. All good. Mere flesh wounds." Drolla tapped the bandage around his head.

"We lost everything! How is that alright?" Palama hissed through clenched teeth.

"We live, thanks to you."

"Seniarch after all," said Xindro.

Palama groaned and rolled his face away.

"You have several thousand grateful survivors that insist you are," said Dandaron.

"Bendro will be pleased." The edge of Xindro's grin nearly reached his eyes.

Palama ignored them. His gaze was fixed on the escaping catamarans festooned behind them. Two days ago, a hundred followed the monarch's yacht as they snaked out of the Oxxian River into the open ocean. Now, the defeated fleet hugged the coastline just beyond the crashing surf. The sailors kept the land in sight to prevent the army of landlubbers plunging into panic. It was a long, slow voyage back to the sheltered safety of The Kataraxs' bay.

While the horde escorted the beaten soldiers to the waiting boats, Drolla was found by Joltoro. He and Tranna commandeered a squad of trovers and searched the fallen for any comrades that might still live. Away from the eyes of any authority, a rowdy cluster of battle-drunk thugs taunted a dazed and confused Drolla. He tottered about with a face streaked with his own blood. His eyes were curdled shut. The kladgers goaded the injured fool with broken lances, then jeered at him blindly slashing his blade through the air. They meant to wear him down until he bled himself out. One spat in his face. Drolla rubbed his eyes and the slobber softened his bloodied lashes. His eyes blinked open. In a moment of clarity, the weary haze that stifled Drolla also lifted.

His gaze saw wrists and elbows. The air whispered. In four flurried strokes, those nearest lost hands and forearms in a flash. Their comrades reeled back awestruck. Just as quick, the haze returned and wrapped Drolla like a weighted net. Spent, he collapsed. Surprise turned to revenge and vows of murder filled the air. Drahni rescuers swooped in and encircled Drolla. While the unconscious evacuee was hoisted onto his saviour's shoulders, Joltoro and Tranna confronted the shivering blades of the angry foes. Now they rattled more from worry than from vengeance.

Tranna laid an undaunted threat and pointed from the severed limbs to the opponents' own. Joltoro pointed towards the half-built funeral awning where Vrerth would honour the fallen. The tacit choice was put to the insulted goons, dare they risk mortal injury and breach their Imperator's truce? Wisely, they held their stead. A begrudging nod allowed the Drahni squad to withdraw and join their retreating army. As they made their hasty exit through the mournful battlefield, the Miokhi morticians gathered corpses for the pyre.

The small company brought Drolla directly to Torono. The royal surgeon oversaw his medics. Each vessel was assigned a nurse with a small makeshift sickbay for their patients. Most were squeezed in below deck, between rations and tackle. After Torono's interns washed and dressed his injuries, Drolla was laid to recover in the grand saloon atop the monarch's yacht.

Pure Vitron glass, as clear as air, plated the oval cabin. The windows were swiveled open and the sweet salty breeze washed through the upper deck. The cooling ocean mist settled like dew across the wall shelving. Waist high, its tapered edge ringed the cabin and sat above a dado of polished grasswood cupboards. Tiles of slated stone covered the floor like an outdoor patio and an enormous round pouffe of smooth brown suede dominated the middle. It stood as high as a knee and as wider than the tallest person. Drolla squatted in the middle like a boss. His legs were trapped within the tangled pile of soft woolen quilts.

Glendoro placed his precious parcel on the wall shelf. The monarch's royal toga was washed and crisp. It wrapped the glass embalming jar with a series of black segmented pleats, the first seamlessly tucked into the last.

"The morticians have prepared Soltoro."

All eyes in the cabin fell on the tiny cloaked coffin and paused in respectful silence for a moment. That little jar and its lifeless royal contents uprooted the uncomfortable future that had remained as yet unspoken. But, it was a future they would all soon face.

"Vondaka has not yet left his cabin," said Glendoro. "Fontaza bars any interruptions."

"Good," said Palama. "Let him fester in his own self-imposed house arrest."

"He is wise to stay out of sight," said Dandaron.

"Let the city marshals take him to the Prince," said Drolla.

"I just want my twins safe," said Palama.

"You will get them back," said Xindro. "Krantolo knows the penalty if not."

Hurried footsteps scrambled up the cleated ramp into the saloon. The ship's caterer brought up a large tray covered with open bowls of delicious picnic dishes and sparkling drinks. He placed the meal on the wall shelf next to the black parcel. He slammed his eyes shut and thrust his face high. With hands over his heart, the mourning subject curtsied the reverent remains of his beloved monarch.

"Woe to his demise," he whispered. He stood and informed the group. "Lunch, with compliments from Viceroy Vondaka."

"Viceroy," Xindro laughed "to who?"

"He moves quickly," scowled Palama.

"Take it away," said Dandaron. "Bring us sealed jars from the pantry. Nothing opened." The nervous caterer nodded a frown and disappeared back downramp. "No one is safe with Vondaka aboard." Dandaron began an unnecessary explanation. His voice soon trailed off and mingled with the others. Their political blather was of no interest to Drolla.

He was lost in his own thoughts. He stared vacantly at the horizon ahead and pondered his destination. A place where his own liberty awaited him. He was rescued from his childhood prison, he had served his kindom in battle and liberty was his reward. Free to live his own life. He would never return home, except maybe to visit and gloat. He was now master of Quetono's country estate. No, his own estate. He would release Dandaron of his fateshield vow, he deserved freedom as well. He should take Quetono's city mansion.

I'll gift it to him, he vowed to himself. Palama can have his realm. Leeporp can have his army. Drolla wanted leisure. He wanted staff. He wanted pampering and his new manor sounded perfect.

Slow heavy footsteps tromped up the rampwell. Fontaza's ugly mug appeared from the floorline first. His head bobbed higher with each step, not unlike the first of the enemy rising from the lichen gorge. This arrival was even more unwelcome. His wheezing frown of mistrust scanned the room and eyed the faces of his rivals. His stony glare insisted they behave. From behind his wary fateshield, Vondaka grinned wide at Palama and stepped from the ramp. He lowered his curtsy with every step and crooned,

"Congratulations."

"Par'. Can you not even offer one handful of grief?" said Palama, nodding toward Soltoro.

"I will save my tears for the funeral." The smile fell from his face. "We have no time to mourn. The prince awaits us all at The Kataraxs. There is much to do."

"There is," said Palama. "The prince said your Amber assassins await their fee."

"What fee? The Creed has conned the fool," said Vondaka.

"No. A zealot demanded payment from me. The Consultorium hold their own witness under arrest. We all know you are guilty and they mean to prosecute you," said Palama.

"Poh. You are the sovereign-designate now, you will veto any such nonsense."

"Will I?" said Palama. With a flick of his wrist he let a scroll unfurl in front of Vondaka.

"The Declaration of Peace? Seen it. I wrote it," said Vondaka.

Incredulous yelps jumped from every throat in the room, except the impassive Fontaza. His dull grin relished their surprise.

"Par'. You have committed the most treacherous betrayal in history."

"I saved Drahn."

"You lost Oxxia," said Xindro.

"Oxxia?" quizzed Vondaka. "They are no loss, no better than a rabble of brags. Let the Miokh suffer them."

"You have lost us our sand," said Dandaron.

"We have a decades worth of ingots in reserve," Vondaka stabbed a finger at Drolla. "You have seen them. You also know what else is down there, don't you?"

"Yes, I smelled it. You are growing Red Spore."

"An easy fortune, worth a dozenfold more than hardmade glass," said Vondaka. "The prince has lost his Oxxian income."

"The twins are lost as well, unless I hand you over. President Krantolo holds your own grandchildren hostage," said Palama.

"Yet still safekept from you by Oxxian Guards," said Vondaka. "Perhaps they too have reason to blackmail you?"

"How dare you," seethed Xindro. Fontaza gripped his hilt and swallowed hard. Vondaka held up a hand and silently begged for calm.

"I am sorry about the children," said Vondaka. "I did not mean for them to be kidnapped, but that complication has not altered the plan."

"What plan?" asked Palama.

"Why, to put you on the plynth, of course."

"Drord's Guts. This again?" said Palama. "It is ridiculous. I know nothing of royalty."

"I promised it on your birthing pillow," said Vondaka.

"Why?"

"Despite being the youngest, Bontoro assumed the throne. He had already birthed Soltoro and exercised an heir's right. The monarchy should have been mine. I was the eldest, but I was childless. When Quetono birthed Drabana, the insult was worse. At last, I birthed you Palama and vowed then to retake the royal line and make you monarch."

"You idiot," laughed Xindro. "You betrayed your greatest ally. Oxxia had already endorsed Palama as sovereign."

"And now the entire army supports him," snapped Vondaka. "Krantolo's illegal marshalry will not stand a chance. The prince is doomed."

"You misunderstand. I care only for my twins. I do not care about the throne. I don't even care about you. You betrayed your kin, and they will judge you themselves."

"You ungrateful brat. Everything I have ever done was for you..."

"No," Palama interrupted. "It was all for you and your own gloating vengeance. For decades you have made yourself a puppet master. Well, I am cutting your strings. I renounce all you have done," his scowl leaned in closer, "and I renounce you."

The slap across Palama's face startled everyone. Without hesitation, he retaliated.

His fist landed squarely on Vondaka's mouth. The force of the blow knocked him down hard and fast. His neck crunched on the edge of the wall shelf. Vondaka fell to the floor in a clumsy heap and did not move again. A runnel of blood crept from under his twisted neck. Vondaka was dead.

3.8 - THE PAINLESS AGONY

Yesterday's washing hung on the deserted balconies.

Every local boat had left the bay empty and the silence of the vacant city was louder than the roar of the lonely waterfall. The soldiers were baffled. Like the boiling mists at the base of the falls, their faith evaporated when the expectant flotilla rounded the cape. Neither a wave nor a cheer. Not a single flag or pennant. Nothing but forgotten rags on the occasional neglected clothesline. No kindness greeted their humble return. Surely, their generous billetors did not resent them still?

The terror of the battle and the shame of the rout weighed heavy on their sodden hearts. Despite their failure, had they not done their duty? They wished to revisit their former hosts and craved the warmth of a reassuring hug. Many boasted the hopeful promise of fresh food and strong drink and fluffy cushions on a terrace lounge. Keen eyes searched for any activity on the patio that pampered them last time. Perhaps they themselves were not forgotten, even if everyone else was. Alas, the hundreds of porchyards carved into the lofty cliffs showed no signs of any life. Dejection corroded the hopes of even the most optimistic. The place seemed abandoned. Something was wrong.

While the army slipped away down the Oxxian River like truants, the mariners took to their helms and steered the convoy over the crashing surf and into the open channel. The self-appointed chauffeurs prided themselves that they would deliver the fleet home safe. The past is mourned, let the broken rest and await the friendly harbour. They had timed their departure well. The great monthly tides had passed and would not return for weeks. As the ocean flowed west chasing the Petramon, the channel winds blew the voyagers east. They would drop anchor long before the mighty waves returned.

The monarch's yacht sat in the middle of an invisible web. Pilots steered their laden craft into an ordered array around the royal hub. For days they held a steady course out of consideration of the queasy landlubbers. But, the drudgery of the dawdling voyage soon enticed the jolly sailors to compete. The tillers would challenge their mates and playfully weave in and out of the convoy. The catamarans veered close enough to tease anyone who dared to leap across. With a hilarious dousing of sea spray, they sped off to retake their position in the great floating herd. Shrewd quartermasters commandeered the mischievous sport and hopped from boat to boat. Caterers took stock and ensured the food was rationed where needed. Soon, emboldened passengers would follow them to find missing comrades and spread any news.

Palama countermanded Zonara's stay order. "Let them mingle."

Day after day, cruising east, the black coast was a constant and bitter reminder of what they had lost. The terms of surrender had leaked, details were sketchy but the guts of the story had spread to every vessel. Everyone knew why they had lost, and they hailed Palama as seniarch because they themselves were not. Without him, they too would be funeral ash wafting across the Verdant Prairie. They owed him their lives and they were thankful to do so. As the distance to their sanctuary diminished, the praise of Palama increased. He could do no wrong in their eyes. This forgotten noble was finally in his rightful place. Regal by merit, rather than by birth. Their fortunes now lay within his stately care.

Their chatter had reached Palama. He commanded his herald to send messengers out across the flotilla. They deserved the facts and he wished to quell their speculation. Thus, an official report of events was read to all followed by a personal note.

'Greetings, noble warriors. A clear sky and fresh breeze are the perfect weather for a lazy jaunt along the coast. Once past our lost black sand, we rest at The Kataraxs. I trust the heralds have relayed the ruthless terms of the Declaration of Peace.

Also, I am bound to inform you that the culprit of our betrayal and the architect of our national disaster, the traitor Chancellor Vondaka, my parent, is dead. Killed by my hand. A family quarrel ended with a lethal clash. Despite his villainy, I beg time to mourn my loss. The Consultorium will expect justice, thus I will face the consequences soon enough. An uncertain welcome awaits us all behind the waterfall, so we shall proceed with due patience and care.'

"How was it received?" asked Dandaron.

"Not as you expected," the herald replied. "The warriors insisted the messengers return and make their sentiments known."

"Do tell," said Palama.

"Vondaka was never much liked, now he is utterly despised. No one cares you killed him, even if he was your own parent. Most boasted they would have done the same thing."

"Anything else?" asked Xindro.

"Every catamaran swore, by their hands, Palama will never be tried for parricide. They vowed none shall harm their saviour. More than that, they are determined all will curtsy before their glorious seniarch."

A week later the catamarans clustered tight around the monarch's yacht. They were moored together at the far end of the bay. Far enough away to survey the panoramic view of the vast lagoon. The air was still and the waters were as calm as glass. Bewildered eyes faced the abandoned waterfall city. Unlike the impatient soldiers, Palama and his crew were not so keen to disembark too soon. For the time being they would err on the side of caution, thus all were forbidden ashore. Zonara climbed the ramp into the saloon.

"The order is issued. The troops are not happy, but they will not land until given leave," he said.

"Where is everyone?" asked Drolla.

"Prince Diltoro is behind this," said Palama. "Our warriors shall not be sent into another trap."

The sun had not yet traveled once around the horizon before the weather turned foul. A heavy grey sky rolled in from the south and gathered the cold winds across the bay. The cautious climbed below deck and hid beneath their battened hatches. Drenched to the bone on deck, the sailors flaunted their indifference to the lashing rains. Once they had tied the canvas and rigging down, they stood vigil and ensured the squalling waters tore no vessel from its mooring. Hours later, the sun finally peeked through a crack in the clouds. The rain had moved on, but a gusty zephyr wafted still.

From behind the waterfall, a tiny black sail sped toward them. The curious emerged from their cabins to see the advancing craft. The hope for news from the city was too great for some to resist. In a scrambling frenzy for a better view, a few catamarans tipped so high they might capsize. Furious sailors fought to level their crafts and threatened to let the idiots slide overboard. The terrified passengers realised their folly and crawled over each other until the boat was stable again. By the time the panic had subsided, the royal craft had reached the outer vessels. The pilots steered aside and opened a courteous wedge all the way to the monarch's yacht.

"Here we go," said Palama with a nervous sigh. Xindro followed him down the ramp with Dandaron and Drolla in tow. Glendoro met with them as they assembled on the rear landing. With a face of stone, he clutched the monarch's black jar tight to his chest. Fontaza emerged and joined the reception. He had overseen the morticians embalm Vondaka, and until now had remained isolated within his cabin. He seemed to have lost his bravado. He nodded to the company with an unnatural deference and approached Palama. Xindro stepped between them, hand on hilt. His vow of revenge was not forgotten.

"Not now," said Palama. Xindro grunted his displeasure, but obeyed his commander. Hateful eyes remained fixed on his grandpar's murderer. The masterless fateshield stood by Palama at the platform's edge. The cold bay water gently splashed their feet as they watched the envoy approach.

"Thyre, Prince Diltoro knows everything," said Fontaza.

"What do you mean?"

"After the battle, Vondaka sent a courier. He carried a copy of the Declaration of Peace with a note reporting Soltoro's demise and your promotion."

"How did he think that would help? He bites like a dead serpent," said Palama.

"Until his grandchildren are safe, the city must not know Vondaka is dead." Never before had this filthy beast ever muttered compassion. Palama sighed, and his shoulders fell.

"It was an accident you know. I hope you do not begrudge me," said Palama.

"I saw it happen, young thyre," said Fontaza. "I know what he was like. Forever scheming, he was nasty and he was dangerous. I loved it. He often said, 'Malice is a sharp tool for a blunt task'. He only had one task, to keep his promise to you."

"To make me monarch."

"While I live, no-one will undo his life's work," vowed Fontaza.

The little royal skiff docked sideways between the towering sterns of the royal catamaran. The coxswain and his mate dropped their sail and secured the mooring ropes. Vrandala and three marshals stepped off their little hull onto the open rear deck.

"Salutations, Commander Palama," said Vrandala. His tone and curtsy seemed fake and arrogant. "I greet you in lieu of the regal heir apparent, Prince Diltoro. He is grateful you have all safely returned."

"We are thankful to be welcomed home," said Palama.

"Yes, but my time is short and my errand specific. As empowered by the Consultorium, I am to arrest Vondaka and deliver him ashore immediately."

"Where are my kids?" asked Palama.

"What?"

"Did you not phapping bring them?" snapped Xindro.

"President Krantolo holds my children hostage. He promised to exchange them," said Palama.

"Apologies thyre, that was not my brief. You must hand over Vondaka first. He is to answer for his crimes against the kindom."

"His crimes?" said Palama. "For decades his crimes went unchallenged. Cowardice and neglect by a corrupt nobility encouraged him and brought us all to this ridiculous situation."

"Inform the elders, the army has declared Palama seniarch," said Dandaron.

"They know," said Vrandala. "Nevertheless, the prince is the heir to the monarchy. The elders will never reinstate a seniocracy."

"Tell them that," he jabbed his fingers at fellows behind him. "I shall not parley until my children are released to me."

"Then end this farce," said Vrandala. "The news of the battle forced the Consultorium to consolidate. They will refute your false sovereign claim. The marshals have the city under armed curfew. Hand over the royal army and endorse Diltoro as monarch. I beg you, submit to their demands so we can avoid any bloody violence." His words floated in the air like fragrant advice, yet they stank like a menacing threat.

"Thank you for your counsel, Vrandala," said Palama. "You are a true and loyal officer. Please arrange a meeting so we may exchange the guilty with the innocent. Tell Diltoro I am willing to accept their terms, when my children are returned to me safe. We shall bring Vondaka."

He held up a palm to quash any arguments from his friends. Without a word, Vrandala nodded a smug smile and motioned to his colleagues. They boarded their little boat and departed.

"Summon a scribe," said Palama. "I need to document a defense."

Xindro's finest rowed a captain's catamaran past the fog of the crashing falls into the cavernous harbour. Hundreds of clear glass rods as thick as thighs poked through the enormous vaulted ceiling. Sunlight was piped through from high above and spotlights peppered the vast internal wharf. Endless rows of watercraft berthed side by side along the far left wall. Yachts were stuffed together with trawlers and ferries within the congested marinas.

To the right, the dock itself was lined with black sandstone mooring posts, the busts of past dignitaries were sculptured from the living rock. From them, across the great tiled esplanade, walls were lined with recessed offices and warehouses. Their facades were covered with painted crests and chiseled logos denoting clans and commodities. Normally, these halls would have bustled with merchants, clients and officers all busy with industry. Today, a few yawning sentries stood about pretending to keep watch. At the farthest end, past the last row of stores, the portcullis was locked shut. The pedestrian's passage to the narrow shore that skirted the bay denied all access in or out.

The captain sidled his catamaran up to a mooring post. His mate jumped ashore and wrapped the rope tight around the neck of an ancient stone patron. Two dozen hectarions of the Cyan Corps, crawled onto the docks like pale blue ants and formed a guard of honour. A semi-circle of determination protected their seniarch-elect and his attendants as they disembarked.

Dandaron tenderly helped his secret lover step from the boat to the wet stone ramp. With one warm hand within another, he steadied Drolla's rise onto the tiled landing. They joined their assembled peers, Palama was flanked by Xindro and Glendoro. He carried the monarch's jar with rigid solemn reverence. Fontaza remained aboard, the fateshield stood guard over Vondaka's swaddled corpse.

Prince Diltoro and President Krantolo emerged from a shadowed corridor by the travelers' kiosk. Vrandala led an escort of four dozen marshals. Tromping out of step, the straggling troop of misfits were an embarrassment to the dignity of a prince. The serious cyan soldiers struck a proud smirk and formidable pose. Straining knuckles wrapped their ready hilts. They glared scorn at these pitiful probate plastic police.

The twin children saw Palama. They yanked their hands from Krantolo's grip and ran squealing with delight to their parent.

"Par', par'." He crouched onto one knee and they ran into his open arms.

"Have you come to rescue us?" asked Nolana. Palama could only nod a weeping smile. His swollen heart choked his words.

"Then why are you so sad," asked Tindara, wiping his par's tears.

"He's not, silly. Look, he's smiling," said Nolana. His eyes passed from Xindro, to Dandaron and Drolla. "Are these your friends? Those aren't. They're mean, they locked us in the dark for ages."

Krantolo cleared the uncomfortable guilt from his throat. Xindro stroked the hilt of his shard. Another vow yet unkept.

"You are both safe now," whispered Palama.

"Where is Vondaka?" asked Diltoro.

Xindro whistled to his corps, two looked over and clapped in unison before running back to their boat.

"Diltoro." Glendoro scolded the child. "Surely you wish to receive the monarch?" He held out the black clad jar.

"I shall venerate the dead later, first we must deal with the living," said Diltoro. Glendoro's face fell like molten wax. He grunted disbelief and stared wide eyed at a prince he did not seem to recognise anymore. Glendoro clutched his monarch even closer.

"You have the kids now," said Krantolo. "Hurry with Vondaka."

"There is something you should know," said Palama. "There was an accident."

The porters returned with a thorn over their shoulders. Slung beneath it and bound in funeral tape, the squatting corpse swayed back and forth. Fontaza escorted his dead master. He unrolled a small woolen pelt and laid it hide side down. Vondaka was gently placed at Vrandala's feet. Fontaza grinned at the marshal's silent fury.

"Dead? This is not what we agreed," howled Krantolo.

"It's what ya phapping getting," spat Xindro.

"Still oozing civility, I see," said Diltoro.

"We argued. I hit him. He fell," said Palama. "He died in an instant."

Diltoro sighed and put his forehead in his palm. After a pause he calmly spoke.

"Well, it has saved us all a hostile indictment, I suppose."

"Palama," said Krantolo, "you are still expected to explain yourself. The Consultorium might label you a murderer, or worse, a parent killer."

"We assumed you might take that stance, here are the witness affidavits," said Dandaron. He produced a bundle of scrolls from the folds of his toga and handed them to Krantolo. "You should not ignore these. It would be desperately unwise for you to even consider prosecuting Palama."

"Do not threaten me child," said Krantolo. "The President is exempt from violence by his juniors." His eyes flared as Xindro burst into laughter at the empty boast.

A party of caterers arrived and diluted the tension. Without a prompt, they laid out an array of stools. Five surrounded the one in the middle. With open palms the caterers invited the dignitaries to be seated. Drolla moved the central stool and placed it alongside the others. He took the time to even the spaces between the six seats. The chief caterer shrugged a frown. With a snap of his fingers, he summoned his head attendant. He nodded at the whispered instructions and ran off with the remaining caterers.

"What are you doing," said Krantolo. "Do you expect the prince to sit on the floor?"

"None of us will sit in centre," said Drolla. "We parley as equals." He winked at Palama. Even dead, Soltoro was still monarch. No one else had the right to assume seniority yet. The action kept Diltoro's assumption of power in check and proved Palama's neutrality.

The caterers had returned with a large round table. It was knee high and placed within the circle of stools. Glendoro reached over the table and placed Soltoro's jar in the middle of it. Shaftlight glinted off the creases of the folded pleats.

"It's ridiculous," scoffed Krantolo.

"It's unusual," said Diltoro.

"It's decided," said Xindro.

He climbed onto a stool and sat. The rest did likewise. Dandaron shot a sideways glance, he smiled and shook his head at Drolla. Glendoro stood behind Dandaron while Vrandala loomed behind Diltoro. Between Drolla and Xindro, Palama sat and the twins climbed onto his lap. Defeated, Krantolo took his seat with a huff.

"Why are The Kataraxs in lockdown?" asked Palama.

The question was posed almost as if he was indifferent to the answer. Eyes darted back and forth from this unexpected query. The prince and the president stammered like naughty children caught stealing.

"For the safety of the citizens," said Vrandala. "We expected the royal army to return with an illegal usurper. We feared your intent." He stared directly at Palama and made no attempt to hide his mistrust.

"As you see, the army remained aboard," said Dandaron. "Perhaps we should discuss the issue of sovereignty after we arrange the monarch's funeral."

"The monarch was assassinated during the battle," said Krantolo. "The same battle the chancellor staged. We find it all too convenient you now challenge the rightful heir."

"I challenge no one," said Palama. "My goal sits here on my knees."

"How do we know you were not in collusion with Vondaka?" said Krantolo.

"Because the army would have stormed the city and thrown your pathetic shardhire cadets from the falls by now," said Glendoro.

Grunts of complaint rose from the ranks of the marshals. In an instant, two dozen blades of the Cyan Corps squeaked from their sheaths and stood pointed at the offended amateurs. No amount of pretended intimidation from the city marshals could force Xindro's elite to break their ring of defense around the party.

"Control your minions before my soldiers do," said Xindro.

"Everybody, ease back," roared Dandaron. Utter silence gripped the dock. The voice had yelled with such command, all present obeyed by pure instinct.

The caterers took their chance and swarmed the squabbling titans. They adorned the scarlet cloth with jars of assorted delicate treats. Various racks of herb-and-spice vials were placed within each diner's reach. Carafes of nectar water stood next to stacks of long stemmed bowls and fluted crystal goblets. Drolla huffed his disappointment at the obvious lack of any brewberry syrup. An attendant caterer passed the bowls around and filled them with a portion from each jar. Dandaron gently pushed away the bowl placed in front of him.

Palama ignored the party at the table. His attention returned to his children. Together, they cheerfully tasted each treat with relish. Feeding each other tidbits, sampling the various spices and laughing at sauces smearing their cheeks.

"Commander Palama," said the prince. "Vrandala informs us you intend to reject the endorsement of the army, and you propose to pledge their support to me."

"He can't reject," said Xindro. "He's got no phappin' say in it. The army has vowed to put him on the plynth."

"That army lost us everything in Oxxia, from the border to the falls," said Krantolo. "They have no right to demand anything, except forgiveness."

"Those brave kids gave their for the likes of you," snapped Palama. "What poor dupes they were."

"They died for the monarchy, and the monarch's rule must be maintained. Or do you consider yourself the Paladin Bode?" snarled Krantolo.

"He may not, but his warriors do," said Xindro.

"Soltoro named me his successor," said Diltoro. "I intend to follow the law."

"Surely you uphold the same laws, magistrate?" said Vrandalor.

"Of course. But I am a judge no more. I have learned that people are quite capable of umpiring themselves. I recuse myself from this mess."

"The prince has the support of the Consultorium and the Doyen Assembly," added Krantolo.

Xindro threw his head up and laughed a fake laugh. He became serious in an instant. He unbuckled his shard from his middle and held it out to Krantolo by the sheath, upside down.

"But, does he have these?" He rattled the weapon to highlight his message. The shard fell from its scabbard and sang as the pommel punched the stone floor. After a still moment, it fell in a twisting arc and the blade chopped at the tiles with a clang. Krantolo pulled his feet away just in time. Xindro quickly grabbed his shard and resheathed it. "And we know how to use them."

"We have other weapons," sneered Krantolo as he slid his stool a little further from his aggressor.

A quiet moment took hold. The caterers refilled goblets and bowls. Palama reached to the nearest spice rack. Krantolo held out a small vial of blue salt and passed it to Palama. He stood it up between thumb and forefinger.

"What is this?"

The president pinched a corner of his mouth into a snide little smile.

"Ocean's Delight, from my own spice mines. It enhances seafood perfectly."

"Oh, I have heard of this," said Palama. He sprinkled the tiny sapphire crystals onto his bowl of pickled fish. Nolana offered his bowl. "Nope, finish your mushrooms first."

Drolla's forehead slowly furrowed into a frown, the spice sounded familiar.

"Palama," said Diltoro. "I beg you to abide by the laws of succession. Please reconsider before it is too late."

"It already is," whispered Krantolo through clenched teeth.

"I do agree. Your argument is with the soldiery, not me," said Palama licking his fingertips. The twins had finished their mushrooms and they all took a deep drink of the cool sweet water.

"Then you must officially reject their claim," said Diltoro.

Palama stared hard at the prince for a moment, then gagged. He squinted, and he retched. Pale pink vomit fizzed up and out of him like an overflowing cup. For a moment he froze, his eyes flared and his confusion turned to worry. He could not breathe. His fingers wrapped about his own throat. His airless torso jerked before he swooned and collapsed onto the floor. An endless foam snake, the size of his arm, slithered from his mouth and wobbled as it gathered like a fat pink pile of rope in front of him.

Drolla fell to his side and held his head, desperate to nurse him somehow.

"It stinks like fish," cried Tindara.

"Summon a medic," screamed Drolla.

Nolana squealed. Their poor par' still had not taken a breath and the froth would not stop. Wiping the stuff away made no difference, it just kept on piping out. The others gawped in stunned silence.

Dandaron and Xindro seemed to guess the crime moments before they looked to each other. Once their eyes met, it was obvious who the culprit was. Krantolo shot a nervous glance back and forth between them as they turned their suspicious gazes upon him. All three looked down at the half empty vial of blue salt.

"What have you done?" cried Xindro.

Without warning, the flow stopped. A spasm ripped through Palama, his body tensed and he coughed. Suds spattered everywhere. Air whistled down his throat and filled his starving lungs. His chest heaved and fresh life rushed back into him. He sat up giddy, wiped his mouth and forced a small smile of relief. His twins bawled, glad their dear par' was alright now. He exhaled a heavy sigh and his guts gurgled loud enough for all to hear.

He took another drink of water, and the nausea erupted again. This time the foam was pinker, thicker, and slower.

Tears streamed from his pleading eyes before they rolled back in his head. He slumped into Drolla's lap. His limbs stretched and strained, craving precious air. Soon they were still, and Palama never drew another breath again.

3.9 - THE CERTAIN DOUBT

L eeporp's face shattered like a dropped glass.

He sprang at Krantolo. Instinct raised a fearful arm in defense, but it was a futile gesture realised too late. A severed hand slapped the floor and blood wept from his stinging wrist. Another arm dropped from its shoulder and a bloody arc sprayed from the screaming armpit. Krantolo reared back and stumbled to his feet, trying to evade the pitiless blade. His shrieks echoed throughout the cavernous chamber.

Vrandala jumped aside and pulled Diltoro away from the butchery. The marshals moved to rescue the president, but the blue guards closed ranks and fenced them out. The Cyan Corps were outnumbered by the city marshals, but not outmatched. His loyal guard would not allow Xindro to be interrupted.

A leg fell away from under its knee and the president dropped onto the raw stump. Driven by pure adrenalin, he desperately scrambled backwards. Three swift strokes separated foot, shin and thigh. Despite his blind fury, Xindro amputated with the accuracy of a field surgeon. He was famous for it. His protectors looked on grinning at their mentor's talent. Krantolo lay floundering amongst his dead limbs, squealing and squirting and squelching about in his own bloody puddle. Then he stopped. A final strike had his severed head spinning on the floor. Xindro kicked it toward Vrandala. It struck him squarely in the midriff. His reflex caught it face up, and the dying eyes blinked at him. The marshal captain squealed with fright and dropped it on his own foot.

Leeporp struck a pose, blade ready. His victim's blood dripped off his brow like sweat. The pit of his elbow wiped his face, and panting tears began to well. He swallowed bile with gritted teeth and stared deep into himself. His reputation was lost. An oath in vain. His vow to protect was dead. No matter how furious or just the reprisal, the fateshield had failed. Palama lay as dead as Krantolo. Dandaron placed a palm on Xindro's shoulder, a friend's empathy broke the spell. He flicked the blood from his blade and sheathed it.

"Corps, enfold."

The cyan wall withdrew its boundary and pulled in tight around their envoy. A fence of black blades stood adamant, promising instant murder at these petty city guards. Their nervous faces searched for any direction from Vrandala. They too drew their weapons, but their stances were far more defensive. The guards held stead, and intensified their intimidation toward the marshals.

In a distracted moment, Vrandala acted. He pulled Diltoro close to him and boldly elbowed through the cyan barrier. The blue guard let them pass, retreat was no threat. The marshals pulled them behind and jostled the prince and the captain until they were far from the front lines.

The standoff stood motionless. The marshals became a little braver as reinforcements poured out of the great corridor behind them. Many within the first few rows glanced about, as if to spur each other on. Xindro drew their gaze to the butchered corpse and smirked a pointing finger at the closest of the cocky city guards. The colour drained from their bought faces. What price was their courage? They swallowed deep, but held their skittish ground.

For a moment, time froze. Drolla nursed the body of Palama and consoled the weeping twins. His heartbroken expression met Dandaron's look of dismay.

"Get us out of here," insisted Drolla.

Dandaron stared a blank pause, then nodded and replied.

"Get the twins to the boat."

Fontaza scooped up Vondaka and ran to stow him below deck, he climbed back up in time to help Drolla lift the twins aboard. He hurried back to Palama and gently threw his corpse over a shoulder.

"Leave him be," screamed Xindro. Fontaza ignored him, and carried Palama's body to the boat.

"Xindro, defend our retreat and follow us aboard," yelled Dandaron.

The pale blue protectors slowly herded the party back to the safety of their vessel. Thirsty blades threatened slaughter as they steadily stepped away from their advancing foes. Both factions were ready to strike at the slightest misstep. During the distracted melee, Soltoro sat abandoned.

"Do not let them leave," ordered Vrandala.

The fools obeyed him and moved to attack the defenders. Xindro's finest repelled the marshals' pathetic attempt to enforce their captain's command. The soldiers' blades kept their fatal promise. The speed and determination of the blue ants' stings shocked the naive marshals and their bloody screams echoed throughout the harbour. The wiser of the brave city guards hung back and kept a safe distance from the retreating hedge of shards. They cautiously stepped over their howling limbless comrades soaking the harbour floor. As the last of the corps boarded the catamaran, Diltoro scooped up the monarch's jar from the parley table and ran to the edge of the dock.

"Pass him to me," yelled Glendoro.

"You were fateshield to the monarch. You know par' named me successor. Why do you desert me for these rebels?" cried Diltoro.

"I was his only intimate," said Glendoro. "Soltoro trusted none of you. He knew Vondaka planned the war. He knew you were Krantolo's little puppet, you brainless dupe. You are not his heir, he left no Bequeath."

"Liar! He promised..."

"He fooled you all. If he survived, he aimed to punish everyone who betrayed him. He left the plynth vacant on purpose. 'Let the traitors squabble over it' he said. I wish he was here now to see it."

"You are the traitor. I *will* be monarch, and you will be the first I put on a pole."

Diltoro screamed like the brat he was. In a final petulant act, he raised his arms above his head and threw the black clad jar into the murky harbour waters.

"Soltoro," cried Glendoro. He jumped from the boat as the oars pushed it from the steps. Before anyone could stop him, the monarch's fateshield hugged the prince. He pulled him off the edge and plunged into the harbour. The frigid waters swallowed them both. No-one moved. Everyone watched. They waited what seemed an age until the splashing ripples subsided.

"Row," yelled Dandaron. A dozen oars stabbed the water and began their escape. Glendoro alone burst though an eruption of breathless bubbles. He swam to the boat and hauled himself aboard. As they paddled toward the sunlit exit, Diltoro bobbed to the surface and floated upside down.

"Take your fleet and go," roared Vrandala. "The city is now mine. The civilians are mine. If you return, they die."

The catamaran launched past the crashing falls into the stark cold daylight. The rowers beat their steady pace, pounding the choppy waters. They did not slow their stroke until the sail was hoisted. The wind pushed them with all speed from the disaster they had barely escaped. As the clustered fleet became ever closer, a sea of expectant faces covered the deck of every vessel. Through the gaping wedge, the captain steered the cat' toward the monarch's yacht. The frowning faces of the curious warriors stared at the open cockpit, their seniarch was missing. Bold voices demanded answers, they shouted their questions from every quarter.

"Where is Palama?" "Why do you return without him?" "What happened in there?"

"The kladgers killed him," screamed Xindro.

A howling roar of surprise and sorrow sped across the flotilla. Angry warriors clambered everywhere, vowing revenge and promising murder.

"Now look what you have done," said Dandaron.

The hectarions did their best the quell the rampant fury, but the enraged soldiers proved a wild beast to tame. Rational minds helped calm the witless anger of their peers, but the warriors dressed and prepared themselves. Their intent was clear, they would soon assail the city.

A chill breeze wafted through the saloon of the monarch's yacht. Creaking footsteps climbed the solemn ramp and the doctor joined the assembled mourners.

"I gave the kids a draft. They will doze through their grief," said Torono.

"And Palama?" asked Drolla.

"The morticians are washing him down, ready to embalm. He'll not be disturbed once they are done."

"I think we all need a little time to grieve our loss," said Dandaron.

"We don't have time to mourn," said Drolla. Dandaron flashed him a disgusted glare. "The civilians are in danger. We can't just leave them. Palama wouldn't."

"We cannot rush back. Vrandala vowed to kill them if we return," said Dandaron.

"How are you going to stop the army?" said Xindro. "Now they know, they are scrambling to avenge Palama and rescue the people. Nothing will stop them."

"Zonara will. He is with them now. He'll report back soon," said Dandaron.

"Vondaka's grand plan has spun out of control," said Drolla.

"It's a pity he is dead. They'd have him sky dancing by now. Everything he did has turned to shit," said Dandaron.

"Not everything," said Fontaza.

"Trust you to defend him," spat Dandaron.

"We know he was bad. Of all his evil deeds, he did them to fulfill his plans for Palama. You were the only selfless thing he ever did."

"Me?"

"Yes, to atone for the death of Drabana," said Fontaza.

"What?"

"Poor Drabana," said Torono. "Murdered so young, I buried him embracing Quetono's arm. It was a private affair, family only. Apart from the sky dancers, of course."

" *'Under one cairn, an innocent assailed. On seven thorns, the felons impaled. This scene of sorrow, proof lives will cease. An omen for others, to keep the peace.'* The plaque is still there," said Fontaza.

"Quetono said there were eight," said Drolla. Fontaza blushed a guilty glare.

"Tell us," said Dandaron.

Fontaza sighed and and dropped his shoulders.

"I was the eighth. Vondaka sent me to oversee the ambush. He hired cheap cutthroats and the idiots fumbled it. Quetono lost his arm fighting to protect Drabana. They chopped the kid up pretty bad. I gave them masks, but they showed their faces. They had to go, so Vondaka double-crossed them. I tore out their tongues and he turned their punishment into a memorial. One fit for a nephew murdered, and a sibling betrayed. The remorse haunted him until he could make amends. So Dandaron, you owe your existence to Vondaka." The fateshield nodded at Drolla. "And you. Your parent met Quetono, and the sluts fucked..."

"Drord's Guts. Enough," said Xindro.

"Your family kept the secret too," said Fontaza.

"Pondra suffered for decades keeping that secret and you took his head as a reward."

"Would have taken yours too, but we still needed you. You hide the proof."

"What secret?" demanded Dandaron.

"Quetono's baby was not stillborn," confessed Xindro.

"Vondaka could not stand another rival heir," said Fontaza. "Nor would his conscience let him kill it. Not again. So he stole it."

"He forced the babe into Pondra's care. We're a big clan with scores of kids of all ages. We hid the child among them."

"Four seasons later," said Fontaza, "that pathetic Zintrix runt, the one Drark gave Quetono, died in the orphanage. Vondaka hushed it all up. He took back the stolen child and swapped it out with the dead one. Quetono never knew. He always thought you were just his foreign ward. His little foreign pet." Fontaza paused, his gaze scanned the audience and settled on Dandaron. "You are not Krodangan. You are Quetono's birthchild."

In a cloudless sky, the thunder clapped.

Dandaron and Drolla both glared at Xindro, his sober nod confirmed the truth.

"Sworn to secrecy," he said.

Drolla gasped, his face flushed hot and he locked a gaze with Dandaron. Deep within their muted stare, for the first time ever, they saw themselves staring back. Tears welled in their searching eyes. With a sudden hearty embrace, Dandaron threw his face into Drolla's shoulder and sobbed like a child. They pulled apart and clutched each other's forearms.

"They lied to us," gasped Drolla, "all our lives."

"An emptiness I never knew existed, has just been filled to overflow," whispered Dandaron.

"Ugh, Vondaka did right to keep this long-lost filth a secret," said Fontaza.

Shard glass squeaked, a lung hissed, and blood spattered. Fontaza grasped the blade that Xindro had pushed into his chest. He raised a foot to Fontaza and pushed him away. Fingers dropped to the floor as the blade slid out through his hands. With a groan, he tumbled backwards and rolled down the saloon ramp. He came to a rest and sprawled onto the rear open deck below. Xindro sprang down after him. He gripped an ankle and dragged the dying fiend to the water's edge. With a heave, he slid him sideways overboard. Fontaza floated for a moment, staring disbelief. He slowly disappeared as he sank to the cold, black depths of the The Kataraxs Bay.

"For Pondra," said Xindro.

An ocean wind picked up and blew across the bay, north toward the falls. It seemed nature itself wanted to send the grieving soldiers to the city as fast as possible. Every loaded catamaran had weighed anchor, hoisted sail and sped to the cavern's entrance. It was an organic reaction to the news of Palama's death and dread of the citizens' fate. No command sent them, nor could any hold them. Nothing would stop them. If there was no wind, they would row. If there were no oars, they would swim. They could not save Palama, but they were determined to defy Vrandala's threat and free their beloved pamperers. Anyone who tried to prevent them, did so at their own peril.

"Half had left before I got there," said Zonara. "The rest lashed their rigging and wished me good luck. I could only watch them go."

He was the last to step aboard the little catamaran. He joined them in the open cabin and grabbed the handrail. The skipper fussed about setting ropes ready to sail.

"You are their general," said Dandaron.

"I am not Palama." No, he was not. None of them were, and they knew it. None were held in such high esteem as he. The army would have waited for him. They trusted him. Their devotion wavered just shy of worship. He was their smolderstone in the deepest, darkest halls. But now, without him, the blackness shrouded their reason. Their wild emotions blindly carried them toward certain slaughter. "Even Xindro went with them," said Zonara.

"There won't be many marshals left by the time we get there then," grinned Glendoro.

"Who knows what mess we shall face," said Dandaron.

"Xindro commands the Cyan Corps and the rest follow them," said Zonara. "The people are safe enough."

"The people have lost their monarch, a faction has lost their prince and the army has lost their seniarch. Without a sovereign, the Doyen Assembly might revive their ancient animosities. Another clanlord might try to make himself tyrant," said Glendoro.

"Zonara, you must call your forces to order," said Drolla.

"When the heralds left, with them went my orders to the officers and some instructions to Xindro," said Zonara. "But you must realize many of the warriors now consider themselves civilians."

"Resigned to rescue and revenge," said Drolla. "What about the enforcers?"

"They are with the soldiers," said Glendoro.

"It cannot get worse," said Drolla.

"The Doyen Assembly and the Consultorium are also in the city," said Glendoro.

"What?"

"It is obvious they were invited early," said Dandaron. "The prince intended to install himself monarch as soon as possible."

"The marshals thought they owned the city, now bloody anarchy runs through their halls," said Glendoro.

"The nobles and the elders must be secured," said Dandaron.

The discussion ended with a jolt. The wind filled the sail and lurched the little boat on its way. Between them and the screaming maw of the harbour entrance, the view from the skiff was a wall of rudders, like a herd of hind-ends galloping ahead. The sail shifted and caught more wind. Both hulls lightly skimmed the water as the bows sliced a smooth path. The run was swift and the breeze was fresh.

A new unforeseen dread welled up within Drolla. Somehow, now everything mattered. An urge to protect, or at least realize where the danger lay, prefaced every thought. Need begged to know how it should be avoided, or made safe by any means. Sea spray splashed his face, and for the second time, mortal peril awaited them. This time there was more to lose. *You'll not lose Dandaron*, his heart vowed. Drolla smiled. The miltlings found each other, and they loved each other. His throat was warm. It felt blue, even though it wasn't. Yet.

Sooner than expected, their little catamaran joined the vast reassembled fleet. Every sail was lowered. The naked masts clustered like a forest of dead trees. The skipper and his mate lashed their vessel to the nearest craft, adding it to the great interlocked pontoon. The boats were crammed together cheek by jowl all the way to the harbour's cavern. Hundreds of warriors scrambled still across the floating walkways, spilling inside past the thunderous base of the falls.

"By your leave, good thyres," said the skipper. His mate emerged from below with weapons. Both strapped a shard to their middle. "Good luck to you all."

They curtsied and ran off, leaping and bounding across the decks, away to join their peers. Zonara paused and studied the jumble of hulls that lay before them. "What a maze," he moaned.

"Follow me." Glendoro led the small party of elites along the crazy path. He stopped now and then to re-assess the best course to take. They trotted along decks and leaped from one to the next. It was no easy stroll. Lashed together, the boats bobbed and heaved in turn as they undulated from the shifting weight of the clambering mass ahead. It was like running across floating stepping stones. Half an hour later, they reached the shade of the looming cliffs. From where they stood, gazing up, it seemed the black wall reached to the sky. The last of the soldiers had entered the city and the raft of dancing boats was now deserted.

"A hop, skip and a jump and we shall be inside," said Glendoro.

The unexpected crash nearby stopped them where they stood. A body tangled in yellow silk lay on the roof of a nearby catamaran. It had fallen from the sky. Another crash further away startled them again. Then another, and another and more. It was raining people.

"Look," yelled Drolla. He pointed high up the cliff face. More bodies dove from the hundreds of balconies that peppered the cliff face.

"They are all marshals," said Glendoro.

"Our kids are purging the city," said Zonara, grinning wide.

After each enemy was ejected from a balcony, residents hung out family pennants. The flag boasted their own house arrest had lifted. One less captor meant one more citizen freed. They leaned over their banister and waved to their neighbours. Everyone shared the joy of seeing their jailers hurled from so high. Some swam screaming through the air. Others fell like dolls, already dead. Either way, their bodies snapped alike when they hit the decks below. The spectators above cheered at the crash of every landing, like children watching lightning.

"oy." A faint voice squeaked through the roar of the falls. It was distant, yet familiar.

"OY!" It squawked a little louder. "Up here." Five stories above them, Xindro leaned out over a balcony and waved. "Look out." He tipped a lifeless body over the handrail. It spun end over end toward them. Two boats over, bones cracked aloud when the torso struck the stern. The broken body slid off feet first and sank without a splash. "See you down there."

His face disappeared and the tenants took his place. They hung a blue pennant striped yellow over the railings of their apartment. They waved and smiled down at Xindro's friends, then returned indoors.

Outside the cavern, the water was cloudy like a milky broth. Inside, it was stained blood white, as thick as paint. Bodies were stacked a dozen high and lined the run of warehouse foyers. Medics and morticians dashed here and there. Soldiers escorted them like bodyguards, forever maintaining a ring of protection. Gore poured through spouts, fed by the drains of boulevards and apartments above. Piped river water gushed from open faucets and washed down the bloody wharf. A huge smile and welcoming arms ran towards them.

"The city is ours," said Xindro. "You have missed all the fun." An escort of blue ants swirled around him.

"Have you killed them all?" asked Glendoro.

"Would have, but the cowards surrendered."

"We shall send them over the falls later," growled Zonara.

"Were any people hurt?" asked Drolla.

"Some. They saw us coming, and started the fight without us."

335

"Brave fools," said Dandaron.

"Once we arrived, the soldiers elbowed them aside and took over."

"What about the others?" asked Drolla.

"Who?"

"The elders and the clanlords," said Dandaron.

"Oh, them. Tranna rounded them up, for their own safety like," Xindro grinned. "His hectary guards them in the Seniarch's Hall."

"Debating the sovereignty already, no doubt," said Glendoro.

"They were counting a quorum."

"I take my leave, young thyres," said Zonara. He faced Xindro. "Where are my officers?"

"They commandeered the royal apartments of the prince."

"Of course they did." He paused. "Once I have the soldiery back in hand, we shall join you in the hall."

"Thank you," said Drolla.

Zonara strode toward a few free ranging warriors and called them to him. His new armed escort grunted their assent and trotted away with their general.

"Glendoro," said Drolla. "Would you go ahead and inform the Consultorium that Quetono's Heir requests an audience? You were fateshield to the monarch, sway them to wait for his cousins."

"They may not welcome a prince killer," said Dandaron. "Not without this."

From within his robes, Dandaron held out Quetono's sceptre. The tri-winged baton rendered its bearer Persona Amnestate. A royal agent in lieu of the monarch.

"When did he give you that?" asked Drolla.

"I was Quetono's fateshield," Dandaron shrugged. "I always held it for him."

"They will wait." Glendoro hid the baton in his robe and dipped a shallow curtsy. Within a moment, he blended into the crowd and disappeared.

Xindro called after him. "Tell Bendro, he may have his royal contender yet."

3.10 – THE QUESTIONED ANSWER

P ast the last kiosk at the far end of the wharf, an immense passage ramped deep into the upper cavern.

Ancient tapestries hung stiff with age and draped the corridor walls. The noisy thoroughfare ran frantic with traffic, twenty people wide. Drolla led his escort into a queue going up. Those running down lugged dead marshals. Morticians had enlisted warrior and citizen alike as porters to help clear out the bodies. Dead marshals not hurled from the upper decks were brought to the lower docks. The piles grew by the hour and the wharf was filling up. Overloaded funeral barges would soon ferry their lifeless foes out onto the water, and dump them into the bay. Ropes lashed stone about the feet of some. Dozens more, strapped ankle to wrist and strung together like bunting, would pour overboard like an anchor's rope. Their tethered corpses will sew the bay like orchards of meaty kelp. A timely glut for the hungry shoals. By next haul, the seafood fattened on the murdered marshals will clog the trawlers' nets. What a feast awaits, everyone loves fish.

"Leeporp, take me to the shops," said Drolla.

"But," said Leeporp, "the Seniarch's hall?"

"We need better robes."

"Why? I'll stay in uniform." Dandaron smoothed some wrinkles and scratched at a stain. He did not notice his upper chest. Like spitting rain, blue flecks glinted across his white skin.

Drolla shouldered him into the rampway wall and pulled a draping carpet around them both. The warm purple velvet hugged them against the cold black stone. Dandaron flicked an eyebrow. The corner of his mouth pinched into a cheeky grin. Drolla silently agreed. It was cozy. It was naughty. He pushed Dandaron's palm onto his chest. The smutty grin disappeared. Drolla swapped hands, and they felt the other's flash.

"They're spiky," whispered Dandaron.

"We are starting to show. We need to cover them," said Drolla.

Leeporp yanked the drape aside, and Drolla slapped away Dandaron's caressing fingers.

"We cannot be pregnant," mumbled Dandaron.

"Are you serious? You phapping sluts." He frowned a quizzing grin.

"See?" said Drolla. "We need a tailor."

"Come on." Leeporp pulled them out and pushed them forward.

The top end of the ramp opened into a vast oval mall. An endless colonnade carried a curved arcade that ringed the entire lower level. Beyond the balconies, arches led to the deeper galleries of the residential suburbia. Behind the columned portico, many shops still traded. Some bartered their goods while many others served their protectors free. What the marshals once extorted was now offered willingly. No warrior could pass without salutations or gifts thrust upon them. The civilians gratitude had yet to wane. Despite civil violence, the blood, and the horror of the corpses, city life bustled on unabated. A broken curfew brought carefree liberty.

A fake glass sun set high in the ceiling flooded the place with endless daylight. Little verdant booths were dotted everywhere. The semi-circle herb planters sat in the manicured shade of laden fruit trees. Between the sprinkling fonts, tiny carmine saptongue bats fluttered amongst the manna blooms. The grotto floors were carpeted with a familiar luxurious white fungus. Resting civilians and soldiers alike shared snacks in the shade of their snug little nooks.

Drolla spied his mark and ran off. Weaving between the scattered gardens, he stopped and waited as a troupe of warriors tromped past in squad formation. No rest for them yet. Past the entrance curtain, the mercer's store smelled wonderful. Reams of cloth, woolen pelts and grasswood matting laid stacked in separate piles. Rows of ready made gowns hung on racks. Dangling mantles adorned either end. Feathers, furs, hair and leather. Drolla flipped through them in a flurry. Time was short. He plucked out two and held them at arm's length. A white feather stole for him and a grey fur shawl for Dandaron. They will do. He stepped toward the exit.

"Is looting," croaked an ancient voice, "now part of your marshals' privilege?"

Drolla froze. He threw his head back over behind him and stepped toward the shopkeeper. He scowled with angry fists perched firmly on his hips. He was Brokka's age, but nowhere near as friendly. His pinto kilt fluted sturdy thighs and its wrap draped one of three broad shoulders. The cloth failed to hide old silver battle scars across his torso.

"I am not a marshal."

"Oh, I see. A soldier's privilege then, is it?"

"Sorry. You are right. I was in a hurry, please forgive me."

"I might have given them to you, soldier, had you asked. Now you can pay."

"I have no money." Drolla unclipped his belt. "Please, take this." With two hands, he presented his shard.

"I already have one." His fingers gently wrapped the scabbard. "Although, it has been years since I held it." The old tailor squinted as he withdrew the blade close to his face. His cloudy eyes admired the spalling veins that crackled along its spine. "Beautiful, and near new." He slammed the hilt home and held it out to Drolla. "Like blade and sheath, the spaller and shard are made as one and neither suit another."

"Thank you," whispered Drolla.

"What's so urgent?"

"I'm due at the Seniarch's Hall."

"What do you want to go there for? Those fools are squabbling like children. We have lost the royals, and without a monarchy the clanwars are bound to start again."

"Not all the royals are gone. The hall awaits Quetono's Heir."

He burst into laughter. "Don't be ridiculous. I knew Quetono. He left no heirs."

"You didn't know him very well then, did you?" said Drolla.

"I am Vindra," he boasted, with a hand over his heart. "I served with Quetono as a shardhand during the Zintrix War against the Tamzi Kith. You think you know him better?"

"I know his child lived."

"Who?"

"Me, for a start. I am his sporling."

"Drord's Guts! How do you guess that?" He laughed again and shook his head.

"Quetono told me everything on his deathbed."

The old soldier narrowed his eyes. "Alright, so maybe the rumour was true. Maybe he did seed that pretty country puff after all. What was his name?"

"Hlammi."

"Hlaaammi, that's him. What a ponce he was. He wronged his own siblings too, didn't he?"

"My uncles?"

"Were they? Yes, I suppose they were." He paused to reminisce. "Yes, I remember them. That young slut begged them to avenge his fake outrage. Afterwards he ran home crying, the young Protorians stayed behind and the fools kept their vow. They lured Quetono into an abandoned latrine. They meant to murder him and hide their crime in the sewer. But they were neither smart nor skilled, were they? They forgot to disarm him, didn't they?" Vindra smirked at the memory. "He turned on them and smothered their stupid Oriennan pride. They were never seen again."

"No. I heard they drowned at sea."

"They drowned in shit."

Drolla stood speechless. The old fellow shuffled over to the hangers and rummaged amongst the gowns. The clothes danced along the rail like someone trapped behind a curtain.

"If you are Quetono's Heir and you are about to face the gentry in the Seniarch's Hall, you will have to suit up better than that. You cannot top grimy battle rags with fine dress mantles like these." From the far end, he showed two shimmering silks draped across a forearm each. "For you and the grey fur shawl." He handed Drolla a long deep blue gown, bleeding into matted white spider web at one corner. Under the white feather stole, Vindra held up a glossy orange robe with a faint honeycomb pattern. "Who are these for?"

"My miltling," said Drolla, stripping out of his crusty duds.

"Your what?"

"Dandaron."

"Drark's runt?"

"He was never the Krodangan. It died, he lived."

"Is that so? You are well informed, aren't you?" said Vindra. The old fellow paused, and gazed into the distant past. "I held that sickly child. I brought it from Drark's tower to the waif's Lodge. I learned the truth of it when I returned home. We all kept Pondra's secret. The truth never left the forest."

"You knew Pondra?"

"Our silence kept him alive. My loyalty was tested back then. I admired Quetono, but I adored my cousin more."

"Poor Quetono," said Drolla. "He never knew Dandaron was his."

"I convinced myself, he would never have believed it," said Vindra. "My silence has been a great burden these past two decades."

"We have to tell them all, but we only have our word to vouch for who he is."

"You will need more than that. The Consultorium have known Dandaron all his life."

The foyer was choked with a hundred nosy citizens. Their curiosity and their pride demanded entry into their own hall. But none of them were gentry and the hall was already full. Civil servants barred the entrance and ushered the unwelcome out like bouncers. The disgruntled mob milled about complaining and comparing their pathetic ill will. Leeporp elbowed between them and incited even more objections. He led Dandaron and Drolla. Old Vindra followed closely behind.

A waist-high velvet chain hung across the wide doorway from one arched jamb to the other. Inside, two teal hectarions stood silent guard watching their betters down at the podium. This side of the cord, a bureaucratic fop leaned back on two legs. His third was perched forward on tip toe. A white bearded baublepouch laid proud across his naked thigh. The officious fool stepped forward to bar their way.

"None may enter."

"Except your slimy fist," said Leeporp.

The dandy was insulted. "How dare you," he bleated.

"How dare I? You're the one standing there dangling your wanker's purse."

"So?"

"Forever touting. It's disgusting," Leeporp sneered.

"You could look away."

"You could put it away." Leeporp snatched hard, the dainty copper chain snapped and flung from around a startled waist. In one fluid motion the hairy handbag flew across the room, over and beyond the crowded onlookers. For a moment, he considered running off, but a grinning colleague safely caught it. The servant pretended his civic duty held him at his post. He was now adamant.

"No entry. By order of the president."

"So you say."

Vindra pulled Drolla to the doorway.

"Look at this place."

The grand amphitheatre laid open before them. Embossed into the vaulted ceiling, a dusty relief of Throthm gazed down from his senioral plynth. From behind the frieze, hidden light shone across the shallow sculpture. The casting shadows defined the ornate details of the image. Arms seemed to reach down, each hand held an emblem of the seniocratic kinfold. In one palm, the smolderstone geode was a mark of craft and industry. In another, a handful of brewberries boasted harvest and excess. His third, dominant hand held the weapon of power and law, the fuglstone bladestaff. The carvings praised the intellect, wealth and order established by the ancients. Drolla marveled at the massive edifice hewn raw into the black rock above him.

"What a lie," snarled Vindra. "It was poverty, starvation and tyranny for all, except for the seniorial clan of the day."

"It didn't start like that," said Dandaron.

Seniocrats had always reserved the right to rule for a term. When altruism reigned, seniarchs would retire and cede their power to another clan. This was long before ambition became a virtue. The competition for the plynth became ever more bitter. 'The bout was rigged', the losing clans would cry. Animosity festered between the cousins close and distant. The clandoms closed their ranks and then they closed their borders. Warlords sought power through conflict, and the Doyen Feud began. For five dozen decades, ascension to power depended on military victory and holding power meant quashing dissent. The hostilities were now permanent and they were tradition. And yet, it got worse.

During the Kentrex Spree, the plynth sat a hundred seniarchs in as many years. The rising youth tired of endless war. Xendaka the Monofier brought co-operation or punishment, and the monarchy held sway ever since. The royal family bound kith to kin. But today, in the hall of the syblings' ancestors, those binds were unraveling.

The grand oval amphitheatre tapered a gentle slope down to the central podium. Filtered sunlight bled from the smolderstone in Throthm's palm. Its light faded as it reached to the walkway encircling the perimeter of the darkened walls. Eight more foyers sat behind throughways at the high end of nine tapered lanes. Segmented squatting sections sat several serious stern seniors. The place was packed.

The noise rumbled like water over rocks. While half the crowd listened, the other half yelled across themselves. Together, the Elders of the Consultorium, Doyens from their Clanlands and the recently freed denizens of the city gentry squat apart. Their factions filled three sections each and soldiers lined the spaces in between. A lone soul draped in grey stood on the podium. His attempts to preside over the rampant mob had faltered.

Across the hall, pompous voices bellowed their virtue and just as many cynical echoes laughed them off. The place was rowdier than a berry den on payday. An old senior rose from his haunches. His bright emerald gown shimmered like windy grass. He struck an orator's pose and looked a little too proud.

"All that aside," he said. "Why are half the Doyen Assembly and the Consultorium Elders absent?"

"Because Councillor Hentra," said Joltoro, "they have deserted you and fled home. As fast as they could, they clambered up the spiral ramp to Rivertop Plaza. Without doubt, the cowards are running still."

The soldiers thought that was hilarious. Not many of the rest enjoyed the joke, though. Some even chose to take insult at the irreverence of these cheeky, yet well armed, brats.

"President Bendro, is this true?" demanded Hentra.

"Only those who supported the prince have departed," replied the grey clad compere. "They hoped their absence might prevent a quorum and hinder our proceedings."

"Well, it won't," said Hentra. "Only those in attendance can resolve a Senorial Bout."

At floor level, by the podium, Joltoro cast about a casual eye. He spotted Drolla and a bright grin tore across his face. He tapped a shoulder and a mute command sent a cyan tunic up to greet the visitors. With a measured gait, the happy hunk trotted up the lazy ramp to the velvet cordon. Drolla shivered. Frost ants ran up his spine and melted into his heart. Boohala survived. Of course he did, he was far too pretty to kill. He nodded a broad smile at Drolla.

The doorkeep stood froze in awe of Boohala. His open jaw had a slight smile and his lopsided eyebrows could not hide his glaring lust. Mesmerised, he saw Leeporp unhitch the barrier. He watched them all walk past him into the hall. He glowed and gushed when Boohala handed him the clip. He gazed on as more sneaked past after them. He blinked and flared. "OY."

"My lords." Boohala pulled his skirt aside and curtsied.

"Stand hectarion," said Dandaron, admiring the new status of an old comrade.

"It's true, you made it out," said Drolla.

"And you."

"I knew we would."

"Of course," smiled Boohala. "Shall we?" His upturned palm reached out an invitation to join the podium. They left the bouncer squabbling with his ejected foisters.

Another round of laughter shamed a foolish speaker back onto his haunches. Joltoro watched Boohala's errand descend the ramp between the Doyens and the Elders. He elbowed Glendoro and nodded toward them. Drolla waved as if he met strangers in a market. Glendoro smiled at his silly friend and leaped onto the podium. He stabbed the winged rod into the air.

"Quell all and heed the royal baton," roared Joltoro.

All talk and laughter stopped when the soldiery snapped to attention. The assembly paused. Their arguments had reached an impasse and they welcomed the interruption. Curious faces dashed here and there until Bendro's gaze showed them where they should look. Every silent eye stared like sunlight at the curious little group approaching the centre piece. The elder coaxed them to join him on the podium. Boohala kept Vindra back. Three soldiers gladly shimmied aside to give him room. He stood among them and patted their young shoulders in appreciation.

Before the nation, this small group enjoyed their little reunion. The elder pulled Leeporp aside. Their whispered glances ran Drolla up and down.

"Drolla, Dandaron. This is President Bendro," said Leeporp.

"Welcome, young thyre. It is a pleasure to finally meet you," said Bendro. "Condolences offered. I knew your par' well." They shared a silent quiet moment. Dandaron blushed. "How opportune." Bendro grinned, and rounded on the audience. "Noble thyres, fresh news." He gazed about and stared down those still wittering. Once he had their silence, he began his speech.

"Today. The realm grieves. Even The Kataraxs pours with tears." Any standing, sat. The audience shuffled and settled to better hear. "Never has such carnage befallen us since before Monofication. Cherish these past few centuries of royal peace. Today, our tomorrow is unknown. So, we must pause to remember yesterday and recount the undue violence brought upon us."

He paused.

"Chancellor Vondaka forced Drahn to her haunches and sought her demise. He forced our syblings to die for sand he had already sold." He spat on the floor and trod on it. His words splintered between his teeth. "Hated forever."

"And ever," the crowd hissed. Before any mumblings could break his stride, Bendro lifted his cheer and lauded their dead sovereign.

"Our Glorious Monarch Soltoro ruled a peaceful realm, as good as any could. And yet, a sly uncle duped His Majesty. Thus, his regal valour led us into a fight we could not avoid."

"Nor win!" a lone voice yelled.

"Aye," grunted many.

Bendro curtsied deep, "Thyre. Bid us time to mourn you soon, but allow us to retire you first."

A moment ago the place howled with discord, now the solemn wept. Tears fled on cue and the custom silence held until Bendro continued.

"Diltoro! Our mad prince meant to seize his own inherent power and tyrannize us all." Now scowling wet faces were wiped dry. "Coaxed by Krantolo, their corrupted shardhires bullied, confined and extorted innocent civilians. Their fate was just. When true royalty arrived, death swallowed the marshals whole." He smirked. "The Prince too was murdered by the monarch's own fateshield, no less."

Every eye fell on the baton holder.

"If you condemn me, speak now," cried Glendoro. "That brat threw the monarch's head into the harbour. Without any remains of Soltoro, his grave is empty forever."

No one spoke for the prince.

"Vengeant Glendoro. Your prosecutors, if any, have fled. Your allies forgive you. The city is grateful."

The noble folk dutifully applauded their young warriors.

"Commander Palama. A nobody who came to rescue everybody. Hailed seniarch by the legions saved and acclaimed monarch by citizens freed..."

"No he wasn't." A lone bold voice dared to interject. Hentra stood to speak.

"He should have, but he was assassinated," said Bendro.

"Lament them all you please," said Hentra. "But the royals lost us Oxxia. We are well rid of the monarchy."

"No." Bendro shouted. "For the stability of the realm, the monarchy must be reimposed immediately."

"How?" scoffed Hentra. "The line has ended. All the royals are dead."

"Not all." Bendro extended a welcoming arm to Drolla. He stepped into the column of sunlight and the entire audience vanished in the white glare. "Syblings of Drahn. Behold Drolla, Quetono's Heir."

Cries of civilian disbelief were smattered between shouts of military approval.

"Who?" roared Hentra. "Last we heard, he died in battle."

"Your news is old," said Bendro. "The monarch recognised Drolla as legitimate, and, considered him family. Drolla was the first to join Soltoro across the river."

"That does not make him fit to rule."

"Fitter than any," blurted Joltoro. Drolla and Dandaron shared a glance, not true.

"Any and all, witness here his adoption certificate."

Bendro held the document outstretched, inviting an inspection. None did. None dare question the verity of Quetono. The authority of the new president held sway.

"By title maybe, but not by merit." Hentra splayed three arms wide and swept open palms around the audience. "Let us waste no more time. A new seniority is due. Doyens, I say we bout."

Hope widened the eyes of the ambitious doyens. A senioral bout meant any could stand, and any could win. The plynth was up for grabs. Drolla sniffed. These city toffs were no better than his own uncles back home. If Brokka were here, he would sway their votes. 'A rich purse always buys poor deference.' He remembered Brokka's favourite boast.

Zonara mounted the middle step of the podium. One level above the people yet one below royalty. Every soldier snapped to attention. As one, short drawn hilts slammed back home. The synchronic crash of glass shut every doyen's mouth and opened every elder's ear. The old soldier frowned like an angry uncle set on scolding naughty children.

"No seniocrat, however noble, will win us Oxxia back," he stated.

"The monarchy lost us Oxxia." An ancient member sat surrounded by an escort of half a dozen great-grandkids.

"And only the monarchy can win it back," said Zonara. "But not if we fight each other. Western Drahn will be Eastern Miokh soon enough, and our occidental syblings await deliverance. Or do we just let Oxxia go? Should we all sit back here and watch the leftover clans squabble again over the sovereign chair?"

"The war is not over. The royal army is still gathered," said Drolla.

"Do not use our kids to enthrone yourself," scowled Hentra.

"Nor you," Drolla spat back.

Leeporp bound onto the podium. He wrapped a sideways hug around Drolla.

"You old kladgers must be phapping kidding. I saw none of you cross the river with Soltoro. Clanlords you may be, but warlords you are not. You could not even stand up to the marshals. You have earned no right to an election. So beware, the next seniarch you vote in just might be the hundred and first on the Kentrex list."

Hentra flared and huffed. "So be it." The threat stung. "I move to defer. There will be no accession today, we have no torkh. Another thing Soltoro lost in battle." A reverent hush fell upon the room.

Glendoro rummaged among the folds of his robe and withdrew a fist gripping black regal silk. The slick cloth quietly slid off itself and revealed the royal glass collar. The audience gasped. The sight of the monarch's crown was unexpected. The ring of black Drahn glass sprinkled with embedded smolderstone. Spread between three tusks, coloured gems the size of eyeballs glistened in their copper threaded sockets.

"You hold the torkh?" asked Bendro.

"I was Soltoro's fateshield," Glendoro shrugged. "I always held it for him." He took a step and sidled up against Dandaron and whispered, "I am sorry old friend. You know a claim without proof, is no claim at all." Dandaron nodded in solemn agreement.

Glendoro passed the torkh to Bendro and presented the baton to Drolla.

"Here stands royal blood," crowed Glendoro. "Even a royal sporling is legitimate."

The doubtful silence of the audience seemed to last hours.

"Syblings, please," Dandaron blurted. "Resolve this now. You have argued enough. Crown your monarch today so we might liberate Oxxia tomorrow. The army lusts for revenge. Who here would deny them?"

Shouts of agreement and proud applause followed. These few words from an unexpected statesman, uttered by a foreigner, humbled them and resolved their sentiment.

Hentra stood silent. Bendro nodded and Joltoro called. The Cyan Corps slammed their hilts home again, the audience glared about, peeved at the unnecessary hint.

"Despite your doubts, Drolla is the last legal heir and due the monarchy," said Bendro.

The hall erupted. Spurred on by daring soldiers, the cheering folk almost sounded genuine. Those bribed by a blade were no different to those bribed by a purse. But even so, they applauded him.

The adulation was overwhelming, yet strangely not unwelcome. Dazed, he muttered to himself, "Monarch Drolla." For a moment, time stopped. His imagination ran wild and figments of it streamed past like driving rain. A life of majesty laid before him. Lord of all, serf to none. Not even... Hlammi scowled through the daydream blur. 'What a fraud you are,' he mouthed. 'Would you cheat our dearest?' The chiding image vanished and the roar of the hall returned.

Dandaron was as still as a statue. His head nestled in his white feather mantle like an egg in a nest. He is the true monarch, and a far better warlord. Drahn needs him. Par' was right. Drolla was just a lazy mushroom farmer, who really would rather retire.

"Wait," yelled Drolla. "There is someone else."

"What?" Hentra thought he heard a wild claim over the din.

"Who?" yelled Bendro.

"Syblings. Silence," roared Hentra.

"The birth child of Quetono outranks me," yelled Drolla.

"It seems we cannot give the monarchy away," jeered Hentra. Awkward laughter rippled across the crowd.

"Drolla, what are you saying?" said Bendro. "I knew Quetono his whole life. His first child was murdered and the second was born dead. You make no sense."

"You don't understand, that's not true. The baby wasn't stillborn. Vondaka stole him away and hid him in plain sight. He has been in front of you all the whole time."

"Who?" called the old grandpar' as he stood. His fussy great-grandbrats shushed him and pulled him back to his haunches.

"The rightful heir is Dandaron," Drolla announced again.

The adulation of moments ago now turned into ridicule. The uproar and the incredulous laughter choked the hall like the heavy fumes of a shardsmith's forge.

"Who told you this?" jeered Hentra.

"Fontaza," said Drolla.

"Fateshield to Vondaka?" Can he verify this?" asked Bendro.

"Ye... ah, no."

"Why, where is he?"

"At the bottom of the bay." Drolla looked to Leeporp. "Xindro sent him there."

"Penance for Pondra," he snarled back.

Hentra cleared his throat and puffed himself up.

"These proceedings have become a mockery," he roused. "Bendro, before your candidate is even crowned, he abdicates his inheritance to the Krodangan runt. Is this the monarchy you propose?"

"He is not Krodangan! He is my miltling. Quetono was our par'."
Drolla flushed hot. His frown beseeched Leeporp to come to his
defense. "You were there, you heard it. Tell them."

"Words will not be enough to sway this lot," said Leeporp. He
bowed his head and turned away.

"Why are you doing this, Drolla?" asked Bendro.

"Because it is true. Dandaron is more monarch than anyone
here."

Dandaron stood at attention, proud and unmoved. His upward
face pretended to ignore the ruckus around him, but his darting eyes
betrayed him. He watched it all. Drolla held out Quetono's baton and
declared.

"Your claim is true, even without proof."

Dandaron curtsied and gripped the base of the rod. His welling
eyes stared admiration at Drolla. He gently took a hand and squeezed
his affection. Drolla near choked on his own heart. If everything else
in the world was wrong, at least this was right. Dandaron rose proud
from his haunches, the wings of the Trohr Bat rested in an elbow.

"Syblings, can you credit this ridiculous stunt?" called Hentra.
"These amateurs seek to make fools of us all. They cannot even
agree who should usurp the monarchy. Let us waste no more time
and defer this assembly now. Bendro we shall reconvene later, when,
if ever you have proof."

Leeporp unclipped the phial from his belt. He held it high
between thumb and finger.

"Proof, Hentra? Here is your proof."

A thumb snapped the waxed seal, and flicked the stop cork
away. Slowly, glistening white grains poured like fine sand past
paperbark scrolls.

"This is the original certificate. It proves Dandaron is the birth
child of Quetono. Signed by Vondaka and witnessed by Pondra. He
stole it when Vondaka forced him to hide the baby Dandaron. My
family kept his secret while Pondra spent his life imprisoned."

Drolla and Dandaron locked gazes, sharing the disbelief. They
turned as one and both glared once again at Leeporp.

"You knew all along?" gasped Drolla. The Oxxian brat just smiled and shrugged.

"Registrar Wendama," called Bendro. "Would you examine this document?"

The old fellow gently rose from his haunches. His party of great-grandkids rose with him. He slapped away their hands, and pointed them to sit back down. He smoothed his toga and strode to the podium.

He carefully unrolled the delicate crisp paper curls. His curious eyes flicked and smiled at the faded ink. He spoke as he examined the details.

"The year is valid, and the bark is etchmarked properly. The embossed seals of both Vondaka and Pondra are authentic." He flicked the scroll over and blinked. "Oh, this is my stamp? I lodged this." The old registrar frowned at Leeporp and proclaimed, "It is true. I declare this document as legitimate."

Dismayed, Bendro looked to Dandaron and curtsied deep.

"Thyre," he gushed.

In contrast to the maddening cheers and ridiculous laughter, now the crowd fell quiet. Whispered opinions started like spitting rain. Across the hall quiet conversations quickly turned into loud discussions. Arguments arose and insults were hurled. The people lost control of themselves again. The rumble of the berry-den had returned.

"Look at what you have done," smiled Dandaron.

"Serves them right," said Drolla. "Leeporp, why did you wait so long to vouch for Dandaron?"

"Why did you?" he answered.

Zonara whispered to Bendro. He nodded and called to Hentra, waving him down to the podium.

"Counselor Hentra," Bendro confided. "We beg your support. The monarchy still stands. While it rules from Xendurbia, The Kataraxs will need a new governor. If the monarchy cannot appoint one, a bout of seniors will. We would prefer to avoid that."

Hentra was silent. His gaze rounded the on the seniors in the audience. His peers looked to him with hope and trust.

"Set an example," urged Bendro. "Let Dandaron lead Drahn. Our brave young sybling warriors," he waved a pointing finger, "look at them all, they will follow him west and take back our homeland."

Hentra conceded and Bendro nodded.

"For Oxxia," they agreed.

Zonara blew his war horn. He kept up one long tone until every mouth shut. A few saw a challenge but the rest shushed them down, lest he ran out of breath. Just in time, the air was as quiet as a tomb. He pulled a deep smiling breath and his grin panted at everyone. The compassionate smirked back. The seniors should retire, the adults were in charge now.

"Noble thyres," called Bendro. The elder was still master of these proceedings. "With neither doubt nor delay, the law deems Dandaron is right to rule. We shall proceed at once."

Without ceremony, Bendro gripped Dandaron by his nearest arm and placed him by the plynth. Pulled off balance, he misstepped and stubbed a toe. The black velvet quilt slid from a solid column of water clear quartz. It sat like a short fat frozen fountain.

"Straddle it," said Bendro.

His warm kladger kissed the cold crystal.

Hentra leaned in, frowning at Dandaron.

"Vow you mean it. Vow you mean to rescue Oxxia."

"I mean to rescue Drahn, and to reward my loyal aides."

Hentra leaned out, smiling at Dandaron.

"Look up," said Bendro. By one tusk, his outstretched arm held the torkh over Dandaron. Poised within the skylight's beam, the jewels sprayed down shafts of coloured light. They skirted him like a rainbow curtain. Dandaron reached into it. Beam and shadow danced beneath his twiddling fingers. Like a fascinated child, he smiled at Drolla. How did this happen, his eyes asked. Drolla shrugged. All the royals had killed each other off. A pair of lust spawn miltlings were the only ones left. The serfs were kings after all.

Bendro turned to Dandaron and faced the crowd. The elder lightly touched his shoulder like a comforting mentor. Coaxed by Glendoro, Drolla left the podium and joined him with Joltoro and Boohala among the inner circle of the reverent gentry. Solemnity always stank of obedience, but today Drolla clutched his pride swollen heart and was glad of the allegiance directed at the podium.

"Syblings of Drahn", the president called, "the Consultorium duly names Dandaron as monarch." A lone hushmoth fluttered above the heated air. Its silent wings were deafening. The noble elder turned to General Zonara. The soldier sniffed and gripped a second tusk. He cleared his throat.

"Every folk-soldier and clanbrave, every warrior of Drahn bind their fate to shield the monarch and his realm."

Bendro and Zonara turned to Hentra. "Join us, represent the clans of Drahn?"

He ignored them both and studied Dandaron. An uneasy pause waited for the agent of a free people to accept a new governing liege. The sea of anxious faces and the glare of expectant soldiers made his decision for him. He clutched the final tusk.

"The syblings offer their loyalty, equal to the fidelity of the monarch."

All three slowly lowered the torkh over his head and rested it gently onto the shoulders. They swapped glances, released their grip and stepped away from the plynth.

"Behold!" yelled Hentra. "Dandaron, Monarch of Drahn."

PART FOUR

MUNIKA

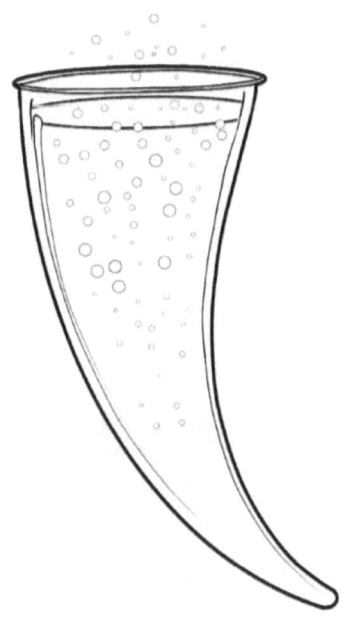

4.0 - THE PRUDENT FOLLY

T he dappled shade of the waternut tree danced to-and-fro, and the grey breeze cooled the graveled patio.

Beyond the shaded curve of the winding path, unseen footsteps crunched their approach. Drolla drained his goblet dry and held it out for more. Nolana reached for the carafe. The orphaned twin princes of Palama turned ten years old last Pannatalia and were now royal wards to Monarch Dandaron. The unfortunate waifs had inherited vast estates from both Vondaka and Palama, but it remained in probate until they turned fifteen. For now, they were permanent guests within the palace.

Dandaron assigned them separate royal tutors and indentured them into their pre-teen servitude. Tindara, the younger, serves as a junior steward. He adores the hectic work of attending to the Consultorium Elders and the Doyen Assembly. His youthful ambition revels within the halls of the political machinery. Nolana is a far more mellow soul. He welcomed the genial duties of a personal valet. He has a great affection for the close friends of his lost parent. It is a great personal comfort and privilege to wait on them, and to stay safe by their side.

Nolana gladly refreshed Drolla's empty goblet. The sparkling fruit water splashed and fizzed like a crystal pond under a bubbling streamfall. Dandaron held up a smiling palm and declined a refill. By chance, a lone Aurora Bug fluttered by and gently landed on his upright fingertips. The youth smiled at the monarch's good fortune, it was a rare thing for the shy insects to grace any creature with such trust. This simple act always forebode a bright and happy future. Satisfied it's portent was read, three shimmering wings flew the colourful mite away to hide again deep in the garden shade. Nolana sighed contented, and placed the carafe back on the table between his patrons. They then all looked to the path, and waited for their unknown guest to appear.

The day was lush and ripe. The palace gardens in Xendurbia were an ocean of colour. A confused bouquet of a hundred different pollens teased the nostrils. The frantic drone of countless swarms seeking mates deafened any who cared to listen, and those who didn't. Tiny hovering nectar bats darted from flower to flower. They squabbled and floundered amongst the powdered honey blooms. Their greedy fur was laden thick and weighed the little things down. Only the strongest could still fly and mate.

Birds swooped and danced to impress their hopeful partners. A maze of winding paths meandered between hundreds of flowering beds and shaded lawns. Fountains sprinkled within dozens of private little grottos hidden throughout the expansive grounds.

Everything was bright and fertile. The auroras had arrived. From north to south, the ghostly clouds snaked across the sky like twisting, churning, rainbow rivers. Once again it was mating season around the world. Every living creature, tame or wild, hurried to breed.

Fateshield Xindro stood nearby. He had not left their presence since the impromptu torkhification.

On that day, he was the first to drop to his haunches and pledge himself to His Majesty. In front of them all, Dandaron oathbound the Oxxian on the spot.

Enthralled, the fateshield encouraged the syblings to vow a new fealty. How could they not, the soldiers around them were already on their haunches. From the gentry's inner circle to the outer rim of soldiers, they curtsied like a rippling pond and cheered their new monarch. When the jubilation died down, Dandaron spoke.

"Honourable syblings, today you mended Drahn. Broken from without and torn from within, the truest hearts and wisest minds stood here and chose stability. From this moment on, we move forward united. I bid your leave to rest and recoup. Go home, holiday and relax. Inform your kin of what transpired here today. In five days time, we shall all assemble atop the Golden Plaza. We will host a national memorial for Soltoro and a state funeral for Palama." And thus the Warrior King and the Lord Commander would be honoured by the Last Monarch and his Royal Consort.

He thanked them all for their support and called an immediate council. The soldiery evacuated the hall. The elderly took their time and any who caught the monarch's eye, curtsied him again with smiling deference. With regal calm, Dandaron waited until he was surrounded only by his principal adherents. At last the heavy doors groaned and shuddered as they closed.

"Noble thyres, we few survived." Their nodding silence agreed. "What turmoil have we endured. What sorrows have we suffered. But that has passed, and now we all have a part in the new regime. Today we start afresh. President Bendro, please bear witness to those still present." Dandaron cast his gaze like a fisher's net.

"Zonara. You have served the nation well. Drahn thanks you for your long and magnificent service, but..."

He interrupted, "Thyre, I welcome my retirement. It is long overdue. Please allow me to resign with pride." Dandaron bowed a solemn nod and squeezed a respectful smile.

"Joltoro, Khillionaire extraordinaire," said Dandaron. He could not hide his smirk. "Lord of the Black Legion. Master of the Orienna Horde. I appoint you Commander of Churon's Pen, if you consent."

Zonara reached out to Joltoro. Thumbs and fingers wrapped clasping palms. The old commander squeezed his grip and nodded his approval.

"Of course he will," said Zonara. "I could wish for no better successor."

"You both honour me. I accept, my liege."

"You may reward your officers as you see fit," said Dandaron, "except Boohala."

Dandaron ignored the disappointed silence, and rounded his gaze on Boohala.

"I would have you as my chancellor. Bring the Cyan Corp with you, I need a new royal guard."

"Your Majesty, we are yours." He curtsied deep and winked a hidden eye at Drolla.

"Hentra. Clanlord of the Kataraxs. Director of the Doyen Assembly. How does that sound?"

"Too much, my king."

"I know, but I promised. I need you. Oxxia needs you. Plan her rescue. Commander Joltoro will supply the troops and President Bendro will advise you."

"The consultorium will delight in offering their counsel," said Bendro. "We must mount an offensive before the enemy has time to settle."

"Fateshield Glendoro, your onus is lifted. Your life is now your own."

"I would stay captain of the enforcers, thyre. Your new laws will need policing."

"So be it. Thank you syblings, I am grateful for your participation and look forward to our future, we have much to arrange. We shall reconvene here in two days so I may officially induct you all."

Except for Leeporp and Drolla, the newly exalted colleagues bid their adieu to the monarch. Dandaron cut a lonely figure on his little plynth sat in the sunken middle of the vast Seniarch's Hall.

"What about me?" asked Drolla. "Do I not have a place on your new royal bureau?"

"My dear Drolla, you have the most important task of all."

"What's that?"

"You are my most trusted confidant. I cannot do this without you."

Every eye of the little group watched Boohala brush aside the shimmering featherbush fronds. They whispered as they swayed and jostled to overhang the path again. Dandaron sat upright to receive his chancellor.

He curtsied and crooned, "Greetings your majesty, noble Drolla. Lord Xindro, Nolana."

"No need for that pomp," said Drolla. "It's only us."

Boolaha remained on his haunches and rolled an eye toward Drolla.

"At my induction as chancellor, I vowed my devotion to decorum. I insist on always observing the courtesies. I will not be seen as another Vondaka. None shall have cause to ever doubt my fidelity, young thyre."

"Stop it, you boast too much," grinned Drolla. He waved his hand, coaxing Boohala to his feet.

He withdrew two message tubes from the satin folds of his sepia gown of office.

"A dispatch from Churon's Pen," said Boohala. "The administrative reports have been logged. These are private letters."

Leeporp stepped forward and inspected the glass seal of the first message. He broke the tube open and slid the scroll into Dandaron's palm.

"Joltoro reports the army and the clanguard militias have held the western forests and secured the civilians from the central plains to the northern mountains. Killionaire Tranna and the Orienna Horde are conducting a rampant guerilla war of harassment along the black coasts." Dandaron paused to ponder. "I find it strange we have had no diplomatic complaints as yet."

"Our foreign agents inform me the Premier forbids any retaliation, bar defense."

"That's not what their Imperator promised," said Dandaron.

"They are amassing a fortune," said Boohala. "The miners are ordered to extract as much sand as they can, as fast as possible."

"Meanwhile, our store of ingots dwindle," said Dandaron.

"We need another income," said Drolla.

"We may already have one," said Dandaron. "Patr' told me a tale once."

Vondaka presented two clear vials to Quetono. One was filled with red powder, the other black sand. 'Which is of more value?' he asked.

Quetono pondered the riddle.

Black Sand fueled industry and prosperity, whereas Red Spore fed recreation and pleasure. Each was a distraction from the other. Both had merit and satisfied different desires. Work and play were equally important. Therefore,

'Neither,' he replied.

Vondaka scoffed. The vial of Red Spore powder was weight for weight ten times the value of their precious black sand. Vondaka insisted an immense revenue was ripe for the plucking. Quetono replied, 'we're miners, not pharmers'.

"And yet, Vondaka still seeded the secret gardens under the Churon's Pen," said Drolla.

"He was content to lose the sand," said Boohala. "It seems our enemy has a great hunger for the 'shrooms."

"Vondaka was vicious, but he was no fool," said Drolla. "His market was ready to buy."

"But for him, we could have had both," snarled Leeporp.

"There's more," said Dandaron returning to his note. "Joltoro asks when we might mount a royal visit to inspect the renovations at Churon's Pen. He asks on behalf of the troops, for their morale."

"Soon," said Drolla, patting his belly.

"Yes, we definitely cannot go in this condition," agreed Dandaron. "Boohala, please send our apologies."

"Yes, thyre," said Boohala. "This also came with the courier."

He handed the message tube to Drolla. He recognised the handwriting and blushed.

"This is from my par'."

"Well, it has been two months since the war ended. He must wonder," said Dandaron.

"Nolana. Please read it out," said Drolla. The seal snapped. The scroll slid from the tube and unfurled into his palm.

'News reached us the war is over, yet there is no word from you.

Everyone looks forward to your swift return. You are greatly missed.

We have not harvested since you left, there is so much to do.

Hurry home.'

"They miss you," said Dandaron. "That's nice."

"They haven't harvested yet. That's what they miss," scowled Drolla.

"We should go," said Dandaron. "I'd like to meet Hlammi."

"You already have," snapped Drolla.

"I don't remember him, though. I should like to get to know him, I think."

"Why would you want to do that?"

"He is my parent as well," purred Dandaron.

The sweet afternoon suddenly turned sour.

"You can go, I won't. I have too many awful memories, and I do not wish to make any new ones."

"I would like our children born there."

Drolla's skin went cold.

"A moment ago, a visit to Churon's Pen was too distant. Now you want to travel twice as far. I doubt we would even make it."

"Ever the optimist," frowned Dandaron. "We shall go. I have decided."

You are his child aren't you? thought Drolla. His very soul fought hard to hide his disgust.

"On that note," said Boohala, "I have duties to return to."

"If only," muttered Drolla.

"Thyre," said Leeporp, "I am loath to leave you unguarded, but I would like to attend the conjugation for a while. I hear the new beaus this year are particularly gorgeous."

"Leeporp, you have a dozen kids. I thought your mating days were behind you," said Drolla.

"They are, but I still like to watch."

"Go," smiled Dandaron. "I have the mighty shardhand Drolla to protect me."

"Glendoro has enforcers scattered throughout the gardens," said Drolla. "The monarch is perfectly safe. Take Nolana with you, he needs the experience. Let him serve refreshments to the fornicators." Nolana dropped his shoulders and groaned at the idea. "It will do you good," he insisted.

Drolla and Dandaron watched all three curtsy and disappear through the gardens.

"I am sorry. Now is not the time to argue," said Dandaron gently.

Alone, the two hearts melted into one. Under the streaming auroras, they held a loving hand and admired their swollen bellies. They were both far too pregnant to orgy.

DRAHNFOLK

ORIENNA

DROLLA (24) GRANGER
KWINNO (22) HEIR
SRODDI (7) NEPHEW
ȞLAMMI (40) DOYEN
BROKKA (57) ELDER
ZONNA (21) PATROLLER
TRANNA (33) HECTARION
PENNO (26) FISHER
GLUTTO (28) DEPOTIST
VRATTO (44) SHARDSMITH

OXXIA

XINDRO (29) WARRIOR
PONDRA (61) PRISONER
JANDRA (28) QUARTERMATER
KLORDRO (44) INNKEEPER
SONTRO (31) SAPORIST
BENDRO (59) VICE-PRESIDENT
ȞENTRA (55) DENIZEN
VINDRA (60) MERCER

MEZZINA - MUNIKA

PALAMA (29) ARBITER
SOLTORO (42) MONARCH
QUETONO (58) RECRUITER
VONDAKA (59) CHANCELLOR
DILTORO (20) PRINCE
GLENDORO (32) FATESHIELD TO SOLTORO
FONTAZA (44) FATESHIELD TO VONDAKA
KRANTOLO (53) PRESIDENT
ZONARA (56) GENERAL
JOLTORO (38) KHILLIONAIRE
TORONO (44) SURGEON
BOOHALA (25) SOLDIER
VRANDALA (38) MARSHAL
ZAKALA (26) PROTORIAN
DANDARON (24) FATESHIELD TO QUETONO

FOREIGN

VRUNE (41) TAMZI TRADER
DRARK (37) ZINTRIX DIRECTOR
VRERTH (47) MIOKH IMPERATOR
THLARSH (26) AMBER CREED ZEALOT

THE KINDOM OF
DRAHN

THE DEAD MOUNTAINS

LAKE MOUNTAINS

Kaeliton

Dolchiner

THE NORTHERN MOORS

Efferon Grange

KNOLL RANGE

Northarm River

Nothfeld

SAPHYRE RAPIDS

Auravian Steppe

Beast Water

Montlands Spill

Blood Hurst

SkyWright

Mykoria

Hillky River

Skeloron River

Luprok

Kyth

GRAX'S STREAM

The Nectarlands

Lake Kyth

Loggers Grove

Lithia

Shafham

Spondia

Midfeld

Makhraal

Xylla

Midlands Rush

The Austr...

ORCHARD FOREST

Arbos

MIOKH REPUBLIC

OXXIAN RIVER

Hoarhelm

Shardshire

OXXIA

Scarfort

KATARAXS

Kertford

VERDANT PRAIRIE

Grannix Docks

Grey Cove

Red Bay

Sudfeld

★ EBON SHORE

EQUATORIAL CHANNEL

THE GREAT CONTINENT OF
KRODANGA

HINDROX RIVER

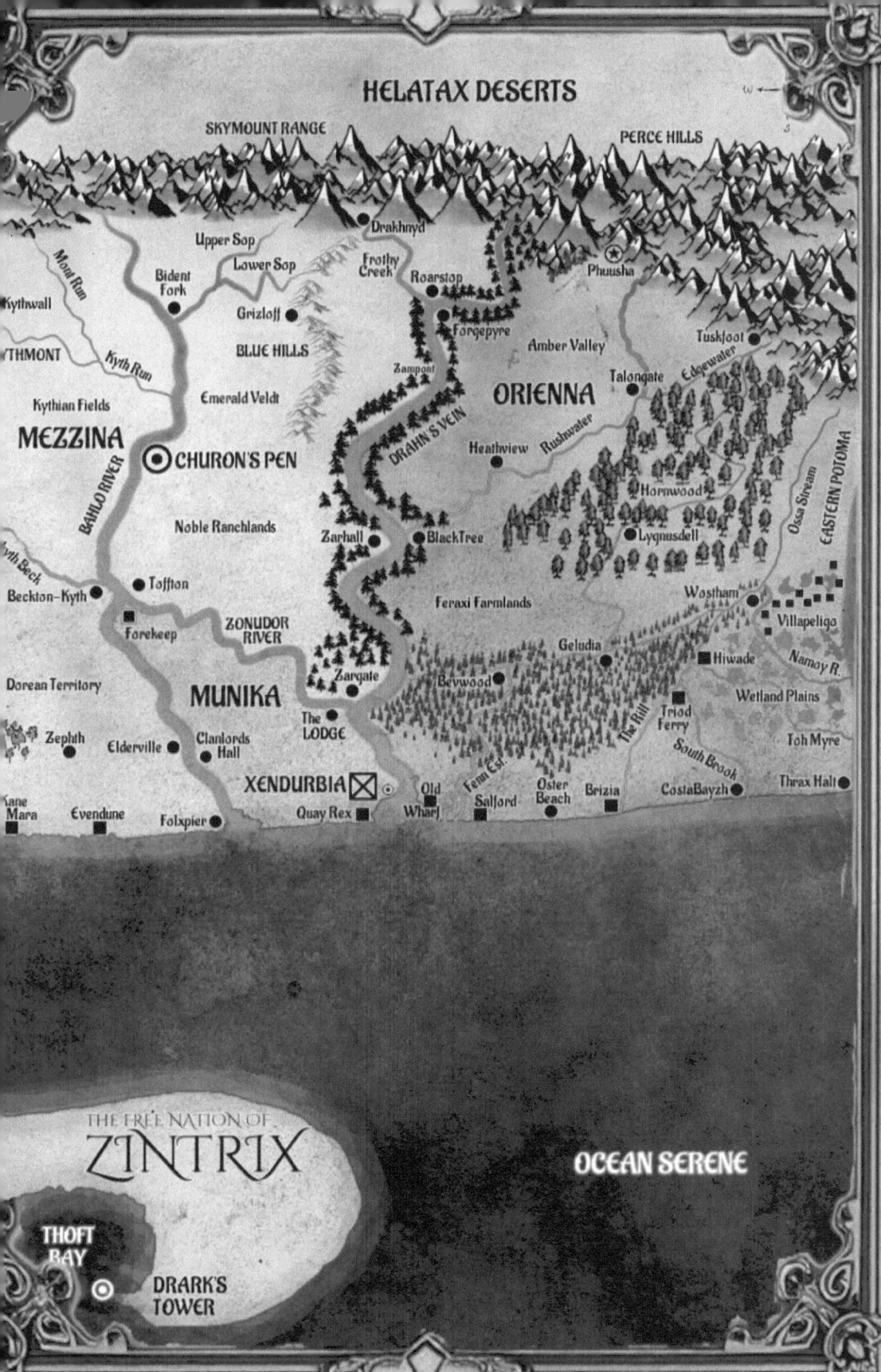

HELATAX DESERTS

SKYMOUNT RANGE   PERCE HILLS

Drakhnyd

Upper Sop   Phuusha
Bident   Frothy
Fork   Lower Sop Creek   Roarstop
Kythwall
Grizloff   Forgepyre   Amber Valley   Tuskfoot
RTHMONT   Kyth Run   BLUE HILLS
Mout Run   Edgewater
Kythian Fields Emerald Veldt   Zampont   Talongate
                                                    ORIENNA
MEZZINA   DRAHN'S VEIN   Heathview   Rushwater
              ⊙CHURON'S PEN   Hornwood
                                                                        Eastern Potoma
                                                                Lygnusdell
         Noble Ranchlands
                              Zarhall   BlackTree
Kyth Beck   Wostham
Beckton-Kyth   Taffton   Feraxi Farmlands   Villapeligo
              Forekeep   Geludia   Hiwade
Dorean Territory ZONUDOR   Bevwood   Namoy R.
              RIVER   Zargate   Wetland Plains
   Zephth   MUNIKA   The Rill Triod
                  Clanlords   The   Ferry   Toh Myre
Elderville   Hall   LODGE   South Brook
                                                                                      Thrax Halt
XENDURBIA ⊠ ⊙   Old   Oster   Brizia   CostaBayzh
Kane   Quay Rex   Wharf Salford Beach
Mara   Evendune   Folxpier   Fern Est.

THE FREE NATION OF
ZINTRIX   OCEAN SERENE

THOFT
BAY
      ⊙ DRARK'S
         TOWER